CAPSULE

Library of Congress Control Number: 2019918355

ISBN 978-1-7341745-3-3 (paperback)
ISBN 978-1-7341745-5-7 (hardcover)
ISBN 978-1-7341745-4-0 (ebook)

Cover design by Cakamura Designs
Interior formatting by Formatted Books

Published by Lost Island Press
San Jose, California
www.lostislandpress.com

CAPSULE

MEL TORREFRANCA

LOST ISLAND
PRESS

For Brandon

PRESS START

#201

THIS ONE'S FOR a boy I've chosen not to name. The anonymous student annoys me to the core, but I can't get him off my mind (and neither can you, judging by the fact that you're reading this). He strives for perfection when he knows he'll never get there, climbing and fighting but never reaching the top—never even seeing it. This obsession destroys him. His friends are gone, his family's more dysfunctional than they are in those cringey television dramas, and now he has no clue how to escape the deep hole he's dug himself into.

Sometimes I look at him and think, *My god, what a mess.* He's got nothing to live for. He keeps going and he has no idea why.

Moon.

8:20 AM

"READY FOR ANOTHER day behind bars?"

Jackie Mendoza ignored the boy seated to her left. Somehow it'd become a running gag that Mr. Berkshire's class was a prison, students even coordinating days to show up in matching orange t-shirts, but they were exaggerating. Sure, the windows were covered in blackout curtains and the class had an eerie yellow glow from the dying LED lights, but it wasn't at all a torturous environment. Mr. Berkshire simply didn't bother plastering his walls with funny posters or setting stupid knick-knacks on his desk for kids to point out in the middle of an important lecture.

"Really?" The boy leaned over the aisle, catching a glimpse of Jackie's screen. "Clash of Clans? That game's ancient."

Jackie set her phone onto the wooden desk and faced him with her lips pursed. She'd been cursed to arrive ten minutes early on the same day as the most relentless boy in class. He was always testing creative ways to get Jackie to talk as though breaking past her social barrier were a video game level he was dying to beat, and it made her blood boil.

The only interesting element about the boy's appearance was his odd-colored eyes, and he seemed to know it too. He framed them with these ridiculously oversized round glasses, two golden rings resting on his cheeks. Every time she made the effort to face him—which was only occasionally—she'd find herself lost in his eyes, struggling to distinguish their color. The hue was trapped between a dull blue and a grayish green. *If only I had a picture,* she thought, envisioning a color picker in Photoshop extracting the exact hex code of his irises.

"What are you staring at?" He leaned further over the aisle, widening his eyes. Flaunting their color.

Jackie broke free from his trap, lifting her phone from the desk and suppressing the echo of *blue or green or gray or blue* running in the back of her mind. Less than two months until the end of the school year and she still hadn't learned his name, but odds were he didn't know hers either. The only times he'd ever spark a conversation with her was when he was bored, and judging by the janky arrangement of empty desks around them, his only shot to squeeze in maximum social interaction before class was to converse with the intentionally quiet Jackie Mendoza.

"Well someone's awfully moody this morning. I don't blame you though. It's a lot to take in." His own phone unlocked with a *click.* "So what do you think happened to him?"

Jackie opened Clash of Clans and tapped her barracks, deciding which troops to train. She knew the boy would only grow more annoying if she didn't feed into his conversation, so she asked, "Who?"

"You know, that Peter kid."

Jackie's thumb paused after tapping the dragon icon only once.

"You seriously haven't heard?" He raised his voice to a near shout. "You know, Peter Moon? The *kid-who-sits-right-next-to-you-this-period* Peter Moon?"

Two girls entered the room with their hands wrapped around hot Starbucks drinks. Their chattering stopped, eyes crashing onto the empty desk to Jackie's right.

Peter's plastic seat sparked Jackie's memory. Pale skin, wavy brown hair—Peter was the only student who used free time during class to work on homework instead of mindlessly scrolling through a screen like everyone else.

Jackie turned to ask the boy with the golden glasses why he'd brought up Peter but was greeted with nothing but the back of his t-shirt. The two girls jumped onto the wooden desks in front of him, swinging their legs as they talked over each other.

Never mind.

Jackie's fingers grew numb against her phone screen as she surveyed her Clash of Clans base, gusts of morning air poisoning the room as the door swung open and closed. Students filled the empty seats until only Peter's remained abandoned, thirty three of thirty four teenagers occupying the room—a normal class size for Brookwood High. Although every bordering city and town in Northern California was at least an hour away, Brookwood had outgrown its small community years ago. The school district, however, had yet to keep up with the ever-growing high school student body of now nearly three thousand.

Jackie swiped out from Clash of Clans, about to unpack her textbook and notes, but a new app resting in the third row of her home screen distracted her. The icon featured a red and black gel capsule glowing under a starry night sky. She brought the screen to her face and squinted. *Don't remember installing you.*

The bell rang. Mr. Berkshire dragged his feet to the front of the room, a clipboard trapped in his sturdy grip. As the teacher's eyes bounced between the desks and his roll sheet, Jackie held her thumb on the Capsule icon and tapped **Remove App.**

Jackie had never considered math her favorite subject, but she preferred Mr. Berkshire's class over her others simply because she found him relatable. He marked attendance from a seating chart made of boxes that represented desks so he wouldn't have to learn anyone's name and even chose raised hands by pointing out physical characteristics such as hair color or clothing. She heard he was unmarried, childless, and had no interest in pets, so he didn't seem like the type of man to choose a career that involved talking to snarky teens all day. And although she'd never shared a private conversation with him before, she had a feeling they would get along well.

"Hey, girls in the back." Mr. Berkshire raised his chin from the clipboard. "You have chairs for a reason."

The girls chatting with the boy to Jackie's left hopped from the desks onto the crumb-infested carpet, ending their conversation with him. Now that the boy with the golden glasses wasn't smiling, his eye bags popped against his creamy skin.

Jackie's phone buzzed with a Discord message from Eugene, the only online friend she bothered keeping in touch with daily.
You down for Mystery Bullets later?

Jackie peeked at Mr. Berkshire, who was still focused on attendance. She faced her screen once again and responded with **Always.**

"I'm sure many of you have heard the news."

At the sound of Mr. Berkshire's raspy voice, Jackie tossed her phone back into the leather rucksack that rested on the floor. The man's gaze paused on Peter's empty desk, and the entire class went silent at once for the first time this school year. He cleared his throat as he lowered the clipboard to his side.

"Two students from Brookwood High, Peter Moon and Kat Pike, were reported missing on Friday night." He walked to his spotless desk and took a seat, setting the clipboard by his laptop. "If you have any information about them, please go to the *school office*—not your friends, not your parents, and definitely not me. Only a few people at the office are directly involved with the case."

The boy to Jackie's left raised his hand.

Mr. Berkshire took a deep breath, knowing to expect trouble. "Yes, kid with the glasses."

"Do you think they ran away together?"

The class erupted with darting heads, eyes meeting, breaking apart, and meeting again. Students were restless, some with deep dimples from their grins and others with jaws hanging wide open. Jackie leaned back in her seat, watching the chaos unfold from the back row. For the entire school year, she'd never seen anyone in Mr. Berkshire's class talk to Peter—yet now that he was gone, they cared.

The teacher shook his head as he opened the textbook in front of him. "Let's turn to page 332. I have a review assignment for you."

Jackie stared at Peter's empty desk as the other students pulled their seats together, gathering into groups to *collaborate* on the review assignment—another word for *goof off*. Mr. Berkshire knew the students weren't getting any work done, but he didn't care. He shut his laptop and scrolled through his phone.

Jackie had never paid attention to anyone in math class before, but considering how this was the first time someone from Brookwood had gone missing, she couldn't deny her curiosity about Peter's absence. Now that she thought about it, she and Peter were the only students to ever choose to work on review assignments alone. Peter Moon, a boy who never used his phone in class, who always turned his homework in on time—surely he wasn't the type to rebel and run away.

Friday night. Jackie had shared geometry class with Peter on Friday morning, exactly three days ago, which meant everyone in this room had seen Peter the same day he'd disappeared. She frowned at the shapes on her textbook page, trying to recall how he'd spent his time during first period. All she remembered was that Peter had shown up half an hour late, and everyone laughed at how flustered he was from interrupting Mr. Berkshire's lecture.

The two girls to Jackie's left tossed their empty coffee cups into the nearest trash bin, one missing but not bothering to pick it up. They were sitting in front of the boy with the golden glasses again, this time with their desks pushed together. Jackie leaned forward at the sound of Peter's and Kat's names, her silky black hair falling over the sides of her face as a natural shield.

"I heard it was Peter's birthday on Friday," the boy said. "Now tell me, why would he go missing on his birthday? Kind of a weird coincidence if you ask me."

Jackie watched the girls between the strands of her hair. They tossed statements back and forth until it started to sound like the only possible truth.

"I don't get it." One of the girls had her arms crossed and her back hunched over as though anyone in the room could have murderous intentions. "I know Kat's a K-pop fan, so it wouldn't be hard to believe she has a thing for Korean guys, but Peter? There's no way she'd go anywhere with him. Doesn't she hate his guts?"

"Would make for an interesting story though." The second girl's tight grin left her voice strained. "Popular girl elopes with the nerdy bad-boy. A perfect Wattpad plot."

"You read Wattpad?"

"But let's focus on what we *do* know. Peter and Kat went missing after school, and on his birthday too." She pointed a finger around the air to emphasize her point. "Obviously Peter's the one behind this."

The first girl's stiff posture loosened. "Maybe Kat was some kind of sick birthday present."

"Exactly, and I heard Peter sometimes goes to that restaurant she works at."

"Wow, okay." She nodded, processing the information. "He really is obsessed with her."

"Guys, shut up. That doesn't make any sense." The boy with the golden glasses raised his voice, ensuring the entire class could hear. "I was joking when I asked about them running away. We all know Peter hates everyone. He's not the type to waste time on romance."

The room fell silent, everyone too afraid to acknowledge what he'd said. It was much more fun to spread rumors about Peter and Kat being responsible for their disappearances. It was safer. But the fear of a third party being involved left the students with goosebumps on their arms. What if whoever was behind their disappearances would find themselves a new pair of targets?

Jackie tucked the strands of hair behind her ear, refocusing on the textbook page in front of her. Well, trying to. The diagrams and numbers blurred until Jackie could only see a strange fuzz of black lines. This was the most interesting event she'd witnessed at Brookwood High, even more than when her PE class had found the gym windows smashed out her freshman year.

Jackie's eyes twisted to Peter's desk. She didn't know him personally, but she couldn't help but wonder where he'd gone.

And this Kat Pike girl—who was she?

4:41 PM

JACKIE THREW HER back against the front door, slid to the floor of the porch, and reached behind her dripping hair to tear the AirPods from her ears. Her gasping breaths spread in billows from her face—proving the cold weather—but the air burned her throat as she watched the water stream over the edge of the roof in a waterfall. The rain hadn't started until she was halfway through her run, but by then it'd been too late to avoid the ambush.

I'm a poser, and a loner.

Triple check my, persona.

The rock music buzzed in her left hand, dulled by the wind, but she'd heard the Cuffed Up song *Small Town Kid* so many times the lyrics remained clear to her. She hummed with the vocals as the uneven pattering of rain threatened to knock her off beat.

Outside is a little more substance.

Inside is a little big lie.

Jackie raised her phone to her face, blocking sight of the drizzling water. With a few swipes she closed the apps on her phone—including Spotify—and cut the music from the air completely. After tucking the AirPods into the zippered pocket of her wet jacket, she stood with broken balance and opened the front door.

The entryway greeted her, its walls blocking sight of the dining room only a few steps away. Her thawing fingers stung in the house that now felt twenty degrees too warm for comfort.

"I know. I can't believe she's gone. Do you think it's connected to what happened back then?" Jay's voice trailed away as Jackie kicked the door shut behind her. "Maybe I could..."

Jackie reached the end of the entryway to find Jay sitting at the dining table, a phone sandwiched between his ear and his shoulder and a stack of wrinkled papers in his hands.

"I'm so sorry, Whitney." Jay's eyes jolted from the papers in his grip to Jackie, head remaining still. "I'll call you later. Promise."

Jay's phone clinked against the dining table as Jackie tossed the running shoes off her feet. She almost walked to the stairway before remembering the last time Mrs. Mendoza had exploded when she'd forgotten to place her shoes onto the rack. Jackie leaned over to pick them up and rose to find Jay's pages spread across the dining table.

"Did you hear what Dad said on the phone?" Jay twirled the stud in his right ear, scanning the pages, hungry for *something*. "He really didn't want you running today."

Jackie slapped her shoes onto the rack. "Then don't tell him."

Mr. Mendoza had called Jay on their way home from school, stressed over the email he'd received about Peter and Kat's disappearance. After a long day of listening to rumors in every class, Jackie was sick of hearing their names.

"Are you hungry?" Jay's hand fell from his ear as he gathered the papers back into a stack. "I can warm up the chicken adobo Mom made for us last night."

No, the food she made for you, Jackie thought. Jay had always embraced their Filipino culture more than she had, an easy way to win favorite points with Mrs. Mendoza. Their mom always made an effort to prepare Jay's favorite dishes for dinner, and although Jackie enjoyed them too, something felt off about eating food that hadn't been cooked for her.

She headed for the stairs.

"Wait. Jackie, please." Jay stood from the table, his chair scraping against the hardwood floor beneath him. "Could we just—just talk for a minute?"

Jackie's foot paused on the first carpeted step. Jay had driven her home about an hour ago without so much as saying a word, and now he was in the mood for a sibling chat?

"I said I'd call Eugene at 5:00." Jackie checked her phone for the time as she pivoted to face Jay, one foot glued to the first step. It was already 4:42. "Maybe later?"

Jay's focus fell to the stack of papers in his hand, the cursive writing of the phrase *Dear Stranger* written across the top. Judging by the aged look of the pages, he must have been going through his old song lyrics from when he would create original music in middle school. It'd been years since he'd last done that.

Jay sat to reread the front page, slumping forward so drastically Jackie could hardly see his face.

She continued up the stairs. *Okay then.*

The first object she noticed upon entering her bedroom was the desk leaned against the wall. A neon purple glow illuminated from the LED lights behind her PC, the keyboard, and even the logo of her favorite lavender headset. She flicked her bedroom lights on with the intent to dull both the mesmerizing illumination of her desk as well as her temptation to sit there. She had to get rid of her soaked clothes first.

After changing into a pair of black sweatpants and a gray PE shirt from eighth grade, she entered the bathroom across the hall to wash off the makeup that had now smeared onto her cheeks. It wasn't the best for her skin to leave makeup on during her runs, but it wasn't something she worried about. It wasn't like she wore as much as some of the other girls at school—that stuff was practically on in piles.

Jackie raised her chin to face the mirror in her dimly-lit bathroom. She yanked the violet scrunchie from her ponytail and parted her damp raven-black hair off to the side. Frowning at her reflection, she thought back on how much time she'd spent choosing outfits in middle school. By the time she reached ninth grade she'd stopped putting an effort into her appearance because she wasn't trying to impress anyone. Not even herself.

Jackie busted through her bedroom door and flicked the lights off, filling her room with a sacred purple haze. Now for the best part of the day.

She hopped onto the gaming chair and pulled her knees up to her chin. "Hey Siri." Phone in hand, Jackie hugged her legs with one arm, pressing her free palm against the desk to give her chair a spin. "Call Eugenie."

"Calling...Eugenie," the robotic woman replied.

The chair slowed to a stop in front of the computer screen as the phone vibrated softly in her hand. She kicked her feet off the chair and clicked the speaker button, the ring intensifying. After setting her phone onto the desk, Jackie shook the life out of her mouse to wake the PC and typed her password at a racing speed.

"Hey! If it isn't JackieLantern. What's with the call?"

"You gonna start with that every afternoon?"

"Absolutely."

Jackie double-tapped Mystery Bullets, and EugenieGenie popped up immediately. "Ready for a round?" she asked.

"Well, I just finished a dumb bio assignment, so I guess I'm down."

"You've been waiting."

A pause. "Have not."

Jackie shook her head as she opened Discord. "Let's switch over?"

Eugene hung up without a response, and a Discord voice call appeared on her screen. Jackie lifted the weighted lavender headphones from their stand, slipped them over her ears, and accepted the call.

Eugene's voice was crisper now. "What mode are we playing?" It almost sounded like he was right next to her.

"Bro, what mode do you think?" She hovered over the first three options, the cursor landing on *Challenge.*

"Should've known." Eugene gave an exaggerated sigh as their screens landed together at the starting location.

Jackie had been friends with Eugene for nearly four years now. They'd met on a Fortnite game—you know—back when people thought Fortnite was cool. They gamed together daily, using the time to catch up on each other's personal lives. All she knew about his family was that they'd moved to Florida when he was three and that he'd been attending online school since fifth grade. Other than the fact that he lived in a subpar school district, she wasn't sure why he no longer went to a *brick-and-mortar school*—as he liked to call them—but he seemed to enjoy learning from home, so she didn't question it.

"How's the run time?" Eugene said as he customized his default inventory pack—she could tell by the violent taps of his keyboard through her headphones. Setting up inventory was the only part of the game he didn't suck at, but Jackie wouldn't be the one to tell him.

"Let's just say it's worse than your aim in COD." She hovered between a few new starter packs before clicking her usual one, too lazy to deal with testing new keyboard combinations. "But in my defense, it was *pouring* today."

"Sounds like you're not trying hard enough." The opening countdown came to an end, forcing Eugene to start with his weapons half-customized. A subtle whimper escaped from his lips.

"Yeah, whatever dude." Jackie got in position for battle, her right hand on the mouse and her left stretched over the most common keys in Mystery Bullets. "Like you exercise."

"You haven't seen my abs?"

Jackie stifled a laugh. She wasn't sure whether Eugene *did* have abs or not—she'd never even seen his face before—but the joke was funny either way.

"So, anything interesting happen at school today?"

"Surprisingly." Jackie thought back to the announcement Mr. Berkshire had made this morning. "Two kids went missing over the weekend."

"Weird. You know them?"

"Obviously not."

"Right, obviously." He chuckled. "So I'm guessing that means you still haven't made any friends."

"Don't have to."

"Jackie," he said in a mothering tone.

"I'm serious. I already have a best friend."

"Well," Eugene said, "I hate to break it to you for the millionth time, but I definitely don't count as a *real* best friend." He darted to the top of a hill, a dumb move that left him in plain sight, an easy target for anyone spawning on the other side. "Hey, there's a group approaching from down there. You have good ammo?"

Jackie rolled her eyes. "I'm good." Of course the group would approach them if he peeked over the hill like that!

"Look, I'm online schooled, so I can tell you from first-hand experience that there's a big difference between internet friends and real-life friends. I told you about Kevin, right?" He continued anyway as Jackie approached his avatar on the hilltop. "He was so snarky in our virtual classes that our teachers had to permanently mute him. Somehow we started a streak on Snapchat and I thought he was the coolest dude. Then we all get together for this field trip at some stupid aquarium and turns out he's the most annoying kid I've ever met. He smeared peanut butter on the back of my shirt thinking it'd be a funny prank. Who the hell does that?"

Jackie peered over the top of the hill and switched to a heavier weapon. Two against four—this wouldn't be easy. "So you're saying we'd hate each other in person."

"All I'm saying is that online friends and real-life friends are completely different. They have to stay separate. If someone— grab it!"

A limited item appeared to her right. Jackie tapped the keys fast enough to retrieve it before it could disappear. Unlimited ammo for thirty seconds. Just what they needed.

"Yes!" Eugene continued where he'd left off. "But like I was saying, they have to stay separate. If someone were to ask me who my best friend is, you know who I'd say? Nolan. Nolan Russo, the kid I met at the Twenty One Pilots concert. I don't say Jackie Mendoza, the girl I met playing Fortnite Battle Royale."

"Well you don't have to put it so harshly."

"Just being honest. Maybe it's time you make some new friends." He tossed a few power-ups to her, and they hovered over the computer-generated grass. "The world doesn't revolve around the internet. We have the sun for a reason."

"How poetic." Jackie threw the power-ups back, ignoring his support. He was always like this, asking if she'd talked to anyone at school recently or if she'd considered joining that high school community service club Jay was in. No, she hadn't talked to anyone—and no, she wasn't joining.

"I just don't get why you do this to yourself. I find it hard to believe you're avoiding people *just cause*. It's like you're scared to put yourself out there, and I don't know why."

You try living with a perfect older brother.

The other group rushed up the hill, and soon Jackie and Eugene were talking about nothing but the game.

"Faster!" His shout was so loud it distorted through her headphones.

Jackie cringed. "I'm trying here." She aimed at the closest player in the group ahead of her, ready to shoot, but before she tapped the final key, a new window popped over the game. Eugene groaned with the disappointing hum of the **GAME OVER** screen.

"Why didn't you shoot?"

Jackie leaned over her desk. The pop-up was navy blue with the title **CAPSULE** written across the top in a simple, bold font—the same name of the app she'd deleted from her phone in class earlier. A smaller string of text appeared beneath the title. **TIME IS AN ILLUSION.** When she hovered the cursor over the window, the pop-up disappeared, revealing the **GAME OVER** screen of Mystery Bullets.

"What the hell? We were so close." Eugene's keyboard clicked again as he finished customizing his default inventory. "Hey JackieLantern, you there?"

Jackie grabbed her phone from the desk, unlocked it, and swiped to the final page of her home screen. There—right next to Clash of Clans—was Capsule. She was positive she'd deleted it earlier this morning in Mr. Berkshire's class.

"Yeah, I'm here," she said softly. "Have you heard of Capsule before?"

"Is it a game?"

"Not sure." Jackie frowned as she tapped the icon. "What about an app randomly downloading itself onto your phone? Has that ever happened to you?"

PLAYER, WELCOME TO CAPSULE. The white text overlapped the dark blue screen—the same shade of blue as the computer pop-up. The font was the only defining design feature so far. It sprung across the page in the style of an old generated text adventure game.

"Nah. Like I said, Apple's a complete scam. You should make the switch to Android." The sound of the Mystery Bullets menu screen chimed again. "I'm starting another round."

A block of text faded onto Jackie's phone. **PETER MOON. MALE. HIGH SCHOOL JUNIOR. AGE 17.**

Jackie nearly dropped her phone. Peter Moon? As in, *the-boy-who-sat-right-next-to-her-first-period* Peter Moon? *The-boy-who-went-missing-on-Friday* Peter Moon? Was it really a coincidence?

To the right was a second block. **KATHABELLE PIKE. FEMALE. HIGH SCHOOL SOPHOMORE. AGE 16.**

Kathabelle. Jackie gulped, making the connection. *Kat.*

THE SUBJECTS ABOVE ARE IN DANGER. COMPLETE THE LEVELS IN TIME TO WIN THE GAME, ERASE THE MEMORIES, AND REVERSE THE DAY. READY FOR A CHALLENGE?

A bold button slid upward from the bottom of the screen. **START THE COUNTDOWN.**

No, this couldn't be a coincidence.

"Dude, I gotta go." Jackie dropped her phone onto the desk and exited from Mystery Bullets, leaving Eugene without a teammate.

"You okay?"

"Yeah, just gotta take care of something. Let's talk later?"

"Hey, watch it." Jackie lifted the headphones from her ears, Eugene's voice fading. "I know a *later* from Jackie means *never*."

She held the headphones close to her mouth, muttering into the mic. "Fine. Tomorrow then." After hanging the headphones onto their stand, she ended the call and closed every window on her PC.

Whatever this app was, it wasn't a modern game. She snatched her phone from the desk, leaned against the backrest of her gaming chair, and pulled the screen to her nose. The app had no graphics. Nothing but text and lines. The strangest mystery was how it had possibly downloaded itself onto her phone in the first place. And that pop-up on her computer—how did it get there?

She exited to the home screen, held a finger over Capsule's icon, and tapped **Remove App** for the second time.

Jackie blinked. She'd tapped to remove the app, but Capsule stood with pride.

"Hey Siri."

"Good evening!"

"Is my phone hacked?"

A familiar ding. "Interesting question."

Yeah. Jackie narrowed her eyes at the screen. *Interesting.*

She pressed her thumb onto the Capsule icon to delete the cursed app once again. This time, it disappeared.

A quick swipe to the right, then back. There it was again.

Jackie viewed her settings to find that Capsule took up no storage on her phone. It wasn't even on the list of applications. After another unsuccessful attempt to delete it, she resorted to Google Chrome. Surely other people had experienced this. Perhaps it was a glitch with the new IOS update. Jackie searched for **iPhone installing apps without permission** and **unable to delete app from iPhone**. Both scenarios had occurred before, but they never seemed to occur at the same time. Perhaps she could be more specific. **Unable to delete app I never installed on my iPhone.**

Nothing matched.

Jackie Googled the phrase that had popped onto her PC during the game earlier. **TIME IS AN ILLUSION.** She found various articles studying the idea that time never flowed linearly. Apparently the quote was by Albert Einstein, who believed time was relative and flexible. In other words, all she'd managed to find online was philosophical trash.

The only logical answer was that she'd been hacked. She did use the same email for her Apple ID and her Microsoft account, so that would explain the crossover of Capsule on both devices.

That's what I get for not installing antivirus.

As her PC downloaded a free security software, Jackie updated the iCloud password on her phone. Although she tried to distract herself by wondering where the app had come from, she couldn't ignore the fact that it mentioned Peter's and Kat's names. Capsule mirrored an outdated game, but Peter and Kat were real, and considering how they'd gone missing three days ago, the claim that they were in danger wasn't hard to believe. What if whoever was behind their disappearances was also behind Capsule?

Jackie's head jolted to the window in a rush of paranoia, goosebumps flooding her arms. She stood from her chair, leaving it spinning softly behind her as she approached the glass and tested the window's lock. It was secure.

Okay, Jackie. She paced around the room, an act Eugene claimed to always help him through stressful situations. *Think.*

It was hopeless. She'd run out of information to work with, and only one place could offer her answers.

Jackie tapped the app. Her thumb hovered over **START THE COUNTDOWN**.

8:08 AM

JACKIE EMERGED FROM the bottom of the staircase with dry eyes and a mere four hours of sleep.

Apparently she wasn't the only one getting a rough start this morning. Mr. Mendoza sat at the dining table glaring at a laptop screen in front of him. Judging by his casual t-shirt and cotton pajama pants, he wasn't ready for work yet.

Across from Mr. Mendoza was Jay. His hair was a tangled mess and he wore the same gray sweatpants he usually lounged around the house in, an empty mug placed on the table to his right. Jay had never been a fan of coffee—he only drank it when he didn't get enough sleep.

"Can you turn those off?" Mr. Mendoza asked.

On Jay's phone was an endless stream of Instagram stories. Students from Brookwood either posted videos with tears streaming down their cheeks, shared photos of their fun moments with Kat, or apologized for hurting her in the past, voices quaking as though their guilt had led them to believe they were partially responsible. Everyone rooted for Kat to come home, but Peter's name was hardly mentioned. When it was, no one had anything nice to say.

"Jay." Mr. Mendoza broke his gaze from the laptop screen, meeting his son's face. "I told you to turn them off."

The volume of the Instagram stories faded as Jackie walked to the front entryway. She grabbed her white sneakers from the shoe rack, forcing herself to contain her grin. She couldn't remember the last time Mr. Mendoza had ever been openly frustrated with Jay, and witnessing it had left her with a cruel satisfaction.

"Dammit!" Mr. Mendoza closed his laptop and held it shut as though the screen might burst with more unwanted surprises. "I can't believe they didn't send us an email until the end of the school day."

Jackie leaned over and pulled her laces tight with a yank. Mr. Mendoza had already been through this. Last night he'd thrown a fuss over how their principal hadn't alerted parents about Peter and Kat's disappearance during the weekend. Anything she'd say either in or against her dad's favor would only rile him up about the matter all over again.

"Yeah, I see what you mean." Jay finally set his phone onto the dining table. "But I guess the school didn't want parents to panic."

"Well, of course we'd panic, and we have a right to." Mr. Mendoza sipped his coffee and pulled the cup away in a jolt. It was hotter than he'd imagined.

Jackie changed the area of focus. "Any updates?"

"Nothing. Four days missing and no leads. It's like they vanished into thin air." Mr. Mendoza set his cup down and faced Jackie with a strange twist of concern hidden behind his grin. "Why don't you two stay home today? I'm not sure I'm comfortable with you going to school before we have more information."

Jay looked at Jackie, wondering what her reaction to Mr. Mendoza's suggestion would be. For the first time this morning she had a clear view of his face. His eyes were bloodshot, lips dry.

Jay's natural youthfulness had vanished overnight, leaving him aged three years older. He definitely wasn't in the right state of mind to go to school.

What a drama queen.

The thought of staying home with her half-alive brother while her parents were at work left her stomach churning. "I'd rather not miss my chem test." She redirected her attention to the laces of her white sneakers and tightened her grip onto the straps of her rucksack. "I can ask Mom to drop me—"

"It's okay." Jay hopped from his seat, walked into the entry-way, and plucked his Converse high-tops from the shoe rack. "I'm comfortable going."

"Dressed like that?" Mr. Mendoza asked.

Jay shoved his feet into his shoes, trying to get them on without untying the laces first.

Mr. Mendoza raised his bushy brows. "Alright then, but I'll be monitoring the situation from work." He set his elbows on opposite sides of his laptop and rested his nose against his interlocked fingers. "Just stay safe, okay? And call if there's an update, because apparently the students will hear it before any of us."

"Of course, Dad." Jay readjusted his laces. "Will do."

As Jackie slipped into the passenger seat of Jay's Honda, all she noticed was how restless he was. Mrs. Mendoza had given him a haircut about two weeks ago, the almost-black hair on the sides of his head now shorter than the top, but he didn't have it gelled to his left side like he usually did. Jay swiped open the mirror on the sun visor in front of him and ran his fingers through the scraggly mess. His skin was still tan, but as he wrapped his trembling hands around the steering wheel, his complexion dulled. A loss of saturation.

This game—or whatever it was—was driving Jackie insane, and the last thing she needed was a mysterious brother to add to her list of questions. She hadn't finished her homework last night and had accumulated a total of five missed voice calls from Eugene on Discord, most likely in concern over how she'd ended the game yesterday so abruptly.

Jackie had stayed up until nearly 4:00 in the morning, stuck in an endless loop of research. She'd started by searching for **Capsule** in the App Store to find nothing but apps for contact management or in relation to pharmacies. From there she'd turned to Google, spiraling down articles of historic time capsules, medications packaged in gelatin pills, and even songs containing the word *capsule* in the lyrics, but none of the results mentioned the app she was looking for. It was almost like Capsule didn't exist.

But why me?

Sure, the app appearing out of nowhere was strange, and the fact that Peter and Kat were mentioned in it was even stranger, but why had it been *her* phone? Why had Capsule chosen to haunt her, of all people? She had no connection to Peter or Kat whatsoever.

After buckling her seat belt, Jackie redownloaded Instagram onto her phone. Maybe if Google didn't have answers about the app, Peter's and Kat's social media accounts would. Jackie's username was the same as in the gaming world—*jackielantern*—and her account was as barren as she'd left it in middle school. No profile picture, bio, saved stories, or even a single post. The only users she followed were Jay, Mr. Mendoza, and a few classmates from middle school. Five followers, six following.

Jackie was about to start her search for Peter's and Kat's Instagram accounts when she realized that Jay hadn't moved the car yet. He stared blankly at the mailbox at the end of the driveway.

"Kuya?" Jackie cringed at herself calling Jay the Filipino term for *older brother.* She couldn't remember the last time she'd called him Kuya, not that she'd started using his first name. She simply had no reason to call him in the first place.

Jay cleared his throat as he turned the car radio on, snapping himself back into reality. "I'm sorry." The car synced with the bluetooth on his phone and blasted the song *Cigarette Daydreams* by Cage the Elephant. Jackie remembered his obsession with that song a couple of years ago. During one month he'd play it on loop every day after school. The singing and strumming had seeped through the walls and into Jackie's room, distracting her from her homework. She still remembered the lyrics today.

Jay's pointer finger paused over the skip button. With a re-hearsed smile in Jackie's direction, his arm retreated to shift the car into drive. He pulled out onto the road, the rustic guitar rhythm filling the silence between them.

Jackie held her gaze on him for a few moments before turning to her phone screen again. Jay followed over two thousand people on Instagram, the majority of whom also attended Brookwood High.

Two Peters emerged on his following list. One had no last name, but the profile picture was a boy with blond hair. He couldn't be Peter Moon for two reasons. First, the Peter who sat next to her in Mr. Berkshire's class had brown hair, and second, he never seemed like the type of person to take selfies. She couldn't even recall seeing him with a phone in his hands before.

Jackie tapped the second Peter, who had no photo, but his profile revealed that his last name was Ackerman. No luck there either.

Jackie typed **Kathabelle** into Jay's following list, reaping no results. She hit the back button until the search bar displayed nothing but **Kat.**

There it was—one result in Jay's following list. Kat Pike's account wasn't even private. She had a total of fifty-nine photos, all featuring herself, and a highly-curated bio.

bhs '23 ~ proud stallion, professional procrastinator <3

"your time is limited, so don't waste it living someone else's life" —steve jobs

It was perfect. A cliché attempt at originality followed by a cringey quote she'd searched for online specifically for social media. Classic.

Reminds me why I don't use Instagram.

Jackie's eyes grew larger with every scroll through Kat's feed. Her style was *out there*. Like, really out there. She'd posted her most recent photo eight days ago, and in it she wore a plaid brown and gray button-down tucked into a turquoise skirt. Neon green socks peeked out from under her combat boots, a knitted cardigan in the same annoying lime color draped over her shoulders. Judging by the arrangement of blurry brick buildings behind her grinning face, she was standing in the middle of Old Town Brookwood—the most historic part of the city.

The caption read, **just two months of school left, but i'm barely hanging in there lol**

Jackie's grip tightened around her phone screen. *Over six-hundred likes for* this *photo?* The comments were filled with support from students at Brookwood High, all of them either complimenting her looks or applauding Kat for her carefree style. Kat didn't bother replying to—or even liking—any of the comments.

What does she even get out of this?

As much as Jackie couldn't relate to the idea of posting dozens of photos of her face online for everyone in school to see, she found herself drawn to one photo in particular.

Kat's first post on Instagram was from over two years ago. She stood in the middle of an ice rink, bulky skates on her feet— the comfortable kind that cost extra to rent—and wore linen shorts despite the chilly air. Unlike the other photos, her outfit was normal.

Overly plain, even.

Next to Kat was a girl a few inches taller than her, blonde hair falling over her yellow hoodie in perfectly symmetrical waves. The caption read, **happy birthday to the most amazing girl i know <3** Most likely her sister, judging by the endless freckles splattered across their faces.

Jackie navigated to Kat's following list and searched for Peter. The only result was Peter Ackerman. No Peter Moon.

"Kat," Jay said. "Do you have any classes with her?"

"No." Jackie turned her phone off. "But I do have a class with Peter."

Jay readjusted his sweaty grip on the steering wheel at the sound of Peter's name. Jackie waited for him to say something or ask a follow-up question, but he never did. He drove in silence, shoulders high, neck tense—the same posture Jackie remembered him having when he'd started driving for the first time.

The Mendoza siblings arrived at school a few minutes early, which was barely enough time to walk to their respective classes. As soon as they landed on campus, Jackie and Jay headed their separate ways. The car rides to and from Brookwood High were the only moments Jackie felt like she and Jay were actually siblings. The commute forced them together in a car with no distractions, barred from the outside world of opinions of who they were in relation to each other. It was just them, just a brother and his little sister, but the car rides were only ten minutes long.

Jackie held her breath as she entered the science hall at Brookwood High, greeting a mixture of near-dead and over-energetic teens. Some stood on their toes or crouched to reach their chipping teal lockers, and others lined up in front of classrooms waiting for the teachers who only opened their doors after hearing the bell ring. The longest stretch of lockers in the science hall—where Jackie's was located this year—filled the wall between two AP physics classrooms to her right. Jackie had nearly reached it when her shoes froze to the ground.

Peter Moon's locker.

It was only a few steps away from her own, but she didn't know that because she remembered seeing him there. Peter had only been announced missing to Brookwood High yesterday and students had already moved past a level of remorse and scribbled cruel messages on the steel in his memory.

I hope they don't find you.

How long until they report you dead?

What have you done to Kat?

About time you disappear.

Each note had been written with different handwriting. Some in pencil, others with Sharpie, and judging by the fact that *bye blogger boy* rubbed off with a quick swipe of Jackie's finger, some had been written with whiteboard markers.

"Can you just go?"

Jackie turned to face a short-haired girl holding a dripping rag. She was slender and about a foot taller than Jackie with checkered knee socks nearly reaching her shorts. The girl stepped forward, forcing Jackie aside as the maroon rag in her hands met the faded blue steel. After a few scrubs, most of the messages came off, but a few had stubborn ink they both knew was going nowhere.

"I didn't write anything," Jackie said.

The girl's bangs jumped as she turned around. Her piercing blue eyes threatened Jackie, but after a moment the sharpness dissipated. "Sorry." She frowned at a string of words she couldn't get off before scrubbing at them harder. "I'm just really sick of this. There's been a lot of hate for Peter lately."

Normally this was the scene where Jackie would make an exit and never speak to the short-haired girl again, but today she couldn't contain her curiosity. Maybe learning about Peter would help her discover why the app had chosen to connect her with two random students from Brookwood High. So instead of walking away, Jackie planted her feet and asked a question.

"One of the quotes…" Jackie rubbed the whiteboard marker ink from her fingers. "It said *blogger boy*."

The girl scraped her thumbnail against the locker, attempting to scratch off a stubborn patch of writing. "They're just talking about Moral Moon."

"Moral what?"

"You know, Moral Moon. It's where he writes about different people from school." She gave up on scrubbing and tossed the rag into a trash bin standing by the nearest classroom door. "Kids act like he's the worst person alive when they're thinking the exact same thoughts. The only thing that differentiates Peter from the rest of us is that he actually says what he thinks."

The girl stepped away, but Jackie's voice stopped her. "It sounds like you know him pretty well."

"Yeah." She looked over her shoulder with a light grin. The hallway lights reflected off her golden brown hair, and for a brief moment, she glowed. "We're in book club together."

Jackie pulled the phone out of her back pocket, opened the Capsule app, and held the screen toward the short-haired girl. "Has he ever mentioned this before?"

The girl frowned. "Mentioned what?"

Jackie pointed to her screen. "The app."

She took the phone from Jackie's hand for a closer look. "Which one?"

"The one the screen's on." Jackie crossed her arms, already growing impatient.

The short-haired girl's eyes trailed over the screen, never landing on one destination. As the hall emptied out, she passed the phone back to Jackie. "I'm not sure what you mean, but trust me, Peter never would've mentioned an app. He hates the internet. Said he deleted his social media accounts before sophomore year."

What kind of person hates the internet but still runs a blog?

"You can't see it?" Jackie raised her phone screen higher, trying to get the girl to focus on Capsule again. "With the text? And there's a button at the bottom to start the countdown."

The short-haired girl blinked a few times, the folds on her forehead growing more defined the longer she stared at Jackie's phone. "All I see is your home screen." She ripped her eyes from the device as a prison bell screamed through the hallway. "Sorry. I need to get to class."

As the short-haired girl disappeared into a swarm of late students, Jackie tightened her grip around her violet phone case and twisted her wrist to double-check. As expected, her phone revealed the elements of the Capsule app, not her home screen.

Lines of students in the hall vanished, the obnoxious chattering coming to an end, leaving the hallway unusually silent. The short-haired girl didn't seem like the kind of person to mess with people for her own entertainment, but she had to be lying.

A boy in an oversized puffer jacket shot past Jackie, fiddling with one of the lockers to get it open. She approached him without a second thought, nothing but the app on her mind. "I have a question."

The boy jumped as he turned to find her standing next to him, not expecting an interruption after the bell had already rung. He continued with his rummaging, arms tense. "Yeah?"

Jackie raised her phone to the height of his head. "What do you see on my screen?"

The answer was clear in her mind. On the top was the phrase **PLAYER, WELCOME TO CAPSULE** followed by Peter's and Kat's blunt descriptions and a prompt to save them. At the bottom was a bold red button labeled **START THE COUNTDOWN.**

It took a moment for the boy to look at the screen. He obviously had higher priorities.

"Um, I don't know. A bunch of games?" He clicked the lock shut and hurried to his first period class.

Jackie walked down the hall as she pressed her fingers on the volume and lock buttons simultaneously, taking a screenshot of the Capsule page. After exiting to view the photo in her library, she came to a complete halt.

Capsule wasn't there.

All that appeared in the screenshot was her home screen, which didn't even have the app icon. Next to Clash of Clans was nothing. The hallway grew dark, the occasional student walking past her only a silhouette, a menacing shadow. She leaned her head forward on the way to class, blocking her face with her long hair.

Only I can see it? She tapped her home screen, a chill running down her spine as the Capsule app stood proudly next to Clash of Clans. *Is it possible for an app not to show up in a screenshot? What if it's somehow built into Capsule's code? Or maybe it's a glitch.* Her mind buzzed with more scenarios than she could comprehend at once, but her theories had one tragic characteristic in common—they failed to explain why no one could see the app but her.

Overwhelming dread tightened around her throat, wringing her breath away. Someone had to be playing with her. Toying with her.

This can't be real.

Jackie stopped in the middle of the hall, spinning for a sign of someone—anyone—but she was alone.

DEAR STRANGER

Sometimes when I visit my family
They compliment my new car
I don't want them to
But they can't resist the smooth paint
The bright scent
The way the windshield sparkles under the sun

Sometimes while I'm driving my new car
I think of you
I think of how happy you would be
To drive a new car like this
And I hate to admit it
But I start to believe it was meant to be yours

3:43 PM

JACKIE WOULD NORMALLY approach her closet after school to get dressed for an afternoon run, but today she approached her closet to tear it apart.

She raised her chin to a shelf above the hanger rod. On it were layers of middle school notebooks, random board games, and other junk she never bothered using. Jackie dragged her gaming chair to the closet and stepped onto it.

Balancing on the seat cushion put her on high alert—a spinning chair wasn't the best solid object to stand on, its position sliding in response to even the most discreet motions. With one hand she rummaged through the mess of her closet shelf, the other pressed against the wall to hold her balance. Her searching fingers met with the cold buttons of her old digital camera.

Bingo.

Tucked under a sixth-grade PE sweatshirt was an old Canon EOS Rebel T3i. Mr. Mendoza had purchased the camera used on eBay after noticing her interest in taking photos on her iPhone, but this only made her more resistant to pursuing a hobby in photography. Into the closet of junk it went. Another failed attempt of meeting the high standards Jay had left behind for her.

Jackie lowered herself into a seated position on the chair. She flicked the switch on the camera body to find that the battery still had two bars left. With the phone in her extended left hand and the Canon in her right—only inches from her nose—Jackie peered through the viewfinder. In the frame was every element from the Capsule screen—the descriptions of Peter and Kat as well as the prompt to start the countdown.

Jackie pressed the shutter button to take a photo.

Holding her breath, Jackie clicked the photo view button on her camera. The short-haired girl's statement from earlier echoed through her mind.

"All I see is your home screen."

Jackie had seen the app in the camera's viewfinder, but the actual photo displayed nothing but various mobile games. Like the screenshot she'd taken before class, the Capsule icon was missing.

Fine then. Jackie jumped off her gaming chair and abandoned her camera on the sheets of her unmade bed. *Time for Plan B.* She monitored the screen on the way to the bathroom as though Capsule could disappear with only a blink. After shutting the door behind her, she locked her gaze onto the mirror's reflection. The bags under her eyes from last night were stronger than she'd thought.

Should've worn concealer.

Jackie fixed the uneven part in her hair, straightened her back, and took a deep breath. She raised her phone to her cheek— screen facing the mirror—to reveal nothing but—

The home screen. Even Capsule's reflection refused to make itself shown. She flipped her phone around, facing the screen directly. There Capsule was again. Back to the mirror, and it was gone. She lowered her arm, blinking at her clone inside the glass. If this app was real, and this countdown supposedly had something to do with Peter and Kat, she was the only person with a lead on their disappearances.

THE SUBJECTS ABOVE ARE IN DANGER. That's what Capsule displayed below the descriptions of Peter Moon and Kathabelle Pike. **COMPLETE THE LEVELS IN TIME TO WIN THE GAME, ERASE THE MEMORIES, AND REVERSE THE DAY.**

As curious as she was about the game, she had no clue what starting the countdown would do, and considering the fact that Capsule had the power to appear to her and her alone, she wasn't confident that she was ready to find out. She might've been the only person who *could* get involved, but did she really want to go through the trouble for two strangers?

Two strangers whom she didn't even like?

Kat was full of herself, and the students of Brookwood High naively went along with it. They worshipped every one of her Instagram posts, spamming her with hundreds of likes, and she did nothing to even acknowledge her unearned support.

And Peter—well—he was on a whole new level.

Jackie returned to her bedroom, thinking back to the various rumors she'd overhead at school. There were the playful ones— theories that Peter and Kat had some kind of hidden romance and ran away together. Then there were the messed-up ones—the scenarios where Peter was the villain. The kidnapper. The stalker. At first Jackie had found the rumors far-fetched, but after scrolling through Moral Moon during fourth period today, Jackie wasn't sure what to believe anymore.

She dragged the chair back to the PC, sat down, and typed **moralmoon.blogify.com** into the search bar. She scrolled through his entries, blood simmering. Peter posted about twice a week exposing the so-called *truth* behind different students. He ridiculed people's very essence as though he were born a prophet. No one could please him because he never gave them the chance. Who would bother being friends with him after being called *an insecure jock* or *a rich kid who buys attention?* It sounded like he was too good to become friends with any of the lowly students at Brookwood High.

Jackie clicked the filter button in the sidebar to sort the posts in ascending order. She didn't recognize any of the names the entries had been addressed to until she reached **#013.**

What kind of parents name their kids Kathabelle and Emmeline? Probably the same to raise an attention-seeking bitch.

Peter had written this entry about Kat. The date on the blog post was marked **February 17, 2020.** A little over a year ago. Judging by Peter's nasty descriptions of her, it was likely that the two didn't get along, but nothing about the entry gave Jackie the impression that Peter thought of Kat any differently from the rest of the students at Brookwood—to him she was just another teenager riddled with flaws.

Jackie scrolled to the bottom of the entry and read Peter's last sentence. **Kat's family is just as broke and clueless as your neighbor across the street, so stop treating her like she's royalty and study for those chem tests you keep failing.**

The first comment on the post was by a user named *Indigo.* **A little birdie told me you failed last week's chem test,** the comment read, **but you wouldn't share that detail with us, would you? Hypocrite.**

Jackie's phone buzzed on the table. She didn't have to check the screen to know it was Eugene calling. She'd been ignoring him since last night, and he at least deserved an explanation. It took all of her willpower to remove her eyes from Moral Moon.

"Hey, if it isn't JackieLantern." Eugene spoke as soon as she tapped the green answer button. "Finally picking up my call."

Jackie put her phone on speaker mode.

"Yeah. Sorry about that, dude." Jackie scrolled further through the blog posts, tapping a random entry addressed to a name that sounded vaguely familiar. "I've been really busy."

This next blog post had over twenty comments, the first of which was written by that same user, *Indigo*. Students from Brookwood retaliated against Peter, pummeling insults that could easily rival the same degree of hatred he'd used first. Some defended friends under unknown aliases—and others chose to take action without the protective mask of anonymity—but no one had anything nice to say. Maybe Peter wasn't solely responsible for the fight, but he did throw the first punch.

"Busy? Is that the best excuse you can give me, Ms. *I-don't-need-friends*?"

Jackie clicked the back button and rapidly scrolled through Peter's posts, stopping at the sight of her own name in the entry labeled **#389**. She spun her chair around, sheltering her eyes from the dangerous text. After seeing what Peter had exposed about the other students at Brookwood, she wasn't sure if she wanted to read what he'd written about her. How could Peter possibly critique her character when they'd never spoken to each other before?

"Okay look, I'm sorry about what I said the other day." Eugene spoke again, reminding Jackie of the phone call she'd forgotten she was on. "I could've made my point less harshly."

"Dude, I'm not mad or anything. There's just been a lot of drama about those kids who went missing." Jackie squinted at the camera sitting on her bed, remembering her failed attempts to view the app with anything but her own eyes. "Remember that game I told you about? Capsule?"

"Not really."

"The app that popped up on my phone out of nowhere?"

"Oh right." His voice was dull. "What about it?"

Jackie opened her mouth, but nothing came out. She peeked over her shoulder to spot the blog entry Peter had written about her. How could she possibly explain what was going on? An invisible app? He'd call her crazy, and Eugene was the one person Jackie cared about losing.

The door busted open.

Mrs. Mendoza entered the room, still dressed in her blue work scrubs. She had her hair tied back in a ponytail, placing her deep forehead wrinkles on clear display. The downturned curve of her lips pressured Jackie into taking immediate action.

"Hold up, I'll call you back in five." Jackie spun the chair to face her desk again, ended the call, and exited from Moral Moon before Mrs. Mendoza could spot Peter's questionable online content.

"Why did you take it out?" Mrs. Mendoza walked to Jackie's bed and lifted the camera. "I thought you hated taking photos now."

Of course she had to put the word *hate* into Jackie's mouth.

"I never said I hated it." Jackie didn't look at her—she stared at her PC's screensaver, a simple purple gradient.

"Can you not live a few minutes without your screens in front of you?" Mrs. Mendoza's voice stabbed Jackie in the spine. "Sit next to me. Please."

Jackie joined Mrs. Mendoza on the bed. A discussion like this hadn't come as a surprise, but the timing couldn't have been worse.

Mrs. Mendoza tried to massage the folds from her forehead, but she failed. Her stress wrinkles were as malleable as dented memory foam. Impossible to smooth out without reverting back to its imperfect form.

"I wasn't gaming earlier." Jackie rubbed her black socks against the carpet. "I was talking to Eugene."

"I don't care what you were doing. You are never present and I'm starting to get really tired of it." She dropped her hand from her forehead with a sigh. "Sorry. I'm just concerned about Jay. Something is bothering him, but I think he would feel better after talking to his little sister."

Jackie shook her head at the floor. It was true that Jay and Jackie had been close when they were younger, but even back then they'd never been each other's emotional support. They always had their differences. Jackie liked rainy winter days and sipping hot chocolate while she played Minecraft in her glowing bedroom. Jay preferred summers outdoors in the field and biking with friends to the park. Jackie was quiet; Jay loved to talk. Jackie liked taking photos; Jay liked being in them. It was those exact differences that helped them get along so well. They never fought for controllers because Jay was never in the mood for playing video games. They never fought over toys because they never wanted the same one.

It was only a matter of time before the differences that united them morphed into the differences that drove them apart.

"I'm sure Dad could cheer him up better than me." Those two were insanely close. Jay went to Mr. Mendoza for practically everything.

"You always underestimate yourself. Do you not notice how much Jay wants to know his little sister?" Mrs. Mendoza smiled. "Just talk to him for a bit, okay?"

"Kuya can handle himself." Jackie's jaw stiffened. Of course the first time Mrs. Mendoza smiled at her in months had something to do with Jay. "He's fine."

"He is not *fine*, Jackie." Mrs. Mendoza stood from the bed and stared down at her with that familiar chill in her voice. "You would have to be very stupid to look at your brother right now and say he is fine. You are always like this. Hiding in your room with your screens. And so you know, if you were in the Philippines my family would have kicked you out of the house by now."

"Well, we're not in the Philippines."

"So? That does not mean you can neglect your brother." She raised her voice to a near shout. "All you care about are your games."

Jackie held a firm face. She'd learned not to let her mom's outbursts affect her emotionally. "And all you care about is Kuya."

Mrs. Mendoza breathed in a violent huff. Her foot stood planted for a few blinks before she retreated to the bedroom door. "I bet that if someone were hanging off the edge of a cliff, you would not even bother offering them a hand, huh?"

Jackie stared at the wall, refusing to look at her.

"Even if you don't get along with someone, that does not make it right to ignore them." Mrs. Mendoza swung the door open. "True kindness is unconditional."

The door shut softly behind her, definitely an upgrade from the last time Mrs. Mendoza had left her room.

Jackie ran her fingers through her hair, breaking the tangles. No, Mrs. Mendoza was wrong. Surely if someone were in immediate danger, if someone were really hanging from a cliff right in front of her, Jackie would offer them a hand.

Right?

She found herself standing at her desk, heart pounding as she reached for her phone. All she knew about Peter was Moral Moon, and all she knew about Kat was her Instagram page. Judging from their online presences alone, Jackie didn't like either of them. Kat Pike was a narcissist. Peter Moon was a hater.

But they needed her help.

Jackie opened Capsule to the **START THE COUNTDOWN** button.

If Peter and Kat were hanging from a cliff in front of her—if she had no context about their lives whatsoever—what would she do?

Jackie's thumb hovered over the button.

And she tapped.

Simple as that.

LEVEL ONE

23:59:59

PETER MOON'S SEVENTEENTH birthday. He thought his family would be sick of bringing it up by now, but like every awful year they burst into his bedroom singing the same song at the same time, but in different keys. It was even worse than the horrible iPhone alarm that woke him up in a panic every morning.

At least Mr. and Mrs. Moon didn't have their hands wrapped around a camera like they had when he was younger. For years Peter had refused to be in their silly YouTube videos, and they eventually gave up on recording him. It was only a matter of time before they'd give up on him next.

And then there was Grace.

Oh, Grace.

His little sister had always loved singing happy birthday to Peter when they were younger. Surprising him was one of her favorite hobbies. She'd draw Peter surprise paintings, bake him surprise cookies to show off her baking skills—although they both knew it was their mom doing the work, and would sometimes offer him a surprise compliment, but Grace didn't have the enthusiasm to surprise him anymore. Today she leaned against the wall of his bedroom, singing *happy birthday* so quietly he couldn't hear her over Mr. and Mrs. Moon's booming voices. Grace's eyes trailed along a cream-white envelope in her hands.

"Happy birthday to you!"

Peter waited until the vocals faded completely before sliding his feet out from under the sheets. "You guys are up early." He reached for his phone, but his hand met nothing but the cold wood of his nightstand.

"I know you don't get enough sleep."

Peter caught sight of the blood-red phone case in Mrs. Moon's spidery fingers. *Great.*

"And on your birthday," his mom continued, "you really should wake up well-rested."

"I get exactly seven and a half hours a night." Peter gripped the sides of his mattress, eyes on the shaggy carpet. He hated how that was a lie. "What's the time?"

"Hm?"

"Mom." He raised his chin to face her. "Please."

Silence.

"Awesome. I'm late." Peter held his palm out, waiting for Mrs. Moon to drop his phone onto it, which she did. He gritted his teeth, bracing himself before checking his screen for the time. It was past 8:30, which meant school had already begun. "Are you kidding me? My attendance was perfect this year."

"It's a nice day. We were thinking you and Grace could take off school for a family trip to the beach." Mr. Moon smiled.

"Really, Dad? The *beach*, of all places?" Peter frowned at Grace, who instantly crossed her arms, encouraging him to go along with their silly plan. It was easy for Grace to take a day off from school as a twelve-year-old in sixth grade, but high school was much less forgiving. "I can't miss class."

"That's exactly our point. You work so hard, and you deserve a break." Mr. Moon tried to set a hand on Peter's shoulder, but Peter jumped out of bed, dodging his sympathy.

"That's not your decision to make." He headed for his dresser and opened a drawer of perfectly-folded shirts. *Gosh, what should I wear?* Normally he'd wake up at 5:00 to get ready and study before school, but now it was already 8:36. He'd have to accelerate his entire schedule now, and he hated rushing. He wouldn't be able to do his morning stretches, look over his homework assignments for a third pass, or even play his favorite song on the guitar. It took Peter an average of fourteen minutes to bike to class, so even if he left now he'd be at least twenty minutes late. If only his family would honor his schedule for once.

Mr. Moon retreated to the door. "Your favorite breakfast is waiting for you."

I don't have time to overthink this. Peter grabbed a scarlet t-shirt and slammed the drawer shut. "Pancakes, right."

He waited for the receding footsteps of his parents to disappear before scanning the jeans in his second drawer.

"Is this your life now?"

Grace was still standing against the wall. She could never mind her own business. Always asked him questions and tried to teach him morals as though she could possibly understand life more than he could.

"I don't know." Peter grabbed a pair of blue jeans and threw the random outfit onto his bed. "Is it your life to find out?"

Grace held an envelope in the air, locked between her middle and pointer finger. "It's from that girl."

"How wonderful. Another letter from dear Isabella." Peter approached Grace and snatched the envelope from her hand. "When is she gonna stop this?"

"She's trying to be nice." Grace squinted. "I think."

"She's only doing it because her all-knowing parents tell her it's the right thing to do." Peter frowned at the return address. *Ravensburg.* Even the sight of the town's name in writing got on his nerves. Those mega-rich families in Ravensburg always thought of everyone in Brookwood as a charity case.

"Sure, keep thinking that." Grace slowly backed out of the room. "And happy birthday by the way." She paused to close the door in front of her, and her face vanished in a swipe.

Peter tossed the letter into a metal bin standing at the side of his desk. Inside were stacks of unopened envelopes from the same girl. For nearly two years she'd been writing to him and receiving no replies back. When would she get the point? And who even mailed letters nowadays anyway?

I don't know why I bother keeping them.

Peter shook his head to restructure his mind. He needed to focus on getting to math class as fast as possible, not stressing over another stupid letter. After changing into his red shirt and jeans he fumbled to his desk and opened the top drawer to reveal an assortment of supplement bottles. Normally he'd take only a few at a time, but today he pooled a capsule from each bottle into his hand and chucked them into his mouth at once, chugging his tall glass of water to send them down his throat in a steady stream.

His textbooks formed a straight tower on his desk, ready for his next study session. Peter scooped the school supplies into his backpack with a lazy arm and rushed downstairs. He hadn't missed a morning studying session in months, but now he'd broken his streak because his own mom had turned off his alarm.

Mr. and Mrs. Moon sat in the dining room and watched Peter emerge from the end of the spiral staircase. He made a turn for the entryway, his sneakers squeaking against the marble floor.

"Wait!" Mrs. Moon raised her voice, hands landing against the glass dining table louder than she'd meant to, judging by the slight whine that slipped between her lips before saying, "It's your birthday."

Peter stopped, eyes running along the abstract wooden carvings in the front door. He gripped the straps of his backpack tighter as Mrs. Moon spoke again.

"At least have breakfast with us. Look—Grace even made this for you. Maybe you can drink it instead of that gross health tea you always have."

"It's wheatgrass juice, Mom." Peter turned around to see Mrs. Moon holding a mug of mystery fluid with a giant dollop of whipped cream on top. If Grace had made the drink, it had to be hot chocolate. When they were both in elementary school, they'd sit in front of the fireplace together binge-watching episodes of *Avatar: The Last Airbender* by the dozen, topping their drinks with whipped cream whenever the last blob melted.

Peter approached the stretched dining table, a majority of the cushioned white seats resting untouched for years. He was embarrassed to admit that the concept of drinking hot chocolate was enticing—but it was.

"Mom made it," Grace corrected with a glare. "Not me."

Mrs. Moon set the mug onto the table and sat. "But it was your idea." She'd say whatever it took to bring Peter and Grace together, and it made them both eager to crawl into a dark cave and die.

Grace crossed her arms as Mr. Moon pushed the hot chocolate across the table—closer to the side that Peter stood by now. Peter took the mug, but the moment he brought the drink to his face, the smell wasn't as pleasant as he remembered it being. The sickly sweet aura of sugar killed off the spark he'd originally felt, and nausea struck him. He lowered the drink from his lips.

The stack of pancakes on the table told him the true story. He knew what this was really about. His parents weren't being nice to him because today was his birthday. They were using his birthday as an opportunity to push him to change. Their real mission was to bring back the old Peter Moon, and he wished that for once they'd accept him for who he was. But if they couldn't grant him acceptance even as a birthday present, when would they ever?

"Do you want some bacon too?" Mr. Moon asked.

Peter noticed himself slouching and straightened his posture. "You know I'm pescatarian."

"And why?" Grace hadn't touched the plate of pancakes in front of her. She drew lines in the syrup with the prongs of her fork. "Why are you avoiding meat all of a sudden?"

"It's not *all of a sudden.* It's been almost two years." Peter shook his head, regretful for approaching the dining table in the first place. He set the hot chocolate onto the transparent table with a satisfying *click* and took a step back. "I gotta go."

"I'll drive you." Mrs. Moon stood from the table a second time. "It'll be faster."

"Not worth the trouble."

"Your school's on the way to work."

"I already sit in a classroom for seven hours a day." Peter slipped his white sneakers on and leaned over to tie them, sparing an extra moment to ensure that each lace hung at an equal length. "At least biking can make up for some of it."

At exactly 8:42, Peter stepped onto the tiled terrace and shut the door behind him. He checked the time on his phone as he approached the glimmering red bike leaned against the exterior wall. It was one of his personal goals to have perfect attendance this year—he wrote it in his planner and everything—but now he'd messed it up. And on his birthday too.

Yay seventeen!

23:38:42

JACKIE RAISED HER heavy head from the cushion of her arms to find herself at a wooden desk. The boy with the golden glasses had playfully poked her with his pencil, students staring at the back of the room as she rubbed the confusion out of her brows.

Where am I?

Mr. Berkshire snapped the cap onto his whiteboard marker, drawing her attention to the front of the room. "Dozing off, are you?"

The digital clock on the wall read 8:57, twenty-seven minutes after the start of class, but she hadn't remembered falling asleep. She also couldn't remember choosing her outfit this morning, which was apparently a ribbed blue top tucked into her black jeans. The only memory she had from earlier was the car ride to school with Jay, but even that was a blur.

Jackie studied the room for something *off*, some explanation behind her sudden slumber in the middle of first period, but Mr. Berkshire's class matched its usual levels of gloomy and bland.

The teacher's focus drifted away from Jackie, landing on the empty desk to the right of her. His shoulders relaxed as he uncrossed his arms. "That's strange. He's always on time." Mr.

Berkshire referred to the seating chart resting on his desk. *"Peter Moon.* Does anyone know if he's sick?"

The boy next to Jackie broke into a laughing fit, the lemony lights of the classroom shimmering on his golden glasses. "He's been sick since 2004."

The class joined him in laughter, leaving Jackie with a dull ache in her stomach. Could it be deja vu? She was almost positive she'd heard the boy next to her say that exact line before.

Mr. Berkshire frowned at the sea of cackling students, not that it would result in a silent room. Before he could raise his voice on the obnoxious kids, the door busted open, and Peter stepped inside with eager footsteps and a shaky voice.

"Sorry I'm late."

Peter slammed the door behind him, drowning the laughter to its end. Judging by the way he flinched at the silence that fell across the room, his intrusive entrance had been unintentional.

Some students whispered while others sniggered, both groups eyeing Peter as he weaved around desks to the empty seat next to Jackie in the furthest row. Mr. Berkshire sat and marked Peter present on his roll sheet.

Peter unpacked his belongings at record speed. His urgency to catch up with the class after his late arrival was so strong it even left *her* anxious, which was odd considering how he'd always come across as over-confident and self-righteous in his blog entries.

Wait, his blog. Jackie faced the numbers Mr. Berkshire had left printed across the whiteboard in computer-font handwriting. *How do I know about Moral Moon?* They'd never even spoken to each other before. And now that she thought of it, how did she know that he didn't use social media? How did she know that he disappeared?

Jackie set her hands around the book resting in the corner of her desk, but she lacked the willpower to open it, a muddle of crazy memories spinning through her mind. Mr. Berkshire had announced Peter Moon and Kat Pike missing on the same day that strange app had appeared. Jackie leaned over and plucked the phone from her rucksack. She swiped to the home screen's final page, and there—next to Clash of Clans—stood Capsule. It really hadn't been her imagination.

Jackie rested her phone onto the desk and observed her class-mates closely. *Why is everyone acting so normal?* Peter had been missing for days, but the class reacted as though the only strange thing about Peter showing up to class was that he had shown up to class *late.* The real mystery was why he'd shown up at all. What happened to Peter Moon being gone? Why did the rumors disappear? And the fear that once filled every inch of Brookwood High—where was it now?

Mr. Berkshire sat at his desk, scrolling through his laptop to find notes for the next part of his lecture. Jackie scooted her plastic chair to the right, catching the attention of her classmates seated nearby, but they lost interest quickly and returned to skimming through the pages Mr. Berkshire had assigned for them to read.

Now a few inches closer to Peter, Jackie leaned over the aisle. At first he didn't see her—he sat hunched over his notebook as he took notes—but when Jackie whispered, his pen came to a halt.

"Dude," Jackie said, "where were you?"

Peter raised his brows, but he still didn't face her. It wasn't common for someone to choose to speak to him, especially not the quietest kid in class. His eyes drifted to the whiteboard again, pen bolting into action.

Jackie would normally linger over his rude choice to ignore her, but she instead scooted her chair back into place and directed her attention to the boy at her left. He caught her gaze instantly, as though he were simply waiting for a ball of gossip to be thrown his direction.

"Does that mean Kat's back too?" Jackie asked under her breath.

The boy with the golden glasses grinned too eagerly, excited for some exclusive news. "Back from where?"

Jackie's face went red. She was about to reach for her textbook to mask her strange behavior when a date written near the corner of the whiteboard caught her attention. Friday, April 2nd. Perhaps Mr. Berkshire hadn't updated the board? Jackie checked the calendar app on her phone. Friday, April 2nd—the day Peter and Kat had disappeared. How was that possible?

Jackie tapped the Capsule app to reveal a page she hadn't seen before. **THE SUBJECTS PETER MOON AND KATHABELLE PIKE WILL MEET THEIR DEMISE AT THE END OF THE COUNTDOWN. COMPLETE THE LEVELS IN TIME TO WIN THE GAME, ERASE THE MEMORIES, AND REVERSE THE DAY.**

Following those brief instructions was a draining string of numbers that appeared to be counting down from twenty-four hours. Five lines stood below the countdown, each labeled the name of a level. **LEVEL ONE** was the only line written in bold.

On April 5th, Mr. Berkshire had announced Peter Moon and Kat Pike as missing.

"I'm sure many of you have heard the news," the teacher had said. *"Two students from Brookwood High, Peter Moon and Kat Pike, were reported missing on Friday night."*

But according to the date on the whiteboard as well as the date on her phone, it was still April 2nd. Peter Moon—the boy who had gone missing—was still here.

Jackie couldn't focus on the geometry lesson. She analyzed Peter's every move, although she didn't have much to analyze. He tapped his foot against the floor and spun his pencil when he wasn't writing, but he never once averted his attention from the whiteboard or his notebook. He was obsessed with school like any other day.

The bell rang. Peter shoved everything into his backpack faster than he'd taken the items out.

Jackie grabbed her rucksack and followed Peter to the door. Although she despised the idea of talking to him, especially after he'd ignored her earlier in class, she knew that if she didn't, she'd never find answers to the game.

Just say it. Jackie trailed behind Peter down the hall, trying to rally the courage to call his name, but failing. *Come on, dude. How else can you figure out what's going on?*

As more students exited from their classrooms, the hall grew more crowded. Jackie struggled to stay close behind Peter as students cut and shoved past her. She used his red shirt as a guide to direct herself, but all it did was remind her of the growing distance between them as the block of color shrunk.

Envisioning the countdown in her mind, Jackie shouted his name—which luckily only brought a few extra stares in her direction—but had Peter heard?

The blob of red in the distance came to a halt. Peter turned around, their eyes linking clearly, occasionally broken by a student or two who shot between them in a flash.

It was the first time she'd ever looked Peter in the eyes, but it wasn't at all how she'd imagined it to be. His face was too soft to be the kind of face to call people such horrible things on his blog. She couldn't imagine those words leaving his mouth—or even his fingertips. A strike of guilt sliced through her at the image of Peter's locker. People had seen the worst in him, but Jackie couldn't imagine him being guilty of what they'd accused.

Peter walked against the hallway traffic on the way to Jackie, but she took a step back, unsure of what to say now that she'd caught his attention. In a panic she turned sharply in the opposite direction, crashing into a girl breezing by.

"Shit!" The girl winced and wrapped an arm around her shoulder. "You don't just turn around in the hall like that."

"Sorry, I..." Jackie regained her balance and froze at the sight of the girl's perfect blond locks dangling from her ponytail, her glittering green eyes, and the artistic arrangement of freckles across her cheeks. How was it even possible for someone to be so photogenic?

"Oh yikes, bad luck." Peter planted himself by their sides, arms crossed. "Looks like you bumped into the famous, entitled feline." His words sounded like something from Moral Moon, but the smile on his face cushioned the phrase to nothing more than a playful jab.

"You're Kathabelle Pike?" Jackie could hardly believe the resemblance to her Instagram photos. It was like her two-dimensional self had been cloned into the real world, her features identical down to the angle of her winged cat eyeliner. Even her outfit was accurate to the funky style Jackie had seen online—a white top with a sunflower embroidered at the chest, neon pink socks, and her classic faux leather combat boots. She did look shorter in person, though. Not much taller than Jackie.

"It's *Kat*." Her transparent windbreaker rustled as she tightened the grip on her shoulder. "But yeah, of course I am."

"Well *of course* she is." Peter raised his brows, leaning forward with a crooked grin. His voice was long and drawn-out, letting each vowel fill the air with maximum volume. "*Of course* you're

Kat Pike. Everyone knows who you are. You're like a *god* around here. I guess your only imperfection is an extremely low pain tolerance."

His voice grew raspier. More condescending. Jackie might've even used the word *aggressive.* Maybe he really did mean everything he wrote on his blog.

"Oh shut up, Peter." Kat released her arm with red cheeks, and Jackie stepped away, afraid Kat might resort to physical violence.

Peter bowed. "As you wish, Your Majesty." When he straightened his back, he had a hand over his mouth and nose, but his squinting made his concealed smile obvious.

Jackie's focus jumped between Peter and Kat. The two had sent the entire school into a panic. Their disappearances had been a huge ordeal, but apparently Jackie was the only person who remembered anything about it. Students passed Peter and Kat as though seeing them in the halls again was completely normal.

Kat took a deep breath before storming off, throwing herself into Jackie's own shoulder in the process. Jackie stared at the wall in shock, fazed more by the girl's rude behavior than the numbness in her arm.

When Kat's pineapple-colored backpack disappeared at the end of the hall, Peter dropped his hand from his mouth. "Well, that was unsurprisingly dramatic." He shook his head as he reverted his focus to Jackie. "Do you need something?"

Jackie opened her mouth, but only air came out. What was she supposed to say? Where could she even start?

Peter nodded at her confusion. "Nice talk." Creases formed between his brows as he turned in the same direction of the hall he'd come from.

Jackie scoffed, half annoyed by his behavior and half in disbelief that Peter was walking away with no memory of ever going missing.

She merged with the bustling crowd of students leaving the math building and entered the main outdoor hallway, nothing but a long stretch of concrete leading to the different wings of Brookwood High—history, science, math, language, art. Jackie rubbed away the goosebumps on her arms as she entered the science building and slowed her pace by Peter's locker near the middle of the hall.

Jackie leaned forward, searching the metal for signs of the nasty messages people had written, but they weren't there. The cruel phrases the short-haired girl had failed to remove no matter how hard she scrubbed had now vanished without a trace.

Jackie's phone vibrated. She pulled the phone out of her back pocket and leaned against Peter's locker.

How's brick and mortar school going?

The hallway finally started to clear out, a sign that Jackie should probably be in history class by now. **Fine**, she typed. **Btw, do you remember those two missing kids I told you about?** She gripped her phone tighter as the *typing* icon appeared from Eugene's side of the Discord chat.

What missing kids?

The hallway grew colder, and the lockers lost their teal color, fading into a dark gray. Eugene's message had confirmed her new reality. Starting the countdown had brought Jackie back in time, which meant she had less than twenty-four hours to complete the levels and prevent Peter and Kat's *demise*—whatever that meant.

Jackie swiped out of her conversation with Eugene and navigated to the Capsule app. She held her breath as she tapped

LEVEL ONE beneath the countdown, triggering a pop-up with the phrase **BOOK CLUB.**

Like, the one at Brookwood? Jackie knew her high school had a book club, although she had no clue what room it was located in. *Am I supposed to go there?*

The bell rang, and Jackie looked up from her phone to find herself in an empty hall. Although she had the urge to search for the book club meeting room, she'd most likely get caught by one of the school admin scouring the halls, so she headed for her history class instead.

Lunch. Jackie tucked her phone into the side pocket of her rucksack as the bell faded away. *I'll go at lunch.*

#013

WHAT KIND OF parents name their kids Kathabelle and Emmeline? Probably the same to raise an attention-seeking bitch. You do realize Kat only pretends to hate her full name to get unnecessary compliments, right? I can't count the amount of times I've heard people say, "Why does she go by Kat? Kathabelle sounds so pretty!"

Let me tell you a sad fact: Brookwood High has exactly 2,976 idiots. Every single one of you falls into her manipulative traps. She's nothing more than an entitled feline with a fake smile. She demands attention, and people hand it to her in endless supply. She posts a picture, people comment. She switches up her style for the millionth time, everyone notices. But guess what? Kat's family is just as broke and clueless as your neighbor across the street, so stop treating her like she's royalty and study for those chem tests you keep failing.

Moon.

19:40:17

JACKIE SQUEEZED BETWEEN sweaty students in the history hall. She had nearly twenty hours left on the countdown, which averaged to four hours per level, but she had no clue how they worked, let alone how long they'd take.

She'd thought about finding Peter and Kat to clarify whether they knew about Capsule or not, but she'd figured it would be a smarter use of her thirty-four minute lunch break to investigate book club on her own. Why? Well—first, she had no clue where they were, and finding them in a sea of nearly three thousand high schoolers dispersed throughout campus would be nearly impossible. Second, she'd spent the entirety of world history class drowning in her own curiosity of what this level entailed and couldn't wait any longer to find out. What would she have to face? A monster? An obstacle course?

Jackie pressed the phone tighter against her ear, Jay's voice interrupting a long *ring*.

"Is everything okay?" Jay answered the phone with an un-natural urgency, which Jackie couldn't blame him for. It wasn't a normal occurrence for her to call her brother during school, or at all, for that matter.

Jackie escaped through the exit of the history building and squinted under the beaming sun. Luckily the outdoor hall wasn't too crowded as most students spent lunch inside classrooms or at the school cafeteria scrolling through their social media feeds.

"I'm fine." Jackie walked along the side of the brick history building, which was honestly more paper than brick, ripped posters and cheesy quotes covering nearly every inch of the wall. She searched the collage for a club list. Surely there had to be one paper hidden among the mess that held information as to where book club was located. "By—uh—by any chance, do you remember Kat disappearing?"

Doesn't hurt to ask.

"Kat? Like, Kat Pike?" Jay paused, and Jackie could hear the distant slamming of basketballs from his end of the line. He was in the school gym. Of course. "Well, what do you mean? Did something happen to her?"

Jackie stopped at the side of the English building, a grin entering her face at the absurdity of it all. Even her brother, who'd been broken down senseless after Peter and Kat's disappearance, didn't remember a hint of it. As though the moment were timed perfectly—as though it were fate—a tangerine paper labeled *Book Club* called to her from its hiding spot half-tucked behind an advertisement for the yearbook.

"Jackie?" Jay asked. "Is Kat okay?"

"Guess it's just a rumor. Bye." Jackie ended the call and slipped the phone into her back pocket. The flyer stated that book club took place at Room 43.

Jackie headed further down the concrete walkway until she met the language wing, which was identical to the other buildings besides a wooden plaque over the entrance labeled *Language.*

She pressed her hands against the door, entered the hall, and approached Room 43.

Standing at the classroom door, her arm refused to reach for the handle. Most clubs at Brookwood met during lunch, so it wouldn't be a stretch to assume they had a meeting today, and the last thing she wanted to do was walk in on a group of nerds in the middle of a reading session.

"Are you going inside or not?"

Jackie turned around to face Peter Moon. For a moment his eyes widened, perhaps realizing she was the same girl who had called his name in the hall earlier this morning. He had a book in his right hand and a face frozen in time, so unnaturally stiff Jackie decided the unapproachable person he presented himself to be was completely intentional.

"We're in book club together."

That's what the short-haired girl had told Jackie four days after Peter and Kat had disappeared. April 6th, 2021.

The game had brought Jackie to the exact location Peter was heading to, a coincidence that meant one of two things—either Capsule had intended for them to work together, or Peter really did know something about the game.

Jackie pulled the phone out of her back pocket, opened Capsule, and held the screen toward him. "Does this look familiar to you?"

Peter leaned forward. "What am I looking at here?"

"This app." Jackie pointed to the first block of text, where Peter's and Kat's names were mentioned. "You're in it."

He raised his chin to reveal a half-sincere grin. "And you made this?"

He can see it!

Jackie shook her phone. "How would I make this?"

"Well you're on your phone in class all the time, so I wouldn't be surprised if you've dipped your toes in app development." Peter read the first line of text aloud. "*The subjects Peter Moon and Kat Pike will meet their demise at the end of the countdown.* Oh, so it threatens our lives too? Creative concept, I applaud you for that."

"Bro, can you just listen for a sec?" Jackie pushed her phone screen closer to him. "I've searched all over the internet, and this Capsule app doesn't exist."

Peter glanced at the door handle behind her. "Look, as much as your app intrigues me, I think it'd be better if you leave me alone. I'm not really in the mood for playing some silly RPG game with you."

"Wasn't asking you to."

"Then I'm not writing your history research paper." He gestured for Jackie to step aside from the door to Room 43, but she stood planted. "And if that's not it either, I think I know the real reason why you won't leave me alone today."

"You do?" Jackie lowered her phone.

"Yeah, and I'm flattered, but I'm not ready for a relationship right now." He reached for the doorknob, and this time, Jackie stepped aside. "I get it—shy girls have a thing for guys like me. You know, slightly above average in the looks department. Overly critical, cold, and hard to win over—but also really intelligent. Hence the book in my hand and the fact that I'm standing at Room 43."

"It's kind of weird that you'd assume—"

"So what's this really about then?" He opened the door a crack, lowering his voice at the sight of a cluster of students. "Actually, no. Don't answer that. I'm leading the discussion today, and I'd like to live out my full glory in discussing the morals behind Lou's betrayal, so I'd rather you try that weird timer threat on someone else." Peter swung the door open completely and disappeared into Room 43.

The wind ruffled Jackie's hair as the door slammed shut in front of her. *Does he know about the game or not?* If he did, he certainly wasn't taking it seriously enough. Jackie's fingers met the door's cold handle. *You got this. Just go inside.* She closed her eyes and took a deep breath. *It's just a game.*

Detaching herself from reality did the trick. Jackie entered the room, opening her eyes to meet a circle of students. Their heads jolted in her direction.

The desks had been pushed out toward the edge of the room, forming an empty space in the center for a circle of chairs. Students sat facing each other, identical books in hand. Jackie recognized the short-haired girl who she'd seen rubbing the notes off Peter's locker. The girl glanced at Peter for a brief moment, a grin smacking her face as she looked away.

The club advisor spoke with a voice made of soft cream. "Hi, do we have a new face today?"

But what really attracted Jackie's attention was *inside* the circle.

Jackie turned to Peter, who had stopped halfway to the group of chairs, his jaw too heavy for him to close. He swung his backpack off his shoulders and dropped it onto a pile of the other club members' belongings.

Hovering inside the circle of students was a giant aluminum capsule. The two-foot long object hovered a few feet above the carpet, but cast no shadow beneath it. The capsule was static, merely pasted within Jackie's vision.

"What the…" Peter stepped forward and pointed at the capsule. "What is that thing?"

The other club members looked for what Peter was pointing at, but their eyes never landed on the same destination. Some gazed through the window while others stared at the students a few feet in front of Peter's fingers, but none seemed to take notice of the capsule.

"Is no one seeing this?" Peter's voice was shakier than earlier, and it made Jackie smile.

Karma.

The short-haired girl closed the book in her hands, giving Peter her full attention. "Seeing what?"

Jackie passed Peter at his right. She ignored the curious eyes in her direction and squeezed between two chairs.

It's just a game, she reminded herself. *It's just a game.*

"What are you doing?" Peter raised his voice. "Hey, don't touch it. We don't know if it…"

Peter trailed off as Jackie's hands met the mysterious object.

The capsule wasn't cold like Jackie had expected it to be. It lacked temperature. The air simply pressed back against Jackie's palms. Her strange stance in the center of the circle and Peter's unnatural dialogue left the students with raised brows, but Jackie didn't care. She'd been knocked out of reality. Capsule had given her a controller, and now all she could do was play.

Jackie tried to move the capsule from its place in the air, but it wouldn't budge. Only after a few failed attempts did she notice a split running horizontally through the middle, right where the two colors of a gelatin capsule would meet. A crease. She wrapped one hand around the top, one around the bottom, and gave it a firm twist.

The capsule popped open, slipping from her grip.

LEVEL ONE

PETER MOON WAS in bed, one of the many blankets tucked to his chin to keep him safe from the unknown air of night. The others melted off the sides of his mattress, threatening to completely slip away. His face was noticeably chubbier, and despite the chaos of blankets encasing him, something about the way he rested looked as though he were having a pleasant dream.

A mess. Posters on the ceiling. Knick-knacks and gadgets he'd received as gifts taking up more space on the bookshelves than books themselves. Dirty clothes piled in heaps over the area rug, and his desk displayed a scattered art piece of unfinished math homework, a few droplets of coke, and a scarlet notebook he hadn't bothered to write anything destructive in yet.

Footsteps filled the hallway. The door swung open to reveal Nicholas Moon. He grinned at his now fifteen-year-old nephew before glancing over his shoulder and into the hallway behind him. Nicholas lowered his chin and whispered, "Ready?"

Trailing behind Nicholas was Grace. She wrapped her arms around her uncle's leg with a giggle, attempting to stop him from entering Peter's room.

Mr. Moon followed behind Nicholas and Grace, his hands wrapped around a Nikon DSLR, which he pointed at Peter's bed.

Mrs. Moon leaned over his shoulder, watching the viewfinder with an open-mouth smile.

Nicholas flicked the lights on. The little parade marched deeper into Peter's disorganized room.

"Happy birthday to you," they sang in unison. "Happy birthday to you!"

Peter's eyes snapped open. He grinned at the scene before pulling the sheets over his head. "Stop!"

"Happy birthday to Peter." The group laughed, and Grace jumped onto Peter's bed to shout the final line. "Happy birthday to you!"

"You ready for some pancakes?" Nicholas stepped closer to the curled figure of Peter.

Peter flipped onto his side, wrapping the sheets tighter around himself. "Can Dad turn off the camera first?"

"But it's your birthday," Mr. Moon said.

"You haven't been in one of our videos in months." Mrs. Moon peeled the sheets from Peter's grip, and he wailed as though she were ripping off his skin. "Oh, stop with the drama. People want an update on our boy."

Peter sat up, the sheets falling to reveal the Pikachu art on his maroon pajama shirt. He pouted at his uncle for support.

"Oh Brother, just turn it off." Nicholas nudged Mr. Moon in the arm. "The kid needs some time off the interwebs."

"Alright, Grandpa. We'll be downstairs then." Mr. Moon flicked off the camera and pointed at Peter before leaving the room. "Get ready. Your favorite breakfast is waiting for you."

Mrs. Moon gestured to the door. "Come on, Grace."

Grace whined as she hopped off the bed, and Nicholas waited until Mrs. Moon shut the door behind them before commencing his lecture. "Look at this place." He gestured to the room with a half-joking, half-disappointed laugh. "What did I tell you about cleaning your room? Clean room, clean mind. Clean mind, clean soul."

It wasn't often that Uncle Nicholas came to visit. He spent six months of every year in Korea visiting family or traveling for humanitarian projects, and during the time he spent in California he was usually busy with freelance photography work. Both Peter's dad and Nicholas loved cameras, but unlike his brother, Nicholas didn't feel the need to record everything. Photography was for work and work alone. The man knew his boundaries.

Peter crossed his arms. "All they care about are their stupid YouTube videos."

"That's not true." Nicholas sat on the edge of Peter's bed. "Everyone has a different way of storing memories. Think of your little sister. She's kept every single Christmas card and school Valentine's Day candy she's received since kindergarten. Your great-grandfather would scrapbook everything. And my mom still loves daily journaling."

Peter's frown loosened. "Then what do you do?"

"Poetry." He shrugged. "I'm a softie, what can I say?"

"Well, I don't do anything like that." Peter uncrossed his arms and shook his head. "I'm not really sure how I store my memories."

"Well…" Nicholas lifted his chin to reveal his downturned lips and unusually wide eyes. "I'm guessing it's not with video."

After a moment of processing his statement, Peter broke into laughter. Nicholas joined in, their humor uniting to dissolve the tension in the room.

"I'm really not sure if they're doing this for the memories though." Peter grabbed his phone from the nightstand and pulled up his parents' YouTube channel, his humor fading. Moon Monkeys. Over 12,000 subscribers. Peter scrolled to the most recent video titled **Grace Moon's First Piano Recital.**

"Last week they told us they wanted to get ice cream in celebration of my sister's first recital, but the real reason we went was because they wanted to spend the next week scrolling through comments about how cute their daughter is. I'm not jealous of Grace or anything. They'd do the same to me if I allowed that camera near my face, but there's something about this obsession with YouTube that gets on my nerves."

"Jeez kid. You're only a freshman in high school. Hang on to your cheerful spirit as long as you can." Nicholas leaned back and rested his shoulders on a pile of unevenly-layered blankets. "But I do see why that would bother you. Everything's about sharing memories now. Creating moments for the sole purpose of hearing what others will think of them. But you can't change that—it's built into the system. The only thing you have control over is yourself." He peeked at his analog watch and stood. "Let's head down before those pancakes get cold."

Peter pried the blankets off his legs and slipped out of bed. "You're really gonna wear that tie?"

His uncle had a red and blue striped tie hanging from his neck. He was dressed better for a business meeting than a coffee date.

"You're trying too hard."

"You're right." Nicholas frowned at himself in Peter's bedroom mirror, removed the tie, and frowned at himself some more. "I really am trying too hard."

Nicholas hadn't had much luck in the dating department. Practically every week he went on a new date, and he never met with the same person twice. Sometimes a few would ghost him, and on a special day someone might clearly communicate their disinterest. The rest, however, which accounted for the majority, Nicholas would forget about by the time they'd text him the next day. And yet every time, he was nervous for the next date. Nervous he might meet the one.

"Why do you try so hard if you always end up rejecting them anyway?" Peter crammed his feet into a pair of fluffy slippers. "You know, if you keep searching for perfection, you're never gonna find it."

"Maybe, but I do find it hard to believe a high school kid is giving me relationship advice." Nicholas rolled up the tie and tucked it into his front pocket. "Why do you think I have a date?"

"You told me that you only have dates on Saturdays." Peter pointed at his uncle's head. "And today's Saturday. Plus you have gel in your hair."

"You're quite the detective." Nicholas opened the top few buttons of his white shirt and ran a hand through his hair, unsticking the stiff figure he'd molded the strands into. "But that's not why I'm dressed up today. After breakfast I'm heading on a trip."

Peter dropped his arm. "Where to?"

"Not sure yet. Planning to let the world guide me on this one." Nicholas turned away from the mirror, and for a moment his face fell off-balance from its usual symmetrical figure, his right side drooping lower than the left. He set a hand on the doorknob. "Come on, let's eat."

LEVEL TWO

19:27:21

"HOLY SHIT, WHAT'S wrong?"

The smashing of basketballs drilled through Kat's brain. She leaned forward, her head spinning, pressing her palms against the sweaty gym floor as though she could penetrate the polished wood.

"Kat?" A warm hand met her shoulder. "Are you okay?"

Kat boosted herself back to her feet, the unwelcome hand on her shoulder falling in the process. What was she supposed to say? That she remembered something she never remembered happening before? That she remembered something she wasn't supposed to remember? Kat dusted the dirt off her blue mom jeans and readjusted the crooked glasses on her nose.

Peter Moon. The boy she'd argued with in the hall this morning. The idiot who ran that stupid blog and tore students from Brookwood down as a twice-a-week hobby. Why did she know that his uncle's name was Nicholas, or that his little sister's name was Grace? Why did she know that his birthday was on April 2nd?

That's today, isn't it?

A girl hopped into her field of vision. Kat had the instant impulse to turn around, but she concealed her inner distaste with a quick rub of her forehead. "I'm fine."

Whitney Navarro. In everyone else's eyes, Whitney was Kat's best friend, but Kat never saw Whitney that way, and she was positive Whitney didn't see herself that way either. The two had gone to school together since fourth grade, and although they'd tried to make plans together in their last year of middle school, Whitney had always flaked. She hadn't shown a real interest in Kat's life until their last semester before freshman year, when Kat had finally switched up her style. Sure, maybe she was overthinking it, but the idea that Whitney liked the role she played in Kat's tragic story more than Kat herself always lingered in the back of her mind.

"Is this about..."

Kat shook her head as Whitney trailed off, a smile growing on her lips. Of course Whitney thought it was about *that*. Gosh, it would have been so nice to dump Whitney and find some new friends. Unfortunately she didn't have anyone else to run to. No backup. No alternative option. For the past two years Kat's entire social life had been hanging by a string—that string being Whitney Navarro.

"Can you take your seizures somewhere else?" Aaron approached them with a basketball cradled in his arms. "We're trying to play a game here."

"That's incredibly offensive." Whitney turned to him, her auburn locks jumping gently on her shoulders. "And Kat's having a bad day."

"Well, Kat's *always* having a bad day." Aaron dribbled the ball as he stepped deeper into the court, blowing a kiss with his free hand in Kat's direction. "Still love you though."

Kat gave him a fake smirk as she stepped behind the court lines, nothing moving but her glossy lips. As she backed up—her boots clicking against the gym floor—she finally took notice of the eyes in her direction. Did these people really have no better way to spend their time than observing her pathetic life from a distance?

Kat's fake smile washed away as the half-court games picked up speed again. Questionable migraine or not, coming here every day during lunch was starting to get *really* boring. Supposedly Whitney only liked to hang out in the gym to watch the cute guys play basketball, and by *cute guys* she really meant Jay Mendoza.

"Hurry." Whitney grabbed Kat's wrist and dragged her to the wall a few feet away. "Jay's coming."

Kat followed Whitney's shimmering eyes to find Jay walking over from a court on the opposite side of the gym. He'd changed into basketball shorts at the start of lunch but was still wearing the same t-shirt and checkered flannel from earlier. A strange combo, but charming in its own way.

Whitney fluttered her eyelashes only inches away from Kat's face. "Is my mascara flakey?"

Kat shoved her away. "Back off, you creep."

"You're no fun." Whitney pouted and leaned against the wall.

Jay high-fived a few of the other guys on the way over, and Kat scoffed. Jay was just as popular and mysterious as she was, but the only difference was that he genuinely didn't realize he'd befriended ninety percent of the school's population. He was always focused on who *didn't* like him, trying to fix his relationships with the drive equivalent to a drugged cult leader.

"You realize Jay's a jerk, right?" Kat plopped her backpack onto the floor and leaned against the royal blue wall mats.

"Name one guy who isn't." Whitney grinned at her peach-painted nails. They were a different color than yesterday—and they weren't even chipped yesterday. This girl was overkill. "It comes down to percentages, and I'd say Jay is only about twenty percent jerk."

Jay waved in their direction, and Whitney waved back. She looked like the Cheshire Cat from *Alice in Wonderland*, and not in a cute way.

Jay stopped a few feet in front of them and fumbled with his hands. First he crossed them, then held them behind his back like he was posing next to his friends for one of those cliché pre-prom Instagram photos. Kat raised her brows as Jay settled with dangling his arms awkwardly by his sides.

"I'm sorry about Aaron. He can be insensitive sometimes." Jay glanced over his shoulder and held his gaze on the nearby game as though that might somehow decrease the tension in the air. If anything, it only made it worse. "Are you doing okay, by the way?"

It took Kat a moment to process that Jay was speaking to her and not Whitney. *Right, the fall.* She'd nearly succeeded in blocking the event from her short-term memory. The last thing she wanted to think about during lunch break was the heartless Peter Moon. She didn't even know the guy. Maybe once a week she'd hear people rant about his latest blog entry as she walked through the hall, and sometimes after school she'd see him at Halos, the restaurant she worked at, but other than those rare instances, Peter would never cross her mind.

When she dropped to her knees earlier, she'd seen a peek into Peter's life. It was vivid, like a picture in her mind. She knew exactly what his uncle looked like, but she was confident she had never seen the man before. It did make her curious, though. The Peter in that memory wasn't at all how she'd imagined him while reading his Moral Moon entries. The boy he'd been exactly two years ago on his fifteenth birthday was much more energetic. Charismatic. Now why would a perfectly normal freshman with nothing to hate but his parents' YouTube channel suddenly show up sophomore year with a blog to hate on people he hardly knew?

"You're not gonna say hi to me?"

Whitney's raspy voice knocked a smile onto Kat's face. There it was—Whitney's insufferable personality. Her need to confront people was perhaps the *only* thing Kat liked about the girl. She had a talent for stirring up unnecessary drama to get her way, and whenever Kat found her life looping the same song—no matter how catchy it was—she thrived with having a girl like Whitney around to shuffle the playlist.

Jay's lips twitched a few times, struggling to spit out whatever words were on his mind. "It's not that, it's just—"

"I'm tired of your bullshit excuses, Jay." Whitney stormed past him and disappeared through the front door of the gym. A few boys *oohed* from the courts, and the color drained from Jay's face.

Kat knew Whitney wasn't *actually* mad. Her act was nothing more than a method to manipulate Jay into chasing her down, texting her *sorry*, or at least spending more time than usual thinking about her. Classic Whitney move.

Kat plucked her backpack from the ground and tossed a strap around one shoulder. "Well, that was fun." The *Big Hero 6* keychains dangling from each zipper clinked against each other, drawing Jay's attention. "Why don't you go tell her she's pretty and give her a hug or something?" Kat offered Jay an encouraging pat on the shoulder before walking toward the propped-open back door to the gym.

Footsteps echoed behind her, and Kat's neck went tense.

"I really don't wanna pry," Jay said, "but you're still curious, aren't you?"

"If you don't wanna pry, then don't ask. And no. I'm over it." Kat emerged into the afternoon air, meeting the school track in front of her and the parking lot to her right. She had a free sixth period and her shift at work didn't start until 2:00, so she had about forty-five minutes to kill.

"Are you sure?" Jay's smooth voice was right behind her now. "Those keychains on your backpack tell me otherwise."

Kat made a sharp right. Literally anywhere was better than here. She squinted and held a hand up to her forehead. The light reflecting off the windshields was strong enough to blind her after standing in the due-to-replace gym lights for so long.

Jay's voice grew louder, but his soothing tone hadn't been compromised. "Can you at least tell me why you fell earlier?"

"None of your business." Kat squeezed between two cars and swerved around the next one, trying to lose him.

"Kat."

"Is this a game or something?" She spun around, Jay hardly stopping in time to avoid running into her. "You're just gonna keep following me until I say exactly what you wanna hear?"

Jay turned to the side, resting his hands on the roof of an old Nissan. "I don't like bothering you, but I'm worried." A smile broke through his lips, which felt wildly out of place.

Kat crossed her arms. "What?"

"It's nothing."

Wow. So you expect answers from me, but you won't reciprocate?

Jay must have sensed her annoyance, because he sighed and turned his chin to face her. "I heard something about you disappearing?"

Kat nodded, encouraging him to explain.

"I'm sorry. It's stupid, isn't it?" He reverted his focus to the car as he rubbed the dust off the roof in patterns with his thumb. "I didn't think much of it at first, but when you fell earlier I thought there might be something going on. I was just concerned that—"

"Stop acting like you're my brother, because you're not."

"I know."

"That was two and a half years ago. Get over it."

"I know!" Jay pushed himself away from the Nissan, nearly shocking Kat into losing her grip on the one strap of her backpack she clung to. "But can you honestly tell me that *you're* over it?"

Kat gulped at his narrowed eyes and tense jaw. She'd never seen Jay so worked up before.

"I was in eighth grade," Kat said. "It's time to move on."

"So? I was a sophomore and I'm still not ready to let it go." The stiffness in his jaw faded away, and his voice lowered to its normal volume. "We can figure this out. I'm sure of it."

"But the world doesn't owe us answers, Jay."

Here they were, two students from Brookwood High held together by the past alone. Jay did that stupid thing where he twirled with the edges of his flannel, and as Kat watched his fidgeting hands, her oversized glasses slipped down her nose.

"I'm planning to go back." Jay tucked his restless hands into his pockets. "See if there's any more clues."

Kat pressed her glasses over the bridge of her nose to keep them from falling.

"You can come if you want. It'll be like old times."

A knot formed in Kat's throat as she released her glasses. *No way. Why am I even considering it?* She offered Jay a quick smile—a genuine one—before sliding her second arm through the dangling strap of her backpack and turning around. She held her breath as she navigated through the packed parking lot, and with her focus glued to the sidewalk in the distance, she reminded herself that she'd never find answers. Jay's blind optimism couldn't fight the fact that they'd already slammed into a dead end.

19:15:54

STRANDS OF HAIR glued themselves to Jackie's sweaty forehead as she ran down the outdoor hallway, her feet burning from the impact of her pounding steps. She'd abandoned Peter in Room 43, leaving as soon as she'd found herself standing inside a circle of students, the capsule in her outstretched hands no longer there.

What she'd experienced in book club hadn't been normal. She'd zoned out into a memory of the past, except it wasn't *her* memory of the past. Jackie remembered Peter's fifteenth birthday vividly. She remembered Nicholas giving Peter advice on accepting his parents' method of storing memories, and she remembered Peter telling Nicholas to stop trying too hard for his dates. She remembered other random details too—that Peter's parents ran a family YouTube channel called Moon Monkeys, that his little sister's name was Grace, and that his birthday was today—April 2nd.

All of this she remembered as though the memory were her own.

Jackie headed for a field of sparkling grass past Brookwood's art wing—the furthest building on campus. She sprinted the last few steps to the end of the cement walkway, adjusting to the soft dirt beneath her feet as she pivoted to the right and hid herself behind the brick wall.

With her chest rising and falling at a rapid speed, Jackie threw her back against the art building and slid onto the grass. First Capsule had brought her back in time, and now *this*? Now she was seeing memories that weren't even hers?

The morning chill had been replaced with a raging afternoon sun that roasted Jackie's cheeks, but she had too many thoughts on her mind to care. After catching her breath, she lowered her chin to face the empty field of grass. Not one student had bothered to enjoy their lunch out in nature, not to her surprise.

Jackie opened her iPhone to the Capsule app. **LEVEL ONE** now had a line running through it to mark its completion. Before tapping **LEVEL TWO**—which was now written in bold—a blinking arrow on the right side of the screen encouraged Jackie to swipe left, revealing a second page to the game, where a red button labeled **EMERGENCY** faded in with a brief description. **EACH USE REDUCES THE COUNTDOWN BY THREE HOURS.**

Below the emergency button was a section labeled **POWER-UPS** featuring only one badge, a gray circle labeled **ONE**. Jackie tapped the badge, triggering a pop-up.

POWER-UP ONE: BONUS MEMORY

COST: ONE HOUR

EXPERIENCE A BONUS MEMORY FROM ANOTHER MIND. THE MEMORY OF INTEREST MUST BE STATED UPON ACTIVATION. The button beneath the description read **ACTIVATE.**

So this really is a game.

Capsule had been structured with a goal, levels to complete, and costs to using different power-ups, but everything took place in the real world. No one could see the game but her, Peter, and potentially Kat. A human couldn't be behind this—the power was too strong, godly even. Yet as curious as she was about how this game had appeared on her phone in the first place, she had to prioritize completing the levels. Capsule hadn't lied yet, which meant Peter and Kat truly were endangered by the clock.

"What the hell was that about?"

Jackie nearly jumped when a shadow cast over her.

Great. She gripped her phone tighter, the sharp edges of the case threatening to penetrate the skin on her palms. *It's him.*

Peter stood on the grass next to her with his arms crossed. He'd abandoned his belongings in book club to run after her, and although Jackie knew that he had questions haunting him, she didn't have the answers either of them sought to find.

"It was like I saw something. Like—I don't know—a vision? Or a memory, but more clear. A dream maybe? I was watching myself." Peter stepped in front of Jackie, trying to catch her gaze. He moved his hands around in front of him as he spoke. "Did they see it too? Why did it look like they had no clue what was going on? And why did you just run off like that?"

"I don't know, okay?" Jackie swiped back to the first page of Capsule. "I'm just as confused as you are."

"Do you at least know why we're the only people who saw it?"

"Probably because we're the only people in the game." Jackie held the screen out toward him. "Looks like whatever just happened was Level One. Four more levels and we win."

Peter chuckled. "You think this is real? How cute." He leaned over and snatched the phone from her grip. "No, we bring this to the police. Whoever's behind this app is trouble."

"Wow, what a great plan. Never thought of that one before." Jackie stood from the grass and dusted the dirt off her palms. "I'm sure the police will believe something they can't see."

"They may not be able to see that weird floating thing, but they can at least see the app." Peter lowered his arm, the sanity in his eyes fading. "Can't they?"

Jackie held her hand out in front of her, and Peter reluctantly gave her phone back. She tapped **LEVEL TWO**, revealing a new pop-up with the phrase **CHERRY ICE**—the same name as the only ice rink in Brookwood.

The warning bell for their next period rang, marking the end of lunch. Jackie tucked her phone away. "Can you drive?"

"If you don't value living, sure."

Is that supposed to be a joke?

"I don't have my license," he clarified.

Jackie rolled her eyes and passed him, heading for the sidewalk.

"Why do you ask?" Peter called after her.

Jackie glued her lips shut. The last thing she needed was to waste time explaining the confusing aspects of the game to Peter.

Let's get this over with.

Peter ran after her, his footsteps loud even against the soft dirt. "Look, I already messed up my perfect attendance this morning. May as well destroy it."

Jackie walked faster. What was that supposed to mean? Now that he'd seen some weird memory of his past, he was suddenly interested in believing her story? Less than half an hour ago he'd accused her of creating the app and having a crush on him, and now he wanted to follow her to Level Two? This guy was a complete fraud, and if she weren't determined to prove Mrs. Mendoza wrong, she could have easily sat around and waited for the countdown to expire.

He matched her pace as he walked next to her. "So where are we going?"

"The next level's at Cherry Ice."

"Cherry Ice?" Peter smiled. "And you're planning on walking there?"

Jackie reached the sidewalk at the end of the field. "What other option do I have?" She stopped and looked left and right, wondering which direction was east.

"You've got to be kidding me. That's like—a ten minute *drive* from here. Let's get a Riderr." Peter pulled a phone out of his pocket. It was the first time Jackie had seen him with it before. "My dad logged into his account on my phone for emergencies."

"Don't you have to be eighteen for that?"

Peter tapped the screen, revealing a black-and-white photo of Nicholas Moon. His uncle wore a button-up shirt, his grin vibrant enough to fool Jackie into thinking the image was colored.

"I can pass." Peter swiped up and tapped the Riderr app on his home screen. "I'd say this counts as an emergency."

DEAR STRANGER

Sometimes I wonder what your life could have been
Had you never left that day
I think of the love you had
The naive faith in forever
And everything I took
When you left
That day

Sometimes I wonder how I can move on
When the love I pursue is stolen from you
And my faith in forever relies on lies
I wonder how I can possibly deserve
Everything I took
When you left
That day

19:05:29

KAT ENJOYED A few things about Halos. First, a part-time job couldn't be located anywhere better. Halos stood directly between Brookwood High and her house, which was convenient for a student without a license or a stay-at-home mom willing to be her personal taxi driver. The second perk was the free and discounted food. Nearly every evening she'd get to bring leftovers home with her. It wasn't gourmet or anything, but it was free, which somehow made it taste ten times better.

No, scratch that—those pros were meaningless. Kat had been trying to remind herself of why she enjoyed Halos on her walk there, but she'd only managed to cloak the real reason why she'd applied for the job at the beginning of her sophomore year.

Life had been so boring lately. She'd do absolutely anything she could to spice up her life, and finding a mediocre job was one of those things. Halos came with coworker drama, annoying customers, and the most frustrating boss someone could have. His jokes were annoying as hell, and he'd always end up acting passive aggressive if her and her coworkers didn't pretend he was the funniest man in the world. But those little sparks only made her life more interesting for a brief moment, and then they were gone.

Kat arrived at the front of Halos thirty minutes early for her shift and stood between two white fences overgrown with buzzing lavender bushes. The wooden sign above the door had *HALOS* scribbled in splattered ink to reference ketchup but had ended up looking more like blood. Kat's focus drifted to the two plant boxes at the front door to give customers the impression that their ingredients were fresh, which wasn't at all the case, but she smiled thinking about how many people it subconsciously fooled.

Smiled. But just for a moment.

I'm bored.

Kat took a step back as a bee landed onto the rim of her glasses. She turned around, heading toward the main strip of Old Town Brookwood. If she showed up to work now she'd most likely end up scrolling through Instagram at a grimy booth, and although a little social media stalking could be fun, she'd rather burn her free time somewhere else.

No sting? Kat frowned as the bee flew away. *Rude.*

Only a block from Halos was Pepperdine, one of the many identical brick buildings bordering the main road of Old Town Brookwood, but also the most popular. Brookwood students flooded the cozy candy store after school, but luckily it was hardly past 1:30, so it'd be a fast trip.

Kat entered Pepperdine with the quick chime of a bell dangling from the door. The aroma of sweet chocolate and artificial fruit struck her in a soothing rush. The complex scent relaxed Kat more than her occasional unnecessary dose of NyQuil.

"Hey Kat, what's new?"

Kat lowered her head from the lollipops dangling from the ceiling to the cashier standing behind a shiny wooden table. Choppy hair, awkwardly skinny arms. Yep, he was the guy who sat two seats away from her in English class. Fairly popular, but a real nerd too. This would be fun.

"Oh, you know." Kat swiped a strand of hair behind her ear. "Just doing anything I can to satisfy my raging sweet tooth."

The boy smiled, his teeth glimmering under the pink-tinted lights.

Kat skipped to the wall on the right side of the room. Everything from the brick floor to the ceiling was covered in rows of plastic containers, neon scoopers, and a colorful assortment of candies. The three containers on the left exclusively held chocolates—dark, milk, and white—and the rest were comprised of gummies, sour candies, and those hard ones shaped like fruits that literally no one but serial killers enjoyed.

Kat yanked a candy bag from the dispenser and reached for the container of Sour Patch Kids. "What do you know about Peter?" She poured a few solid scoops into the bag before glancing over her shoulder. Besides her and the cashier, Pepperdine was emptied out. *Perfect.*

"Peter Ackerman or"—the cashier paused, his voice deepening—"the other one?"

Kat tied the stuffed bag, tossed it onto the floor, and grabbed a second bag from the dispenser. "The other one." She took a few steps to the chocolate section and ran her fingers along the containers. *Some variety would be nice.* Her hand paused on the chocolate nonpareils—those weird-looking flat ones with the white dots.

"Moon, huh?" The boy's voice raised a pitch unintentionally in glaring enthusiasm, lighting up the old-fashioned store. "I happen to know quite a bit about him. When you get the chance, look up *Moon Monkeys*. People say he doesn't have a social media presence, but that's not entirely true if you scroll back far enough."

"Oh yeah?" If Kat hadn't remembered Peter's fifteenth birthday earlier today, she wouldn't have known anything about his family's YouTube channel. "And how exactly did you find out about this Moon Monkey thing?" It definitely wasn't common knowledge. Even if their audience of 12,000 subscribers had grown significantly over the past two years, family-focused content would easily go undiscovered by the students at Brookwood who were much more interested in watching Jubilee social experiments or PewDiePie's Minecraft Hardcore Series.

"Believe it or not, I was friends with Peter a couple years ago. You know, back before he went all psycho on us sophomore year. So I happen to know some blue things about him that most people don't."

Kat stuck the scooper into the bin of candies, stopping at the word *blue*. Her mind flashed with the username she'd seen in the comment section of every entry of Moral Moon. Blue—*Indigo*. First of all, what a lame username. Second, the user by the name of *Indigo* was the only commenter who seemed to know personal information about Peter while everyone else simply raged. He had some of the nastiest replies, not that he was in the wrong or anything. Peter had it coming.

"No way. You?"

"Yeah, me." A hint of pride snuck into his voice. This boy was practically an anonymous celebrity at Brookwood. Everyone wondered how he always managed to calculate the most perfectly-crafted insults to spur back at Peter. "But don't tell anyone, obviously."

Kat spooned a heap of dotted chocolates into the bag. "If you don't want your identity spilled, maybe you should think twice about sharing your username with the most careless girl at Brookwood." She paused after a second scoop. "Kidding, of course."

The boy let out a broken laugh as Kat tied the second bag and leaned over to retrieve the heap of Sour Patch Kids from the floor.

"It's stupid. I know I'm on the right side here, but I'm scared if people find out they'll turn on me too. But you? You're cool, Kat. Wish I could just do whatever and stop worrying about what other people will think."

"Yep, thanks." Kat slid her shoulder through one of the straps of her backpack and unzipped the main compartment. "That's me."

"Uh—I have to weigh them first."

"You don't *have* to." Kat tossed the bags into her backpack, zipped the compartment shut, and headed toward the entrance.

"Wait!" The boy held his tense hands out in front of him and glanced at a door on the other side of the room, where his boss probably was, or at least another employee. He leaned forward and whispered, "What are you doing?"

"Leaving. What does it look like I'm doing?" Kat adjusted her glasses before stealing his line. "But don't tell anyone, obviously." She flashed a peace sign and threw her back against the door, using her body weight to swing it open.

He gulped. "See ya."

"Bye Indigo," she said before the door closed in front of her.

Kat spun around the corner with a grin uncomfortably wide for her face. Oh gosh, it was too great! A perfect threat. If he told anyone about her petty crime, he'd be risking his school reputation. She'd gone in with the intention of sneaking out, but she didn't need to do any sneaking. The nerd set up his own trap and fell right into it. Crazy how students thought they knew her based on the strings of comments on her Instagram photos.

Kat rushed down the empty sidewalk and approached a nearby park a few buildings down. She usually came here after her stops at any of the innocent shops in the area to decompress.

Well, not decompress exactly. More like *deescalate*. Waiting for the excitement to slowly drain from her veins. The fun moments never lasted.

She stopped at the edge of the grass clearing. The park was too small to have a name, nothing more than a single bench under an old oak tree. It was only included in Old Town Brookwood because a group of environmentalists wouldn't let the city cut it down. Fair. Funny, but fair.

Kat checked her phone. 1:41. She still had nineteen minutes until the start of her shift, so she figured it wouldn't hurt to rest for a while. She approached the bench, sat, and tossed her backpack onto the grass by her boots. For a moment her fingers lingered on the zipper, considering whether she was in the mood for candy or not. She wasn't.

Kat's phone buzzed in her hand.

what did jay say after i left, Whitney asked. **he still hasnt txted me yet :(**

nothing important Kat leaned her back against the prickly bench. **leave me alone**

A lady in a frilly white dress flowed down the sidewalk in front of the grass. She stopped as the phone in her hands chimed. A girl around the age of five tugged at the lady's arm, attempting to drag her back in the direction of Pepperdine.

"Candy!" Tears streamed down the girl's face as she pulled harder. "I want candy!"

The mom held her stance firm, eyes glued to her phone screen. "Will you stop that?" She yanked her arm away.

The little girl crying in her long-sleeved, strawberry-colored dress mesmerized Kat. The girl cried effortlessly. Her tears were genuine. She was truly bothered by the fact that she didn't have candy, so she cried.

How does she make it look so easy?

Kat reached for her backpack, remembering how she'd cry when she was younger too. She'd cry whenever her older sister received the attention she wanted. Cried when Mr. Pike worked overtime instead of taking her to the mall like he'd promised to. She'd even cry when she'd watch those stupid rom-com movies over the summer. But for some reason, it was so hard to cry now. Hard to feel anything anymore.

"Hey." Kat held the bag of chocolates in the air, the girl dropping her mom's hands instantly. "You want these?"

After wiping the tears on her sleeve and smoothing out her auburn hair, the little girl held her arms out in front of her as though she were receiving a hug.

"Ready?" Kat pulled her hand back and launched the floppy bag of candy across the grass.

The chocolates landed in the girl's grip as she jumped with excitement.

Kat smiled, but it felt fake. "Nice catch."

The lady finally tucked the phone into her purse and stepped forward, the little girl following her calmly with chocolate already smeared across her lips. As the lady wrapped an arm around her daughter's shoulder, she turned her head in Kat's direction and mouthed the words *thank you.*

Now Kat sat alone on the bench, the adrenaline from her theft fading. She'd been constantly pushing her limits. Acting a bit more rude. Stealing one more thing. Saying whatever she dared. Everything helped bring more spice into her life, but nothing made her feel guilty. Nothing made her feel *bad.*

Kat lifted her boot to reveal a trampled patch of grass.

18:51:44

"LET ME GET this straight." Peter leaned his head against the headrest, chin facing the ceiling. "Kat and I went missing on the same day, and the whole school was talking about it?"

Jackie nodded.

"Sweet!" Peter threw himself forward, a wide grin meeting his knees. "That must have driven people crazy. I can't even imagine the theories behind that one."

Jackie crossed her arms and stared through the Riderr window. *Move faster.*

They were currently on Altemir Avenue in Downtown Brookwood, the busiest road in the city. The sidewalks featured mostly middle-aged adults wearing anything from casual jeans to full-on business suits as they merged into coffee shops, the mall, commercial banks, and overrated restaurants with lines trailing through the front doors. They'd been stuck bumper-to-bumper on this same road for at least five minutes, a new group of impatient pedestrians crossing every time finally had a chance to move forward.

Peter had taken Jackie's story surprisingly well. She'd explained how she found the game on her phone the same day Peter and Kat had been announced missing and the fact that she'd gone back in time after starting the countdown.

Peter's smile faded. "Do you have any idea who could've created a game like this?" The confusion in his voice blasted through the car in a bullet of dread, but Jackie was unfazed.

"Trust me, dude. I've done my research." She rested her head against the window and instantly regretted her choice as the car jolted forward without warning and forced her cheek into the glass. She pressed a palm onto her throbbing face as she explained her long night of Googling for anything related to the game.

"But there has to be a logical explanation behind that—that *thing* we saw earlier." Peter pulled his phone out, resorting to the internet in the same way she had. The fact that he didn't take her word for it left Jackie fuming, but he could search the internet to his heart's content for all she cared. He wouldn't find anything.

The car finally reached the end of Altemir Avenue, and the driver signaled to make a right turn toward the east side of the city. "Are you two alright?" He adjusted the rearview mirror to catch sight of their faces. Jackie let Peter do the talking, considering how he was a pro at running his mouth.

"Oh, we're good." Peter scrolled through the first page of the 163 *million* search results for **capsule app.** He'd be trapped in the research bubble for a while.

"Are you two"—the man paused as he made the turn—"high school students?"

"We go to the junior college, actually." Peter winked at Jackie, proud of his choppy lie as though he'd managed to convince someone he was a giraffe.

The driver held his gaze on the rearview mirror for an unsafe amount of time before pasting his focus onto the road. The gentle rumbling of the car on the rocky street brought Jackie into a trance of her own thoughts. She'd spent less than an hour with Peter, and although she wouldn't dare say she knew him, she couldn't deny the fact that part of her wanted to. After opening the first capsule, she understood him on a new level and was itching to get to the next one.

"So, your uncle." Jackie paused in shock by her willingness to ask him a question so effortlessly. "Did he ever find anyone?"

Peter tapped an article. "I don't think so."

"Are you guys—"

"Why book club?"

"Huh?"

"Out of all places, why was the capsule in Room 43?" Peter shut his phone off. "There's absolutely no correlation between book club and my fifteenth birthday."

The car swerved to a stop. "Here you are," the driver said as Jackie stepped out of the car in front of Cherry Ice. "You kids stay safe now."

"We'll try," Peter muttered before slamming the door shut. He crossed his arms as the man drove away. "That guy should learn to mind his own business."

The ice rink was located only a few minutes from Downtown Brookwood, but the sidewalks were nearly empty here. If it wasn't for the cheesy cherry logo hanging above the sliding front doors, the building could easily be mistaken for a mansion. Cherry blossom trees bordered the massive length of brick steps leading to the front door of Cherry Ice—perhaps a subtle joke left behind by the building's landscape architect.

Peter stopped at Jackie's side. "I haven't been here since a worthless third-grade field trip."

"I don't think this level has anything to do with you." Jackie recalled a photo from Kat's Instagram account, the one with her and that other girl—most likely Kat's sister—at Cherry Ice.

"I sure hope not." Peter headed up the stairs. "Do you have any cash on you? I think they charge general admission."

Jackie followed behind him, watching the chestnut hair jump on his head with every step. "Aren't there bigger problems to worry about?"

A group of elementary students had gathered around the door—most likely the wealthier homeschoolers that flocked the east end of Brookwood. They ran around sipping chilled water from Hydro Flasks and tossing branded duffel bags between each other in a game of hot potato. Skate sessions were often divided by age, so the group was likely waiting for their turn on the ice.

Jackie and Peter passed the kids and entered the packed lobby through the automatic sliding doors. To their right were two cut-outs in the wall to form booths. Above the first hung a wooden plaque titled *Admissions* followed by a list of prices. Behind the booth next to it stood two teen girls dressed in glittering black shirts and crimson jackets handing out skates. Jackie scrunched her nose at the mixture of sweat and artificial cherry that filled the air.

Across the other end of the lobby was a second set of glass doors, and through them was a massive field of painted red ice. Teenagers twirled in circles, adult coaches sprinkled evenly among them.

"Are you here for the Connexus Academy skate trip?" A boy around their age poked his head through the admissions booth, his voice nearly a shout to overpower the chattering in the lobby. Connexus Academy—one of Brookwood High's rivals, a private school on the eastern side of the city where more vineyards and wineries existed than actual homes. Jackie flashed the boy a grin before grabbing Peter's wrist and shooting in the direction of the second glass doors. They lost themselves in a crowd of teens wrapping paper bracelets around each other's arms and workers handing out complimentary packages of cherry-shaped gummies.

"Glad we're skipping the skates," Peter said as the glass doors slid open for them. "Let's make this quick. This place is filled with nothing but snobby rich kids. What kind of high school has field trips to go skating?"

Jackie released his arm with a frown. Based on the memory she'd seen in book club earlier, Peter's room was huge. Chances were *he* was the rich one here.

"Don't give me that look." Peter gestured to the swirling skaters through the transparent fence. "In my defense, my family is pretty well-off, but we're not rich. And we're certainly not snobby."

Jackie headed toward the entrance to the rink. *I'd argue that you're much snobbier than anyone here.* The temperature by the ice was chillier than in the lobby, so she crossed her arms to keep the goosebumps at bay.

"What do you think we're looking for?" Peter held a hand over his head as though shielding the sun from his vision, which was completely unnecessary considering how they were indoors, but she didn't bother saying anything.

"Not sure." Jackie stopped at the rink's entrance and stared at her sneakers, which were only inches away from the blood-colored ice. She narrowed her eyes at the cluster of skaters in the center of the rink, jumping and holding their arms out in elegant forms. A girl in a velvety black dress practiced the same combination of twists and spins. Her body slipped back and forth through a shimmering aluminum object.

A capsule.

Jackie took a step back, stumbling away from the ice and leaning forward, the fake cherry smell in the air striking her with a massive headache. Not only could no one else see the capsule, but they couldn't touch it either. The skater had gone through it as though it'd never existed in the first place.

When Jackie raised her throbbing head, Peter was still standing in front of the entrance to the ice rink. "Jeez, Jackie." He pinched his arm and winced, rubbing the redness away as he looked over his shoulder. "What kind of nightmare have you dragged me into?"

Jackie gulped as the girl skated through the holographic capsule once again. "I wish I knew."

Almost every ounce of color drained from the air, the saturation in the room concentrating into the red field of ice. The cheesy pop music that blared from the ceiling's speakers left Jackie with chills running down her spine. *No, don't fall for it.* Jackie's lightheadedness faded as she took a solid step forward. *It's just a game. Not a nightmare. That's all it is—a game.*

Jackie passed Peter, her sneakers landing onto the ice. Although the rink was slippery, it certainly wasn't as challenging as skating on a thin blade.

One step after the other, Jackie walked across the rink. She avoided the occasional incoming skater, taking a few side-steps out of their way. By the time she was halfway to the center, Peter had caught up to her.

"I really don't think we should be doing this." His pupils bounced around as though a demon had possessed him. For someone reckless enough to run a blog like Moral Moon, he didn't handle breaking rules very well.

"Hey!"

Jackie spotted a young woman standing at the entrance to the rink. She wore the same black shirt and coat as the two girls wore at the skate handout booth, signifying that she was a Cherry Ice employee too.

"No shoes on the ice!" The woman set her right skate onto the rink, her red curls flowing behind her as she skated in their direction.

Jackie's eyes widened. "Sorry, we—"

"Hurry up!" Now it was Peter's turn to take the lead. He ran past Jackie, shoes tapping against the ice in bold strikes.

As Jackie followed him, the breezy air rushed along her skin, calming her in the same way her runs would calm her during a cool afternoon. The skaters in the center of the rink cleared the area, frowning at the unwelcome shoes from a distance, but Jackie didn't care. They were background characters in a video game. A bunch of Koopa Troopas in a level of Super Mario Bros.

Only a few feet from the capsule, the silver ellipse lit her vision, blocking everything else from sight. She swam through a pool of black ink and red-tiled floors, the capsule her only object of focus. Her only choice. She leaned forward and stretched her arm out, the music around her shattering in dead silence.

But her fingers swiped nothing but air.

Stumbling to keep balance, the pop music faded back into her senses. She was in the real world again, the colors in the air blinding. The capsule was still in front of her, but an arm stood pressed against her ribs, blocking her path.

Peter stood to Jackie's left, his arm outstretched in front of her. "Don't get any closer." He raised the phone in his left hand— its case perfectly matching the shade of ice beneath them—attempting to steal a photo of the capsule. Jackie's breaths lengthened as the adrenaline faded away. The capsule remained invisible on Peter's screen.

The air grew hot. Jackie wasn't sure if was from her sprint or her rage. She pushed his arm away, eager to end Level Two. "We don't have time for this."

"Wait!" The fear in Peter's voice froze her arm in the air. "Can I see the app again? I'll be quick."

Jackie couldn't ignore the desperation in Peter's eyes, a strange glimmer she'd never seen in him before. He was curious. Scared. Those were two feelings she'd grown far too comfortable with the past few days. Maybe Peter was right. Maybe it wouldn't hurt to give him a chance to find answers. She reached for the phone in her back pocket.

"You can't be here without—"

Jackie's hands jumped at the piercing voice behind her. The phone slipped, landing onto the ice face-down and knocking the breath out of Jackie as though she'd been the one to fall. She stood frozen, breathless in the middle of the rink, staring at her violet phone case resting on the ice as though reaching for it might end the game, as though a broken phone meant Peter and Kat were done for. Before she could reach for it, the phone had already been swiped from her vision.

Jackie raised her chin to the freckled face of the red-haired woman. She held the violet phone up to her cheek. "Can you explain what you two are doing on the ice without your admission bracelets?" Her high-pitched voice sounded sweet, but the down-turned curve of her lips proved otherwise.

Jackie nearly shouted at the sight of her phone in the woman's hand. A few thin cracks spread across the screen, but considering the fact that the capsule was still floating to her left, the damage hadn't interfered with the game. *If the phone isn't working properly, how can we know where the next locations are?* Repairing the screen would be a huge time burn—at least a one-hour hour stop at the electronic repair shop in the downtown mall.

The woman headed toward the rink's entrance. "Why don't you come with me?"

Jackie clenched her fists as the woman calmly walked away. She assumed a teenage girl would do anything to avoid separation from her phone, but to Jackie that phone was far more than a source of addiction. This woman was unintentionally using Peter's and Kat's lives as leverage. Two *futures* were in that phone.

"Shit." Peter tucked his own phone away. "How do we get it back?"

We don't. Jackie turned to the capsule. *Not yet.* She took a step forward, but as soon as Peter caught on, he jumped to block her way.

Jackie's face burned. He'd already tried to stop her once, and she wasn't going to slip up and fall for his stupid ideas again.

"Move." She spoke through gritted teeth.

"Just let me take a closer look before we—"

"Move!"

In pure instinct, like a few clicks on a controller during an intense battle, Jackie pressed her palms against Peter's chest and shoved him to the side. Neither had time to react. Before Peter's back slammed onto the ice, Jackie rushed forward and wrapped her hands around the capsule.

LEVEL TWO

KAT PACKED A *few granola bars into the turquoise skate bag resting on the dining table in front of her. Her hair was wrapped into a bun—a hairstyle no one from Brookwood could imagine her with anymore. She wore contacts instead of her silver-rimmed glasses, leaving her emerald eyes less vibrant. Even her outfit—leggings, an oversized gray sweater, and a maroon scarf wrapped around her freckled neck—was surprisingly simple for someone with a style as radical as Kat Pike's.*

She was about to zip her bag compartments back up when her phone buzzed with a text from Whitney. **my moms running late agaainnn...lets do 5:30 instead?**

Of courseee :) *Kat sat at the table.* **Dw about it.** *This was the fifth time Whitney had postponed their plan to hang outside of school for the first time, but Kat didn't mind. She was honored Whitney had bothered reaching out to someone like her in the first place. Whitney had a million friends, impeccable style, and could even do a perfect cat eye—which Kat had always failed at—so it'd been a surprise when Whitney had sat next to bare-faced, bed-headed Kat in the cafeteria last week and asked, "Wanna hang out?"*

Another text from Whitney. **actually let's do 6**

Kat had been running her hands through the frizzy waves in her blond hair, trying to decide how to reply when the doorbell interrupted her train of thought. She looked over at the entryway and sighed. "Emmeline?"

A moment passed. Nothing.

"Emmeline?" Kat shouted. "Can you get that?"

The floorboards creaked, breaking the silence, but Kat knew it wasn't a sign Emmeline was planning to come downstairs anytime soon. She scrolled through her past text conversations with Whitney, ignoring the door. Obviously Emmeline had heard her and chose to act as though she hadn't. Surely that also meant Kat had the right to obviously hear the doorbell—and choose to act as though she hadn't.

Her phone buzzed again. This time it was a message from her sister. **You're closer**

Kat slammed her phone onto the table as she leapt from the chair. With heavy steps she approached the wooden door and swung it open to reveal an unfamiliar face.

The boy looked to be around the same age as Emmeline, possibly younger. He wore black jeans, converse, and a navy blue shirt with the illustration of a chess piece on it. A few droplets of sweat had accumulated on his forehead, his breathing was a bit too fast to call normal, and he still had a backpack dangling from his broad shoulders—all signs he'd walked here straight from school.

"Is Emmeline home?"

Kat nodded. Having strangers arrive at the Pike household wasn't necessarily a strange occurrence. Emmeline always had people stopping by to hang out with her, but Kat—well—making friends had never been easy. She was about to run upstairs to get Emmeline when the boy raised his hand in a slight wave.

"I'm Jay."

She gripped the edge of the door. "Kat."

"You go to Brookwood too?"

"Brookwood Middle," Kat said.

"Right." He tilted his head as he ran a hand across the top of his gelled hair, revealing a glimpse of his black stud earring. "Eighth grade?"

Kat nodded. Her eyes wandered into the kitchen as she debated inviting the stranger inside or not. At first Kat had assumed he was another one of Emmeline's boyfriends to add to the waiting list of her growing collection of exes, but the way he twirled with the corners of his black-and-white checkered flannel made him appear less confident than the other boys Emmeline had invited over. Emmeline's exes usually followed the same formula—they dressed the same, smiled the same, and even spoke with the same voice—but Jay was an outlier.

Kat's face grew hot. She remembered shouting for Emmeline after Jay had rung the doorbell. He didn't hear me, did he?

"Looks like you've met my adorable little sister."

Emmeline's bright voice emerged from the stairway, and her hair tumbled gently with every step toward the door. She wore her normal go-to outfit—a dulled-yellow long-sleeve under her overalls, which she always denied was a reference to the Despicable Me movie, but Kat seriously questioned that. Judging by her glossy pink smile, Emmeline evidently knew who Jay was, but Kat couldn't figure out why she wasn't surprised by his arrival. Jay was all sweaty and nervous with tense wrinkles in his forehead while Emmeline was—completely comfortable.

Emmeline squeezed between her little sister and the door, forcing Kat to release her grip on the wood. Now standing next to the mystery boy on the patio, Emmeline reached for the handle of the front door and pulled it toward her. "Give us a minute?"

Kat flinched as the front door closed in her face.

As she took her seat at the dining table again, Kat tried to convince herself that she wasn't curious, but it didn't work. Emmeline had always been a mystery to her. Although they'd spend plenty of quality time together, they never seemed to grow any closer. A certain barrier loomed between them that Kat could never cross. A level impossible to beat.

Her phone buzzed on the table. Another message from Whitney.

sorry, something came up…let's do it next week

Kat sat in the dining room, listening to the muttering of Jay and Emmeline's voices from outside the door. She tried to make out what they were saying—and she might have been able to, if she were actually focused—but Whitney's sudden change of plans distracted her. What if Whitney never wanted to hang out with her in the first place?

What if I'm just a part of some joke?

The front door swung open, and Emmeline stepped inside alone. "Hey Sis." She dangled her Baymax keychain in front of her, the Big Hero 6 character's head clattering against her car and house keys. "You ready for a drive?"

Without a second thought, Kat joined Emmeline at the door.

No, she wasn't in the mood for a drive, but what made her agree had nothing to do with her personal preferences. Emmeline would only go on drives when she needed to clear her mind. Sometimes she'd be gone for hours. No one knew where she went, but no one disrespected her privacy enough to question her.

Sitting in Emmeline's car, Kat realized the real reason why she'd decided to join was because Emmeline had never invited her before.

Kat buckled her seat belt, and Emmeline twisted the key into its lock to get the engine running.

"Do you know where I'm taking you?" Emmeline asked as she pulled out of the driveway.

Kat pursed her lips and nodded. "On a drive."

"Well yeah, smartass, but where?"

Kat shrugged.

"Drum roll please." Emmeline made a turn out of the neighborhood, not bothering to wait for Kat to reciprocate the excitement before making the big reveal. "We are headed to Lothen Heights." She pointed to a duffel bag in the back seat. "I brought some extra clothes, towels—everything we need."

"Lothen Heights? I'm gonna guess that's in Lothen."

"You got it, Sherlock. It's a campground by the ocean a few hours from here. One of my favorite spots." Emmeline took one hand off the steering wheel, waving her fingers through the air as she described the scenery. "There's a gorgeous cliff there overlooking the ocean. And you know what? It'd be a perfect weekend vacation spot. We should bring Dad there sometime."

Normally Emmeline's drives were impulsive, but this one was planned. Kat narrowed her eyes at the dashboard. She couldn't put her finger on it, but Emmeline wasn't herself today, and although Kat understood that she was the younger sister of four years—that she was supposed to be the one receiving advice, not giving it—she longed for Emmeline to open up to her. Even just once.

"Who was that guy earlier?" A little prying wouldn't hurt.

"Hm?" Emmeline glanced at Kat and returned her focus to the road with a straight face. "Oh, Jay? He's a friend of mine."

A friend. Maybe she'd been overthinking this. Maybe there really wasn't anything going on and Emmeline finally wanted to spend time with her outside of the house.

"Is he from school?"

"Yep, we have trig together. A sophomore in trig, can you believe it? That guy makes me feel like a complete idiot. Fifteen years old? More like fifteen years smarter than me." Emmeline's jaw dropped while she sorted through her memories. "Actually, now that I think of it, you might know his little sister. I'm pretty sure you're in the same grade. Gosh, what was her name again? Jamie?" She settled down, the prickly enthusiasm in her voice softening and the folds on her forehead spreading further apart. "I'm pretty sure it's Jamie."

"I don't think I know her." Kat searched Emmeline's eyes for a clue as to what could possibly be running through her sister's mind. "But why'd he stop by earlier?"

"Not sure. I think he was looking for answers." Emmeline smiled and tightened her grip on the steering wheel. "Who isn't?"

LEVEL THREE

18:35:12

PETER'S BACK SLAMMED onto the ice. A sharp pain shot through his tailbone, the chilling strike leaving him breathless, eyes locked shut. He lay on the rink, grimacing in pain, but the piercing blow faded with nothing but a dull ache.

"You good?"

Peter opened his eyes to find Jackie leaning over him with an outstretched hand.

The memory of Kat, Jay, and Emmeline invaded his mind. He hadn't known Kat in middle school, so the memory left him brimming with questions. Eighth-grade Kat was way too serious. Unnaturally calm.

"Hurry!" Jackie emphasized her outstretched arm. "My phone."

Peter raised his back from the ice and propped himself onto his feet, ignoring Jackie's arm. *Of course your first thought is your phone.* With numb fingers, he dusted the ice chips from his jeans. *That's what addiction does to a person.*

The capsule was no longer in the center of the ice rink. It had disappeared once again, leaving behind nothing but a memory that wasn't his. A memory that never should have been so vivid, even if Peter were to describe it with the talent of every author in history. All that remained in the center of the rink were the skaters who had reclaimed their space, staring at the intruders with furrowed brows. He and Jackie had overstayed their welcome, and now the frustrated employee had nearly reached the rink's entrance.

Jackie lowered her arm and caught Peter's eyes. They needed that phone back, and fast.

The pair rushed in unison toward the entrance. As they caught up to the employee, Jackie swooped around the woman's right, plucking the phone from her grip. She ran forward before the worker could say a word, and as Peter followed her toward the sliding glass doors to the lobby, he looked over his shoulder to see the woman step off the ice onto the rubber-coated floor, hands empty, jaw dropped.

Peter and Jackie entered the chattering lobby. The heat melted away the soreness in his lower back as though he'd walked into a sauna. The two split up, weaving between different workers and avoiding packages of cherry gummies held out in their direction, but by the time the front doors slid open, they were standing side by side.

The two jogged down the front steps, turning around the corner to a long stretch of sidewalk with more blooming cherry blossom trees on their left and the road bordering the parking lot to their right. As they slowed to a walking pace, the spring sun beamed onto their faces. Pink petals fluttered to the ground in a soft gust of wind.

They walked next to each other, and their breaths slowly fell into sync. That's when the laughter set in.

"That was crazy." Peter reached for the back of his shirt. The cotton fabric was still wet from the ice. "So crazy."

"Bet they hate us now." Jackie had a nice smile. A shame she didn't use it much.

"For all we know they'll be putting up wanted signs in our honor." Peter gestured out in front of him and quoted his vision. "Warning! Two crazy kids seen with *shoes*. Avoid at all costs."

Jackie's grin tumbled from her face as she remembered the phone in her hand. She raised the screen, which instantly revealed the time—2:04. Jackie sighed with relief. "I thought for sure we'd have to fix it."

Peter should've been worried about getting to the next location, but the memory from the ice rink distracted him. He knew Kat in high school as the careless bitch who said whatever whenever and fished for compliments her self-esteem didn't need, but now he wasn't sure what to believe.

"That memory just now." Jackie was about to swipe up on her screen, but she hesitated and turned her phone off instead. "Why did my brother show up at Kat's house that day?"

Peter frowned. "No way."

Jackie Mendoza? *The-girl-who-sat-right-next-to-him-first-period* Jackie Mendoza? *The girl-obsessed-with-screens* Jackie Mendoza? Had Peter really not noticed it before? They shared the same last name, same eye shape, same complexion—but he'd never put the pieces together.

"You two are siblings? Wow, I guess I didn't make the connection because he's so—I mean—you don't really—"

"It's fine." Jackie stopped on the sidewalk and looked back at him. "Everyone knows my brother. Everyone loves him. And I'm just—"

"No no no. You better stop right there." Peter crossed his arms. "Of course Jay has haters too. Trust me, I've got my problems with the guy. All I'm saying is that you two are practically from different worlds."

"Nice symbolism."

"Just hear me out, alright? You're walking around wondering why your brother showed up at Kat's house that day, but everyone knows." Peter frowned at his sneakers. "It's been nearly three years since it happened and even now the story gets tossed around. I mean, I get that he might not talk to his sister about personal drama, but like I said, you'd have to be from a different world not to hear about it."

"Hear about *what*?"

"Everyone knows Jay had a huge crush on Emmeline. She was in cheer, student gov, debate club, drama. Pretty too, in a really generic way, so practically everyone found her attractive. And she was just nerdy enough to come off as genuine."

Peter hadn't been there himself, but he'd heard the story a million times. Jay Mendoza, star of the school. One of the most well-liked students at Brookwood High. He was the kind of guy no one really had any issues with, unless they had low self-esteem, in which case they were madly jealous and hated his guts. Even the upperclassmen thought Jay was cool. As a sophomore he was friends with countless juniors and seniors, and one of those senior friends was Emmeline Pike.

"Jay asked her out to homecoming in September of 2018. Had a huge poster and everything, got his friends involved. And she said no. In front of a huge crowd of people. That's probably what he showed up to talk to her about—to ask her why she rejected him. Cause—you know—not knowing why someone doesn't like him really drives a guy like Jay nuts. You haven't heard any of this?"

Jackie showed no sign she was even listening, so Peter took that as a *no*.

"You've got to be kidding me. Even random freshmen at Brookwood know the story. News spreads. Your brother had a crush on Emmeline Pike at the absolute worst time. *The* Emmeline Pike."

"Cool story, dude." Jackie held her free hand out, a petal falling into her palm. "But what's so special about Emmeline?"

"Well, there's one thing." Peter plucked the petal from Jackie's hand and ripped it in half. "She's dead."

Jackie stopped. "Dead?"

Peter continued down the sidewalk. He really was right when he'd written that blog entry about Jackie. She'd trapped herself in video games to the point of complete social isolation.

Jackie caught up to him. "What do you mean *dead*?"

"It's complicated. We all know *how* she died, but no one really knows the full story. The *why*."

Jackie broke their brief moment of silence when she turned back to the phone in her hands. "We need to check the next location." She made her way to the edge of the sidewalk and sat on the curb, facing the road.

Peter followed and sat next to her. She'd lasted surprisingly long without checking her phone, and he was almost impressed.

He leaned over her shoulder to find that **LEVEL TWO** was now crossed out. Jackie tapped **LEVEL THREE** to reveal a pop-up with the third level's location—**PELLE COVE.**

They sighed in unison. Pelle Cove was a California State Park located on the coast of Ravensburg—over an hour's drive away.

Peter raised his brows as Jackie swiped to a new page of Capsule she hadn't shown him before. On it was an emergency button as well as a section labeled **POWER-UPS**, where a circle labeled **TWO** faded in next to **ONE**. Jackie tapped the second badge.

POWER-UP TWO: BATTERY RECHARGE
COST: ONE HOUR
RECHARGE THE PLAYER'S PHONE BATTERY TO
100% AT ANY POINT DURING THE GAME.

At the bottom of the pop-up was a button labeled **ACTIVATE.**

Peter snatched the phone from her grip. "Why haven't you shown me this page before?"

Jackie reached for her phone, but Peter scooted away. Obviously she didn't trust him. Did she really think he was going to click the emergency button and risk three hours of the countdown? He wasn't the reckless one here. No, what he needed to figure out was if there were any clues inside the game. Something alluding to a creator. There had to be a person behind this. It was the only semi-logical explanation.

Jackie settled her restlessness, sitting a few feet away from him on the curb. Peter swiped at different angles across the screen, searching for a new page, tab, pop-up—anything really. Unfortunately there were only two pages. First, the countdown. Second, the emergency button followed by the power-ups. He held the worthless phone back to Jackie, which she grabbed instantly.

"Look." Jackie's voice was deeper now, catching Peter off-guard. She leaned toward him, her deep eyes shimmering under the blazing afternoon sun. "I need you to tell me what you know."

Really, is this girl serious? Tell her what I know? She was the one who had been following him around at school all day. She was the one who burst into his book club meeting, opened a floating capsule, and gave him a memory of his past. It was Jackie who reeled him into this mess, and now she was questioning whether he had something to do with it? This girl was a hypocrite. An absolute hypocrite.

"Tell you what I know...regarding?" Peter leaned away from her, pinching a pebble from the road and rolling it between his fingers. "Let's see. I'm pretty good at physics. I also know a lot about musical theory, if that's something you're interested in. And if you don't care about my valuable knowledge, I do have information on the latest gossip. I'm a master at observation."

Jackie faced the ground, her silky hair falling in strands across the side of her face. "I thought you were on my side here."

"You obviously don't, judging by the fact that you don't trust me." The worries he'd been pushing away all day started to seep in, leaving him light-headed. He rubbed his temple, thinking about the bed he'd forgotten to make this morning. He'd absolutely butchered his daily routine. "I should be at home studying for the SATs right now, but no. I just snuck into an ice rink with a complete stranger and now I can't get the thought out of my mind that there are giant floating capsules only *we* can see that give us visions of the past and that this stupid game, or whatever it is, might actually be real. If I wasn't as confused as you are, I wouldn't be here."

A few more strands fell loose from behind her ear, blocking her face from him completely.

Peter relaxed his hand, the pebble falling onto the road with a *click.*

A car raced by, creating a breeze that ruffled their hair. Jackie turned to face him, and as they locked eyes, her hair floated around her in wisps. It was the first time Peter wondered why she was doing this in the first place. Why would Jackie try to help him—the most despised student at Brookwood, or even Kat—the girl who didn't earn one ounce of the popularity she was drowning in? Sure, maybe someone like Jay would jump at the opportunity to save someone's life, but Jackie? The girl was the opposite of a people-pleaser. She spent every minute of her free time in Mr.

Berkshire's class playing mobile games and ignoring anyone who made an effort to talk to her.

"So everything you said in the car earlier. All of the time travel stuff. You really meant it, didn't you?"

Jackie shrugged. "I lived it."

Peter nodded slowly, finally processing the story she'd told him earlier. On the Riderr here he'd been scared by the first level's memory, and sure—he did crack some jokes about it—but he wasn't fully on board with the idea that it really happened. Now that he'd seen a look into Kat's life—a memory that wasn't even his own—Jackie's story was starting to sound believable.

"Okay, so we're obviously both really confused," Peter said.

"Obviously."

"And I know you're fully convinced this is a magical game, but we can't rule out the possibility that Kat knows something."

Jackie stood from the curb.

"Where are you going?"

"The next location." Her footsteps trailed down the sidewalk. "Alone."

"Yeah?" Peter stood and followed her. *So dramatic.* "You really think you have superhuman walking abilities, don't you?"

"I'm taking the bus."

"With what money?"

Jackie stopped in her tracks, dead silent.

"You left your backpack in the Riderr earlier." Peter stopped at her side and pointed to the phone resting in her hand. "That's what happens when people get too addicted to their phones. They forget what really matters. Like their wallet, and their geometry textbook, and their—"

"You knew I left it and didn't tell me?" She stared at Peter, her face a striking red.

"Look, I can get us a ride to Pelle Cove a lot easier than you can. It's in both of our best interests to win the game. Plus, I may come in handy later. You never know when you'll need a big strong man to sweep in and save you."

The redness in her face faded, replaced with furrowed brows.

"Joke." Peter sighed. "That was a joke. But anyways, I'll be here to help you with this. All I ask is that we make a quick stop to see if Kat knows anything."

"Dude, when are you gonna catch on? I've tried to understand this game before, but it's hopeless. All this investigating is wasting our time. Look at what happened at the ice rink. If it weren't for you, my phone wouldn't be cracked."

"Whoa, okay. I didn't know the quiet girl had a temper." Peter took a step toward Jackie and spoke painfully slow. "But really, there's no reason to get all worked up over this. I know exactly where Kat is. One hour detour, tops. I'll ask her a few questions, see what she knows, and we're done. In and out, we're back on track. If it turns out she's just as clueless as we are, I'll drop my so-called *investigation* and focus on the levels. Deal?" Peter held his hand out. "And to be frank, you really don't have any other options."

Jackie glared at Peter and shook his hand. Not necessarily firmly, but not hesitantly either.

"Great, I'll get us a ride." Peter pulled his phone out of his pocket and navigated to the Riderr app.

"Isn't she in class?"

"She has a free sixth period. Works part-time at Halos."

Jackie crossed her arms. "Weird knowledge."

"Great, it's ordered." Peter tucked his phone away. "Now we wait."

#129

WHEN IS BROOKWOOD going to wake up and realize that Jay Mendoza is mediocre at everything he does? He's made out to be a prodigy, but he's not. The only thing he has going for him is the fact that he's two years ahead in math and science, but have you seen his grades? Hardly above average. He's not the smartest student in class, he's not the best athlete on the varsity basketball team, and he's certainly not the best guitar player at school. Yeah, I've seen his YouTube covers.

The only thing that stands out about Jay is that he knows how to give compliments, but having good people skills doesn't make him talented. All he does is dress pretty and call people nicknames. And to think Emmeline would rather die than go to hoco with him. Obviously she recognized the phoniness everyone else was too blind to see.

Moon.

17:49:02

TWO HAMBURGERS AND a large order of fries. Only five minutes into her shift Kat had somehow managed to drop an entire tray of food onto the floor, plates shattering, food splattering. One moment she was living in her ordinary world, the next she was trapped in the past, and before she knew it she was thrown back into reality, knees buckling from the impact.

Her loss of balance had felt just like her fall in the gym during lunch, but this time, Kat couldn't stop thinking about the first time she'd met Jay Mendoza.

After cleaning the mess and gathering stares from literally *everyone* in the room, Kat situated herself at the least desirable booth in the corner of Halos—the one she sat at now, phone in hand. The booth had a broken light fixture dangling above it, leaving the ambiance in the corner dark in comparison to the other seats in the restaurant. Unless Halos seats were in demand, the grimy booth was open for employees during their breaks. Not that it was Kat's break or anything.

Remembering the image of fifteen-year-old Jay standing at her doorstep was definitely strange, but it was explainable. She'd been there. The memory was hers, so it didn't leave her panicked, but it did help her realize how unexplainable it was that she'd remembered Peter's fifteenth birthday in the first place. How could she possibly recall a memory that wasn't hers? How could she possibly recall a memory when she wasn't even there?

Kat scrolled through responses to a Reddit post from eleven years ago. It was written by a nineteen-year-old college student who claimed to have a memory that didn't belong to him. The student explained that he remembered his father taking him fishing on his fifth birthday. When he brought up the trip one summer evening, his father clearly stated that he'd never taken him fishing before. The man did, however, take the nineteen-year-old's brother fishing for his fifth birthday—the brother who was nine years older than him. When he called his brother to ask about his fifth birthday, they both recalled the same exact memory.

This college student was now fully convinced he had one of his older brother's childhood memories and was turning to Reddit—of all places to request medical advice—for an explanation behind this strange phenomenon. There were only seven replies in response to his post. Two users called him crazy, one claimed to have a similar experience but shared no context, and the other four displayed a genuine concern for his mental health. Kat stopped scrolling when she reached the final reply.

Sounds like psychosis to me.

Psychosis? A group had mentioned the term during a schizophrenia presentation in biology class last year. Kat didn't remember what it meant, so she Googled a definition.

psy·cho·sis /sī'kōsəs/: a severe mental disorder in which thought and emotions are so impaired that contact is lost with external reality.

Kat tossed her phone aside and slammed her head onto the sticky table. She focused on the light chattering of customers in Halos in an attempt to calm herself. Maybe she really was losing touch with reality. Maybe her mind had made up an imaginary birthday for Peter Moon to mess with her. But even if that were true, why would her mind fake a memory about Peter? What a random choice.

Kat's temple ached from the pressure of her own head.

"Hey." A bold voice slid through her ears, overpowering the buzz of the room. "What's wrong?"

Kat raised her throbbing head to find her coworker Owen sitting in front of her. He leaned forward and rested his chin on his palm. Owen was a junior at Brookwood High, and although they didn't have any classes together, they'd shared quite a few fun conversations at work.

"Let's just say I'm having a weird day."

"Yeah, I figured. You're not usually the clumsy type." Owen adjusted the maroon apron over his black shirt—the same uniform Kat was dressed in. His eyes jolted to her phone screen, and Kat ripped the device from the table, but she was too late. "Psychosis, huh?"

"It's nothing."

Owen faced the window, his dark skin glowing as the golden light struck him at the perfect angle. "I don't know what's going on with you, but I'm worried."

"Don't be."

Owen tapped his fingers on the table and stared at the hills in the distance. He always had this strange caring nature. Looked out for her, gave her advice, was always the first to offer her a hand, but if Owen knew who she really was, he wouldn't be eager to call Kat his friend anymore.

"I haven't really been sure how to bring this up." Owen shut his eyes, bracing himself. "But have you been—like—I don't know—"

"Just spit it out." Kat exited from the Reddit page before shutting her phone off.

Owen stopped tapping the table and opened his eyes to meet Kat's. "Have you been stealing spoons?"

A grin grew across Kat's face as she set her phone face-down onto the table. Someone had finally noticed. She'd been slipping spoons into the sleeves of her jacket on the way home from work after every shift. She now had a total of thirty-seven spoons sitting in her desk drawer at home. Seeing the confused looks on her coworkers' faces on the rare occasion a customer ordered a soup had comprised sixty percent of her work entertainment for the past month.

"Stealing spoons?" Kat shook her head. "You're crazy."

"I know I shouldn't point fingers." Owen held his head firm, pasted in the air. He wasn't convinced. "But we all know something weird is going on with the spoon count. I just want you to know that if you're struggling with something right now, there are better ways to cope with it. You can talk to a friend, like me, and there's also professional help, like therapy, or..."

Kat reached for his hand and folded his fingers against his palm until only his index finger was pointing at her. "You say you shouldn't point fingers, but that's exactly what you're doing."

"No." Owen pulled his hand away from her grip and crossed his arms. "What I'm doing is making sure our customers don't have to eat soup with forks."

The front door to Halos swung open, and her eyes widened at the sight of Peter Moon. Behind him was that same girl who had run into Kat in the math hall this morning. It couldn't be a coincidence. Peter occasionally came to eat at Halos after school, but never during sixth period, and certainly not with another person. Yet here he was.

"I'm here for you, okay? If you need help with anything—anything at all—let me know."

Kat ignored Owen, watching Peter and the mystery girl walk their way to one of the open booths near the door. Was she a friend? Kat hadn't heard of Peter having friends before. Not since freshman year, at least. Who would choose to be friends with a guy like him?

"You should think about skipping your shift." Owen slid out from the booth, pausing before heading to the kitchen. "I'll find a way to cover for you. Get some rest."

"No need for that." Kat tucked her phone into the front pocket of her apron and rushed toward Peter. "I got table three!"

At the sound of Kat's voice, Peter looked over and smiled at her. Surely he had to know something about the memory she'd seen this morning.

"I see you've brought a date today." Kat approached the edge of the table and studied the girl sitting across from Peter. Tan skin, infinitely dark eyes, and hair that draped across the sides of her face like wet shower curtains. Kat was positive she'd never interacted with her before this morning, but she seemed familiar.

"I'll take a salad," Peter said. "Balsamic vinaigrette."

Kat had already made a mental note of his salad. That was all Peter ever ordered at Halos. Salad, salad, salad. He didn't even switch up the dressing. But what Kat really didn't understand was why he came in the first place. The salads at Halos were nothing special.

"You?" she asked the girl across from him.

"I'll pass."

"Well if you're going to sit here and take up space, you better buy something." Kat tapped her foot as the girl frowned at the table, contemplating her order. These two likely didn't have a free period, which meant they were skipping class to be here. Skipping class for a meal at Halos was wildly out of character for the punctual Peter Moon, and hanging out with Peter at Halos was wildly out of character for anyone with even a pinch of sanity.

"Fine, I guess." The girl rested her head against the wall. "A chocolate milkshake then."

"Wow Jackie, a chocolate milkshake?" Peter spoke with a loose lower jaw and raised brows. "Doesn't get much worse than that."

Jackie frowned. "What's with the salad?" Her voice was dull, uninterested. It was almost like she didn't want to be here with Peter in the first place.

He raised his chin, eyes glowing. "I try to be healthy."

Kat raised her voice. "That all for you then?"

"For the order. But I do have a question for you regarding something else." Peter leaned toward her, refusing to blink. "What's my uncle's name?"

Kat pursed her lips, waiting for him to say something else, but he simply sat with a slappable grin on his face.

"Nicholas." Kat plopped herself onto the booth seat next to Peter. "Why the hell do I know it's Nicholas?"

Peter's voice reduced to nothing more than a mumble. "You saw the memories too."

"Your fifteenth birthday?" Kat asked.

"And Jay showing up at your house." Peter turned to the girl across the table, prompting her to hold her phone out toward Kat. On the screen was a countdown and a sentence explaining that Peter and Kat—the *subjects*—would meet their demise unless they completed the levels in time.

"Do you know anything about this app?" Peter pointed at Jackie's screen. "Does it look familiar to you?"

Kat shook her head. "What does this have to do with the memories?"

"Told you she wouldn't know." The girl pulled her phone away, eyes drifting to the door. "We should get going."

"You're right." Peter tried to get up, but Kat refused to move, locking Peter in the booth.

"Going where?" Kat asked.

Jackie stood next to the booth. "Pelle Cove."

Kat laughed. First Peter showed up at Halos with a girl, next he finally displayed a hint of having answers, and now he was leaving to go to the beach before even finishing his salad? Oh man, now this was getting interesting.

Peter pulled his phone out from under the table. "I'll get another Riderr."

"That won't be necessary." Kat made eye contact with both of them, her smile growing so wide it made her cheeks ache. This entire situation was bizarre, and although she was wildly curious and had no idea what was going on, she couldn't stop the excitement from seeping in. What loser would turn down the opportunity to hang out with the Brookwood crazy boy and his awkward girlfriend, two kids who were somehow involved in giving her visions of the past? "I can help."

"No." Peter shook his head. "No, you are *not* coming with us."

Kat pressed her glasses closer to her face. "And why not?"

"I don't know why you'd decide to join us when you don't even understand what's going on, but I don't care. You're not coming. Let me explain this really simply for you. You and I are both in danger, and if you'd like to wake up tomorrow morning with a beating heart, you'll get out of my way so Jackie and I can do what we have to do. You can stay here, keep up with your little shift at Halos, and assuming the next three levels are more of those weird floating capsules we have to open, brace yourself for three more random memories. Besides, we can't mess around with time anymore. Level Three is at Pelle Cove, but the last two locations could be in Italy for all we know."

"Which is exactly why you need my help." Kat knew what Peter was doing. He wanted to scare her out of coming along by blabbering nonsense he knew she wouldn't understand, but all he'd managed to do was intrigue her further. Chasing down floating capsules to unlock memories of the past? Gosh, this was either really dangerous or these two kids were messed up in the head, and both options were a lot more interesting than her usual shift at Halos. "I can get us a car."

Before Peter could oppose, Jackie spoke up. "A car would be helpful."

Peter blinked at Jackie a few times before turning back to Kat. "And what's in it for you?"

"People do weird shit when they're bored." Kat stood from the table, finally letting Peter out. She turned to see Owen staring at her from behind the bar, his brows furrowed.

"You two can wait outside." Kat offered Owen a subtle wave. "Give me a few minutes to change and we're out of here."

"Aw. What about my salad?"

Kat frowned at Peter, and he raised his hands as though she were holding a gun to his head.

"Relax." Peter raised his brows. "I'm kidding."

17:27:32

THE TIME WAS 3:08 in the afternoon, nearing the end of Brookwood High's last period of the day. Peter stood next to Jackie at the front of Halos with perfect posture, eyes frozen, lips pursed. He'd finally stopped running his mouth, and although Jackie should have enjoyed the silence, his strange behavior left her uncomfortable, so she escaped reality by checking her phone.

Eugene had messaged her on Discord over an hour ago. **So what's going on with that missing kid situation?**

Normally Jackie would never take so long to reply to Eugene. So much had happened in the past few hours that Jackie could hardly comprehend how on a normal day she'd be solving a LIMBO level in the middle of a boring language arts lecture right now.

Her thumb rocked back and forth over her screen, debating how to reply. She didn't want to scare Eugene away with her personal problems, and in less than twenty-four hours this would be over with anyway, so did it really make sense to tell him about Capsule?

What if he doesn't believe me? Jackie's thumb paused. *What if he calls me crazy?*

Before Jackie could make up her mind, a second Discord message appeared from Eugene's side of the screen. **I have plans with my friends today...let's play earlier? Like 4?**

Sorry. Eugene could sniff lies from a mile away, so she refrained from messaging him a stupid excuse. **I'll be free tomorrow**

Jackie bit her lip as Eugene's *typing* icon appeared. **Tomorrow? There's no way your busy**

Jackie responded with **you're*** to dodge his indirect question. The ironic part was that she actually *was* busy. Probably for the first time in years. She couldn't remember when she'd last turned down a gaming session with Eugene, if she'd even done so before. Calling Eugene had always been the highlight of her day.

"Eugenie?"

Jackie flinched at the sound of Peter's voice in her ear. She turned her phone off and tucked it into her back pocket. "It's Eugene." She spoke quickly, avoiding eye-contact with Peter, who stood leaning over her shoulder. "He's an online friend."

Jackie's own phrase caught her off-guard. She'd called Eugene an *online* friend. That was a first.

"Online friend, huh?" Peter leaned away and stared at the boring parking lot again. "What do you guys even do? FaceTime all day?"

"We don't FaceTime." Jackie thought back to the PC in her room. Part of her wished she could quit this stupid Capsule game and play a round of Mystery Bullets with Eugene instead, but death was much more challenging to ignore when it stood right next to her.

"Really? No FaceTime?" Peter crossed his arms. "So I'm guessing that means you don't know what he looks like."

"No, I don't."

"And how old is he?"

"Sixteen."

"*Sure.*"

Jackie rolled her eyes. It was true that she'd never seen Eugene before, but that didn't mean he'd been lying about his identity for four years.

"You're being catfished." Peter's face grew angular, the softness fading until his skin morphed into the mask of the boy behind Moral Moon. His complexion hollowed, leaving him lifeless.

Plastic.

"There's nothing I hate more than fake people," he muttered.

"Eugene isn't fake." Jackie took a side-step away from Peter's unfamiliar face. "He's my best friend, but I guess you wouldn't know what that's like."

Ever since Jackie had met Peter this morning he'd caused nothing but trouble, yet none of his annoying acts had ever bothered her as much as the insults directed at her best friend. Peter didn't know anything about Eugene and had already managed to judge him and accuse him of being a liar. The blood rushed to Jackie's head, and her jaw went tense to restrain herself from shouting. For a moment Jackie considered handing him her phone and placing the responsibility of Capsule between his hands instead of hers.

Peter can save himself.

But Jackie couldn't do it. She couldn't give Peter the controller mid-way through a level. No, she was too invested for that. The first two memories framed Capsule as a narrative game. Surely the memories hadn't been random. Capsule had a story to tell, and the game had chosen Peter and Kat as the main characters. If Jackie dropped out now, she'd never understand the story's significance.

She'd never understand why she'd been chosen as the player.

No, I'm doing this. She folded her fingers around her screen as though she were clutching a joystick at an arcade. She'd clicked play, and now she was in this to win.

Now she was addicted.

The front door to Halos swung open. Kat stormed past them with steps daring enough to be mistaken as gunshots. She no longer wore her black work apron, but the same outfit from this morning—a white top with a sunflower embroidered into it and a pair of bright pink calf socks, the left scrunched a bit more than the right. Cartoon keychains dangled from every zipper of her pineapple-colored backpack. Among them Jackie recognized the same Baymax keychain Emmeline had clipped to her keys in the Level Two memory.

"Let's go." Kat gripped a key in her right hand in the same way she'd grip a knife.

Peter's and Jackie's eyes met, and the tension between them shattered. They followed Kat to a white Toyota Highlander a few rows from the front of Halos. Jackie still hadn't gotten over the fact that he'd slandered Eugene, but they were in this game together, and she could at least try to get along with him until they reached the end.

Kat unlocked the SUV and held the key toward Peter. "Let's get to Pelle Cove."

Peter's face went red. "Wait—no—I don't—"

"Just spit it out." Kat pressed the key's tip against Peter's chest.

"I don't have my license."

"Well neither do I."

Peter pointed at the SUV. "Then why do you—"

"My friend Owen's letting me borrow it." Kat pulled the key away from Peter and grinned. That shade of lip gloss—it was the same shade of pink Emmeline had worn that day.

Peter crossed his arms to protect himself from a future key attack. "And he's trusting you with a car when you don't even have your license?"

"Well it's not like he knows that part." Jackie flinched as Kat pointed the sharp end of the key toward her. "I hope you can drive, because if you can't, we're out of options."

Jackie took the key from Kat with a loose grip. "I have my permit."

"Nice." Kat headed for the other side of the car. "I call shotgun."

"You know what?" Peter stepped in front of the driver's seat, blocking Jackie's way. "Why don't we just call another Riderr?"

Jackie guarded the key safely inside of her fist. This was their best option, and Peter knew it. They had no idea how challenging the next few levels would be, so it'd be smarter to maintain as much control over transportation as possible.

Peter sighed and stepped away from the door. "Fine."

Jackie hopped into the driver's seat and tightened her face to keep from smiling as Peter mumbled his complaints from the back. It was strange to think that someone as rule-following as Peter could create Moral Moon. Legally, he was a goodie-two-shoes, but socially, he was an overconfident rebel.

Peter slammed the back door shut as Jackie started the car. She wrapped her fingers around the steering wheel with a death grip, the urge to smile fading. Her only driving experience was a few trips with Jay and Mr. Mendoza back and forth from home to Brookwood High. She had actually only received her permit two weeks ago, but she wouldn't mention that detail. As long as she drove safely, they'd be fine.

Jackie shifted the car into reverse and backed out of the parking space. "Can you pull up directions?"

Kat reached into her backpack for her iPhone. It didn't have a case. "I'm on it."

"I still think this is a horrible idea," Peter said from the back seat.

"Don't worry, dude." Jackie forced herself to loosen the grip on the steering wheel. "I can drive."

Kat turned the volume on her phone up. "Starting route to Pelle Cove State Park," the robotic voice spoke.

"Great." Peter threw his hands in the air. "All the way up those windy cliff roads with an inexperienced driver."

Winding roads? Jackie had never driven on anything more than the calm streets between Brookwood High and her house, but she cloaked her nervousness. She'd rather not deal with Peter overreacting any more than he already was.

According to Kat, a majority of the trip to Pelle Cove took place on a single road starting on the far west end of Brookwood. All they had to do was get there and the remainder of the trip to the wealthy beach town of Ravensburg would be smooth sailing.

Jackie carefully followed the phone's directions, her driver's confidence increasing with every stoplight she'd pass. Soon enough they'd left the comfort of Old Town Brookwood and entered the west end of the city, Brookwood's commercial district. The roads here had multiple lanes in both directions, cars frequently turning into vast parking lots for big-box stores and popular restaurant chains.

There weren't many trees on this side of town. The SUV was out in the open, sunlight beaming through the windshield and blinding Jackie's vision. She flipped the sun visor down and focused strictly on the lane in front of her, trying to ignore the cars zooming too close for comfort to her left and right. *I have to drive faster.* She almost applied more pressure on the gas, but the phone ringing in her back pocket interrupted her. With one hand remaining on the steering wheel, she grabbed her vibrating phone and passed it to Kat. "Who's calling?"

"Kuya?" Kat frowned at the screen. "Weird name. Want me to answer?"

"It's my brother." Jackie glanced at the time on the SUV's display screen—3:37. The school day had come to an end seven minutes ago, and she'd forgotten to tell Jay that she didn't need a ride home from school today. For a moment she considered ignoring the call, but the last thing they needed was her overprotective dad trying to chase her down, so she gave in. "Yeah. Put him on speaker."

Kat swiped to answer the call, and Jay's voice filled the SUV without delay. "Jackie? Where are you?"

"Oh sorry, I'm…" Jackie paused to focus on completing a left turn. "I'm uh—walking to Pepperdine. With a classmate."

"The candy store?"

"Yeah." Jackie cringed. Not because she couldn't have come up with a stupider destination than Pepperdine, but because she'd never gone anywhere with a classmate outside of school before. She half-expected Jay to call her out for lying right on the spot.

"Oh. Well, okay then. That's great, Jackie." His heavy breathing concealed the pinch of enthusiasm in his voice. He almost sounded like someone was timing how long it'd take him to reach the car. "Do you think you could get a ride home? I'm planning to visit a friend."

Jackie nodded before remembering that he couldn't see her. "Yeah."

Kat's phone boomed with the robotic voice again. "In 1.3 miles, turn right onto Pelle Road." Kat shuffled to stop the navigation before it could speak again.

"Was that—"

"Phone's being weird," Jackie shouted. "Alright, just got to Pepperdine. Have fun with your friend."

"Thanks. I'll see you—"

Kat ended the call before Jay could finish, lowered her arm, and whispered, "Wait."

Jackie's eyes wandered around the road, sensing Kat's stare in her direction.

"That was Jay, wasn't it?" Kat's booming voice burned Jackie's ears. "Like, *Jay Mendoza* Jay? *Varsity-basketball* Jay? *Accepted-into-Stanford* Jay?"

Jackie sighed. "Bingo."

"Jay's your brother?" The SUV slowed to a stop before turning onto Pelle Road, so Kat ended the navigation on her phone. "No way."

Peter laughed. "That's what I said."

"But you two are so different," Kat said. "Jay gets all nervous for no reason because he's afraid of letting people down. But you're like—too chill for that kind of stuff."

"Right?" Peter said. "At least Jackie's quiet. Jay's alway getting involved with other people's business. And those damn flannels—how many does he own?"

"He definitely likes his flannels." Kat looked over her shoulder at Peter. "But I will admit he's pretty good at guitar."

"Jay, good at guitar?" Peter leaned forward. "You should see me play sometime."

Jackie ignored their blabbering and focused on the road. Everyone always had something to say about Jay, even during a life-threatening game like Capsule. Of course Jay had to show up in the Level Two memory of Kat and Emmeline. Video games were the one thing Jackie had managed to keep to herself, and now

Jay had to trickle into it and outshine her just like in everything else.

The massive buildings of Brookwood's commercial district grew more infrequent the further Jackie drove down Pelle Road. The lanes narrowed, but luckily there were hardly any other cars around, so Jackie didn't have to stress about driving too slow. Eventually Peter and Kat's conversation trickled off, and Kat asked Jackie for her iPhone password so she could explore the Capsule app on her own. Kat whispered the different power-up descriptions to herself as the commercial buildings completely left Jackie's sight.

The road grew windier up the hills of shriveled dead grass, the rocky ledge to her right leaving Jackie slightly uncomfortable, but biting her lower lip calmed her nerves.

"There's one thing I really can't wrap my head around," Peter said.

Jackie caught Peter frowning in the reflection on the rearview mirror, which had been pointed too low. Her heart pounded as she took one hand off the steering wheel to adjust the mirror to suit her height.

Once Jackie had returned her full attention back to the road, Peter continued. "I know I said I'd stop my investigation and all, and I am. But let's say we ignore where this game came from. Let's say it's magic. Or some weird form of mother-nature or something. Let's say this game is completely unexplainable, which is really hard to believe, but I can maybe get on board with it. Even if that's the case, why would the game choose us? I can't get that question out of my mind."

The car fell silent.

Why us?

The question hadn't left Jackie's mind either. Why would this mysterious game target three strangers from the same school?

"And then there's that weird phrase," Peter said. "*Clean the mess, erase the memories, and reverse the day.*"

Jackie had been too busy focusing on the chaos of the game that she hadn't spent any time analyzing what the phrase meant. "Maybe it's talking about our memories of the levels."

"Or our memories of the game." Peter's voice grew louder, more confident. "Think about it. Whenever we try searching anything up, it's like the game doesn't exist. What if other people have played Capsule too, but they just don't remember? In that case, maybe the *mess* Capsule refers to is the game itself. *Clean the mess,* as in clean up the weird, unexplainable things that happened today. *Erase the memories,* meaning our memories of said mess."

"*And reverse the day,*" Jackie added. "Like none of this ever happened."

"We already know that you're technically from the future, right? But only you remember what happened. Obviously Capsule has control over time—and our memories." Peter's enthusiasm settled, his voice hard to hear over the rumbling of the car on the rocky road. "We win the game, and our lives go back to normal. We can relive this day the way it was supposed to be. Kat and I won't be threatened by some countdown, and you won't have to deal with the app."

Kat's booming laugh warmed the car. Jackie hadn't noticed the goosebumps on her own arms until they'd disappeared.

"So you're from the future?" Kat pointed her thumb at Jackie. "Wow. This keeps getting better."

For the remainder of the drive, Peter brought Kat up to date on everything he and Jackie knew regarding the game. He explained Jackie's experience with traveling back in time, opening the first capsule in book club, and the craziness at Cherry Ice. The information didn't bother Kat one bit. She grinned the entire time, asking questions and challenging the obscure facts Peter spouted in her direction.

"So you're saying we have"—Kat checked the time on the Capsule app—"about seventeen hours left before we die?"

"Yes," Peter said. "Exactly."

Jackie wasn't sure whether Kat believed them or not. Surely if she trusted what Peter had explained she'd be petrified, or at least confused. It almost seemed like she'd only decided to come along for entertainment, and if that were the case, Kat would be in for a treat.

The twists of Pelle Road eventually settled as the ocean emerged at the horizon. An emerald green sign by the side of the road read *Welcome to Ravensburg* in bold white letters. They drove past the few dingy buildings located by the coast—a surf shop, a seafood restaurant, and a souvenir store of worthless keychains and postcards.

Almost there.

In a few minutes they'd run straight into Pelle Cove State Park. Jackie wanted to be proud that she'd driven so far from home, but she couldn't move on from the fact that after the game, she wouldn't remember anything from today. This memory right now, of her driving on Pelle Road with the water glimmering in the distance—was she really okay with forgetting it?

16:43:05

THE SAND DUNES formed a wall at Pelle Cove, separating the barbecue grills and empty picnic tables from the shore. Every stride up the dune they'd chosen to scale left Jackie more exhausted than the last. The sand sank under her shoes, shifting her lower and stifling her progress.

Kat dodged one of the many ankle-slicing shrubs. "I used to come here with my family all the time."

"Really? I never pictured you as the outdoorsy type." Peter counted the traits with his fingers. "Kat Pike—professional drama queen, aspiring Instagram influencer, climate change activist, and—you know what?" He dropped his hand, ceasing his count. "I think I'm starting to see it now."

"Clever one, Seinfeld," Kat said.

"Do you know what I do for some time out of the house?" Peter patted his shoulders. "I go to the gym. Gotta get these muscles somewhere."

Jackie lengthened her strides, taking the lead up the dune and filling her sneakers with sand in the process. If Peter and Kat would rather share a worthless conversation instead of being mature about the game, Jackie would have to play the responsible role. She scanned to her left and right as she climbed, searching the adjacent dunes for a hint of an aluminum capsule.

"Yeah?" Kat chuckled. "What gym?"

"Joke." The enthusiasm in Peter's voice fell flat. "That was a joke. But in my defense, I bike religiously. And I mean *religiously*. I could start a bike cult if I wanted to. I mean, I'm talking twelve miles a day. Then there's my nightly exercise regimen. Mostly pushups and sit-ups. Personally, I think body weight exercises are healthier and easier on the joints. The machines at the gym aren't natural. Read a whole book about it."

Jackie stopped at the sand dune's peak. She hadn't visited Pelle Cove since August of last year, a time when the beach roared with laughter and half-naked bodies, beach towels, and umbrellas covered every inch of sand. Today the beach was deserted, discomforting, yet still undeniably beautiful. Seagulls soared in flocks over the shore, and the waves twisted in the distance. White clouds pasted themselves against the gray sky, creating the illusion of a sunny day.

"Whoa." Kat appeared at Jackie's right. "It's really pretty."

Kat looked younger than usual, and despite her makeup, she resembled the eighth-grade Kat Jackie had seen in the Level Two memory.

Peter nearly lost his balance on a loose plant on the way up, catching Jackie and Kat's attention. They stared him down as he joined the dune's peak, brows pointed toward his nose even though he smiled to crack a joke. "I'm surprised you're not Instagramming this right here." He held an imaginary phone up to Kat's face. "I can totally picture it—you posing on top of this sand dune with the caption *summer vibes*. Actually—no. You'd be more dramatic. Something like, *the sky brightens my world*." He waved his hands in the air, emulating a rainbow.

Jackie bit her cheek to keep from smiling. Although she held a distaste for Peter's judgmental attitude, she couldn't deny that his impression of Kat's Instagram caption was spot-on.

"So we're here to twist open a floating pill?" Kat asked.

Jackie forgot why she'd almost smiled a moment ago. It made sense that Kat was skeptical, but Jackie couldn't stomach that sparkle in her eyes. This game was dangerous, and Kat refused to acknowledge that Capsule was threatening her life.

"Yeah. That's what Peter explained earlier." Jackie crossed her arms. "The capsule has to be somewhere nearby. We just have to find it."

"Sounds exhausting." Kat reached into her backpack, retrieving a handful of granola bars. "Always keep emergency snacks on me. Want one?"

Jackie gladly took a bar from her, the thought of food lightening her spirits. She couldn't remember what she'd eaten this morning, but judging by the rumbling in her stomach as she opened the granola bar's packaging, whatever it was hadn't been enough.

Kat held a bar toward Peter, her eyes lingering on Jackie to avoid his gaze. Peter bowed with his hands outstretched, grabbing the bar in the process. "Why thank you, Your Majesty." He flipped the granola bar over as he straightened his back, scanned the nutrition label, and held the bar back to her.

"It's vegan." Kat pushed his arm into his chest, insisting he keep it. "Healthy," she stated, as though *healthy* were a synonym for *vegan*.

"Yeah, I'm not sure if I consider vegan healthy." Peter tossed the granola bar at Kat this time, forcing her to catch it. "But sugar? I know with complete confidence that sugar is toxic, and this energy bar you call *healthy* has loads of it."

Jackie headed down the other side of the dune, a much more gradual path than the way up. Peter's and Kat's voices followed her back.

"Oh, so you're anti-vegan now?" Kat dropped Peter's rejected granola bar into her backpack. "I'm not even vegan, you know. I just try to get healthier snacks because—"

"I'm not anti-vegan. I'm *anti-sugar*. All I'm saying is that there's no way an egg is less healthy than a few teaspoons of sugar. Or that a cup of milk causes more damage than one of those ridiculously sweet vegan cinnamon buns they sell at Halos. Not to mention chicken teriyaki. Really? Is society so corrupt that we need to season our meat with sugar now?"

Jackie tuned out their argument as they reached the base of the sand dune. The only object in sight was a lifeguard tower in the distance, a single ring-shaped buoy hanging off the side of its deck.

Jackie had found the first two capsules in obvious locations. The capsule in book club had floated inside the discussion circle, and the one at Cherry Ice hovered boldly over the rink. What if Capsule had spoon-fed them the first, like the beginning levels of a game or the introductory trial? What if tracking down the next three capsules would end up being more challenging than she'd been anticipating?

"I thought I heard you were vegetarian," Kat said.

"Low-carb pescatarian, actually. It's a very specific—"

"Can you guys focus? Please?" Jackie couldn't remember the last time she'd interrupted anyone like that before, but she held no remorse for doing so. Jackie took another bite of her granola bar, and this time the taste distracted her. Peter's argument deserved some credit—the bar could've easily been mistaken as a dessert.

"About that." Peter's voice dragged along, delaying his point and leaving Jackie itching for time to move faster. "Yeah, so—I was thinking. Why don't you two handle this one? I already helped out with the level at Cherry Ice, so it's Kat's turn to take over as sidekick."

Jackie stopped chewing. What kind of idiotic reasoning was that? Peter's life depended on completing the levels before the end of the countdown, and he wasn't in the mood to give the game his all?

"We're doing great on time," he added. "That stupid countdown is the underdog at this point."

Jackie swallowed her half-chewed bite, the oats scraping her throat. "You're being ridiculous."

"Well maybe this game is ridiculous!" Peter made eye contact with Jackie, and she couldn't help but feel rightfully attacked. "Did you ever think of that? This whole game is a serious invasion of privacy. I'd much rather be at home right now stressing over homework—not a magic game, but here I am."

"Aw." Kat set her hand on his shoulder with an exaggerated pout. "Poor Peter."

"You don't get it, okay?" Peter yanked his shoulder away from her, averting his focus to the sand. "I have a bad feeling that whatever this capsule's about to show us won't be pretty, and I hate that I have no control over it." His voice softened as he raised his head to face the waves. "But fine. Let's get this over with. I'll head back and search by the picnic tables. You two can cover the dunes and…"

Jackie followed Peter's gaze, eyes landing on a shimmer in the distance. Floating above the waves was a capsule, swaying slightly, matching the motion of the water. It hadn't been there the last time Jackie looked.

No words had to be said—they all knew what to do. The trio kicked their feet forward, running to the shoreline. The sand accumulating in Jackie's shoes and the wind pressing against her face threatened to slow her down, but Jackie fought against the pressure and took the lead. Her breathing fell into a rhythm, and when the damp sand below her started to squish, Jackie stopped. The three panted out of sync, watching the capsule that hovered a solid twenty feet away.

"Holy shit," Kat muttered under her breath. "You guys weren't kidding."

The capsule shook.

It trembled mid-air before jumping an inch higher, driving itself into the water, and vanishing from sight.

Jackie didn't waste time in her jungle of thoughts. There had been far too much of that today already. Now was time for action. She ripped the shoes from her feet, sand fluttering to the ground in gentle streams.

"What are you doing?" Peter took a step away from the water as a wave approached him.

Jackie rolled her socks off, offering Peter nothing but a quick glance. What did it look like she was doing? Dancing? The only way to beat the level was to open the capsule, and they didn't have any other options. She reached into her back pocket and grabbed her phone. "Hold this?"

Kat took the phone from Jackie's hand with a subtle smile on her face, but her stance read that she wasn't comfortable—shoulders tight, raised against her chin. She stepped away from the water with Jackie's phone in her hand.

Her own life in her hand.

"I'm starting to hope this really is psychosis," Kat said.

Jackie frowned, and Kat shook her head.

"Nothing."

Jackie shut her eyes and inhaled the salty air, reminding herself that this was just a game. *Right.* Another breath. *That's all this is. A game. I'm great at games. I got this.* She opened her eyes and stepped forward.

"Wait!" Peter's voice stopped her in a panic. He normally spoke with an artificial confidence, but now his voice trembled with the wind. "What if it's a trap?"

Jackie shook her head. "It's not."

Games normally increased in difficulty. The first level of Capsule had been a walk in the park, the second required a little more effort, and this one lured her into a short swim.

"The water could kill you." Peter took a step toward Jackie, challenging her plan. "It's freezing."

"Well yeah, smartass." Kat ran a hand through the hair of her ponytail. She was smiling, but her arm was tense. "Maybe if Jackie spent four days soaking in it."

The color drained from Peter's face. "You can't go in there."

Jackie raised her voice and turned around, facing him. "We need to finish the level." How much longer did he plan to get in the way of opening the capsules? He was overthinking this and trying to control what he obviously had no control over.

"What if it's not even there anymore?" Peter gestured to the water behind Jackie. "What if it—I don't know—teleported or something?"

"What's going on with you?" Kat asked.

"Nothing. I'm being logical, because apparently I'm the only one here with an ounce of common sense."

Jackie faced the water again. *Focus.* She took a few solid steps forward, frowning as a hand wrapped around her wrist. She looked over her shoulder to find Peter's colorless eyes searching hers in desperation. She'd never seen him like this before.

Not in the Level One memory, not during class, not even today. Something different caught her attention this time. Was it fear?

Peter Moon, the boy who somehow managed to be condescending in every way, was afraid?

"Calm down." Jackie pulled her arm out of his grip. "You know I have to do this."

"No, you don't. It's dangerous." Peter took a step away from her, and the wind ruffled through his brown hair. "Just trust me on this one. Please."

"Hey jerk!" Kat's grip tightened around Jackie's phone. "Chill out. She'll be fine."

Peter inhaled a broken breath as he took a few steps back. He spoke deeper this time. "Be careful."

Jackie wasted no time analyzing his strange behavior. She turned and immersed her bare feet into an approaching wave, gritting her teeth at the sharp sting of the icy water. April wasn't the coldest time of the year to visit Pelle Cove, but that didn't mean the ocean wasn't uncomfortable to swim in. Even in the peak of summer many considered the water untouchable.

Without giving herself time to back out, Jackie took a few bold steps forward. The water trickled up to her knees.

Jackie paused in the endless pool, trying to remember the exact location of the capsule. She struggled with gauging how far away from the shoreline it was. Had the capsule submerged itself at an angle? And how deep had it gone?

She leaned forward, launching herself into an incoming wave as her feet went numb from the cold.

The ocean thrashed the hair around her face. For a moment, Jackie could hardly move, shocked by the motions—the violent current, the diminishing air in her lungs, the inescapable chill that trapped her—but she eventually remembered her mission and reached forward, swiping her arms through the water and kicking with every ounce of energy she could conjure.

Nothing.

Jackie oriented herself vertically and popped her head through the surface. Flailing her limbs to keep afloat, she took violent breaths, occasionally coughing the unwelcome droplets of salt water from her lungs. Peter and Kat stood at the shore a decent distance away, so the capsule had to be close. She propped her burning eyes open and drilled her face into the water.

The visibility was horrible, and her heart pounded when she realized that she couldn't see the bottom of the ocean. Jackie exhaled the last of her reserved breath as her eyes landed on the aluminum figure hovering gently a few strokes away.

Jackie emerged at the surface a final time for a refill of air, but the waves crashed into her and spilled salt water into her mouth. After a few violent coughs Jackie inhaled a deep breath, slipped below the surface, and locked her eyes on the capsule. Air escaped from her lips when she kicked forward into the darkness, her tense muscles relaxing as her hands pressed against what felt like glass.

A final stream of bubbles trailed from her mouth as she twisted the third capsule open.

LEVEL THREE

THE BEDROOM WAS empty.

Not in a way where nothing remained. Of course the necessities stood plainly—a full-sized bed with a simple wooden frame, a glass of water resting on a desk below the window trim, and a few pairs of clean sneakers lined against the wall. But Peter had nothing significant to look at. No spark. No glow.

He sat at his desk with a scarlet notebook under his palm. In today's journal entry he wrote about how in some other dimension, with some other Peter, he lived in a perfect world. A world where he'd come home to a nice house on Carnelia Drive with roses in the front yard and a playful family waiting inside to greet him. He'd place a shiny red bike on the front porch, step inside the house, and lay his shoes on the delicate rack by the door.

But even in this dimension, he did do all of those things. He even had pizza and cake on the evening of his fifteenth birthday a few months ago. A pizza he and his sister had baked themselves that turned out better than they'd expected, and a cake he blew the candles out from after his family had sung him happy birthday. He had turned fifteen in this magical world, but the world didn't feel magical anymore.

He had everything he needed and so much to be grateful for, but the void never disappeared. He had poured everything into this pit with the hope of filling it. Stuffed the void with hours of guitar lessons, endless studying, and countless books of all genres. He had even sacrificed parts of his life that he thought might have contributed to this pit. He deleted his Instagram account. Distanced himself from friends who made poor choices—even the occasional poor choice—which was all of them.

He strived to eliminate his bad habits. It started with No Netflix and continually escalated from there. He had to cleanse his life. Rid himself of any distractions so he could fill the void with worthwhile things. But next came no video games and no staying up past ten and no junk food and pretty soon it was all spiraling out of his control. In his effort to fill the void he had only deepened it. It grew with a force so strong it sucked the rest of his life away, and before he knew it, this void had devoured everything he loved.

And soon I found myself fighting the void, Peter wrote. He set his pen on the table, shut his journal, and stood. The glass of water on his desk quivered in his presence.

It was all part of the routine.

He opened the first drawer of his desk to reveal a collection of containers. He took them out one by one, delicately, as though the plastic might burst from too much pressure. The inner pieces rattled inside as he set them on his desk. Click. Click. Click.

Ten pill containers. He snapped the lids open in the same order he'd retrieved them in and placed a pill from each container on his desk in a straight line. For a moment he stared at the line, his eyes trailing across the pills back and forth, mesmerizing himself. But when he heard footsteps downstairs, he twisted the lids back on, nearly spilling a few bottles in the process.

"Peter?"

A woman's voice.

As the footsteps grew louder, Peter gathered the line of pills into the palm of his hand, raised his fingers to his lips, and slid a few into his mouth. He lifted the glass of water to sip the gel capsules down his throat.

A knock on the door.

"Peter?" Mrs. Moon called.

He popped more pills into his mouth. Four this time.

The door opened. Peter tightened his fist around the remaining pills in his hand and chugged a gulp of water to clear his throat.

"She's here."

His hands grew sweaty around the remaining few pills, but he kept his fingers locked tightly around them. He spotted a Tesla through the window in front of his desk. Obviously this girl's family didn't need any charity. They could handle the news fine on their own. If he could do it, they could too.

"They're here to help you," Mrs. Moon said.

"Sure they are." Peter raised the glass to his empty mouth.

"We all need this." His mom took a step back into the hallway. "Get your act together. She's coming upstairs."

As soon as Mrs. Moon shut the door behind her, Peter opened his fist over his mouth, the last few capsules landing on his tongue before he drowned them with a stream of water.

He wasn't ready for this.

Peter sat. As he stared at the bottles in front of him, he rested his chin on his palm and his elbow on the wooden desk. Now that he'd started taking the supplements, he couldn't stop. A perfect diet and exercise regiment was impossible to maintain—there would always be something missing—but taking the supplements was the one habit he knew he was doing right. Why did the world have to work that way?

Why was perfection, even in such a minute aspect of one's life, so wildly impossible to achieve?

Light footsteps trailed upstairs. Peter gulped, his mouth now dry, but he had no water left to quench his thirst.

The door creaked open. The brat hadn't even bothered to knock first.

Even without looking at Isabella, he could picture her face. He'd seen it far too much in all of the photos Mrs. Moon had shown him. She was only twelve years old with curly golden hair and the purest smile. Of course Nicholas had to step in and save her. How could such a sweet child be left to die?

But it didn't make sense.

Isabella had only one thing going for her—an innocent face. Everything else was flawed. She was selfish—he could tell by the way she spoke in her letters. Everything was always about her. For all Peter knew Isabella's mom was forcing her to write them.

Why hadn't Nicholas seen her flaws? If he had only noticed them, maybe he could have saved himself. People always focused on the wrong things in life. They found the sun beautiful, so they flew an inch too close to it. How could Isabella deserve life when Nicholas had spent the entirety of his working to be the best man he could possibly be? He'd thrown it all away for a young girl who—in hindsight—probably helped the world a whole lot less than he had. She was a taker. She not only got what she wanted, but she got what she didn't deserve. Right when the universe had pressed a knife against her chest, Nicholas jumped into the water. And for what? The loss of his sweet life to maintain hers?

"What are those for?"

Peter jumped at the sight of Isabella's hand reaching across his desk to point at the perfectly-aligned supplement bottles. He could hear the smile in her voice.

Peter shut his eyes. "Pills." He wanted to disappear.

"Are you sick?" she asked.

Peter dropped his hand, feeling the weight of his own head dragging himself down. As the girl pulled her arm away, he turned his seat to face her. He'd hoped to find something different from the photos he'd seen, but she matched her images perfectly. Isabella was the same devil he'd always envisioned.

"Your uncle was really nice." Isabella pulled at one of her curls. "He saved me, you know."

How many times did she have to say that? Did Isabella have to brag about her near-death experience like she was some kind of saint brought back from the dead? Did she have to take advantage of Nicholas' story by turning it into her own?

Peter frowned. "And he'd still be here if it weren't for you."

Isabella's smile fell. Something about the look on her face left Peter eager to take it back, but he was too late. Her lips were already dropping, and she lowered her head with a sniffle.

Peter opened his mouth to say something to cheer her up, but he wouldn't let himself speak. What was he supposed to say? He hadn't lied.

"You didn't have to go in the water." Peter found his lips trembling. "What kind of idiot goes into the water when they can't swim?"

"I thought it was shallow." The girl's voice shook. She gasped for air.

"And where was your family? Taking photos of each other for Facebook?" Peter wiped the moisture from his eyes before any tears could fall. "If they even cared about you maybe they'd get their mind off their stupid social media accounts and spend some time with you."

Isabella couldn't contain it anymore. With tears streaming down her face, she ran to the door and paused with unsteady breaths. "You know what, Peter?" She raised her voice until she was screaming so loud all of Brookwood could hear. "I was trying to be nice, but I hate you. You're awful!"

The bang of the door left the room even emptier than it'd been before she'd arrived.

Peter tossed the supplement bottles back into his desk drawer.

Nicholas had been perfect. He'd lived elegantly, but his one mistake—his one act of kindness that had led to his downfall—that mistake had also been the perfect conclusion to his story. A perfect man with perfect intentions. A perfect hero. Tragic ending and all. How could Peter possibly live up to that?

He shut the drawer and abandoned his desk. Standing in the middle of his bedroom that day, he couldn't help but notice all of the imperfections. The wrinkle in his top bedsheet, the unevenly-sized pillows, the crooked paintings on the wall, the soda stain on the cream carpet by the leg of his desk. It was all such a mess.

So much cleaner than before, but still a mess.

LEVEL FOUR

16:14:33

JACKIE APPROACHED THE SUV with dripping clothes and a million raging thoughts.

A few minutes ago she'd reentered reality underwater, nearly inhaling a gasp of air before realizing where she was. As soon as Jackie had swum back to the shore and stood on the sand, she slid her socks and shoes back on and rushed toward the dunes. Peter and Kat followed her, and for the first time today, existed together in silence.

Jackie unlocked the SUV and sat at the driver's seat, soaking the upholstery. Through the windshield was the same mass of water that had drowned Nicholas Moon two years ago. Peter's strange behavior before she'd gone into the water was likely because he'd seen it coming. And he was right. Capsule had found a bruise from the past and had burrowed a fist right into it, renewing the pain. The memories did have a purpose. A pattern. The first level had introduced Nicholas, and the second had introduced Emmeline. Capsule was turning Peter's and Kat's grief into a game.

Peter slammed the back door to the SUV, locking himself inside. As Kat joined Jackie in the front, Jackie pressed her back against the cushion of the driver's seat. If only she could chuck her phone into the sea and make the game go away. They were nothing but three kids being toyed with.

Three lab rats.

Jackie jammed the key into the lock, but she didn't turn it. The key sat there, waiting for action but never moving. The memory had been too dense. Too difficult to absorb. She remembered aspects of the memory only vaguely implied, like the reason why Peter took each of the supplements lined up on his desk. Vitamin D, because he believed it was impossible to get sufficient sunlight considering how much time he'd spend inside the curtained rooms at school. Potassium, because bananas had too much sugar for the benefits of obtaining it naturally. Lysine to fight off cold sores, oregano to boost the immune system, and the list went on.

She knew he'd decided to become a pescatarian. That he'd stopped baking sweets with his little sister. That he'd stopped watching anime with her in the evenings, topping off their mugs of hot chocolate with whipped cream whenever it dissolved into the fluid. She knew that he'd started biking to school, that he worked on homework in the backyard whenever it was warm enough to get as much natural sunlight as possible, and that because of his new choices, he no longer ate the same meals with his family at the same time and table as his family.

"Well maybe this game is ridiculous!" Peter had said. *"Did you ever think of that? This whole game is a serious invasion of privacy."*

Jackie had learned so much about Peter with only a single glance at one of his many memories. Jackie and Kat had seen a part of his life that they never should have seen, especially without his permission, and yet here they were. Now they knew more about Peter than they'd ever wanted to.

Jackie's tight shoulders loosened as Peter's voice broke the tension.

"Apparently Isabella's family was vacationing in Pelle Cove the same time my uncle was." Peter's voice flowed so delicately from the back seat that Jackie had to focus to make out what he was saying. "It started raining, and she got pulled in by the current. Her family was busy panicking over their drenched towels and it was Nicholas who rushed into the water to save her. He grabbed a buoy that hung from the side of the empty lifeguard tower and swam out to her. But my uncle—he didn't make it back. He was only thirty-two."

Jackie blinked. Her mind was blank.

"That's sad, but it's no excuse for making her cry," Kat said. "Nicholas died saving her. Have you ever stopped and thought about how guilty Isabella must have felt?"

Peter didn't move from the back seat. He was a rock. Inanimate.

"Of course you didn't." Kat scoffed. "Moral Moon, huh? When do you ever look in the mirror?"

Peter's head tapped against the back seat window. "More than you think."

"Dude." Jackie had pried open her dry lips, but the words struggled to break loose from her mind. "You really can't blame him." Her voice croaked, resisting the fact that she was defending Peter Moon, the same boy who had written such horrible entries on his blog about the students at Brookwood. He had even made an innocent girl cry, but for some reason, Jackie took his side.

"Yep. I get it." Kat's blazing emerald eyes locked on Jackie's with a snap. "He had a reason to be mad, but you act like he's changed. You act like he's somehow better now than he used to be. But no—he's still like that. He still says whatever the hell he wants. You've read his blog, right?"

Eager to escape Kat's threatening gaze, Jackie cast her focus to the back seat. Peter still had his head rested against the window. *Yeah, I've read his blog.* Peter's breaths were unsteady, chest rising and falling in hiccups. *But something's off about Moral Moon.*

"Isn't that right, Peter?" A huff escaped Kat's downturned lips. "You hate everyone, don't you?"

"Yeah." Peter unglued his head from the window and stared at the back of Kat's headrest. "I do."

Jackie searched his expression as though a single feature of his face might give her a clue as to who he really was. It was like Peter wanted Kat to hate him. Like he wanted to be seen as a horrible person. Her head flashed with images of the notes students had written across Peter's locker. They despised him. They all did. But maybe they were missing something.

Peter's focus hopped to Jackie, catching her stare. She faced the windshield and twisted the car key with a gulp.

The engine rumbled.

"He's been sick since 2004." That's what her classmate had said in Mr. Berkshire's class this morning before Peter arrived late. The boy with the golden glasses implied that Peter had been sick his entire life, that he had something innately wrong with him, but what was wrong? His sickness—was it really being judgmental?

Jackie wrapped her hands around the steering wheel. "I need some dry clothes."

"Good idea." Kat reached into her backpack resting on the car floor and raised her head with Jackie's phone in her hand. "I'll find something downtown."

Jackie backed the SUV out of the parking space. The lab rats were back in action.

Back in the maze.

Jackie stepped out of the car, her damp clothes leaving her miserable in the chilly Ravensburg air. They had driven ten minutes from the shore and into the town center of Ravensburg, but the air here smelled even more like the ocean than at Pelle Cove, most likely a result of the nearby restaurant grilling fish on an outdoor barbecue.

"Trust me guys, we don't wanna test the game." Despite the bright sun above them and the lack of trees, the ocean breeze left Ravensburg much colder than Brookwood. With a shaky hand Jackie slipped a few coins she'd found in the cupholder of the SUV into the parking meter, kicking it up to nothing but five minutes. "Let's make this quick."

Jackie had managed to claim a parking space in front of a thrift store called Closets & Beyond, which was great luck considering how every other space in sight was occupied. For a beach town as quaint as Ravensburg, it sure was popular. People of all ages—young children to seniors—scattered the cobblestone sidewalks and chattered peacefully. They dressed like they were headed to fancy dinners, which they probably were. Ravensburg was not only a popular tourist attraction for artists like painters and poets, but also a hot spot for nearby Brookwood residents seeking a celebratory meal someplace new.

"Oh relax a little." Peter leapt over the edge of the sidewalk, spun around, and entered through the double-doors of Closets & Beyond with a smirk. Jackie was glad to know he wasn't planning to mope around for the next two levels because of the last memory they'd seen, but she also didn't understand his sudden change in mood. Peter had never been this laid-back before.

The inside of Closets & Beyond was not at all what Jackie had imagined. She'd pictured salmon-pink walls with dusty curtains draped over the windows, flickering lights, and cheap clothes on mismatching hangers. Instead, the room had cream walls with bright lights—including fairy lights surrounding the various black-framed mirrors—and color-coded clothes on rows of glittering silver racks. The young lady at the counter greeted her with a warm smile despite the fact that Jackie's pants were half-soaked.

Money is money, Jackie supposed.

By the time she found a rack of pants her size, Peter had already snatched a bundle of clothes and disappeared through a door by a wall of mirrors labeled *men's dressing room* in fancy cursive on a mini blackboard sign. Jackie rolled her eyes and turned to the prices on the clothes. This was a thrift store? She couldn't find one item under thirty dollars.

Of course. Only in Ravensburg could used clothing be pricier than they were at the mall in Downtown Brookwood.

Kat was too distracted to help Jackie choose something to buy. She ran her hands along a row of yellow tops, searching for something that might suit her.

Jackie found a pair of sweatpants for the *on sale* price of twenty-eight dollars. She wouldn't have been surprised if it was the cheapest item in the store, so she clung to the hanger with an iron grip as she removed it from the rack.

"Hey Jackie." Peter returned from the dressing room with a new set of clothes on. "What do you think?"

Now wearing a pair of khaki pants with a striped orange and blue polo, Peter didn't look at all like Peter Moon anymore, who typically wore jeans and a plain t-shirt. From Jackie's memory of Peter in Mr. Berkshire's class, he never put too much effort into his clothing, so seeing him in such a polished outfit almost tricked her mind into believing he was a different person.

"Isn't it awful? I look like one of those guys who wears non-prescription glasses." Peter grabbed a pair of clear-rimmed glasses from a nearby rack and held a peace sign in the air. "Now all I have to do is dye my hair silver and sign up for TikTok."

The desk clerk, previously trapped within the world of her smartphone, raised her chin to see what Peter was wearing. "I think it looks great on you." She headed out from around the counter and slipped her phone into her back pocket. "Maybe switch to a different color for the shirt though. The orange clashes with the khaki a bit."

"Oh, I wasn't actually—"

"Here, this one looks like it could be a better match." She pulled a hanger from the nearest rack. Of course Closets & Beyond had to have good service too. Considering how insanely overpriced it was, customers had to be paying for *something* of value.

Jackie headed for the counter, stopping when she realized that her wallet was still in her backpack. The backpack she'd left in the Riderr earlier.

"Bro." Jackie took a few steps over to the rack of yellow shirts. "You have cash on you?"

Kat clicked the hanger she held back onto the rack. With the clerk still focused on Peter, she swung her backpack off one shoulder and motioned for Jackie to shove the sweatpants inside.

The desk clerk now had three potential shirt options for Peter hanging on her left arm. She stood facing the opposite direction, so the timing was perfect, but Jackie couldn't do it.

"Hurry up," Kat whispered.

Jackie shook her head with wide eyes.

"You know what?" Peter stretched the polo's fabric from its bottom hem. "You're right. The orange and khaki looks pretty weird."

Jackie nearly gasped when Kat snatched the sweatpants from her grip. She stuffed them into her backpack and coughed to conceal the sound of zipping it back up. The thought of stealing had never seriously crossed Jackie's mind before, and as much as she wanted to speak against it, she knew it'd only lead to more trouble, so she stepped back and gulped down her morals. It wasn't like any of this would matter after beating the game anyway.

"Hey Peter," Kat called from across the room.

Both Peter and the clerk looked over.

"We're not seeing anything. We'll wait for you in the car."

Peter's cheeks drained of color as he spotted Jackie's empty hands. "Uh—sure." He raised his eyes to meet Jackie's, and she nodded slowly to assure him that his worst fear was correct.

As Jackie and Kat walked through the entrance of Closets & Beyond, the alarms blared.

Kat peered at her feet and cursed under her breath. "Open it!" She sprinted across the sidewalk to the SUV.

The store clerk burst through the front doors and scanned the long sidewalk, probably thinking they'd run somewhere further. Jackie unlocked the SUV and disappeared into the driver's seat, heart pounding.

"Of course they had concealed security at a thrift store." Kat was about to use her seat belt, but she paused and let go of the strap. "Damn these rich people."

The engine roared as Jackie turned the key. "What about Peter?" She wrapped her trembling fingers around the steering wheel.

"Who cares?"

The clerk noticed them through the windshield and headed toward the SUV. Jackie backed out of the parking space without checking the mirrors first, nearly running into oncoming traffic. A van beeped behind her, and she stopped just in time.

"She's trying to get behind us."

Jackie focused on pulling out onto the main road. The string of cars was never-ending. "But Peter—"

"We'll deal with it later. Now go!"

A car stopped, pausing the traffic to allow Jackie time to back out. She zoomed in reverse. With a sharp turn of the steering wheel, she straightened the car out onto the main road and accelerated past the speed limit, ignoring the pedestrians waiting for their turn to cross the street. Reflected in her rearview mirror was the desk clerk who stood in the empty parking space with a phone raised in her hands.

"She's taking a photo of our license plate." Kat laughed as she faced the front. "That's classic. She thinks it's our car."

Jackie found herself smiling. "You're so bad."

"Says the girl driving."

The next light turned red, and Jackie stopped. There were enough cars stacked behind her that she wasn't concerned about the clerk anymore. She loosened her hands on the steering wheel. "Okay, so what about Peter?"

"He's not stupid. He can outrun her. We'll just call him and pick him up from wherever he is."

Jackie frowned at Kat. The car behind her honked, pointing out that the light had already turned green. Jackie reverted her focus to the road and pressed her foot onto the gas pedal.

"Oh. You don't have his number either, do you?" Kat pulled her phone from the side of her backpack. "I might be able to find someone who can..." Her phone slammed into the dashboard before striking the floor. Jackie nearly swerved at the sound of pounding against the passenger seat window. Peter ran along the side of the car, managing to keep up due to the slow traffic.

"Open the doors." Kat shouted. "Open the doors!"

Jackie slowly came to a stop in the middle of the road and unlocked the SUV. The driver behind her threw his arms up in frustration. She clenched her teeth, waiting for Peter to hurry inside.

Peter jumped into the back seat, still wearing the same clothes he'd tried on in the store. "Are you guys *crazy*?" He slammed the door behind him as Jackie moved the SUV forward. "We just shoplifted."

Kat smiled. "No shit, Sherlock."

"Kat, no. It's not funny." Peter clicked his seat belt on. "That's a crime, you know."

"It was her idea, not mine." Jackie pressed her foot on the brakes, stopping at a crosswalk for a surge of pedestrians.

"Don't act like you're not happy." Kat lifted her backpack from the floorboard and unzipped it. "You got your sweatpants, just like you wanted." She pulled the stolen item out of her backpack and bit the tag off with her teeth.

"Looks like you've done this before." Peter blew a deep breath toward the SUV's headliner. "Kat Pike—professional drama queen, aspiring Instagram influencer, climate change activist, and shoplifter. Should've seen that one coming."

Kat threw the tags into the empty compartment of the passenger seat door. "Just gives you a nice little adrenaline rush when you need it, you know?"

"No." Peter huffed. "I wouldn't know."

"Oh stop being so sour about it. Our lives are at stake and we have far bigger things to worry about than a little stolen item here and there." Kat pushed her backpack onto the floorboard and leaned against the window. "Besides, you guys needed the clothes and that place set their prices way too high. Like, *scam* kinda high."

"I needed new clothes? No, that was Jackie. Not me. Now I look like a nerd who butters popcorn at the movie theater. And take a look at this crap." Peter took off his non-prescription glasses and tossed them onto the floorboard. "Fifty-nine dollars and I ran off with them. Do you know how scary it was to run out of the store *after* the clerk left to find you? I thought she'd be waiting right outside to catch me or something. But no—then I literally had to chase down the car because you guys go driving off without me. You had me go through all that, and for what? This cheap-looking getup?"

Kat shrugged. "I think it looks nice on you."

That seemed to shut him up.

The trio eventually escaped the luxurious town center of Ravensburg. The long string of cars they'd once been trapped in had now emptied out into gated neighborhoods with two-story homes.

"We have to figure out where to go next." Jackie wiggled her toes, a reminder of her damp socks and jeans. "But I need to change first."

"Ooh, there's an ice cream shop a few minutes down the road." Kat pointed through a tunnel of trees ahead of them. "You can change in the bathroom or something, and I could really use a snack right about now."

Jackie readjusted her grip on the steering wheel. "You don't think we'll get caught?"

"Most likely not," Peter said. "I doubt a small shoplifting crime gets a police force sent on the case."

"That's the spirit." Kat looked over her shoulder. "You're finally talking some sense, Your Majesty."

"Oh shut up." Peter's voice held a foreign kindness to it, and for some reason Jackie imagined him smiling.

DEAR STRANGER

I only met you once before you left on vacation
A brief meeting, but it changed me
I discovered who you were from the stories of others
And the impact you left behind when you disappeared from our lives

Sometimes I wonder if your vacation has been meaningful
I wonder if you ever get homesick
Even if home makes you sick

Sometimes I think of having my own vacation
A long one, like yours
And as I wonder where you went
When you left on vacation
That day
I wonder where I will go
For mine

15:22:54

JACKIE EMERGED FROM the ice cream parlor bathroom with her old jeans draped over her arms. Her feet were awkward in her slightly damp shoes, but it was still a huge upgrade from her previous situation. Kat prompted Jackie to throw the clothes into her backpack and slid a bowl of strawberry ice cream in front of one of the empty seats. "Wasn't sure what you wanted."

"Perfect choice." Jackie sat at the table. "Thanks."

When they'd first entered the ice cream parlor, Jackie had been too focused on getting changed to appreciate its unique atmosphere. The surface area of the walls were more glass than wood, the windows embracing the dark shadows of the surrounding trees. To combat the cold air outside, the heater was set so high Jackie worried her ice cream might melt before she could finish it, and many of the occupied chairs had jackets hanging on them. She held her hair in a ponytail with her free hand, an attempt to cool her sweaty neck.

"So while you were in there, Peter was telling me about some rumors."

"From when you disappeared?" Jackie let go of her hair and took a bite of strawberry ice cream.

"Yeah, the stuff you told me on the way to Cherry Ice earlier." Peter gestured to Kat. "I still can't believe people thought we ran away together."

"I'm sure they had rumors far worse than that, *Moral* Peter Moon." Kat scooped a spoon of strawberry ice cream into her mouth with a grin.

Jackie's tight shoulders relaxed at their bickering, not because they *were* bickering, but because they were bickering the right way. Their words held no malice toward each other. It was equally as hard to believe Peter was the same boy who ran such a horrible blog as it was to believe Kat was the same girl who hated him for doing so.

While Peter and Kat joked about how their families would react to their disappearances, Jackie people-watched to fill the time.

The parlor buzzed with students. It was close enough to Ravensburg's town center to attract a crowd, but far enough to require a car to get there, so most of the customers walking through the door were older teenagers with car keys dangling from their fingertips and the occasional younger sibling trailing behind them.

Over half of the students wore uniforms, which wasn't a surprise considering how Ravensburg had a reputation for well-funded schools. The largest in the small town, Ravensburg University Prep, was involved in the same sports league as Brookwood's. Jackie remembered Jay laughing at how bad their basketball team was. Sure, Ravensburg Prep was never any good, but no one denied that their jerseys were cool.

"Okay, listen closely kids." Peter set his elbows on the sticky table and folded his fingers together. "I'm about to spill some major tea here."

Jackie cringed. "Please don't."

"No." Kat shook her head and stuck the spoon into her bowl of ice cream. "You absolutely cannot pull off that phrase."

Jackie was nearly positive she'd seen Kat conceal a grin.

"Out of all the crazy rumors these idiots could come up with, the one about Kat and I running away together caught fire? I mean—don't get me wrong—I could do much better, but considering my current school reputation, that's got to be the best compliment I've received in years." Peter lowered his hands, eyes sparkling at the mere idea of this alternate reality. "I thought for sure people would throw a party to celebrate my disappearance."

Jackie took another bite of strawberry ice cream. The image of Peter's locker popped into her mind, but she didn't want to ruin this for him. "There was one girl who was really concerned about you." Jackie set her bowl down. "Short hair, book club."

Peter frowned as though he had to fetch her name from the deep recesses of his mind. "Oh, her." A short chuckle. "You guys wouldn't believe it. She reads *so* slow. And she wears those stupid socks all the time. You know, the long ones with those weird designs." He pointed to his ankles, encouraging Jackie and Kat to imagine them.

Kat was about to take another bite of ice cream, but she stuck her spoon back into her bowl and slammed it onto the table. "What's your problem?" Her voice wasn't sharp. It was more of a firm pry than a jab. "And what's your problem with everyone else?"

Peter drew lines through the ice cream with his disposable wooden spoon. Jackie wasn't sure what flavor it was, but it looked plain. Butter pecan maybe?

No, most likely vanilla.

The smile never disappeared from Peter's face, but something was off. Kat must have sensed it too, because the next time she spoke, her voice was softer than before. "If you want people at school to treat you better, maybe you should stop talking trash about them on your blog." Kat pointed her spoon at him. "I'm still not going to forgive you for calling me an entitled feline."

"With a fake smile."

Kat blinked. "What?"

"I called you an entitled feline *with a fake smile*." He stopped playing with his ice cream. "I was at least right about the second part, wasn't I?"

Kat's eyes fell to the bowl in front of him. "You not gonna eat that?"

Peter shrugged. "It's been a while since I last had ice cream."

"How long is a while?" Jackie asked.

Peter jammed his spoon into the ice cream and raised his chin. "Almost two years."

"Two years?" Jackie's eyes doubled in an instant. "I practically live off this stuff."

"Now that," Kat said, taking another bite, "is probably the only thing we have in common."

Peter scooped a bite of ice cream onto his spoon, but something stopped him from raising it to his lips. Jackie wanted to know what that something was. Maybe her interest in understanding Peter was because of the game. Maybe it wasn't. But would it hurt to ask?

"Why'd you order if you're not gonna try it?" Jackie said.

"Kat's the one who ordered. But who said I wasn't?" Peter lifted the spoon halfway to his mouth, chest-level. "It's just weird. I feel like I gave up on ice cream a long time ago."

"Yeah?" Kat asked. "Why's that?"

"It's not healthy, and unlike most kids, I actually care about putting a normalized drug into my body." His gaze was fully focused on the curve of ice cream resting on his spoon. It was the most ridiculously shy scoop of ice cream. A little speck of white on a wooden spoon. But the boy looked at it as though the bite were about to attack him. Was he afraid? What was there to be afraid of?

Peter stuck the spoon into his mouth.

Jackie and Kat continued eating, keeping Peter in their peripheral vision.

"Wow." He chuckled as he eyed the empty spoon. "Interesting."

Silence blanketed the table. Jackie tried to silence her thoughts, but they wouldn't disappear. The memories of Peter flooded her memory. He'd lost Nicholas. His room was neat and organized and practically sparkling, but it didn't seem like his mind was. The memory she'd received from the first level's capsule gave her the impression that something had changed. *What happened to the old Peter Moon?*

"Okay, let's say we win the game, which we will." Peter stuck his spoon back into the vanilla ice cream and pushed the bowl away. "It sounds like we restart the day and forget that any of this even happened. But what if we lose?"

"The jerk has a point." Kat shut her eyes, considering the possibility. "The day won't be reversed. Which means—"

"We *disappear*, to put it lightly." Peter wasted no time. "And Jackie stays in this timeline."

"No." Jackie ate her last bite of ice cream, but it took all of her strength to swallow. The idea of being stranded in a world where she was the only person alive to know about Capsule left her sick. Yet at the same time, the thought of losing her memories wasn't pleasant either. She was conflicted, but she knew one thing for sure—she wasn't losing the game, especially not after everything they'd sacrificed to get here. "That's not happening. We got this."

All they had to do was complete the levels. Three students from Brookwood High challenging an invisible mission together. Whether they hated each other or not, they were a team.

Jackie couldn't stop a smile from appearing on her face.

All three of them were smiling.

A buzz. Kat broke their gaze to check her phone.

"Who's that?" Peter asked.

"It's nothing." Kat turned her phone off and started for the door, tossing her empty bowl and spoon into the trash bin on the way. "Shall we?"

15:05:22

THE INCREASED FREQUENCY of redwood trees towering over the SUV implied that they'd reached the northern end of Ravensburg. They sat in near-silence, nothing but the crackling of the rock radio station filling the empty space between them, but even the music had merged into the background.

Peter sat in the front this time, his head leaned against the seat belt strap, eyes closed. Sleep had overtaken him, and even a mere glance in his direction made Jackie tired. The bags under his eyes, usually cloaked by his motivated nature, were now bolder than ever—his defining feature. In his left hand was Jackie's phone, which he had previously been using to navigate before she'd said, "I know where to go from here."

Jackie concealed her own yawn and focused on the road. *The capsule better be somewhere obvious.*

The Level Four pop-up had read **QUASSO DRIVE**. Jackie had been on the lengthy road before during the occasional family trips to Clay River in Grovestown. Unfortunately they were still an hour away from the start of the road, and once they would arrive, the capsule could be located anywhere along Quasso Drive for miles.

Kat rummaged through her backpack, breaking the silence. "So those power-ups I saw on the second page earlier—what do they do?"

"They're all different. I'm pretty sure we get a new one after each level." Jackie's eyes widened. *Right, I forgot to check for a third power-up.* She turned to Peter, who rustled at the sound of their discussion. "Hey!"

Peter jolted forward, nearly dropping Jackie's phone in the process. Now that she'd seen the bags under his eyes once, she couldn't unsee them. He opened his mouth to question Jackie's urgency, but the words caught in his throat when he saw Kat in the back seat. "Really? Sour Patch Kids?" Peter ran a hand along the top of his head, smoothing out his tousled hair. "Way to rot your teeth."

Kat zipped her backpack, chewing while she spoke. "It's worth the temporary pleasure."

Jackie frowned. "Peter."

"Yeah?" He turned Jackie's phone on and typed her password. Both Peter and Kat had memorized it by now. "What's the problem, *Player*?"

Kat stifled a laugh, and Jackie rolled her eyes. "I think there's a new power-up. Can you check?"

Peter swiped to the second page of Capsule, tapped the badge labeled **THREE**, and read the power-up description aloud. "*Freeze time for five minutes. Surroundings will halt, but the countdown shall remain active.*" He raised his head, humming as he gathered his thoughts. "The first two power-ups only cost one hour to activate, but this one costs two. Don't you think it's sketchy how we haven't had to use any of these yet?"

"Not sure." Kat tossed the bag of Sour Patch Kids onto the floorboard of the SUV. "We really should though. Freezing time?

I'd love to see that one in action. Remind me what the other ones do?"

Peter tapped the first two badges. "*Bonus Memory* and *Battery Recharge.*"

"Bonus Memory?" Kat asked. "Like an extra level or something?"

"*Experience a bonus memory from another mind. The memory of interest must be stated upon activation.*" Peter shook his head. "Seems more like reading someone's mind. Seeing into their past."

"That's sick." Kat laughed. "But like—the good kind of sick."

Jackie could hardly focus on their conversation. Peter was right. Something was off about the fact that they hadn't used any of the power-ups. Normally a game introducing new features would require the players to actually use those features for success, but they hadn't needed them. It was almost like they'd been playing the game on easy mode.

"It's a pattern, isn't it?" Peter caught Jackie's eyes, breaking her train of thought.

A speed limit sign appeared around a curve in the road. Jackie pressed the gas pedal harder, realizing she'd been driving ten miles too slow. "What's a pattern?"

"Level One was my memory, Level Two was Kat's, and then Level Three switched back to me." Peter counted the levels on his fingers. "If the memories alternate between us, the next one's probably about Kat too."

"Maybe." Kat's raspy voice shattered Peter's enthusiasm. "But if there's really a pattern, then how does the fifth level work?"

Peter opened Jackie's phone again, searching the game as though he might find evidence to calculate an answer. Maybe Level Five was some kind of boss, or perhaps one of Jackie's memories.

If it were mine, Jackie thought, *what would it be about?*

All of this thinking about the game was growing exhausting. Jackie turned the radio volume up, forcing her thoughts to clear.

I see your head down there, scared to be unaware.

Jackie recognized the Cuffed Up song as *Danger, Danger*. Hearing the band brought her back to the day Peter and Kat had first been announced missing, when she arrived home from an afternoon run listening to Cuffed Up's song *Small Town Kid*. She hadn't realized how much her life had changed since then. At the time she'd known nothing more than Peter's and Kat's names, and now she was driving them hours away from home when she'd normally be playing Mystery Bullets with Eugene, blanketed under the safety of her glowing bedroom's LED lights.

What's worse than the unknown? Breaking that status quo of yours.

"Oh damn." Kat's voice raised a pitch, freeing the tightness from Jackie's shoulders. "I like this song."

You hate, we love each other, don't we?
You hate, we love each other, slowly?

Jackie grinned as Kat sang along with the lyrics. "You listen to Cuffed Up too?" She glanced into the back seat before Peter tapped her on the shoulder.

"Eyes on the road, Jackie."

She grinned and increased the music's volume, drowning them with the lyrics. As Jackie turned around a few more curves in the road, she thought back to the new memories she'd obtained from the past three levels. She couldn't say she *knew* Peter or Kat, but it was crazy to consider how much she'd learned about them in only a matter of hours, and despite how hard she tried to deny it, she truly hadn't ever wanted to learn more about anyone as much as she wanted to learn more about Peter and Kat.

Relate? To one another, can we?
We're both dangerous.

Peter dropped Jackie's phone onto his lap, unable to focus on his Capsule *research* with the increased volume. "Great." He nearly shouted over the music. "More noise—exactly what this world needs."

"True," Jackie said, trying to avoid another one of Peter's tangents. She failed.

"You know what I listen to? Lo-fi. It's just interesting enough to draw slight attention to its existence and increase focus, but not quite interesting enough to distract you from what you're working on." Peter waved his pointer finger in the air. "Perfect for productivity. I support the hype."

Kat's phone chimed from the back seat. She stopped singing along with *Danger, Danger*. "You're such a nerd."

"And you, Your Honor, are texting when our lives are literally threatened by the clock." Peter glanced back at her. "Who is it?"

Kat typed on her phone keyboard. "It's nothing."

"If it's nothing, let me see."

"You were the one complaining about privacy earlier."

Peter reached into the back seat and ripped the phone from Kat's grip.

"Hey!" Kat swiped for her phone, but Peter leaned forward against the dashboard—out of her reach—and scrolled through her screen. "What the hell do you think you're doing?"

Jackie tried to read the text from over Peter's shoulder, but the font was too small from her distance and she knew she had to focus on the road. She instead searched Peter's tense expression for a clue as to what the messages were about. With every glance between Peter and the windshield, his jaw dropped lower into an eventual sigh.

"You monster."

Peter tossed the phone back to Kat and folded his arms onto the dashboard to use them as a pillow for his head.

"What happened?" Jackie waited for Kat or Peter to speak up, but neither said a word, so she repeated her question louder. "What happened?"

"Kat." Peter's arms muffled his voice. "I thought you said he let you borrow it." He raised his head to turn off the radio, and the lyrics paused during the final repeat of the chorus.

You hate, we love each other—

The car was quiet now. Too quiet.

Jackie faced Peter. "Borrow what?"

He pointed to the windshield. "Focus on the road."

"Fine." Jackie gripped the steering wheel tighter. *What a jerk.* She continued driving, careful to slow before every curve. She tossed the word *borrow* around inside her head, picturing Peter's face from earlier and trying to decipher what kind of text conversion could possibly concern him so much.

Jackie slowly pressed the brake pedal, meeting another sharp curve in the road.

No.

She moved her foot back onto the gas pedal to speed up.

There's no way.

"It's not like Owen suspects me or anything." Kat leaned her head against the window. "It's really not a big deal."

"Not a big deal?" Peter banged a fist against the window. "We're joyriding. We don't even have a proper excuse for doing this. What are we supposed to say? A magical video game made us steal it?"

"No one's gonna find out."

"Well we don't know that!"

Jackie gulped.

I'm driving a stolen vehicle.

This entire time she'd been driving a car that not only wasn't hers, but hadn't been borrowed with proper consent either. She took deep breaths to suppress the oncoming panic. "I don't even have my license yet."

Kat leaned forward, set her hand on Jackie's armrest, and spoke smoothly into her ear. "Everything's fine. Just get us to Quasso Drive. There's hardly anyone out here anyway."

"Shit." Peter covered his face with his hands.

"What?" Kat removed her hand from the armrest, disappearing into the back seat. "Oh."

Jackie's entire body went tense. "What? Did Owen find out?"

"Just focus on the road, Jackie." Kat took a deep breath. "Just focus on the road."

And Jackie saw it.

Oh, she saw it.

In the rearview mirror was the image of a police car. It was right behind them, threatening their entire plan. Threatening everything and everyone. The deep breaths no longer calmed her. She panted, hands turning white from the pressure of her grip on the wheel.

"Calm down. We'll be fine if we don't draw attention to ourselves." Kat spoke with no emotion, nothing but a robotic voice of reason. "You know how to drive. You've gotten us this far, so just keep doing what you're doing."

"I don't have a license," Jackie muttered under her breath. "I'm driving a stolen car and I don't have a license."

"It's not stolen," Kat said. "It's *borrowed*."

"Borrowed without permission is what it is!" Peter's face turned bright red. "Do you know how much this could ruin our futures? We're talking fines and—I don't know—*juvey*."

"If we fail the game we're done for anyway," Kat said. "All that matters is completing these levels, right? After that, it'll be like we never stole the car in the first place."

With every glance at the man's face in the rearview mirror, Jackie's arms grew colder. Her thoughts rushed with all of the possible scenarios. Sure, getting caught for this crime would be horrible—she was the one driving without a license—but this was horrible for the game as well. If they got caught, there'd be no way they could make it to the next two locations in time. It'd be a mess. An absolute mess.

"Slow down!" Kat shouted. "Come on, Jackie. Just hang in there."

"Oh we're dead. We're dead." Peter leaned forward, pulling at his hair. "It's over."

Jackie could hear them, but she couldn't understand what they were saying. Her mind raced forward as the trees rushed by. She had to get out of here. She had to get away from this police car. Their lives depended on it. The *game* depended on it.

"Jackie!" Kat shouted from the back seat. "Are you hearing me? Slow down. You're speeding."

By the time Jackie checked the speedometer, the lights behind her were already flashing. The sirens knocked her back into reality. She slowly set her foot onto the brakes.

"Jeez Jackie!" Peter slapped a hand against his face. "How fast were you driving?"

The car decelerated as the sirens intensified.

"Well slow down faster and pull over," Peter said. "Dammit, we're screwed."

"I don't have a license." Jackie gulped and pressed the brakes harder. "Holy crap, I don't have a license."

The car came to a full stop at the side of the road, and no one said a word.

The trio had run into a dead end.

Through the rearview mirror, Jackie watched the police officer open his car door and slip into the shadows. She readjusted her grip on the steering wheel.

"Jackie?" Peter reached over to nudge her, but by the time his arm was in the air, she'd already slammed her foot against the gas pedal, forcing Peter's head against his seat.

The police officer's figure grew tinier in the mirror as they blasted down the road.

"What the hell are you doing?" Peter watched the endless string of trees rush by the windows.

Jackie's jaw fell loose as she spoke. "I don't know, okay?"

The police car eventually emerged back into sight, shooting after them at lightning speed. Jackie was going sixty, seventy, eighty miles an hour. Twice the speed limit. The curves in the road threatened her control behind the steering wheel, and although Kat shouted from the back seat at the top of her lungs, Jackie was too focused to make out what she was saying.

"Okay, okay." Peter rubbed his forehead as he scanned the road ahead of them, finally coming to terms with the situation. "There's a road coming up. Can you make the turn?"

"At this speed?" Jackie noticed a lime green sign tucked between two trees labeled *Greencrest Road*. She peered at the rearview mirror. The police car trailed behind them, but she had enough time to slow down. After a deep breath, Jackie set her foot onto the brake pedal. The SUV slowed to fifty miles per hour before she made a sharp left turn onto Greencrest Road.

The police car squealed to a stop.

"He's turning to follow us." Peter's seat belt was off now. He had his knees on the seat, fully facing the rear window. "Don't look at me! Focus. We still need to lose him."

Jackie narrowed her eyes at the windshield. Greencrest was surrounded by so many trees the road was dark even at mid-day. She flicked the SUV's high beams on as the police car's lights flickered behind them.

"I'm gonna be sick." Kat leaned forward and hugged her backpack with an iron grip.

"Take the next turn." Peter was still focused on the rear window.

Jackie nodded, taking notice of the upcoming road sign. The sharp turn shoved her against the passenger seat window, but she recovered her posture and straightened the SUV out on the right side of the new road. The surrounding redwood trees trapped them in a woody labyrinth, but the fading sirens left Jackie with more relief than her fear of escaping.

Kat spoke through gritted teeth. "I'm not sure I can handle this."

"Oh really?" Peter faced the front of the car and clicked his seat belt back on. "Looks like the rebellious—"

"No, I mean Level Four."

In only an instant the officer had caught up, and the dark air lit with a familiar mixture of red and blue. It'd be impossible to outdrive him, which meant their only option was to out*turn* him. Jackie raced the SUV toward the nearest road sign and swerved with a violent twist of the steering wheel.

The curve was steeper than she'd expected. The SUV struck a steel trash bin off the side of the road, its two left wheels sliding off into a ditch.

"Shoot." Jackie kicked at the gas, but the car only whined in pain.

"Try backing up first." Peter set the SUV into reverse for her. "Hurry!"

The SUV backed deeper into the ditch. With the sirens wailing behind them, Jackie switched the vehicle into drive and struck the gas pedal. The bottom of the vehicle scraped against the edge of the rocky road as the front wheel broke free from its trap.

But the back wheel locked them into place.

Heart pounding, Jackie removed her hands from the steering wheel. She'd given up, but only on Plan A. She scanned the passenger seat for her phone, and Peter was quick to read her mind. He held it toward her, Capsule already opened.

Jackie swiped to the second page of the app as the police car stopped behind them. Her thumb hovered over the emergency button.

"We'll lose three hours." Peter lowered his voice to a whisper, leaning closer. "Do you even know what it does?"

Jackie met his eyes—two dark pits of fear. "What other choice do we have?"

Peter's skin flashed between red and blue as Jackie tapped **EMERGENCY.**

11:50:03

THE SOUR SCENT of asphalt infiltrated Peter's lungs, luring him back into reality.

His eyes opened.

Above him was a fat clump of gray sky, a single bird shooting past the blinding canvas. Rocking tree branches bordered the far left and right edges of his vision. Unlike the redwood trees they'd been driving between earlier, these were short with smooth bark and spidery arms.

Teleportation, really? Despite having no clue where he was, the lack of sirens was enough to leave Peter melting into the ground with relief. He turned his heavy head to the right, revealing a blur of tree trunks sprouting from thorny bushes. *This day can't possibly get any weirder.*

Peter lay in the middle of an unknown road, contemplating how a phone app could possibly transport him out of the SUV in a way that aligned with modern science. It wasn't until the rumbling of a car engine filled his ears when he acknowledged the sharp pebbles pressed into his shoulder blades.

An approaching car squealed as the driver slammed the brakes.

I'm on a road.

Peter stumbled to his feet and rushed to the opposite lane of the oncoming vehicle. The car came to a jumpy stop right where he'd been lying moments ago. As the wind weaved through his hair, Peter leaned forward, gripping his knees and exhaling a burst of breath.

That would've been a stupid death.

The driver's door popped open. "Are you okay?"

Peter froze, head still facing the ground as he waited for his heart to stop beating so damn loud. *I take it back.* He released the tight grip on his knees and straightened his spine to face the driver. *It can get weirder.*

"Peter?" Jay's brows held still, but Peter could tell from his rapid blinking that Jay had transitioned from genuine concern to pure confusion. "What were you doing?"

Peter's eyes fell to the white line in the middle of the road— the road he'd been lying on only moments ago. "Sunbathing, apparently." He spun in circles, searching for a sign of Jackie or Kat. Fog hovered over the asphalt in the distance, and dew drops occasionally trickled from a branch here and there—remnants of a recent shower. "Where are we?"

Despite Jay's tense forehead, his eyes were calm. "Is everything alright?"

"No, not really." Peter planted his feet onto the ground and stood firmly in front of Jay. "Just tell me where we are."

Jay gulped. "Quasso Drive."

An instant smile struck Peter's face. The emergency button had not only saved them from the policeman, but had also brought them—or at least, him—right to the doorstep of their next level. All at the cost of three hours subtracted from the countdown. Not a grim deal.

Peter shook his head, knocking the pride away. No, there had to be a catch. What if Jackie and Kat were hours away from him? Even if he opened the fourth level himself, without Jackie's phone he wouldn't know where to go next. If only they'd exchanged numbers. Gosh, why hadn't they done that before? His focus landed on the befuddled Jay. "Did you see anyone else from school on the way here?"

"Why would anyone from Brookwood be all the way out here?" Jay reached for the edges of his checkered flannel, avoiding Peter's harsh gaze. "How did you even get to Quasso? There's no way you could've biked."

"I see you're familiar with my preferred mode of transportation."

Jay opened his mouth, but was interrupted by a buzz. Peter reached for the phone in his pocket for the first time since he'd been at Halos with Jackie and Kat. He'd hoped that the call would be from a random number—that Jackie or Kat had somehow found a way to contact him—but the screen simply read **Mom**.

Peter reeled his arm back and chucked the phone at a cluster of trees. The ringing faded into the air as the device flew between a web of white branches.

Jay cleared his throat. "Did you just—"

"Yeah." Peter faced Jay with crossed arms and zero remorse for his probably-broken phone. It was nearly seven in the evening and his family was most likely worried by the fact that he hadn't come home yet. He wouldn't be surprised if they'd contact the police soon, and although he didn't know if it were possible for his phone's location to be tracked, it wouldn't hurt to eliminate the risk.

"Okay, you're obviously not in the right state of mind." Jay took a step back, offering the largest smile he could offer to a boy like Peter—nothing more than a slight tilt of his lips. "Come on, I'll give you a ride."

Jay unlocked the car, and Peter raised his brows. *Did I hear that right?* Jay Mendoza, the most well-liked student at Brookwood High, sitting in a car with Peter Moon, the most well-hated?

Understanding that his other options were hopeless, Peter walked around the front of Jay's Honda and opened the passenger seat door. Resting on the cushion was a bouquet of yellow carnations, tied together at the stem with a golden ribbon. Before Peter could say anything, Jay swiped the flowers from the upholstery and set them gently onto the floorboard by the back seats. He fumbled into his normal driving form, eyes shooting back and forth between the dashboard and the rearview mirror an unnecessary amount of times.

"I see you're on the way to a date." Peter slipped into the passenger seat and studied Jay's reaction. The statement had been designed as a tease, but in reality it was a test.

Jay's expression sat still as Peter shut the car door. Jay was stiff, and that was all the evidence Peter needed to confirm his suspicion. He knew exactly what Jay was doing out here on the foggy road leading to Grovestown.

"I'll take you back to Brookwood soon." Jay set the car into drive and pressed his foot softly against the gas pedal. "I just have to make a quick stop first." The car soared down the road. Only someone like Jay could drive so smoothly.

Peter scanned through the windows for the Level Four capsule, but his thoughts were directed elsewhere. It didn't make sense. He'd been waiting for Jay to explode at him. Waiting for Jay to bring up the blog entry Peter had written about him months ago. He'd been waiting for the moment Jay would change his mind, pull over, and say, *Get out, you freak!*

But it never happened.

It was in Jay's nature to search for answers. He'd do anything he could to win the approval of others, so naturally someone like Peter—someone who appeared to hate him—would bother Jay. The fact that Jay hadn't asked him any questions about the blog entry he'd written was so wildly out of character it left Peter's stomach churning. In fact, Peter was so uncomfortable he brought the topic up himself.

"So about that entry I—"

"Stop." Jay spoke boldly for the first time since the beginning of their encounter. "I said I'd give you a ride, not talk about your problems." Jay flinched as though his words were too harsh for him to stomach himself.

"Actually, the entry was about *your* problems." Peter chuckled at his lap. "But alright."

Jay drove for a while longer. Peter was convinced their conversation had come to an end before Jay spoke again. "New style?"

It took a moment for Peter to realize Jay had referred to his outfit. Peter would never be caught dead in khaki pants and a striped polo, but he went along with it anyway. "I guess you could say that."

Jay took a deep breath and rested his back against the seat, shoulders tense. "By the way, I'm not mad at you for the entry you wrote about me. It's not like I'm the only one you've—you know—disrespected on your blog."

Disrespected. What a delicate word choice.

Jay continued. "I'm mad about the one you wrote for my sister."

Peter froze. "Jackie's entry?"

"Yeah."

"Because it's true?"

"*Yeah.*" Jay grinned. "But I really wish it wasn't."

Peter raised his chin to the windshield, watching Jay through his peripheral vision.

I've never seen one other person at Brookwood who wastes as much time as she does, Peter had written. *She traps herself in video games to the point of complete social isolation.*

It wasn't until the car ride with Jay when Peter finally had an answer as to why Jackie had chosen to help him and Kat in the first place, and this realization stabbed him. *She doesn't actually care about us.* Jackie was playing for the thrill, the satisfaction, the dopamine rush with each completed level. Capsule was all a part of her addiction. It always had been.

Peter didn't know why a part of him died in that moment of understanding, but it did. A warmth inside of him faded into a hole of disappointment. *Why do I care whether Jackie wants to help me or not?* The rage Peter held for himself heated the blood pulsing through his veins. *It's mutually beneficial anyway. She has fun with her stupid game, and Capsule spares my life. All I care about is that she's helping in the first place.*

But that empty feeling in his gut—it wouldn't go away.

For the first time, Peter saw something familiar in Jay's eyes. He saw a frustrated glaze he'd only seen in the eyes of his little sister Grace.

The eyes of his little sister when he'd stopped hanging her drawings on his bedroom wall, telling her he needed to get rid of clutter. "*Clean room, clean mind,*" he'd told her.

The eyes of his little sister when he'd stopped watching shows with her in the living room. When he'd stopped eating her cookies and making her hot chocolate. When he'd stopped allowing her to join him on bike rides because she'd *slow him down.*

It was those same eyes Peter saw in Jay as he drove down Quasso Drive, thinking of the entry Peter had written about Jackie on Moral Moon. Jay was a boy whose entire happiness relied on how people perceived him, and Jackie was a girl with no interest or desire to make time for others—to make time for Jay. All she had time for were her games.

And because Jay relied on people for happiness, he filled the void in his life with more people, like Kat—and Kat's older sister Emmeline.

"You know, I really did mean what I said in that entry about you." Peter slumped forward to balance the lengths of his laces, half in habit and the other half in dread of what he was about to say. "But the part about Emmeline"—he rose with tense arms—"that was uncalled for."

When Peter finally faced him, Jay's shoulders had loosened. His eyes remained focused on the road, but they were shinier now, the longing in his eyes dulled. Not completely gone—but dulled.

"I'm surprised you haven't asked me yet." Jay made eye contact with Peter for a brief moment, and Peter was almost positive he'd seen him smiling.

"Ask what?"

Jay pointed to the road. "Where I'm going."

"Don't have to." Peter's eyes drifted to the yellow carnations resting on the floorboard behind him. "I have a feeling we're headed for the same place."

#001

WELCOME BACK TO another torturous nine months at Brookwood High. I thought I'd kick off my sophomore year by launching Moral Moon, where I'll be exposing the honest truth everyone's too afraid to say themselves. It'll be fun, trust me.

Let's start with Emmeline Pike. Yeah, the dead girl. It's been over ten months since the accident and people are still talking about her in the halls like she left some kind of legacy behind. Spoiler alert: her only legacy is the long list of morons she pretended to love. Emmeline somehow managed to come up with a shitty excuse for every breakup, and her friends fell for it with tears in their eyes. What a bitch. That's all I can say. It's obvious she didn't know who the hell she was. Sometimes I wonder if she ever realized that herself.

Moon.

11:44:14

JACKIE RAN.

She'd woken in a wild panic to a flimsy, low-hanging branch tickling her face. Her location offered no internet, and although her phone still had service, she had no way to contact Peter or Kat. Jackie simply ran and clung to hope that she'd find them.

Her vision flashed with nothing but trunks of thick trees. Their branches reached around for her as she ran, rocking with the wind and threatening to catch her. She tried to dodge them, but despite her evasive efforts, more appeared like respawning fruits in a never-ending level of Fruit Ninja.

The energy Jackie didn't use balancing on the slightly-damp grass beneath her she directed into searching her surroundings. Her original objective had been to find Kat, Peter, or a sign of the capsule, but as more time passed and her panic intensified, she searched for a road, a path—any possible way to escape the foggy labyrinth. The air chilled her bare arms to the point where Jackie believed they were frosted over.

Where am I?

She thought back to when Mrs. Mendoza had lost her at the mall when she was five. It hadn't occurred to her that she'd never felt that same level of fear since then. That unrealistic worry of being lost forever—it impaled Jackie and drained the last few drops of common sense from her veins.

Is this what it feels like? Jackie rubbed her arms as she ran, but all that did was leave her fingers numb. *Is this what it feels like to know the game might kill you?*

Jackie slowed to a stop, head spinning as she rotated in circles, her sneakers pressing softly against the untainted grass. Surrounding her were nothing but trees and the sickening sight of untouched land. For all she knew she was in the middle of nowhere, miles from civilization.

Jackie staggered to the side, her balance failing her as she leaned against a sturdy tree. Mosquitos swirled around the air in flocks, clouding her vision, but she had no energy left to swat them away. What if Peter and Kat were hours away from her? What if the game had trapped her here to fend for herself?

Footsteps squished against the damp grass. Jackie took a dizzy step forward, but by the time the trees stood vertically again, two warm hands had rested onto her shoulders from behind.

"Let go of me!" Jackie tried to pry the palms off her, yelling until the air in her lungs dissipated.

"Jackie!" A girl's voice. "Calm down. It's me."

The hands loosened enough for Jackie to slip away from their grasp. She turned around, heart still racing even though she'd already recognized the voice as Kat's. She needed to see Kat's face in front of her to verify her assumption—to ensure the forest wasn't playing mind games with her.

When Jackie made eye contact with Kat, the shadows on the grass started to look less like skeleton arms.

I should really stop playing apocalypse games.

Kat crossed her arms with a slanted grin. "Hello to you too."

"Dude." Jackie steadied her breath as her heart rate slowed to its normal pace. "This is crazy."

"Is it really? I couldn't tell." Kat turned right and marched between two outstretched branches. "But don't stress any more than you already have. If the emergency button is anything, it's a blessing."

Jackie used Kat's yellow backpack as a guide, following her as she weaved between trees. In the distance, a hint of dark gray taunted her. A road.

"Quasso?" Jackie asked.

"That's it." Kat's arms hardly swung as she walked. "Took us right to it."

Jackie shut her eyes, her last hint of fear washing away. The emergency button had brought her and Kat to Quasso Drive, which meant Peter had to be somewhere close too. Surely they'd run into him at some point, so for now their first priority was to find the Level Four capsule.

Jackie thought back to the police chase earlier. Her hands rolled into fists at her side, imagining the pressure of her fingertips wrapped tightly around the steering wheel of the SUV, the adrenaline rushing through her veins. It was the first time she understood Kat's impulsive nature. No, her risks weren't always justifiable, but Jackie could at least understand the desire to have that feeling again. That feeling of being alive when everything else had lost its color.

"That drive was something," Jackie said.

"Almost as intense as the movies." Kat yanked at her neon pink scrunchie, and her blond hair fell in waves over her shoulders. "I guess the police officer found nothing but an empty car. I'd pay good money to see the look on his face." She tucked the scrunchie into the side pocket of her backpack.

Jackie caught up to her side, walking next to her at a matched pace. She was about to ask Kat about where she'd woken up after the emergency button, but Kat spoke first.

"I've been wondering something." Kat's hair tumbled over her shoulders with every step, reminding Jackie of Emmeline's calming presence in the Level Two Memory. "Why are you doing this?"

"Doing what?" Jackie asked.

"Helping us. You definitely don't have a reason to."

Jackie faced her muddied sneakers. Mrs. Mendoza had yelled at her before she'd started the countdown. She'd played to prove that she wasn't the person her mom made her out to be. That she wasn't the kind of person to see someone hanging from a cliff and refuse to lend a hand. But once she'd gone back in time, had it really been her mom's words that kept her going?

Jackie glued her lips together. No response was better than a false one.

Quasso Drive glowed in contrast to the dark shadows of the woods. The gray sky illuminated the sacred asphalt in a spotlight.

They stopped and stood at the edge of the road in silence.

"By the way," Kat said, accepting Jackie's empty response, "I think I'm starting to understand why Peter didn't want you in the ocean earlier."

"Because he was scared?" Jackie took a step forward onto the asphalt. It was slightly warmer out from under the shade. "After what happened to Nicholas, I wouldn't be surprised if he had a fear of the ocean."

"I doubt that. Peter's not the type of guy to have such a simple fear." Kat made a sharp left turn, passing behind Jackie and stopping in front of a sturdy tree. " I think he was scared of Level Three."

"Why's that?" Jackie caught up to Kat's side and followed her gaze to a thick wooden board nailed to the tree's trunk, a yellow zinnia lying delicately on top. On the wooden plaque was the phrase *In honor of Emmeline Pike.*

A tree. A single yellow flower.

"Your brother had a crush on Emmeline Pike at the absolute worst time. The Emmeline Pike," Peter had told her earlier.

Jackie finally understood the magnitude of the impact Emmeline's death had left on Brookwood High. Two and a half years ago, Emmeline had crashed into a tree—that's what the plaque and flower implied.

"Because I'm scared of Level Four." Kat plucked the yellow flower from the plaque and spun the petals by rolling her fingers along the stem. "Peter knew that if the level took place at Pelle Cove it probably had something to do with his uncle's death. So let me warn you—what I think you're about to see probably won't be my proudest moment."

The zinnia fluttered to the ground as Kat faced her.

Jackie wasn't sure what to say. She searched Kat for a sign of fear—of anything—but nothing was there. She didn't panic like Peter had before Level Three. She didn't try to get out of searching for the capsule. Instead, she watched Jackie as though she were testing her.

Leaves rustled above them. In a jolt Jackie brought her chin to the sky, eyes narrowing on a hint of silver between a few branches. She took a step to her left, catching a clear sight of the fourth capsule. It danced in the air, following the swaying motion of the tree as the wind bullied its branches. Like the third capsule at Pelle Cove, it shook before shooting higher, tucking itself into a network of thinner branches, nothing but a few silver specks remaining in sight.

Kat's chin joined her in pointing at the fourth capsule. "I'm not great with heights."

"Me neither." Jackie took a step back to assess the problem. "But one of us is gonna have to be."

The main issue was the opening span of flat trunk leading up to the abundance of branches. As long as Jackie could get herself onto the lowest branch, she'd have an easy time climbing.

When Jackie reached for the phone in her back pocket, Kat already had her palm out, waiting for Jackie to hand it to her. She knew what Jackie needed without having to say a word, and as Jackie placed her phone in Kat's hand, she thought about her games of Mystery Bullets with Eugene. Sometimes in the middle of battle they'd have to take action faster than they could communicate through words. Their teamwork was strong enough to connect them through nothing but a digital screen, and she recognized a similar connection forming between her and Kat.

Maybe Eugene's right. Jackie took a few solid steps back before running and launching her right foot off the ground. *Maybe there are people out there who could understand me like he does.*

Jackie's left hand locked around the lowest branch. The tree wasn't at all slippery, but it was hard to get a solid grip.

Kat grabbed the bottom of Jackie's sneakers and extended her arms to give her a boost.

"Hurry!" Kat shouted.

"Fine, okay." With a deep breath, Jackie pressed her palms against the branch and pulled her knees forward, slamming them onto the bark. She nearly tumbled over, her heart backflipping inside of her, but she reached for a higher branch to steady herself.

With both hands now wrapped around a secondary branch for support, Jackie pulled herself to her feet and stood.

The thought hadn't struck Jackie until she'd started navigating through the next layer of branches that she was climbing the same tree that had killed Emmeline Pike two and a half years prior. The news sent chills down her spine. Or maybe it was the temperature of the air. Hard to tell.

"What the hell?" Kat said. "What's Jay doing here?"

Jackie looked down at Kat for the first time. She'd climbed no more than seven feet off the ground, but her stomach sank at the mere thought of falling. "What's wrong?" She tightened her fingers around the branches.

"Jay pulled up with Peter in his car." Kat ripped her focus away from Quasso Drive and looked up at Jackie. "But forget about that—just hurry up and open it!"

"Kat? You're here too?"

Jackie's eyes widened. Kat hadn't lied—that was definitely Jay's voice.

Do you think you could get a ride home? Jay had asked on the phone earlier. *"I'm planning to visit a friend."*

That friend. Jackie held her breath as she scaled the next few branches. *Did he mean Emmeline?*

The levels hadn't brought anything good so far, but Jackie wasn't worried for a change. All she could think about was that opening this capsule meant they'd be one step closer to fixing the disaster this game had created. She'd seen the outcome of a world where Peter and Kat had disappeared, and she didn't want to go back to it.

"Are you crazy?" Peter shouted. "Get down from there!"

Jackie balanced herself on a branch within an arm's reach from the capsule. When she looked down for the second time, there were three chins facing her. She didn't know why Peter wanted her to come down, but she didn't have time to bother with his melodrama anymore.

"Jackie?" Jay's face grew pale as he ran his fingers over the buttons of his flannel. "What are you doing up there?"

Jackie redirected her attention away from them. Careful to hold her balance, she moved her steady hands from the branches to the capsule. Her fingers met the abstract surface for the fourth time.

"Don't twist it!" Peter warned.

But he was too late.

LEVEL FOUR

DEAR STRANGER,

Kat sat cross-legged on her bed, five papers spread out over her duvet cover. The lights in her bedroom were off, and she held a warm flashlight in her hand to light up the words. Over the past few weeks, reading the poems had become an evening ritual of hers, but she'd made no progress on deciphering the code.

Her eyes hopped between the pages, reading the lines at random in hopes that it'd form something meaningful.

But they can't resist the smooth paint

When the love I pursue is stolen from you

I wonder if you ever get homesick

Oh, how I wish I could do something right

Sometimes I forget my own face

The door popped open, and Mr. Pike's nose stuck through the gap. "There's a boy at the door." A moment passed before he burst into the room completely, his stiff voice softening. Kat couldn't see his figure in the dark room—only the reflection of light in his floating eyes. "What's wrong?"

Illuminated by the golden lights of the flashlight in her hand, Kat's tears trickled off her chin and dissolved into her blood-orange corduroy skirt. She waited for that feeling of sickness to kick in. Or fear, sadness, anger—she'd welcome absolutely anything with open doors. But the tears were forced, like usual.

Fake.

Kat gathered the papers, layering them on top of each other in no particular order and folding the stack into quarters. She wiped the tears on her oversized black sweater and tucked the papers into the palm of her hand.

"Kat?" Mr. Pike said.

She turned her flashlight off and watched her dad's wide eyes fade into the shadows, but his concerned presence lingered in the doorway. Mr. Pike felt sorry for his daughter. His daughter who was still griev-ing the loss of her older sister. His daughter who cried every night in her dark bedroom in a pit of despair. Emmeline had died, and Kat was struggling to move on. But that was only the story he wanted to believe—what everyone wanted to believe.

Kat tossed the flashlight onto the duvet cover. "Tell him to go away."

"Sweetie." Mr. Pike's soothing voice filled the pitch-black room with a comforting warmth. "He was one of her friends, wasn't he?"

Kat pursed her lips and nodded. She thanked the darkness for cloaking her. She didn't want to disappoint Mr. Pike by allowing him to see her eyes. All dead. Nothing there. As much as she knew her dad didn't like seeing her in pain, she also knew that seeing her without it would leave him more hurt than ever.

Kat was the girl who didn't cry when she heard the news.

Who didn't cry at her own sister's funeral.

Kat was the girl who didn't care. And she was trying to fix that. She was trying to cry. Trying to feel. Trying to be normal, but nothing worked. Every emotion was self-inflicted. Contrived. Unreal.

"You should at least talk to him," Mr. Pike said.

What he didn't know was that she'd already done that. She had sat in the passenger seat of Jay's Honda three times with the false hope that he could help her find answers.

Ever since Emmeline passed away, Kat had been overwhelmed with a million messages. All it took was a dead sister to make the whole world cater to her emotional state. Friends, classmates, strangers—they all told her how sorry they were and checked in with her on a frequent basis. They all tried to empathize with someone who apparently had no empathy in the first place, but Jay—he wanted answers, and that was something he and Kat had in common.

It was Jay's Instagram DM that had stood out to her the most. Among the swarm of emotional messages, his was the only one with enough logic to catch her eye. **I know you don't have answers,** Jay had written, **but maybe we can find them.** He'd sent this message exactly six months after Emmeline's death.

Kat slid her feet off the bed to find that Mr. Pike had already disappeared from her room. She stepped into the hallway, squinting under the bright lights and clutching the paper in her hands. As she walked between the walls of family portraits—many of which featured Emmeline's smiling face—she braced herself for another hopeless meeting with Jay.

Kat entered the dining room, where Jay stood on the patio behind the open front door. When he finally raised his chin and made eye contact with her, the face Kat saw was nothing like the one she'd seen when he'd first appeared at the Pike household to talk to Emmeline that day. He wasn't confused anymore. Now he was nothing but a shell. Not fully there. Incomplete. He was the same as Kat—dying for something to fill the void. Dying for answers.

But why him? Why did this random high school boy care so much about finding answers when it was absolutely not his problem? Why did he experience the same emptiness as Kat when he and Emmeline had hardly been a part of each other's lives?

Kat and Jay had known each other through Emmeline, only for a moment, and that was all. Yet that brief overlap had brought them together four extra times.

Today—their fourth meeting—would be the last.

As Kat approached the front door, Jay's hands reached for the edges of his flannel as though it were instinctive. He grinned with that hopeful glimmer on his teeth. "We'll figure this out."

Too lazy to put on any shoes, Kat stepped forward onto the patio wearing her lemon-colored knee socks pulled over her dotted tights. Jay didn't bother questioning her fashion choice. He rushed down the front steps, fingers rustling through his front pocket for the keys to his car.

The pair sat in Jay's Honda alone that Saturday afternoon. Jay had his hands on the steering wheel, and the key waited patiently in the lock, but he refused to start the car.

Kat suffocated the folded papers in her left hand. "We haven't found anything since the first time we went to Quasso."

Jay and Kat had found the papers three weeks ago by the tree Emmeline had struck that night. They'd been resting under a baby-blue hydrangea, and judging by the sticky end of the stem, the flower had been freshly cut. They hadn't found anything new since then. No poems. No clues. No more blue flowers.

"Your style is different now." Jay's hands fell to his lap. "Nice glasses. I didn't even know you used contacts before."

Kat raised her chin to see her reflection in the mirror of the sun visor. She'd been trying everything to create a few new sparks in her life, and a new style was one of them. She pressed the glasses closer to her forehead before readjusting the banana-yellow headband that held the frizzy blond hair out of her face. Yellow had always been Emmeline's favorite color.

"You've been wearing her clothes," Jay added.

That was only a half-truth. Her new style was much bolder than Emmeline's, but she did incorporate elements from her sister's wardrobe. A few crop-tops, accessories, and even her funky neon socks. Emmeline had started wearing them around the house as a joke ever since Mr. Pike had bought her a pair of hideous donut-themed socks a few years back, but Emmeline had never worn them to school. Kat had even taken the collection of nerdy charms out of Emmeline's bedroom drawers and attached them to her backpack. She rewatched every animated Disney movie that Emmeline binged routinely over spring breaks—Big Hero 6, Tangled, Despicable Me, Wreck-It Ralph— but none of them helped. None of them made her cry.

None of them made her feel bad.

"I'm surprised you haven't asked me yet," Jay said.

Kat nodded at her reflection, impressed with her improving winged eyeliner skills. "Asked you what?"

"Why I showed up to talk to Emmeline that day."

She flipped the sun visor shut, eliminating her reflection and turning her complete focus to Jay.

He traced his fingertips along the lines in his palm. "I asked her why she refused to go to homecoming with me."

Kat had figured it'd been related to the dance. "So what'd she say?"

"She said she wasn't going."

"And the night of the dance—"

"Yeah." Jay nodded.

They sat in the front seats of the car in silence while the sun lit the distant hills with an orange glow. They hadn't gone anywhere. They hadn't even moved from the curve along the sidewalk bordering Kat's home. But it felt as though they'd been driving for miles. They both cared for Emmeline. They had both been close to her, but never close enough to understand her. Neither of them knew why she left that day.

Neither of them knew why she died the night of Brookwood High's homecoming dance.

Kat gulped. She remembered the night clearly. She remembered how Emmeline had snuck to the door with folds across her forehead, eyes glazed over, shiny. "Before she left, she told me she was spending the night at a friend's place."

Jay's eyes fell shut. "She told me she was going on vacation with her cousins."

"My dad was told she was ditching the dance for a friend's birthday party."

"And our other friends were told she was dealing with a family emergency."

Kat clenched her teeth and unraveled the papers in her hands. "This isn't doing anything, is it? No matter how many times we go back to that tree, there's nothing there. Besides a bunch of yellow flowers, these papers are all we have. And they mean nothing."

"What if we go to Grovestown today?" Jay's voice raised to a higher-pitch. "Why didn't I think of that before? Quasso Drive is the main road to get to Grovestown, right? So what if she was meeting someone there? We could ask around and see if anyone knows anything about her. Maybe we could try Lothen too."

"Sounds pointless."

"It's worth a shot."

"We'll find nothing."

"And how are you so sure?" Jay started the car. "Let's keep looking."

"But why?" The pages crinkled from the pressure of Kat's grip. "Why do you care so much about finding answers?"

The smile vanished from his face. His answer required no thought. "Because I cared about Emmeline too." He pressed his foot against the brake pedal and set the car into drive, eager to bring Kat along on his next mission. "We're in this together, you know."

"In this together? You knew Emmeline for what, two years?"

"We were pretty close, and—"

"Maybe she had a pretty face, but you weren't pretty close." Kat didn't bother concealing her unsteady voice. "You're dying to know why she died the same night you were planning to go to the dance with her. You're just frustrated because you wanna know why she said no."

"That's not it." He frowned. "The only answer I want is the reason why she had to leave that night, but I'm also doing this because I care about you. I know this must be a challenge to deal with."

"Well it's not, okay? And maybe that's the problem. Maybe that's why I want answers." Kat's face grew hot. If she knew why her sister left that night, she could understand Emmeline better. And if Kat understood her better, she could finally feel something. She could finally cry and grieve properly. But judging from their last few visits to Quasso Drive, this mystery was impossible to solve. "Whatever this thing is that we're doing, it's over."

Jay had never been extremely close to Emmeline, and he had never been extremely close to Kat either. Yet he cared about Emmeline more than Kat ever could, and he cared about Kat more than she ever deserved. How was it that Jay could care so much, so easily?

He glued his eyes to the sunset at the horizon while his breathing slowed to a steady pace. Kat opened the car door and stepped outside, wincing as a weed pierced through her sock.

"These are yours now." She tossed the five poems onto the passenger seat. "Have fun with your investigation, Sherlock."

Kat slammed the door, the rage slipping between her teeth as she rushed toward the patio. Her eyes watered, and she could tell the tears were real. She wanted to be happy that she'd finally felt something, but she wasn't, because she knew the bitterness inside of her had nothing to do with Emmeline.

Jay Mendoza. She thought he was the one person who didn't look at her like the little sister of a dead girl, but apparently he was just like everyone else.

LEVEL FIVE

11:28:23

JACKIE SOARED THROUGH the evening air.

At first the game had sounded crazy fun, but as Jackie fell from the tree, Kat held nothing but hatred for Capsule. It took their lives, shook them, and spit them right back ten times worse. It had shown Kat a part of herself that she hated. It had shown Peter and Jackie who she really was, and now they'd never be able to see her the same.

Kat's heart pounded as Jackie struck the grass.

Blood.

Jackie had scraped her right forearm against a branch on the way down. Thick droplets of deep red dripped onto the dewy green shards. Jay kneeled by Jackie's side, helping her into a seated position and leaning her delicately against the trunk of Emmeline's murderous tree.

"Jackie?" Jay set his arm on her shoulder. "Jackie, can you hear me?"

Peter kneeled next to Jay, his eyes narrowed, face angular. He resembled the face of the boy Kat had pictured as the cruel blogger behind Moral Moon, but this Peter had softer eyes. He had someone he cared about more than the other students at

Brookwood, and because that person he cared for had been hurt, he was angry. Heartbroken.

Frustrated.

And it was Kat's fault. She was the guilty one here. She should have known from her previous experiences with the dizzying levels of Capsule that having Jackie climb a tree would be dangerous. Level One had left Kat on her knees in the school gym. Level Two had left her spilling food over the floor of Halos. And Level Three had left her stumbling at Pelle Cove, her feet sinking into the sand to regain balance.

Kat should have realized sooner that Capsule had been luring them into danger. She should have supported Peter when he'd shouted at Jackie to come down from the tree. She should have done something to stop her. She should have come up with a safer plan. A plan that wouldn't result with an injury.

Kat knew she hadn't done what was right, but once again, she didn't feel guilty.

Jackie gripped the gash in her forearm with her eyes clenched shut, and as Peter and Jay lifted Jackie to her feet, Kat stood from a distance. Their words muddled as though she were drifting away underwater.

"We need to get you to a hospital." Jay's voice bubbled in the frosty air, and the white puffs sneaking between his lips were so real.

Kat exhaled, but her breath in the air was nothing but a visual effect. A convincing post-production edit made to fool viewers into believing something fake was reality. It was nothing but a breathy lie.

The fourth time Jay had showed up at Kat's home to search for answers, he'd been eager to help. They hadn't found any more clues after the five poems, but Jay had never planned to give up. If he really was the insensitive jerk she thought he was—if he really wanted nothing more than to investigate for his own sanity—he could have driven to Quasso Drive alone on Day One, but he'd reached out and offered to bring Kat along. He had supported her, yet she'd pushed him away.

"Have fun with your investigation, Sherlock."

After the Level Three memory, Kat had criticized Peter for pushing Isabella away when she was only trying to help, but she'd done the same to Jay. For the past two years, Kat had used Peter as an example of what not to become. At least someone worse always lingered nearby. Someone that her level of evil could never top. But this entire time, she'd been exactly like him.

Maybe worse.

Jackie struggled against Peter and Jay. "I'm fine."

"No you're not, okay?" Jay pulled her toward the car. "The wound could get infected."

"Peter, please!" Jackie turned to her right, gazing at him with quivering eyes. "We need to get to the fifth level. I can make it."

Peter shook his head. "You're hurt. We can handle Level Five alone."

Kat stood hidden in the shadows as Peter and Jay settled Jackie into the passenger seat of Jay's car. Jackie no longer fought their help. Jackie's neck went tense before Jay shut the door softly, locking her out of the game. The player's health was drifting away, and right at the end too.

With Jackie safely tucked into the car, Jay turned to Peter with bulging eyes. "What the hell have you pulled my sister into?" He whispered so loud it was nearly a scream.

When Peter didn't reply, Jay faced Kat for the first time since Jackie's fall.

"Kat." He no longer fidgeted with his clothes. He didn't even shiver as a chilly breeze washed over them. Kat knew Jay wanted answers, and Jay knew Kat had them, so he asked, "What's going on here?"

And he deserved answers. He truly did. But Kat didn't know where to begin.

Jay nodded, accepting Kat's silence, and reached into his pocket for the keys. He forced Peter to step out of the way as he walked past him. It was obvious that Peter and Kat weren't welcome on Jackie's evening hospital trip.

As Jay sat in the driver's seat, Kat reached for Jackie's phone in her back pocket. She opened Capsule and watched the time on the countdown trickle away. The game choosing to threaten her life made perfect sense now. It wasn't like she and Peter didn't have the bad karma to deserve it. What had they done for the world, after all?

Peter ran back to Kat. "Where's the next location?"

She tapped **LEVEL FIVE** under the countdown. On the pop-up was the phrase **SUNSHINE AUTO**.

Peter stopped at her side and read the screen. "Never heard of it."

"Me neither," Kat said.

Jay started the engine, ready to steal Jackie from the game.

Neither of them knew where the final location was, and until they reached a place with an internet connection, they wouldn't be able to search for the address. Grovestown was still miles down Quasso Drive, and walking there would take three eternities. They also had to worry about whether Jay would share their location with anyone or not. It wasn't a stretch to think Jay might attempt to reach out to their families. If that happened, it'd be game over.

Kat held Jackie's phone toward Peter.

"What are you doing?"

"Take it." Kat stretched her arm further toward him. "You're on your own."

Peter stepped away from the device, hands in the air, refusing to touch it. "Is this because of the memory?"

Jay's car slipped out of sight in the direction of Grovestown. The engine chuckled as he left the pair stranded off the side of Quasso Drive.

Kat nodded. She didn't pull the phone away.

"Seriously, Kat? What the hell's wrong with you?" Peter pointed to the road, where Jay's car had stood only seconds ago. "Giving up isn't the answer."

Kat squinted at the countdown. "And how do you know we deserve to get out of this?"

"I don't." Peter crossed his arms. "I just have to hope that we do."

Kat found strength in hearing those words from Peter Moon. A boy who had created so much hate and pain through his blog. A boy who had screamed at a sweet girl who had gone through a traumatic experience. To know that Peter still had faith in himself, to know that he still fought for himself even when he had no right to be fought for—that had to mean something. Was it admirable, or selfish? Intelligent, or naive?

Kat wasn't sure, but whatever it was made her pull the phone away from Peter and back to her face.

Maybe he's right. Kat closed the Level Five pop-up and swiped to the second page of Capsule. *Maybe we do deserve a chance.*

Kat wasn't sure what had brought her to tap the third power-up. She wasn't sure if she did it because she wanted to give Jay proper answers for a change, because she wanted more time to get to know Jackie better, or because she simply knew Jay's car was the most convenient way for them to get to Level Five in time and save their lives. Perhaps it was a combination of all three that had led her to tap **ACTIVATE**.

The rumbling engine stopped.

Peter frowned at the lack of sound in the air. The crickets vanished. The wind dropped dead at their feet. He shot a confused glance at Kat before rushing to the side of the road. He looked to his right to find Jay's car resting silently in the middle of Quasso Drive.

"What's he doing?" Peter headed for the car, and it took a moment for Kat to follow him. His voice lacked an echo, as though he were speaking directly into a microphone.

As Kat ran down Quasso Drive, she swiped to the first page of the game. The countdown had dropped two hours.

09 HOURS : 21 MINUTES : 16 SECONDS

According to the directions for the third power-up, they had five minutes before time would resume again.

Before Peter and Kat reached the car, the passenger seat door swung open, and Jackie stepped out. "You wasted two hours." Her hand was clenched tightly against her arm, and the blood had smeared across the fabric at her waist. Her smooth voice had morphed into a raspy one, the pain seeping into her speech. "Smart move."

Kat froze at the sight of Jay through one of the car windows. She'd never seen anyone so still before. He sat in the driver's seat as though he were a picture, eyes open and everything—not a single twitch in his muscles.

Peter rushed to the car window and gasped at the sight of Jay's frozen figure in the driver's seat. "You used the power-up?"

"You're the one who said not to give up." Kat opened the back seat and slipped inside. "Do you have a better idea for how to get to the next location?" She scooted to the opposite window, allowing Peter space to get in.

"Right, the next location." Jackie lowered herself back into the passenger seat. "Where is it?"

"You two are crazy." Peter hopped into the back and slammed the door behind him.

"It's called..." Kat tapped **LEVEL FIVE** a second time. "Sunshine Auto."

Jackie poked her head into the back seat. "I've heard of that before." She spoke fast, and the raspiness faded as though being a part of the game was medicine on its own. "It's a used car dealership at the far end of Grovestown, right on the way to Lothen. It's where my dad bought Jay's car when he got his license sophomore year."

"Why go to a dealership all the way in Grovestown?" Peter asked.

"It's the only used car dealership in the area." Jackie faced the front. "Has the best deals."

That was new. The other four levels had taken place in locations Peter or Kat had connections to, but this one was random. Only Jackie knew where the place was, so the final level had to have something to do with her.

"Kat, I almost forgot to ask," Peter said, his voice finally back to its usual animated tone. "Have your parents called you at all?"

Kat shook her head. "My dad works late."

"How about Owen? Is he still texting you about his car?"

"Yeah, about that. I'm pretty sure he found out." Kat smiled, thinking back to when she'd woken up by the side of Quasso Drive after Jackie had tapped the emergency button. Her phone had flooded with a massive string of chimes—all from Owen. "He wouldn't stop texting me, so I kinda blocked him earlier."

Peter held his palm toward her. "Can I check something really quick?"

Kat pulled the phone out of the side compartment of her backpack and offered it to Peter. Before she could blink he'd opened the car door and chucked the device into the trees.

"What the hell?" Kat reached for her phone through the air as though it might come flying back. Her face went hot as Jackie laughed from the front seat. "That was expensive!"

Peter finally relaxed, resting his head against the door window. "I destroyed mine earlier, so we're even."

"That's not how it works! You can't just…"

The noise of the engine filled the air again. The sudden movement of the car switched Kat's focus to Jay, who continued driving down the road as though nothing had happened. It wasn't until he glanced into the rearview mirror when he caught a glimpse of the two figures in the back seat. He peeked over his shoulder. "How—how did you—"

"What is it?" Peter's voice jumped around as he tried not to laugh.

"I—well…" Jay breathed heavily with his eyes on the road. "When did you two get in here? I thought for sure you were on the side of the road when I drove away."

It didn't take long for Kat to forget about her phone. She grinned, joining along with the teasing. "We were."

Jackie snickered, and Jay's voice grew louder. "Can someone please explain what's going on here?"

Kat opened her mouth to speak, but Peter interrupted her. "For starters, you should probably know that you're nothing more than an NPC."

"A *what?*"

"A non-player character." Jackie gripped her arm tighter, but the smile lingered boldly on her face. "Like a background character in a video game."

"Ignore them." Kat stared at the back of Jay's seat, hoping her gentle gaze would somehow reach him. "I'll explain everything on the way to Grovestown."

Jay deserved answers for a change, even if it was just once.

Even if he would end up forgetting anyway.

DEAR STRANGER

Oh, how I wish I could do something right
To play the hero
Instead of the villain

Oh, how I wish to be proud of my actions
To look back and regret nothing
But I ask for too much

So if I can't be the hero
If I can't do something right
If I can't be proud
Then oh, how I wish
In place of the villain
I play the victim

08:35:16

PETER SCANNED THE parking lot for strangers. One glance at Jackie's bashed arm and bloodied shirt would force any sane person to dial 911.

Only a few cars aside from Jay's occupied the strip mall parking lot. The sun had set during their drive to Grovestown, and the pink-tinted sky made the gloomy atmosphere of the strip mall even more nerve-wracking. Their only source of light came from a collection of building windows to their left.

On the corner stood a gas station, its connected convenience store emitting a nasty yellow glow. Next to it was Grove Aid, a local drugstore where Jay currently rummaged through first-aid supplies. The remainder of the buildings in the area had closed, their light-up store names dimmed and windows blacked out.

Jackie and Kat stared at the busy road to their right. Across the street from the strip mall parking lot was Grovestown High, which meant they were currently in central Grovestown—the most active part of Grovestown—as hard as that was to believe. Peter had never spent time in Grovestown before, but he'd always imagined that it'd be at least slightly more exciting than what people made it out to be. It really wasn't.

"Grove Aid? Really, that's the best name those losers could come up with?" Peter tried to spot Jay through the windows. "Why don't we wait for him *inside* the car?"

"Aw, Peter's scared." Kat tilted her head to the side, eyes nearly red under the orange haze of dusk. "I guess in this scenario it's a good thing that I'm"—she paused—"*broke and clueless*. Helps me feel comfortable in a place like Grovestown."

Peter stood silent, struck by the fact that Kat had quoted the entry he'd written about her during his sophomore year. She'd never seemed like the type of insecure person to bother reading his sick blog.

"I'm not scared because we're in Grovestown, dummy." Peter pointed at Jackie's arm. "Do you see *that*? It looks like Jackie's an extra in some zombie apocalypse film."

Kat nudged Jackie's good arm. "Someone's awfully quiet."

"It's Jackie." Peter chuckled. "Of course she's quiet."

Jackie grinned as the front door to Grove Aid slid open, revealing Jay's silhouette under the dull lights bouncing off the sidewalk. He had a phone pressed between his ear and shoulder, likely on a call with someone.

"Here, hold this." Jackie handed Peter her phone as Jay approached the car with a plastic bag dangling from his grip. Peter spotted a few bottles of water, paper towels, and a package of rolled gauze.

Peter leaned over as he took the phone from Jackie and whispered into her ear. "I'm not sure if I'd trust Jay's doctoring skills."

Jackie stepped away from the car, approaching her brother with a shrug. "Anything's better than risking a hospital."

Jay set the plastic bag on the ground. "Yeah, Jackie's with me." A subtle mumbling came from the other line. "Of course, Dad. We'll be home soon. I love you too." He ended the call and tucked the phone into his pocket before leaning over to retrieve a water bottle that had rolled out of the bag.

As Jay poured water over Jackie's injured arm, she forced her left hand into a fist to keep from jolting away.

"So let me get this straight." Jay stopped pouring, and Jackie sighed with relief. "You three are stuck in a game that only you can see. And it gives you these—these *powers*."

"Wow." Kat gasped. "You finally caught on."

Jay tossed the empty water bottle back into the plastic bag and retrieved the pack of gauze. "And how do I know that Peter isn't behind this?" He struggled to break the package open. "Surely he's somehow involved."

"Good observation. I'm definitely a superhuman who can teleport and stop time." Peter didn't bother hiding the annoyance in his voice.

"I'm sorry. You're right." Jay finally managed to break the package open. He gritted his teeth when his focus returned to the gash in Jackie's arm. After a deep breath, he started wrapping the gauze around it. "I hope you don't blame me for being suspicious. With your—you know—internet history."

"Oh leave him alone, Jay." Kat pushed her glasses up her nose.

"Whoa, the feline standing up for me?" Normally Peter did his best to keep his emotions in check, cloaking everything with a joking tone, but for some reason the humor didn't come through. He sounded more surprised than he'd wanted to. "That's new," he added, the smile in his voice apparent this time.

Peter waited for him to speak, but Jay pretended as though he hadn't started this conversation in the first place. As Jay wrapped Jackie's forearm with the gauze, Peter remembered the phone Jackie had handed him and took a few steps away from the horrid scene. He disappeared behind the trunk of Jay's car, swiped to

the second page of Capsule, and tapped the new badge labeled
FOUR.

"Hey Kat!"

Her footsteps grew louder until she joined him behind the
car. "What?"

"Looks like you missed out on the new power-up. Listen to
this one." He read the description aloud. *"Clear the previous hour
of memory from another mind. Eye contact must be made with the
person of interest during activation.* That would've been perfect to
use on Jay. And it only costs two hours. What a deal!"

Kat had explained everything to Jay on the drive from
Emmeline's tree to Grove Aid, but Peter wasn't convinced Jay had
fully grasped an understanding of their situation, especially because Jay had accused him of somehow playing a role in Capsule's
development. The fact that he'd agreed to forgo a trip to the hospital was proof that at least some of the story had seeped in. Even
the strangeness of finding the trio must have been enough to
partially suppress his common sense. First he nearly ran over
Peter on Quasso Drive, next Jackie fell from Emmeline's tree, and
finally, Peter and Kat magically appeared in the back seat of his
car. *While* he was driving. The poor guy would probably eat up
any answers he could get.

"Actually, I'm happy with the power-up I used. Jay deserves an
explanation for once, even if it's only in this timeline." Kat faced
the road bordering the parking lot, watching the cars rush down
the bustling street. "Remember what Jackie told us? About how
Jay reacted to our disappearances?"

"Your disappearance." Peter shut off Jackie's phone with a bold
click and tucked it into his pocket.

"Fine, my disappearance." Kat leaned her back against the
trunk of the car, watching the dull impression of stars appearing

above them. "Jackie said he was constantly scrolling through social media, searching for clues. But there was one thing that really stood out to me about her story."

"Really building the hype here."

"Jackie said he started reading his own music again. That she saw a page with the words *Dear Stranger* in his hand. But that wasn't his music. It was the collection of poems we found together on one of our trips to Quasso Drive. Two years ago, Jay and I found the poems resting under a—"

"Blue hydrangea. I saw, remember?" Peter frowned. *Where is she going with this?*

"What I'm trying to say is that Jay thought my disappearance had something to do with Emmeline's death. Isn't that crazy? Can you imagine how confused he must have been? He personally knew two sisters. One missing, one dead. I'm sure he wanted answers more than anyone, and I bet it was eating him alive."

Kat had said she couldn't feel anything, but as Peter looked at her that night, her eyes radiated warmth, and it made him smile. Maybe she really could be genuine.

His focus wandered from Kat as chattering filled the air. He peeked around the opposite side of Jay's car, spotting a group of four girls exiting the convenience store next to Grove Aid. He held his breath, worrying they might make a left turn and spot Jay's unprofessional first-aid operation, but thankfully, they walked forward together, cold frappuccinos in hand. The drinks must have come from one of those filthy gas station coffee dispensers.

Overpriced sugar bombs at night. Peter frowned. *How accurate for a group of teenage girls.*

The girls were dressed with clothes slightly too elegant to be labeled as *casual* and had their hair straightened so thin Peter nearly assumed they were malnourished. The only girl with any volume to her hair was the one to the far right of their group, whose natural locks sprouted from her head. She wore a navy corduroy jacket over her dress to keep warm with the logo of Ravensburg University Prep embroidered at the chest. Peter huffed at the sight of it, but then he saw her face.

And it was her.

The girl.

Staring at her glittering gold dress in the parking lot of the Grovestown strip mall, he couldn't deny it. Her hair was longer now—almost obnoxiously long, as it reached down to her waist— and she wore heavier makeup than Peter thought a girl her age should bother with, but it was her.

Isabella.

Peter stepped away from the back of Jay's car to get a better view.

"No way." Kat joined him at his side. "It's her."

She was the girl Nicholas had saved. The girl Peter had shouted at when she'd tried to help him. She was her.

Isabella.

To the rest of the world she was just a high school girl. But to Peter, she was a nightmare.

A tragic miracle.

A wrong place at the right time.

Peter's face grew red. He stepped closer to the group of girls, who were now approaching a car a few empty spaces away. He was eager to catch Isabella's attention, but when her eyes met his, he froze.

Two years.

Nearly two years had passed since he'd last seen her, and people could change a lot in two years. Peter sure had. Isabella was fourteen now, a freshman in high school, and she looked different.

Recognizable, but different. Her honey eyes glimmered under the dull light, enhanced by her tears. She deviated from her group of girls, approaching Peter nearly at a running pace and wrapping her arms around him.

Peter gulped. Why? He'd shouted awful words at her, yet she'd continued to send him her letters. Letter after letter for nearly two years straight. It didn't make sense.

Peter knew how people worked. The pattern was always the same. Always. He'd say rude things, they'd say ruder things back. He'd show hatred, they'd show malice. Some people took longer than others to snap. He thought Isabella simply had a high tolerance for his toxic self, but even now, she'd failed to give Peter what he deserved. After all those months, what he needed was a punch in the face.

But she hugged him.

And for some reason, he calmed his nerves and hugged her back.

The two stood in the middle of a mostly-empty parking lot. Her drink pressed against his back, but he didn't shiver. Neither of them said a word. There were no explanations needed.

Peter's eyes watered, so he shut them and hugged her tighter.

Nearly two years since Nicholas had died, and to each other, they were all they had left of him.

When they pulled away from each other, Isabella reached into the zippered pocket of her jacket. She held the screen of her phone out so Peter could see. "Maybe it's weird," she said, "but I still keep his photo with me." Her lock screen featured Nicholas Moon. It was the same black-and-white photo Peter's dad had given him following his uncle's death—the one Peter had used for his own phone's lock screen. Mr. Moon must have given one to Isabella too.

"Thank you." Peter rubbed his eyes as he took a step back. "I haven't read any of your letters in a while, by the way."

"It's okay." Isabella shook her head. "You didn't have to."

He paused. "Well, what was in them?"

Her smile lit the parking lot on fire. "I wrote about all of the amazing things that have happened in my life—all that I'm grateful for." She zipped her phone back into her pocket as the orange warmth in the sky started to fade. "I have Nicholas to thank for everything, but I can't really thank him personally, so I figured the least I could do was make sure you know that his death wasn't in vain."

Peter wasn't sure what to think anymore. He'd been told by various sources that Isabella must have felt guilty for what had happened that day. Nicholas had died for her. Peter assumed she lived in misery and that her letters, at some point, had shifted from kindness to hate. But that hadn't been the case at all. Isabella was trying to make the most of what Nicholas had gifted her.

"I'm sorry about what I said." Peter looked away from Isabella, his eyes landing on the presence of Jackie and Jay stepping around the front of the Honda. Jackie wore Jay's checkered flannel, buttoned all the way up to cover the stains of blood on her blue shirt. Her arms were shielded by the sleeves, so the only sign of injury was a thin strip of gauze wrapped around her palm. "I just—he was so perfect and I couldn't help but wonder—"

"Why it had to be him," Isabella finished. "Me too."

The three high school girls behind her stared at the scene with grinning faces. Although Peter didn't recognize them, they were dressed similar to Isabella and most likely were also from Ravensburg University Prep. Quite a drive.

"So what are you doing in Grovestown?" Peter asked.

"The high school here is hosting a spring dance."

"Spring dance? Like prom?"

"No, not prom." Isabella's friends burst into laughter, and she offered them a harsh glare. "Grovestown's really small, so they have a spring dance open to all grades."

"*And* all schools," one of her friends shouted. "That's how desperate they are to get a full gym."

"You should come with your friends," Isabella added. "I heard it's pretty lame, but the people are great."

Peter scanned his thrift store outfit. "I don't think so."

"Well, it's Grovestown. Doesn't have to be anything fancy." A car door slammed shut as Isabella's friends loaded into the car, a subtle sign for her to hurry up. Isabella walked backward, making a gradual exit. "Think about it."

"We can't." Peter made eye contact with Jackie. "We're in a bit of a rush."

"It's cool. But Moon?" Isabella pointed at Peter, her hair rustling over her shoulders as she opened the back door to the car. "Write back to me sometime, will you?"

Before Peter could open his mouth, Isabella had already disappeared into the car. He stared at the door long after she'd entered it, his heart pounding, mind racing. None of it made sense, and it was driving him crazy. Why wasn't she mad? How did she manage to be so kind to him despite all he'd done?

Peter couldn't explain what he felt, but he knew he was glad he'd run into Isabella.

As the car with Isabella and her friends pulled out of the parking space and disappeared, Jackie, Jay, and Kat approached him.

"So who was that?" Jay asked.

Peter grinned. "Isabella."

"Okay," Jay said slowly. "And Isabella is who exactly?"

Peter reached into his pocket, unlocked Jackie's phone, and opened the Capsule app. "I need to use the first power-up." He narrowed his eyes at **ONE**, which upon activation would give them an extra glance into the past. A bonus memory.

"Power-up?" Jay asked. "Like the crazy thing that happened in the car earlier?"

"Don't worry about it. To you it'll be like nothing happened." Peter hovered his thumb over the activation button, stopping to seek approval from Jackie and Kat. Jackie didn't protest, and Kat smiled lightly, so he tapped the screen and muttered, "Show me how Nicholas saved Isabella."

BONUS LEVEL

IT ALL STARTED *with a playful sprinkle at Pelle Cove.*

Isabella stepped through the waves, breaking the incoming rushes of water with quick slams of her feet, the damp air gently embracing her. She wore a flowery one-piece swimsuit with her hair pulled back into a thick bun, not expecting a cloudy Ravensburg day in the middle of April, but she didn't mind the surprise. She'd been jumping through the cold water for eight minutes now, and the frosty sea no longer left her trembling.

While Isabella hopped from one wave to the next, she spotted her mom and younger brother resting their stomachs on a dry quilt under a cherry-colored umbrella, phones held out in front of them. Her dad sat on the sand a few feet away, his nose tucked into a fitness magazine. For a brief moment he looked up at the sky, perhaps feeling the vague drizzle—almost a mist—but her dad shrugged it off and turned back to his pages.

A man leaning against the empty lifeguard tower caught Isabella's attention next. He wore light-wash jeans and a white button-up shirt, the top few buttons left open. In his left hand was a leather notebook and in his right was a fountain pen. He had no blanket under him. No umbrella sheltering him from the wind. It was just him and a worn messenger bag resting at his side. The man raised his chin, meeting eyes with Isabella, and she paused, her feet sinking into the sand of the ocean floor as she tilted her head to the side. The man mirrored her, rotating his head at a duplicated angle.

When the man broke eye contact and checked his analog watch, Isabella giggled and resumed her game of wave-crashing. The rain intensified from the occasional sprinkle to full-bred droplets, but Isabella pushed forward, the fresh water streaming down her face and into the salty pool. She trembled as the ocean trekked up to her waist, but in some weird way, the cold returning refreshed her.

With another step forward the sand grew slippery. Less dependable. It slid around under her, the water circling her legs and pulling her down into one of the ocean's many dangerous traps. Her limbs slipped out of control, and the lack of sand under her feet left her choking on her own breaths. She gasped for air as her head returned to the surface. "Help!"

Another wave struck her, the water pulling her further from the shore.

Isabella's head ached as she flailed her arms. Her vision burned with salt water with each return to the surface to gasp for air. She caught glimpses of her family panicking to shelter their belongings under the umbrella, but when she opened her mouth to call out to them, water filled her throat, leaving her coughing and inhaling unwelcome droplets of sea water into her nose. The panic gripped her, refusing to let her float, dragging her deeper. The rain splashed against the ocean's surface and pounded onto the top of Isabella's head with the goal of pushing her underwater—permanently.

As the ocean devoured her alive, Isabella opened her eyes at the sound of a man's soothing voice. She emerged at the surface in time to make out his words clearly.

"You're going to be okay." He spoke loudly, but painfully slow. "I'm about to toss this over to you. I need you to catch it."

As she slipped beneath the surface again, a red and white buoy penetrated the air, landing directly above her and casting a rippling red shadow. She used all of her remaining energy to kick her legs and rush to the air with intention. She wrapped her arms around the buoy and coughed the water out of her chest.

The splattering of the rain against the plastic buoy mesmerized her. She focused on the taps to calm herself.

Several feet away from her swam the man who had thrown the buoy, keeping himself afloat with his elegant circling limps. He was the same man Isabella had seen by the lifeguard tower earlier—the one who had mirrored her. Even now it seemed as though he were breathing in the same panic-stricken rhythm she was.

"Can you kick to the shore?" The man's dark hair flew into his eyes. He reached to push the strands aside, temporarily breaking his swimming pattern.

Isabella had gripped the string of the buoy for extra support when a wave crashed into her from behind, sending her flying toward the shore. As she coasted with the buoy into the shallow end of the ocean, she looked over her shoulder to see the man who had spoken to her only seconds ago. He floated peacefully as a lofty wave snuck up on him from behind.

For a moment, he smiled.

Her scream of horror masked itself as a scream of fear. The other adults at Pelle Cove rushed to the shore, finally taking notice of her dilemma.

Isabella wrapped her arms around the buoy so tight she could hardly breathe. Her tears mixed with the rain that fell across her cheeks and into the deadly water. The image of the man's face seconds before he'd disappeared in the wave ingrained itself into her memory forever.

07:12:13

PETER DIDN'T SAY a word to Jackie and Kat before he ran to the shelter of Grove Aid. The front doors hardly opened fast enough to keep him from slamming into the fiberglass. Jackie tried to go after him, but she couldn't hold her balance well. The asphalt tilted under her feet, and she leaned forward with a scrambled stomach. Seeing Nicholas die that day—seeing that wave crash over his head—it was overwhelming.

Jay wrapped an arm around Jackie, steadying her. "What's wrong?"

"I'll find him." Kat's boots tapped against the asphalt as she stepped calmly toward Grove Aid. Of course Kat was unfazed. She was the only person strong enough to see what they'd seen and act as though nothing had happened.

"Is Peter okay?" Jay asked.

Jackie stepped away from her brother, finally regaining balance. Ever since Level Four at Emmeline's tree, Jay had been the odd one out, but as Jackie faced him in the parking lot, her desire to be more like him rose higher than ever. He hadn't been cursed to live through what they never should have lived through—what no one should have lived through. Not Isabella. And certainly not Nicholas.

Jay hadn't been cursed by the game.

His arms fell to his sides, and he smiled softly. "Go." Jay reached for the car door, surrendering his search for answers for the first time. In that moment, ignorance was bliss, and perhaps he was starting to understand that. "I'll wait for you guys out here."

Jackie smiled as *thank you* before running to catch up with Kat in the parking lot. As the wind tousled Jackie's hair, she thought back to the gentle expression on Isabella's face only moments ago. She and her friends had laughed together as they walked to the car with cold cups in their hands. For nearly two years, Isabella had written letters to the nephew of her savior, the boy who had screamed at her and blamed her for the tragedy.

Jackie reached Kat's side. They didn't speak to each other. They simply walked into Grove Aid as a single unit with a single mission.

Grove Aid was larger than Jackie had been expecting, but the environment was no surprise. Shelves of disorganized toiletries, yellowing discount posters peeling from the walls, and a line of cashiers by the windows who clearly lacked enthusiasm to be working here so late.

Jackie and Kat trailed along the entrances to the many aisles on a search for Peter. They found him sitting on the stained carpet of a discount candy aisle. He had his knees tucked against his chest and his back leaning on several rows of outdated Valentine's Day chocolates.

Jackie sat to his left, Kat to his right. Peter blinked at the shelves ahead of him, not acknowledging their presence.

Before today, Jackie, Peter, and Kat had hardly known each other—if one could even say they knew each other at all—but now they'd shared one of Isabella's experiences from two years ago. They had witnessed the death of Peter's uncle with their own eyes. A sacrifice. A swap of one man for a twelve-year-old girl who had wandered too deep. They were connected in an unimaginable way.

Isabella should have been broken. She should have been shattered a million times smaller than Peter. She had not only heard the news, but she had *seen* it. Yet minutes ago Isabella had stood in the parking lot of Grove Aid, hugging Peter as though he weren't the boy who had blamed her for her worst nightmare.

"I was really close to my uncle."

Jackie flinched at the sudden sound of Peter's voice.

"He was ten years younger than my dad, so they never really got along well," he continued. "Nicholas was into meditation and horoscopes and juice cleanses—all things my dad thought was a load of shit. But you know what? He was the only one who actually talked to me about stuff that mattered."

Kat had her legs extended out in front of her. She clicked her boots together. "Did you see him a lot?"

"Not really, no." Peter inhaled a shaky breath. "During his six months of the year in California he was alway pretty busy with photography gigs, but once in a while he'd pick Grace and I up from school or take me to lunch. I always looked forward to it."

Jackie wrapped her left arm around her stomach, trying to keep that sickening feeling at bay. She hadn't even known Nicholas personally, so she could hardly comprehend how much his death had affected Peter. The man he looked up to the most, the man who took the time to genuinely understand who he was—he was gone.

"I'm sorry," Kat said. "It must have been hard to lose him."

"Yeah. It's different for you though, isn't it?" Peter shook his head, recalling the memory they'd seen at Quasso Drive. "I know you've been trying to cry—trying to feel something—but to be honest with you, the feelings you keep chasing you won't want anyway. Why don't you just accept that you're stronger than everyone else and move on?"

"Because that's not the kind of person I wanna be." Kat gripped the carpet at her sides, her face burning. "Ever since Emmeline died it's just been me and my dad, working through it together. And I love him so much, but when I imagine him gone someday, I can't imagine myself crying."

Jackie had never held so much hatred for Capsule before. The game was here to torment Peter and Kat, to force them to relive the lowest points of their lives. To remind them of everything they'd lost.

"This game is sick. And not the good kind." Kat looked over at Peter and Jackie, that same anger reflecting off her eyes. The one thing all three of them could relate to at that moment was how much they despised Capsule. "These memories keep sending us to the past. And when we're not dealing with that we're searching for the next level, constantly stressing over how much time we have left. When do we get our chance to be Isabella?"

As abstract as Kat's question was, Jackie understood her perfectly. *When do we get our chance to be Isabella?* The fourteen-year-old girl had seen the worst, yet she'd somehow learned to move on. She lived for *this* moment. Nicholas had changed her, but his death didn't *define* her. It would have been nice to stop stressing over the past and worrying about the future. It seemed the trio had been living this way even before the game had begun.

Peter, unable to accept the heroic death of his uncle.

Kat, torn apart by her inability to grieve.

And me—Jackie turned in the direction of the parking lot, where Jay sat in the driver's seat of his Honda, alone—*failing to move on from my jealousy.*

Peter retrieved Jackie's phone from his pocket and handed it back to her. "Kat's right. This game is a trap."

Jackie opened Capsule to reveal the countdown page. The game wanted her to obsess over the numbers. The game wanted to control their worries, their fears, their emotions. The three were ruled by the game. Ruled by the clock. Ruled by nothing but a balance of regret and dread.

"I don't get it." Jackie shut her phone off. "We do what the app says, win the game, and everything goes back to normal. The way today was supposed to be."

The way today was supposed to be, Jackie repeated to herself. If Capsule hadn't appeared on her phone, where would she be right now?

"It's weird, isn't it?" Peter ran his hands along his polo, trying to straighten out the fabric, but he gave up after a few recurring wrinkles. "After everything that's happened, Capsule plans to wipe our memories at the next location. But if we restart the day and don't remember any of this, doesn't that make it all pointless?"

"I guess it depends on how you look at it." Kat shrugged. "You could say that about life too."

The three sat in the gloomy Grove Aid that night, the distant lights from the windows across the street taunting them. Right now, at this very moment, high school students were having a fun time together at the spring dance. They were living.

Jackie set her hand against the floor to push herself back to her feet and winced from the pressure on her wound. "I think we deserve a break."

Peter frowned at Jackie, leaving her uncomfortable at first, but she realized he was simply sorting through his thoughts. He eventually stood and faced her with a smile. "You're right. We do."

"This game wants to have complete control over us." Kat stood next, joining their line. "Let's take one moment for ourselves. Just *one* moment where we aren't trapped in the game."

They left Grove Aid at 8:29 and stood in front of the sliding doors, swatting away the moths circling through the air as they laid their eyes on the school building across the other side of the busy road. To most students, Grovestown High was simply a place to host another silly school dance. A place where they could have a little fun for the night. But to Jackie, Peter, and Kat, Grovestown High was their escape. Their safe place. The present moment in a world plagued by the haunting past and terminal future.

Peter stepped forward, standing in the center of the parking space Isabella had been in minutes ago. It was the first time Jackie noticed how dirty his shoes had become. Earlier this afternoon they'd been pearly white, but now they were covered in dirt. They were muddy. Messy. And maybe—just for tonight—he was okay with that.

"I've been wondering." Jackie stepped off the curb and joined him on the asphalt. "That one entry, the one you labeled anonymous. Who was it for?"

The sky darkened, its orange and pink hues morphing into a deep red.

"I wrote it for me." Peter's light chuckle faded into a frown. "Who am I kidding? It was all for me."

The moon hovered in the bloody sky, a source of comfort among a sea of pain. Before today, Peter hadn't seen the death of his uncle. He had simply heard the news, and that news destroyed him. That news had led him spiraling down a path of self-hatred. A spiral that had brought him back to school his sophomore year as a changed boy. A boy who now ran Moral Moon.

Jackie thought back to all of the horrible things people had said about him. Brookwood High assumed that just because he ran a nasty blog they could say anything they wanted to without being the bad guy.

Because it's okay to bully a bully, and it's okay to murder a murderer.

Right?

07:00:32

THE INSIDE OF the Grovestown High gym was pitch-black, but the dotted lights flashed so frequently it felt as though Jackie were constantly under a spotlight. She blushed at the sight of the students' fancy clothing, their outfits putting her casual sweatpants, muddy sneakers, and oversized checkered flannel to shame.

At least I'm not dressed like him. Jackie grinned at Peter's orange polo and khaki pants. He really did look like a nerd who buttered popcorn at the movie theater.

The four stood against the wall of the gym, Jackie and Jay on opposite sides of the line they'd formed, Peter and Kat sandwiched between them. Together they watched the clumps of students laugh so loud it almost sounded as though they were screaming. The busy chattering mixed with the distorted music from the low-quality speakers formed an ensemble from hell. Jackie hardly recognized the current song as *Talking to the Moon* by Bruno Mars.

"This is the final location?" Jay's voice fell flat. It was more of a statement of disbelief than a question.

"Not quite." Kat took a step forward, breaking their line. She swung the backpack off her shoulders and tossed it at the wall on the spot where she'd stood a second ago. Emmeline's keychains clashed against the polished floor as Kat gestured to the collection of sweating high school students. "We're taking a detour."

To their left, a foldable plastic table against the wall featured an insulated dispenser and stacks of paper cups. At first Jackie thought the tablecloth was burgundy, but the indecisive colors in the air made it hard to tell. A pair of students exited the blur of bodies in the middle of the gym to fill their cups with dark fluid from the stainless steel dispenser.

"Oh wow. Would you look at that?" Peter said. "They're drinking mud in Grovestown. Why am I not surprised?"

Jackie faced Peter with crossed arms, but he took a few steps forward before she could express her frustration with him poking fun at Grovestown. He passed Kat, approached the table, and plucked a cup of his own from one of the many stacks. After pouring himself a serving of hot chocolate, he turned around and raised the cup in the air as though he were giving a toast.

"To the game." He closed his eyes, brought the cup to his lips, and gulped. As Peter lowered his head and stared at the twirling fluid in the cup, he smiled.

Jackie's frustration toward Peter and his judgments vanished, and her eyes narrowed from the pressure of her wide grin. Peter had taken a first step to breaking his habits. His *good* habits. Because even good habits for the wrong reasons did nothing but tear people down.

Peter's choice to drink hot chocolate held no significance to Jay. His mind wandered somewhere else. "I haven't been to a school dance since…" Jay closed his mouth as Kat looked away from Peter and faced him. "I just don't get why we're stopping here first."

"You don't have to." Kat's voice rose to a higher pitch as though she were mocking her own words. "The world doesn't owe us answers, Jay."

Jackie hadn't noticed how tense Jay had been until his shoulders dropped an inch with a light chuckle.

Peter tossed his half-empty cup into a trash bin on the way back from the table. His eyes darted between Kat and Jay. "I'm not so sure Emmeline would approve."

Jay's face grew red, and Kat crossed her arms. "Oh shut up, Peter," she said.

Peter bowed, replicating the same conversation from this morning in the hall. "As you wish, Your Majesty." But this time when he straightened his back with a hand over his nose and mouth, Kat was smiling too.

Looking at the situation objectively was almost comical. Jackie never would have expected to attend a school dance in Grovestown with the impulsive Kat Pike and the despised Peter Moon. She'd spent an entire day with two students from Brookwood High who she'd known absolutely nothing about, but now their wins were her wins, and she recognized a beauty in that.

This was a moment Jackie could never get back, and part of her wished it wouldn't end.

"I'm surprised you're going along with this," Kat said.

"I know, right?" Peter faced the crowd. "But we really do deserve a break."

"Hell yeah we do! Say it louder next time." Kat pointed at the students dancing in the middle of the gym. "Wanna go?"

"Yeah right." Peter shook his head. "Unless you wanna see me perform Taekwondo kata to the beat, I doubt you want me out there."

"Actually, that does sound like something I wanna see."

Peter and Kat disappeared, leaving Jackie and Jay leaned against the wall several feet away from each other with Kat's backpack forming a barrier between them.

"Honestly, I've been really confused." Jay's jaw dropped into an open-mouth grin. "I mean, when am I not? But this has got to be the most confusing part of all. Kat Pike and Peter Moon. Who would've thought?"

"What about them?" Jackie asked.

"I've never seen Kat this happy before. And Peter—well—I always thought he was too stuck in his own head to appreciate anyone else, but look at him now."

Jackie searched the crowd, her eyes running over the twisting students until they finally landed on Peter and Kat. With a few strikes of his arm, Peter imitated a martial arts move before Kat burst into laughter, grabbing his arms to stop him from further embarrassment.

Jackie's and Jay's eyes met again, but they looked away and instead watched the colors bounce off the walls. About once every twenty seconds the air would fill with a bold purple, reminding Jackie of the desk waiting for her back at home. It felt like years since she'd last sat in front of her PC, but strangely enough, she didn't miss it.

"I have a question." Jackie didn't wait for Jay to reply before asking. "After Emmeline died, why did you try so hard to bring Kat with you on those trips to Quasso Drive?"

Jackie now understood that Jay wanted to know where Emmeline was going that night. He wanted to know why she'd told everyone different stories. He wanted to know what she'd planned on doing instead of going to the dance with him. But what Jackie didn't understand was why he had to solve the mystery with Kat.

"She told you about that?"

Explaining the game was getting old, so Jackie settled with saying, "Yeah, Kat told me."

"I see. Well maybe this is stupid, but"—Jay melted against the wall in relief—"I think part of me just wanted to be a brother for once."

Jackie's head darted to her left. The now-orange lights of the room warmed Jay's face as he continued.

"And the other part of me—well—I guess I also wanted to help Kat feel better. But I had it wrong. She didn't need someone to help her. All she needed was a fun time."

Maybe she and Jay were more similar than she'd thought. They were both trapped on the outside. Trying to reach the land of understanding and always getting closer but never reaching the true destination. Peter and Kat had both experienced the tragic loss of someone they cared for, and that was something the Mendoza siblings didn't have. Jackie and Jay could only imagine pain, but Peter and Kat had lived it. As much as Jackie wanted to believe that she was a part of their journey, the reality was that she was the player and Peter and Kat were the pawns. They were in it for their lives, and she was in it for the game.

Jay coughed their wandering minds back into reality. "Well, if we're playing the loners tonight, let me show you how it's done." He boosted himself off the wall, and Jackie sent a final glance in Peter and Kat's direction before slowly following Jay to the snack table. He handed Jackie a styrofoam plate and gestured to the array of cold platters next to the hot chocolate dispenser. "Welcome to the feast."

Jackie couldn't keep herself from smiling. She hadn't seen this playful side of her brother in years, so she went along with it and offered him a curtsy. "Why thank you."

"This here is a quartered gourmet sandwich." Jay plopped a piece onto Jackie's plate. "Classic loner food."

"And what's that?" Jackie pointed to a glass bowl of what appeared to be corn pudding. "That definitely looks like loner food."

They both watched a boy wearing an oversized yellow suit reach for the wooden spoon and scoop the unknown corn substance onto his plate.

"No, that's not loner food." Jay's face grew serious as he leaned over Jackie's shoulder and whispered into her ear. "That's just Grovestown food."

Jackie laughed as the boy faced them with a frown. He grabbed a plastic spoon lying on the tablecloth and walked away, his slacks dragging against the dusty gym floor behind him.

Jay introduced Jackie to a few more foods before they established their spot in the corner of the gym.

"Is this the loner spot?" Jackie asked.

"Not exactly, but it's my favorite spot." Jay tucked himself into the corner as he bit into a dry baby carrot. He set the other half of the vegetable on his plate as he choked the bite down. "If you stand in the corner of any room, you'll learn a lot about the people inside it."

For a moment Jay sounded like Eugene with his poetically-phrased advice.

"But you're an exception." Jay tossed his plate into the nearby trash bin, giving up on the raw carrots and broccoli he'd taken from the vegetable platter. "I could stand in all four corners and not understand any better."

"And why's that?" Jackie took a bite of her sandwich expecting it to be dry, but not *this* dry. It stuck to the back of her front teeth and left her struggling to free it with her tongue. The last thing she wanted to do was reach her fingers into her mouth in front of a bunch of high schoolers.

She set the sandwich onto her plate. *Not eating that again.*

"I just—I could never understand what I did wrong." Jay paused as the song transitioned to a new one. "Freshman year I got really pulled into high school drama. Friends, dances, sports. Then sophomore year came around and there was the Emmeline situation. But I always tried to make time for you, and it kinda felt like you wanted nothing to do with me."

Jackie remembered all of the times Jay had started conversations with her in the car. All of the times he had asked Jackie if she wanted to hang out with him and his friends. Every single time, Jackie had pushed him away. She said no to spending time with him. She boarded herself in her room with nothing but video games and a best friend who didn't consider her *his* best friend. It was all a mess. A sacrifice for nothing.

"I was jealous."

Jay nodded, as though he already knew. "Mom and Dad love you too."

"But not in the same way." Jackie followed Jay's example and tossed the rest of her food into the trash. It really wasn't worth the energy to chew.

"No one ever loves two people the same way." He took a step away from the wall and held his arms out toward her. "Sibling hug?"

"Just this once." Jackie smiled lightly before leaning into him. "Ouch! Bro, watch the arm."

It really would just be once, wouldn't it?

An eternity passed before Jackie and Jay pulled away. That night, standing next to each other at the Grovestown dance, Jackie forgot about the game. She forgot about Capsule's threats and all of Peter's and Kat's memories she'd experienced earlier today. She had successfully escaped from the game—escaped from time.

But it was too sweet to last.

"You're not gonna say hi to me?"

Jay nearly jumped at the girl's voice. "Whitney? What are you doing in Grovestown?"

Whitney. Jackie recognized the name from the Level Two memory—when Jay first arrived at the Pike household to speak to Emmeline. Kat had been planning to meet Whitney at Cherry Ice, but Whitney flaked.

"Oh, you know how I am. I'll go to any school event that opens its doors to me. Even in Grovestown." Whitney's thick hair glowed golden under the pulsing lights. "Nice getup, by the way. Looks like you're heading to the movies."

"It was a last-minute decision to come." Jay looked down at his graphic t-shirt and jeans. "I wasn't—"

"I'm kidding. You make any outfit cute." She pointed at Jackie. "Who's she?"

"My sister." Jay gave Jackie an encouraging smile. "Jackie, this is Whitney. Kat's friend."

"Am I not yours?" Whitney cocked her head to the side, the smile vanishing from her face as she turned to Jackie. "Little sister, huh? What's your name?"

"Jackie." She pursed her lips. *Like my brother just said.*

"Whoa, that's cute. You're really pretty by the way." Whitney was quick to draw her attention back to Jay. "So did you hear the news?"

Jay sighed, expecting drama. "What news?"

"So I was at home trying to call Kat, right? And it keeps going straight to voicemail. Then a few minutes later I get a call from her dad, and he's all freaked out because he can't find Kat anywhere. He's like, about to cry—*that* freaked out."

"Oh yeah?" Jay smiled weakly. "Is Kat okay?"

"So that's the crazy part!" Whitney held her phone out in front of him. On it was a photo of the SUV in the background, the camera focusing on a hand holding a clothing tag from Closets & Beyond. Jackie wanted to observe the photo longer, but Whitney pulled her arm away. "You know Owen, right? From Key Club? He thinks Kat stole his car, and the police found it somewhere in Ravensburg. Totally wrecked."

Jackie rolled her eyes. *That's an exaggeration.*

"They think she's the same girl who shoplifted from some thrift store, and according to one of the employees, there was a guy with her. And you wanna know the craziest part?"

Jay and Jackie leaned forward in unison.

Whitney brought her palm to the right side of her lips. "That *guy* was Peter Moon."

Jackie clenched her fists, trying to keep her fears subdued. "And how do you know that?"

"Easy. His family called the police tonight when he didn't come home from school before five, which apparently is really rare for him. I don't find that hard to believe. But anyways, that thrift store employee saw a photo of Peter and recognized him instantly."

Jackie's heart sank. The three of them had come to the Grovestown dance for a chance to live like Isabella, but this dance in Grovestown—it was only temporary. Unless they won the game tonight, this would be their last chance to ever live in the moment. Maybe, in this case, they really did have to live for the future. Just a few hours of sacrifice—that was all it would take.

It's just a game. Calm down. Jackie's fists loosened, regaining control as the player. "Was there anyone else?"

"Don't think so," Whitney said.

Perhaps Capsule had covered Jackie's tracks.

"Interesting." Jay stepped forward, swooping an arm around Whitney's shoulder and guiding her toward the snack table. "You know what? We should get something to eat." He dangled the keys in his free hand as they walked away, looking over his shoulder at Jackie to prompt her to take them.

Jackie wrapped her warm fingers around the keys as she passed her brother and stormed toward the crowd. She squeezed between students, stepping onto a few feet in the process and not bothering to apologize. It didn't sound like Whitney cared enough to keep a secret, so they'd better not take any chances.

"Oh great." Peter spotted Jackie a few feet away, sensing trouble. "What's wrong?"

Kat went limp at the sight of Jay's keys in Jackie's hand.

"Whitney's here," Jackie said.

Peter took a step closer, turning his ear in her direction. "What?"

Jackie sighed before raising her voice. "Whitney's here!"

"Whitney?" Kat slammed a palm against her forehead. "Dammit! I should've known she'd be here."

"Let's hurry." Jackie turned around, knowing they'd follow her.

As Jackie squeezed out of the crowd, she caught a glance of Jay and Whitney by the snack table. By the time she reached the back door, Jay had caught her eyes. He smiled, and Jackie smiled back. Yes, Jackie wanted to win the game. And yes, Jackie wanted to save Peter and Kat. But at the same time, she also knew that playing the game meant leaving her brother behind. Losing everything they'd gained at the Grovestown dance.

Capsule was finally coming to an end. Both the good and the bad—it would all be over soon.

Jackie burst through the back door of the gym. The air outside had grown significantly colder now, and goosebumps instantly formed on her arms. They'd re-entered reality. Re-entered the game.

"I'll take the keys." Kat plucked them from Jackie's grip.

Jackie turned left, heading down the side of the building and toward the parking lot, but she didn't hear Peter's and Kat's footsteps behind her. When she turned around, they stood with folds across their foreheads.

"Actually, Jackie, we…" Peter took a deep breath, preparing himself. "We were thinking Kat and I could go alone this time."

"At the end of the day this is our problem, not yours." Kat gripped the keys tighter in her hands, knuckles draining of color. "We really don't want to drag you into this any longer."

Jackie shook her head, smiling. "You're not dragging me."

When Kat nodded at Peter, he held his palm out. "This'll be over soon anyways. Last level, right?"

Jackie scoffed at the sight of his palm. She knew exactly what he wanted. Peter wasn't asking for her hand. He wasn't asking for help. He wasn't inviting her along. No—he wanted her phone.

He wanted the controller.

"Worst case," Kat said, "it'll be safer to have you here as backup."

Jackie reached for the phone in her back pocket and unlocked it to check the countdown one final time.

06 HOURS : 49 MINUTES : 21 SECONDS

She placed the phone firmly onto Peter's palm—maybe a little too firmly, because his eyelids flickered at the impact. As Jackie pulled her hand back to her side, Peter folded his fingers around the phone, establishing himself as the new player. Together, Peter and Kat walked past Jackie and into the parking lot of Grovestown High.

They didn't say goodbye.

#389

YEAH, I NOTICE everyone. Even the nobody. It's funny how people think Jackie Mendoza is the smart, quiet kid just because she keeps to herself and turns her homework in on time. She's literally on her phone every time she can be. I sit next to her in math, so I'd know. She's on her phone before class, as soon as she finishes her assignments, and even while walking through the halls. I've never seen one other person at Brookwood who wastes as much time as she does. She traps herself in video games to the point of complete social isolation.

Jackie has the potential to do something with her life, but instead she wastes it away on screen time. But hey—I can't complain too much. We need people like her so the people on top can thrive. Can't have the rich without the poor or the smart without the stupid. That kind of thing. But damn, it really gets on my nerves to see.

Moon.

06:43:43

"BRAKES, BRAKES!"

Peter's screaming nearly made Kat swerve off the road. She jammed her foot against the brake pedal, the car decelerating around a sharp right turn so fast the momentum slammed Peter against the passenger seat door.

Peter gripped his head to ease the impact from hitting the window. "You're slowing down way too late. It's really not that hard." He took unnecessarily deep breaths, emphasizing his discomfort with having Kat behind the steering wheel. "Gosh, you've got to be the worst driver I know."

"Well that would make perfect sense, Einstein, considering how this is my first time on the road." Kat couldn't tell if he was joking around or actually trying to get on her nerves, but she wasn't in the mood for either. "And the stakes are pretty high right now."

"Can I drive?" Peter reached for the steering wheel, and she swatted his hand away. "Please?"

Their final location was at the far end of Grovestown, ten minutes at most from the dance, and they were already halfway there. Kat struggled accepting the fact that she wanted more time in this world, but it was true. She wasn't eager to win the game like Jackie was. Although she knew it was in her best interest to complete the levels, that didn't mean she wanted to. It was a chore. Something that had to be done, but no one wanted to do. She'd felt so at ease at the Grovestown dance—more rested than she'd felt in years—and that was one thing she could thank the devilish game for.

"It took me two weeks to get myself into a car after Emmeline died. I know I come off as reckless and stuff, but to be honest with you, I always thought I'd be too scared to drive one myself." Kat pressed her back against the seat as she drove, her fingers loosening around the steering wheel. "But now I'm starting to get why my sister loved driving. I'm pretty comfortable right now, and I don't even have a license. Or a permit for that matter."

"And you're speeding." Peter pointed to a speed limit sign further down the road. *35mph.*

"And I'm speeding." Kat grinned at the car's odometer, which read *50mph.* "That really says a lot."

Further down the road stood a log building with the name *Sunshine Auto* spelled with light-up letters across the front of the roof. Cars filled the massive parking lot surrounding the building and overflowed along the nearby sidewalks. Although it appeared to be an average car dealership, the location wasn't at all traditional. The dealerships in Brookwood were located within the western commercial district, surrounded by restaurant chains, bustling wholesale markets, and smog shops, but there were no other buildings surrounding Sunshine Auto. Just trees and a few windows glowing from a distant neighborhood.

Kat pulled over behind a string of cars directly across the street from the parking lot. With her foot pressed against the brakes, she pulled at the key. It was jammed.

Peter shifted the car into park and removed the key with ease. "Even I know how this works."

"You know everything, don't you?" Kat snatched the key from his fingertips, smiling as she turned away from him and opened the car door.

The sun had set a while ago, leaving behind nothing but a fading pinkish-purple blur in the sky. Kat crossed the street with her numb hands tucked into the pockets of her transparent windbreaker, which didn't do much to warm her up. Her neck grew tense as she resisted the cold and squeezed between two cars parked way too close to each other. By the time she reached the wire fence that wrapped along the parking lot of Sunshine Auto, Peter was standing by her side.

Kat raised her chin to face the top of the fence—no barbed wire.

"Cosmetic security." She rested her hands against the patterned wires, and the fence shifted with little resistance. Flimsy.

"What?"

"A fence that doesn't keep people out." Kat lifted her shoe, shoving a sneaker into one of the gaps between the wires and boosting herself up. "Cosmetic. It only looks like security."

"Why do I get the sense you've done this before?" Peter's shoes were too large to get a solid grip between the wire's gaps, which left him sliding onto the sidewalk a few times. He placed most of his weight on his arms, breathing heavily as he pulled himself up the fence, feet nearly dangling under him.

"Someone's a bit slow." Kat snickered from the top of the fence before spinning to climb down the opposite side. "And actually—no, I haven't snuck in anywhere before. But I've thought about it. Horrible, huh?"

"What's horrible?" Peter wrapped his hand around the metal bar at the top of the fence.

"That I do bad things when I don't have to. Or at least, when I don't have a reason to." Kat leapt the remainder of the distance, and her soles burned from the impact, but after a few steps the sensation faded. Earlier today she'd stolen candy at Pepperdine when she hadn't even been in the mood for candy. "I feel like I've tried everything to feel bad, but I never do. It's like people think I'm human, but I'm only human when I'm fake."

"You know what?" Peter landed next to her, his feet shuffling as he rebalanced himself. "The fact that you're worried about this in the first place proves that you're human. Me and my blog, on the other hand—I don't have any remorse for what I've done."

They trailed between cars, pretending to search for the final capsule—or whatever the game had in store for them at this level—but they weren't *really* paying attention.

"But that's different." Kat shivered under the cool breeze. "You didn't make your blog to hurt people."

Peter stopped, and when Kat turned around, his eyes widened. She'd reached that conclusion from his memories and what he'd shared back at Grove Aid, but apparently he hadn't even reached it himself. His jaw shifted around, hinting that he had something to say, but his lips refused to budge.

"If people actually knew your story, they'd be able to relate to you." Kat crossed her trembling arms. "But me? I'm like that one character in the movie who everyone likes because they look cool, but no one actually understands."

"No, you're not." Peter shook his head, a grin sliding onto his face. "You're more like the villain's sidekick."

Kat didn't want to, but she smiled.

"In all seriousness though, you're not a monster, Kat." Peter passed her, walking between two cars. "If anyone's the monster, it's me."

Kat stared at Peter's back as she followed him through the parking lot. She couldn't put her finger on what had changed. Earlier today they'd done nothing but throw insults at each other, but now they were fighting to be the bad guy. Now they were defending each other more than they were defending themselves.

Maybe she and Peter weren't as different as she had originally thought.

Maybe no one was.

"Hello?" Peter waved his hand in front of Kat's face.

Kat stopped. "What?"

"I've been asking you where you think it might be." He spun in place, gesturing to the cars surrounding them. "I don't think our walking-between-cars strategy is working very well. It wouldn't be inside, would it?"

Now that Kat was closer to the building she finally noticed how worn-down it was. The log walls made it appear as more of a cabin than a car dealership office, but that wasn't a surprise considering their location. She searched for the silhouette of a capsule through the windows, but with the indoor lights off, it was too dark to tell.

Kat lowered her eyes.

That's when she saw it.

"Oh. Great!" Peter laughed. "It just *had* to be in a car, of all places."

Inside the gray Lexus beside them was the final capsule, hovering gently over the passenger seat. The sticker on the windshield labeled the car for sale at 17,350 dollars.

Kat yanked at the door. It was locked.

Worth a shot.

"Can you find a brick?" She tapped at the driver's seat window.

"Really, a brick?" Peter ran a hand through his hair. "You've got to be kidding me."

"Do you have a better idea, Houdini?" Kat rested her palm on the cool glass. They were so close to the last capsule. So close to the end of the game. Surely one extra crime wouldn't hurt. "The longer we hold off, the riskier it gets."

Peter sighed. "I hate that you're right."

"Then hurry up! We have to find a brick, or a rock—anything." Kat searched the ground of the surrounding area for something strong enough to penetrate the glass with.

As Peter ran to scan the area along the fence, a speaker blasted a warning signal.

"You are trespassing. Remove yourself from the property or the police will be alerted…" The warning repeated itself as Peter returned to Kat with a rock resting between his palms. It was about the size of an apple, but it'd do the trick. *"You are trespassing. Remove yourself from the property…"*

"I'm impressed." Kat searched for the source of the audio warning on the main building, but she couldn't spot the speakers. "Didn't think a place like this would bother with motion sensors."

"Once again, Kat underestimates security." Peter tossed the rock into the air and caught it. "Is this something you always do?"

Kat held her hand out for the rock, but Peter shot his arm past her and smashed it into the window of the Lexus. She clenched her eyes shut at the violent clash of the rock meeting glass.

"Whoa." Kat opened her eyes to the shards trickling onto the dirt in light raindrops. "What happened to Peter?"

"Peter," he said, dropping the rock onto the dirt, "has realized that in about thirty seconds, none of this will matter."

Within an arm's reach through the destroyed Lexus window was the final capsule, but it flew through the windshield without causing further damage, as though the glass hadn't been there in the first place. Kat ran after the capsule, scared of losing sight of it, but it didn't travel far before gliding into another car window. It hovered over the passenger seat, taunting them.

Kat winced as her fingers slammed into the glass. "You've got to be kidding me."

Peter appeared at Kat's side with the rock in his hands again. Kat stepped away, and he swung his arm against the window, shattering the glass. Before he could reach for it, the capsule made its second exit and slipped through the windshield of a third car—a red Toyota.

They'd already smashed two windows. What more was a third? After a few deep breaths, Peter raced to the Toyota and threw his fist into the glass a third time, the sharp edges of the rock in his grip leaving shards of glass fluttering to the ground. Kat held her breath, hoping the capsule wouldn't move again.

And it didn't.

With a humming noise the capsule emitted a vivid blue glow, which Kat assumed was a mark of victory. She joined Peter by the red Toyota's smashed window. The color seeping from the fifth capsule blinded her.

"Not as challenging as I'd expect for a boss level." The rock fell from Peter's grip, permanently this time. He had traces of blood on his right hand, but he didn't reach for the capsule nor bother to study his cuts, and Kat couldn't bring herself to reach for the capsule nor ask if his hand was okay. As curious as she was about what the final memory would entail—if they even had a fifth memory, the dread overwhelmed her.

Is this really the end? Her gaze wandered back and forth between Peter and the glowing capsule as the audio warning echoed around them. *"Remove yourself from the property or the police will be alerted. You are trespassing. Remove yourself..."* At this point Kat had learned to tune the message out. The noise faded into the ambiance of the night, nothing more than a cricket chirp in the wind.

"I guess that's it then." Peter faced Kat, but his eyes lingered on the capsule.

"Yeah." Kat nodded. "I guess so."

They had both agreed that this was the end, but neither of them took action to make the end official. Kat observed Peter's hand, waiting for his fingers to twitch. For him to open the capsule. For *him* to end the game. But Peter's hand didn't budge, and she couldn't gather the strength to budge either.

"I have a weird question for you." Peter's voice was unsteady, lacking the usual confidence he spoke with. His words clashed into each other, struggling to break loose. "Do you feel—you know—like—trapped in the game?"

Kat thought back to the bonus memory. Sitting on the floor of the Grove Aid candy aisle, she'd hated Capsule. She'd longed for an escape, but now the escape exit was an arm's reach away and she couldn't bring herself to step through the door.

"No," Kat said. "I don't feel trapped." What she really wanted to say was, *I kinda like it here.*

Peter frowned at his shoes. "Me neither, and this might be a crazy thing to say, considering the fact that we won't be remembering any of this." He kicked a few shards of glass off his sneakers. "And I don't know—maybe this will freak you out or something—but I've always found you—"

"What? Pretty?" Obviously Peter had nothing else to say. Before today the only sources of judgment he had of her were her

Instagram account and their occasional run-ins at Halos. What else could he bring up besides her looks? It wasn't like he'd known her personally.

"Well, that's obvious. But everyone thinks you're pretty." Peter finally raised his hand, rotating his wrist to survey the cuts. A sliver of glass had burrowed itself into his palm, so he pulled it out with a wince and dropped the invading piece onto the dirt. "What I was going to say before you *so rudely interrupted me* is that I found you familiar. You lost Emmeline six months before I lost my uncle. You knew *how* you lost her, but you didn't know why you had to. In a lot of ways you reminded me of myself."

Peter was right—their stories had plenty of similarities. Isabella and Jay. Nicholas and Emmeline. Kat thought back to the cashier at Pepperdine earlier today—Peter's ex-friend. *Indigo.* Whitney also surfaced to the front of her mind. Both Peter and Kat had been surrounded by people who didn't understand what they were going through—who perceived their suffering in the wrong ways. A boy who had turned *against* Peter after he'd changed, and a girl who had only turned *to* Kat after she'd changed. Neither Indigo nor Whitney had ever appreciated Peter or Kat for who they really were. And yet here the game had brought the two strangers together, as though Capsule were fate itself. Maybe if Kat had known his story all along—if they had somehow crossed paths in the right way before—maybe they could have been friends.

Kat poked his chest. "Well, let me tell you a secret then."

Peter dropped his bleeding hand and raised his chin with a smile. He was wearing that same crooked grin, but this time, something about it was genuine.

"No one says this because they hate your guts," Kat said, "but you're not too bad yourself."

The last bits of pink drained from the sky, their main source of light now the capsule beside them.

"Is it weird that I don't wanna reverse the day?" Kat watched the color ooze from the capsule into the seats of the car, brightening the vehicle.

"No. I don't wanna lose today either." Peter set his hands onto Kat's shoulders, and she faced him again. For a moment she forgot about the capsule sitting in the car. The capsule that was about to end everything. All she saw were Peter's eyes, two twin moons reflecting the soft blue aura that encapsulated them. His smile vanished before he said, "Lose *you*—I mean."

Kat could hear her own heartbeat, even louder than the blaring alarm, and she wanted to smack herself for it. Of all people, Peter Moon? The heartless psychopath who ran a gossip blog at Brookwood High, who tore people down to the point of tears and clenched fists? If it weren't for Capsule, she would have never realized how normal he was. How human he was. How he was possibly the only person who understood what she was going through.

Capsule had given her something special, only to now take it away.

"Peter, we won't—"

"Remember. I know." His brows spread apart, the tension in his face loosening. "But you said it yourself. Just because we don't remember something doesn't make it pointless."

Using her own words against her. Of course Peter had to be clever like that.

The capsule glowed brighter, illuminating their faces with growing intensity. With the light in the sky gone, they were trapped in a sapphire orb, their surroundings fading from view. It was almost as though the game had been designed for this moment, as though the game had been rooting for this from the start.

Peter stepped closer, his grip tightening against her rustling windbreaker, but Kat didn't step away. The Peter standing in front of her wasn't the same Peter who ran Moral Moon, but the Peter who people saw before learning about his past. The cruel filter he'd intentionally placed on himself vanished, leaving his face softer, and the flaming tint in his brown eyes dampened to ash as he looked down at her lips.

Kat gulped as her heart pounded inside her chest. It didn't make sense. She couldn't remember the last time she'd lost control of her nerves like this. For the past two years she'd been fighting for something to make her feel again. Fighting to bring back that sickening rush of fear, sadness, anger—anything really. But today, standing in the middle of Sunshine Auto, she didn't have to fight, and she didn't have to fake it.

Peter leaned forward, and the capsule's indigo haze flickered as Kat mirrored him.

She closed her eyes, and their lips met.

A gust of wind ruffled Kat's hair, and the sharp chill of the night impaled her. Her eyes popped open, and Peter's hands fell from her shoulders as she staggered away from the capsule's glowing aura and into the dark Grovestown air. She turned her back to Peter and leaned forward, her head burning as she faced the flustered clone of herself in the shattered glass by her boots. *There's no way.* She wrapped her hands around her stomach, the colors in her reflection fading to back and white. *I just kissed Peter Moon.*

"Uh—are you okay?" Peter stood still behind her. Motionless.

"Yeah." Kat straightened her spine, eyes propped wide, refusing to blink. "Yeah, I'm fine."

Calm down, Kat thought. *Soon enough it'll be like nothing happened.* The thought left her with a knot in her throat. Was that really what she wanted?

"Well, I guess the rumors Jackie told us about weren't that far off after all." Peter's lighthearted voice morphed into laughter, but the awkward humor crumbled when Kat finally faced him.

There was nothing to say. Sure, Kat wanted to clear things up. She wanted to talk through whatever had happened and understand exactly *why* it happened, but she also knew this moment was temporary. The future was murky. Without the game Peter and Kat would have never been more than two students who attended Brookwood High at the same time for a brief fraction of each other's lives, and after Level Five, that would become their dead-and-revived reality.

Without our memories, this really is pointless, isn't it?

Kat didn't have time to answer that question. The warning signal was still blaring, and they had no choice but to open the fifth capsule eventually, so they might as well get it over with now. Judging by Peter's rapid blinks as he tried to gather something to say, Kat knew he wasn't planning to open the capsule anytime soon. She took a deep breath before approaching the broken car window and reaching inside.

"Kat. Wait, I…"

Nothing.

Kat's hand met nothing but smooth air, slicing through the capsule as though it were a figment of her imagination. She turned to Peter, who had now awoken from his daze and mentally rejoined the game. He took slow, dreadful steps to the car door and reached for the capsule. His fingers disappeared inside the aluminum, reemerging as he pulled his arm away.

"Dammit!" Peter slammed his fist against the roof of the car, wincing as the cuts intensified the pain. He leaned forward and rested his head against his stinging fist.

"We need Jackie." Kat stepped away from the car, breathing into her sweaty palms. "Don't we?"

06:24:09

THE RAGE BURNED.

Jackie ripped Jay's flannel from her shoulders and tied it around her waist. She'd been standing near Grovestown High's gym parking lot waiting for another memory to pop into her mind, but it hadn't come yet, and now all she could think about was the fact that Peter and Kat had left her here alone. The chilly air running along the gauze intensified the sharp pain of her wound.

What a joy.

Jackie peeked around the corner of the gym building, gripping her arm with clenched teeth. Running along the back of the gym was Clay River—a common flooding hazard that often left Grovestown students being sent home early for a few days of every year, but that didn't mean the scenery wasn't nice. Although Pelle Cove in Ravensburg had a pretty beach, and the drive from Brookwood was more convenient, Jackie had always enjoyed the calmness of Clay River. She walked along the side of the gym, hoping some time by the water would help calm her rage.

The back of the gym had no lights against the wall, so it was hard to make out her surroundings with nothing to illuminate her path but the moonlight's reflection on the river. With deep breaths she watched the light ripple across the water, but the serenity did nothing but make her feel even more alone.

Jackie took a few steps to her right and discovered a line of exterior lockers along the back of the brick wall. Most of the doors were still open, signaling that the students of Grovestown High likely didn't use them anymore. Jackie didn't have to wonder why for long. The first rusty locker she opened contained a rotting sandwich bag and more cobwebs than she could count. She slammed the door shut to block the wretched stench, her fingers pressing tightly against the chipping maroon-painted metal. The frustration was comforting. Inviting.

Jackie pulled her hand back, rolling her fingers into a fist. She struck the door to the locker a second time, the cold metal burning her skin, but she didn't care. She forced the air from her lungs in a throat-straining huff, clouds escaping her mouth and billowing in the freezing air. This whole time she'd been misreading the situation.

I should've known they never saw me as a friend.

Peter and Kat had only stuck by her because they needed her to beat the game. Even back when she'd fallen at Quasso Drive, they only used the power-up for a free ride to Sunshine Auto. Now that all of the challenges had been tackled, they could dispose of her however they pleased. It was her fault for assuming they actually cared in the first place. Of course they hadn't. This wasn't her story. Peter and Kat were the real victims here. Ultimately, this was their game to complete, not hers.

Man, I should've realized it sooner. Jackie's hand relaxed, her soft fist falling to her side, unraveling. *Why was I so stupid?* She leaned her forehead against one of the oily locker doors, the sour stench filling her lungs, but she didn't care.

"If I were you I'd try to save your one good arm."

Jackie pried her heavy head from the metal as though her brain were magnetized to it and searched for the source of the voice. One of the lower locker doors slapped itself closed, revealing a boy sitting on the concrete walkway. He'd been tucked behind it, hidden from her sight.

"What happened?" The boy pointed in Jackie's vague direction, but he locked his eyes on Clay River.

Jackie figured he was referring to the gauze wrapped around her forearm and the blood on her blue shirt. "Just a bad fall." She took a step away from the lockers. "What are you doing back here?"

The boy was nothing more than a silhouette in the night, his features hard to recognize. The only information she could gather was that he had curly hair and wore a tie with his collared shirt. He was definitely dressed well—better than most of the other guys in the gym. Unlike Jackie, he had planned to be here, but she assumed he hadn't come to sit alone by a wall of rotting lockers.

"What does it look like I'm doing?" He gestured to the river. "I'm being a loner."

Jackie rubbed her left hand against her shirt. Now that her anger was starting to dull, the pain of her knuckles against the metal kicked in. She approached the stranger, lowered herself onto the ground, and leaned her back against the locker next to him.

The boy's heavy gaze fell onto her. "What are *you* doing?"

"Bro, what does it look like I'm doing?" Jackie rested her two throbbing arms on her lap and mimicked his focus on Clay River. "Being a loner."

As the two sat in silence—the flowing water soothing their minds—Jackie thought back to the pockets of fun memories from today. Laughing with Peter after running out of Cherry Ice. Getting ice cream in Ravensburg before the car chase incident.

And the moment they'd shared at Grove Aid deciding that they deserved a break from the game. Were those all a part of their fake acts?

"Friend drama?" the boy asked.

"I'm not sure if I'd call them my friends."

Jackie had been looking at this all wrong. This wasn't her journey. Her only responsibility was to help them win, and she'd already done her part—more than enough. This was their game. Their life. Not hers. And if they wanted her out, why should that bother her?

"Fair." The boy nodded. "You're not from Grovestown, are you?"

"No."

"Didn't seem like it."

Is that supposed to be an insult?

"So what's your story tonight?" he asked.

"Let's just say I've sacrificed a lot to help two people, and they went off and ditched me."

"Damn. That really sucks."

Jackie stared into his eyes for the first time—two gloomy black holes.

"If it makes you feel better, I don't even have any friends. Thought I'd come to the dance and try to socialize, which was stupid. People come *with* friends, not to make them. Obviously." He rubbed the wrinkles between his brows away. "I'm so done with people."

Jackie wanted to agree, but something stopped her. Was that really what she wanted to decide for herself? Was it naive to think she could find someone like Eugene in person? Someone who actually cared?

Jackie had been sitting with this stranger for far longer than she'd expected to. *What if the fifth level is different?* She thought that by now Peter and Kat would have opened the capsule, but she tried to suppress her worries. After all, they'd said it themselves—this was their problem, not hers. Yet as much as she'd tried to disconnect herself from the game—to hand the controller over to Peter and Kat—she couldn't stop thinking about their smiles throughout the day. At the time they'd felt so genuine, so contagious.

"Jackie!" Footsteps slammed against the concrete slab, coming to a halt at the lockers. "What are you doing back here?"

Jackie squinted at the blinding phone flashlight in her face. The light flew aside to reveal Jay, wiped completely out of breath. He narrowed his eyes as he glanced between Jackie and the stranger. "I've been looking everywhere for you. Why aren't you with them?"

Jackie stood and dusted the dirt from her sweatpants. "Something wrong?"

Jay opened his mouth to speak, but his neck stiffened, the words refusing to leave him. As his breathing slowed back to normal, his throat relaxed and allowed the dangerous sentence to pass. "Peter called me from *your* phone."

Jackie bit her lip.

"They need our help. And I have a plan." In only a blink, Jay's back was turned toward her. He didn't realize Jackie hadn't followed him until he reached the corner of the building, when he turned around and said, "Jackie?"

As much as her body wanted to rush after Jay, she couldn't stop the anger from pulsing through her veins. It paralyzed her. Glued her shoes to the concrete. Left her eyes dry and arms stiff. Peter had called Jay through her own phone to ask for help.

How convenient.

Peter and Kat only wanted her around when they desperately needed her. Like she was nothing more than an emergency button in the game for them to press when they pleased.

"Hey."

Jackie turned around to find the stranger standing now. He was a lot taller than she'd imagined, and with the help of Jay's flashlight pointed in their direction, she could make out more of his features. His locks cast swirly shadows over his forehead, the darkness in his eyes now brightening to reveal hidden specks of gold.

That same sadness cloaked the boy, but it no longer held him down. As he grinned, his posture strengthened. "Your friends are lucky to have you."

Jackie believed him. Not because during their short chat together she'd learned enough about him to take his word as truth, but because she wanted to. She wanted to believe she was lucky. Lucky that Peter and Kat trusted her. Lucky that they were her friends.

The boy waved as Jackie ran from the lockers. *Back to the game.*

Jackie and Jay turned around the corner and slowed at the front of the gym. Jay grabbed a random bike leaned against the brick wall and stepped off the concrete slab onto the parking lot. He dragged the bike by its handles, not stopping to wait for Jackie.

Jackie scanned the other two bikes resting nearby and chose the one that looked more suitable for her height. She rolled the bike off the curb and chased after Jay. Together they guided the bikes through the packed parking lot before eventually reaching the side of the busy road dividing Grovestown High from the Grove Aid strip mall.

Jay was about to get onto his stolen bike, but Jackie's voice stopped him. "Kuya?"

It didn't feel strange to call him *older brother* anymore.

He froze. "Yeah?"

"Why are you helping them?"

A speedy car passed by, creating a wind that ruined Jay's perfectly-formed hair, the strands falling over his forehead in clumps. She couldn't deny that her older brother got along well with people—that he was kind. It was hard for people *not* to like him, but how was he like that in the first place?

"Because I'm your sister?" Jackie added. "And I happen to be a part of their game?"

Jay's stiff face broke into laughter, his grin sparkling as though the answer were obvious. "Because they're people, Jackie." He hopped onto his bike. "I can't just leave them hanging."

As Jackie biked behind her older brother that night, trying to ignore the sharp pain in her arm with every turn, she thought back to why she'd started the countdown in the first place.

"I bet that if someone were hanging off the edge of a cliff, you would not even bother offering them a hand, huh?" Mrs. Mendoza had said that day.

Jay looked over his shoulder and shouted, "You okay if we go faster?"

"Even if you don't get along with someone, that does not make it right to ignore them."

Jackie nodded. The air pulled her hair behind her, forming a natural cape as she pedaled at lightning speed.

"True kindness is unconditional."

DEAR STRANGER

Sometimes I gaze into the mirror
And I see your face
I see your eyes
In my own
Like I peeled your skin and glued it to mine
Like a lonely thief
A life in place of a knife

Sometimes I forget my own face
I gaze into the mirror
I see your life
Your eyes
I feel what you felt when you left
That day
And I wave goodbye

06:10:11

PETER SWIPED AT the capsule again, but his hand sliced right through it. He dropped his heavy head with a sigh. "We really messed up."

"No kidding."

Something about the expression on Kat's face hinted that she wasn't talking about leaving Jackie behind. The raised brows, the tight line her lips formed into—was she referring to the kiss? Peter didn't know what to think about it either, but his mind was occupied with greater concerns—the first being that nasty signal. *"You are trespassing…"* It'd been running for at least twenty minutes now, so he had his doubts about whether the security system actually did notify the police. Perhaps it acted as a bluff to reduce crime, a form of *cosmetic security*, as Kat would call it—but whether or not the threat was real, it was only a matter of time before the ruckus attracted attention. He scanned the main building of Sunshine Auto for the signal's source, hoping he'd have a chance at shutting it off.

Peter's eyes narrowed on the open font door to the building. It swayed in the wind, the hinges weak.

Was it like that before?

Footsteps crunched against the dirt like a monster's bite shattering bones.

Peter and Kat ducked. Staring between the tires, Peter spotted two approaching leather boots. His heart pounded as he pulled Jackie's phone out of his pocket and navigated to Capsule's countdown page.

06 HOURS : 9 MINUTES : 51 SECONDS

They were so close with so much time left, but if the police arrived before Jackie and Jay did, he and Kat would be done for. He swiped to the right, where the emergency button stood. Unlike the power-ups they had already used, it still wasn't greyed out, which implied they *could* use it, but what would it do this time?

"Activate it," Kat whispered.

Peter raised his chin, processing her statement. "Are you crazy?"

Kat brought her index finger to her lips. "Do you *want* to get caught?"

Peter gulped as the crunching from the other side of the car grew louder. He understood that they were running out of options, but the emergency button didn't sound like a solid escape plan. The last time they'd pressed it, Capsule had taken them directly to their next location at Quasso Drive, so what if at this location it did nothing at all? Or worse, what if it brought them back to book club, hours away? Now wasn't the time to take risks.

"Hello?"

A man's voice. Peter pressed his shoulder against the car, trying to hold himself as still as possible.

"Is someone there?" The man's boots neared the opposite side of the Toyota, his voice bolder this time.

Kat stole the phone from Peter's grip. Instinctively he reached for it, but she pulled her arm away in a violent jolt, slamming the back of her hand against the car door. The smack left her grimacing in silence, rubbing her knuckles as the man's steps came to a stop.

Giving up on Jackie's phone, Peter slowly raised his head until his eyes peeked through the bashed window of the Toyota. On the other side of the glowing capsule stood a heavy-set man with his fingers wrapped around a pistol, arms waving as he searched for the source of Kat's strike. Before Peter could duck, the man's eyes locked on him through the glass. He pointed the gun in his direction. "Hey!"

Peter straightened his knees, standing completely. "Excuse me, I—"

"The police are on the way." The man readjusted the gun in his grip, eyes trailing to the broken glass surrounding the nearby cars. "Stay right where you are."

The man's eyebrows were two caterpillars on his head, his eyes dry marbles. Judging by the plaid pajama pants dragging against the dirt, the man had just crawled out of bed. *Really, it took you this long to get up after hearing the signal?* Peter gulped, uncomfortable with the vulnerable situation he'd placed himself in, but at the same time, he couldn't stop his eyes from narrowing at the guy. *How lazy.*

Fearing that the man might pull the trigger at any slight movement, Peter held himself completely still as he glanced down at Kat. She was still crouched on the dirt with Jackie's phone gripped loosely in her hands. She looked up at Peter with a smile that read, *Trust me*, and this time, he did.

Peter shut his eyes, preparing for Kat to press the emergency button, but nothing happened. The ambient noise of crickets and owls never changed. He didn't find his sneakers resting on a different surface or his back placed against the ground. When Peter opened his eyes, the man standing on the other side of the Toyota stared at the gun in his hands. His grip loosened as he took a step away from the car.

Peter turned to find Kat standing next to him with tears rolling down her face. "Please don't hurt us."

He knew Kat's tears were fake—that it was all an act—but he still felt sorry for her. Perhaps he felt sorry *because* the tears were fake.

Peter frowned at the man. "What's wrong with you?" Peter implanted as much shakiness into his voice as possible, probably overdoing it because Kat's eyes landed on him with a watery glare.

Kat was a genius—he couldn't deny it. With the cost of two hours from the countdown, the fourth power-up could erase the last hour of someone's memories, which Kat had used on the owner of Sunshine Auto. Rather than activating the defensive emergency button—which would cost *three* hours with unknown results—she'd found a counterattack instead. Now all they had to do was act the part of two threatened teenagers.

"I didn't, I—well—what's going on?" The man looked back and forth between them, his eyes reflecting the blue glow of the capsule he failed to see. He dropped the gun onto the ground, stepping back as the emergency signal blared through the night sky. *"Remove yourself from the property or the police will be…"* He raised his hands into the air. "I didn't mean to. I'm sorry, I wasn't…"

Kat dove from Peter's side, scrambling over the hood of the car and snatching the gun from the ground. She slipped Jackie's phone into her back pocket as she stood and raised the gun toward the stranger's face. "Don't move."

For a moment Peter almost felt bad for the guy. Sure, he'd been pointing a gun at Peter only seconds ago, but it wasn't like his self-defense hadn't been justified. As the panic dampened the man's eyes, all Peter could see was an innocent car dealership owner in Grovestown. A man who bought and sold used cars to put food on his table. Yet here they were, threatening him with his own gun. This game was changing them.

And maybe not in a good way.

Peter walked around the front of the car and stopped at Kat's side. She tightened her grip on the pistol as Peter leaned over her shoulder. "Are you sure about this?"

"I'm not planning to hurt him," she muttered.

"Even if the police get here before Jackie does?"

"They won't." A remaining tear dripped down Kat's cheek, and this time, Peter wasn't sure if it was fake. "They can't."

They stood for an eternity in the dark air, and Peter's bones ached from shivering. He bit his lip, mind racing as though the gun were held to his own chest. As though it were only a matter of time until the last bit of perfection inside of him died. He'd become the opposite of what he'd been chasing for the past two years. He'd been setting himself standards based on a man who had saved a life, and now he'd become a criminal about to take one.

It didn't matter that the gun was in Kat's hands. All that mattered was that he stood beside her. He stood beside a girl pointing a gun at an innocent man, and he didn't stop her. Who was at fault here? No, it wasn't Capsule. They'd been blaming everything on the game. On circumstance. But the reality was that all choices had been their own. Peter never had to be a part of this, but he chose to be here. He'd chosen a path of broken morals and rotting perfection.

I'm the monster. Peter met the gaze of the heavy-breathed man standing several feet away. *Not Capsule. Me.*

"Peter!"

A shout came from behind the fence. Peter looked over his shoulder to spot two familiar faces, their shoulders rising and falling, breathing heavily.

Jackie dropped the bike at her side. Its handle slammed into the sidewalk, the tires still spinning. Jay kneeled and set his bike gently onto the cement.

"Quick." Kat removed one hand from the gun as Peter faced her direction. She reached into the pocket of her windbreaker for Jay's car keys. "Tell him to wait in the car, just in case the game doesn't end immediately." She held the keys toward Peter, and although he wanted to resist, he took them from her with a firm nod.

Peter ran to the fence, where Jay stood frozen with his jaw dropped in Kat's direction.

"Can you get the car started?" Peter stuck the keys through the wires, offering them to Jay, who woke from his trance and stopped staring at the crime scene several cars away. For a moment he hesitated, his hand stopping only inches away from the keys, but he eventually took them. Jay set his free hand on Jackie's shoulder as a quick sign of reassurance before heading to his car across the street.

Peter made eye contact with Jackie for the first time since he and Kat had left her at the Grovestown dance. He had so much to say—that he was sorry, that he was wrong, that he actually did need her—but when he opened his mouth, all that came out was, "How's the arm?"

Jackie shot a quick glance at the gauze and shook her head. "Fine." She leapt forward, and Peter took a few steps back as she forced her fingers between the wires, the flimsy fence now leaning in his direction.

Thinking about the wound he'd seen on Jackie's arm earlier left Peter with a bitter taste in his mouth. Either her wound had miraculously healed from Jay's half-assed first-aid care or she was purposefully concealing her pain. With each seething breath she forced her way to the top of the fence, and as she turned to climb down the other side, Peter shook his head to force his concern away. Right now they needed to complete Level Five.

"We tried to open it ourselves, but our hands go right through it, like how those ice skaters coasted through the capsule at Cherry Ice." Peter reached out in front of him at nothing, reenacting the experience. "Almost holographic, in a way?"

Jackie climbed down the other side much faster, jumping once she was only a few feet away from the dirt. She took a few micro-steps to steady herself and swiped her hands against each other to clear the dust away. Before Peter could say any more, she headed toward the glowing blue window.

Peter followed. "It's in the—"

"Car, yeah. I'm not stupid."

Jackie's voice was deeper than Peter remembered, and if he hadn't seen her lips move, he might have thought it was someone else who'd spoken.

When they reached Kat, Jackie stopped and raised her brows. Her eyes wandered from the capsule in the Toyota, to Kat standing on the other side of the car, to the man shivering several feet away with his hands in the air.

Kat shot Jackie a red-eyed glance. "Can you stop staring and open the damn thing?"

Peter gestured to the broken window, prompting Jackie to take action. She rolled her eyes and reached for the capsule. Unlike Peter and Kat, her bandaged hand met with the aluminum successfully. She truly was the player of this game.

"So I guess it's over." Jackie's voice had returned to normal now, that raspiness long gone. She'd dealt with Peter and Kat long enough, and she must have been pleased to finally ditch her job as their babysitter.

But Peter still didn't feel ready to end the game. What was the point to all of this? Everything they'd done today was just a bunch of nonsense, wasn't it?

Jackie ran her fingers along the capsule, gripping the top with her left hand and the bottom with her right. "Good game."

Peter stepped forward to stop her, but he was too late.

The capsule split open at the middle, and its light blasted from inside. Before Peter could mutter a word, the dense color swallowed him in a flash, wiping everything from sight and drowning him in a world of blue.

LEVEL FIVE

A BEAUTIFUL DRIVE to Lothen Heights.

It was October 5th of 2018, the night of Brookwood's homecoming dance, but Emmeline had no plans to attend this year. She found power in being somewhere else during such a busy night. She'd been stressed with school, friends, family—everything lately, and to Emmeline a midnight drive topped any form of professional therapy. The splattering of rain across the windshield in perfect rhythm with the cheesy pop music blaring through the car mesmerized her.

Emmeline was a senior in high school, and although she had decent grades, a buzzing social life, and a handful of people who cared way too much about her, it didn't feel right. It didn't make sense to be unhappy, but she was, and the fact that she couldn't understand why left her empty.

A few weeks ago, she'd decided that she'd be skipping the dance for a short trip to Lothen. Senior year was supposed to be her social peak, and so far it had been, but she also knew she needed a break. Maybe she'd go on a drive during prom night too.

Lothen was located one town north of Grovestown. Her favorite part of the ride was heading down Quasso Drive, a foggy road bordered with skeleton-like trees. But even better than the drive was Lothen Heights, a gorgeous campground located on the shoreline.

Her favorite spot, a cliff above the soaring waves, reflected the moon perfectly off the horizon at the right time of the night. Standing on that ledge was just as magical as standing on the border to another world.

Her phone dinged on the passenger seat. A quick glance signaled that the text was from Jay.

Emmeline faced the windshield with a tense throat. She should have given him a proper explanation about the dance, but she didn't want to drag Jay into her personal problems. He was a sweetheart and he didn't deserve that. She removed her right hand from the steering wheel and grabbed her phone to read the text.

Is everything okay?

Another text notification slid down from the top of her screen. One of her classmates. **You going to Sal's birthday thing tomorrow?**

Dad wants to know when you'll be home. That text was from Kat. **He's worried.**

The messages streamed in as they always had. She was the center of attention. The light of the show. Of course there were times she enjoyed it, but now wasn't one of them. She tossed her phone face-up onto the passenger seat. Her eyes skipped back and forth between the road and her screen as a few more texts chimed in.

Hey dude, u coming or what

Let's meet up sometime? I miss you <3

Lmaoo u gotta watch this video

Emmeline flipped her phone over on the passenger seat, eliminating the distraction. She was driving to get a break from the world, not to play a long-distance game. She reached to turn up the volume of the music, blasting it as she drove past the trees in isolation. No, she didn't know when she planned on coming home. No, she wasn't sure how long she'd been driving.

And no, she didn't know why she was crying.

All she wanted was a moment to herself. A moment to live in peace with nature, yet here she was with a phone that wouldn't stop buzzing. The car drifted as she raised an arm to wipe her face with her sleeve. Before she could adjust the steering wheel, her head met the window in an instant blow.

A flash of light.

The car skidded. Faster and faster, out of control.

Emmeline gripped the steering wheel, the color draining from her hands as her head throbbed from the impact. She slammed her foot onto the brakes, but she was too late.

With a crash, her hands jumped from the steering wheel.

A second car had turned around the corner with awful timing. When the driver had caught sight of the oncoming car drifting into the wrong lane, there had been no time to brake. A jolt of the steering wheel had been enough to lighten the impact, but even then the crash had left the oncoming car spinning out of control.

The second car came to a stop. A man stepped out, leaving his own vehicle running with the headlights on. He checked the wheels of his car, the lights, the windshield. Besides a dent in the front that smashed the license plate inward, everything was fine.

The man had been heading home from a dinner date in Grovestown. He hadn't been paying too much attention to the road, but he was sure he hadn't been driving in the opposite lane. Surely the crash hadn't been his fault.

The car he'd struck had slammed into a thick tree off the other side of the road. Under the illumination of his own car's headlights, the man caught a glimpse of a young woman's face through the shattered passenger seat window. He inched closer, her side profile growing more vivid. More real. As he watched the blood drip from her ear, his stomach turned against itself. He leaned forward, choking on his own breaths.

With a shaky hand, he pulled out his phone and dialed 911.

And he called.

Well, he thought about it.

But he couldn't bring himself to press the dangerous green button. The green button that he knew might land him in jail.

With the adrenaline kicking in, the man threw himself back into his car, fiddled with the gears in a panic, and continued on his way home.

It was the next morning when a woman clocked in for her shift at Sunshine Auto. She wasn't in the mood for work, but she greeted a man with a smile as he entered the log building only two minutes after opening. He explained that he'd been planning to trade in his car.

So the woman inspected the car, surveying the damage. The front was completely smashed inward, but there didn't appear to be any major functional issues. Cosmetically, it would take some money to repair.

"The damage was from a previous owner." The man's voice quivered. It seemed he was awfully excited to buy a new car.

"I see." The woman ran her fingers along the dented front. With a deep breath she dusted her hands on her jeans and stood. "We can give you three thousand for it. What's your name?"

The man gulped and set a hand on his soon-to-be-old car.

"Nicholas Moon."

CLAIM REWARD

04:04:33

JACKIE PULLED HER arms out of the car window.

The world was still, noiseless besides the distant echo of sirens. Time stopped to allow the memory a chance to marinate, to really soak into their brains. No malice grew between them because what to be angry about had yet to be understood. The other four levels hadn't been a surprise to more than two people, but this memory had shocked all three of them at once. This was something different. Jackie wasn't the only bystander.

"So he..." Peter shook his head and backed away from the car that now lacked its blue aura. The magic had died, and now all that remained was the bloody truth. "No, there's no way."

Jackie stared at the car window—or the lack of it. She imagined Emmeline sitting in the seat, right where the glowing capsule had been hovering an instant ago. She imagined the blood dripping from Emmeline's ear. What Nicholas had seen that night ingrained itself into Jackie's memory as though she'd been there.

Kat still hadn't faced Jackie or Peter, nor had she lowered her arms. Her face grew red as she opened her mouth and shouted, "Your uncle?" The owner of Sunshine Auto raised his hands higher, misinterpreting where Kat's anger was truly directed.

The nephew of the criminal. The sister of the victim. It'd been that way all along, and no one knew.

"You wanna know why he saved Isabella?" Kat's voice elevated into a scream. "Because he felt guilty! Because he *was* guilty. The only reason he saved her was because he thought it'd make up for what he did. Like some kind of sick penance."

Peter narrowed his eyes at the back of Kat's head. "That's not—"

"He wanted the easy way out of doing the right thing. If he was a good guy, why didn't he tell my family?"

The sirens grew louder.

Jackie pressed her palms against her head, trying to tune out their argument and focus on their next step. This wasn't the right time to lose control. There had to be a reason why the game hadn't ended yet. *What if Level Five's not over?* Jackie's eyes met a sliver of purple peeking out of Kat's back pocket—her phone. *I gotta check the app.*

"Why didn't he call the police?" Kat's voice shook. "Maybe she wasn't dead. Maybe she could've been saved."

Peter slammed a palm against the side of the car, a few extra shards of glass from the window trickling onto Jackie's sneakers. "You saw what happened. It wasn't his fault."

Jackie made her way around the front of the car and grabbed her phone from the back of Kat's pocket. Kat didn't flinch. She was so fixated on arguing with Peter that she had no energy to notice anything else.

"Wasn't his fault?" Kat scoffed. "This whole time. For the past two years you've been trying to live up to your perfect uncle. But your uncle was a murderer. He killed her. You've been trying to live up to the impossible standards of a psychopath. A guy who'd rather maintain his perfect image than do the right thing."

"No, you're wrong." Peter's voice grew softer.

Jackie stepped away from Kat and opened her phone to reveal the first screen of Capsule. A pop-up over the countdown read, **CONGRATULATIONS, PLAYER. YOU MAY NOW CLAIM YOUR REWARD.**

"Nicholas hit her and did nothing to help. Do you know how many times I've wondered why she crashed? Why she ran into that tree? Do you know how many different scenarios I've run through in my head? He could have given us closure."

Claim my reward? Jackie frowned at the screen as she closed the pop-up, revealing a new line under the five crossed-out levels. Following **LEVEL FIVE** was a line labeled **CLAIM REWARD** in bold. She tapped it, triggering a new pop-up with the phrase **LOTHEN HEIGHTS.**

A sixth location.

"I've been trying to be nice." Peter spoke slowly over the roof of the car, ensuring each word reached Kat with painful clarity. "But it was *your sister* who swerved into the other lane. Why should he get blamed for her mistake?"

"Guys!" Jackie shouted as the red and blue flashing lights entered their field of vision. "There's another location. For the reward."

Two police cars stopped in the middle of the road, blocking their path to Jay's car. *Shoot.* Jackie took a deep breath. *There better be another way out.*

"Reward? You really think I care?" Kat turned away from the man, lowering the pistol to her side. "I just found out why my sister died, and you wanna get to some sixth location?"

"That's all you care about, isn't it?" Peter ripped his eyes from Kat and laid them on Jackie with no hesitation. "You're just in this for the game."

The rage that Jackie felt after they left her in Grovestown came pummeling back. She forced herself to loosen the grip on her phone, concerned that she'd break it.

"We're just your entertainment," Kat said. "Aren't we?"

"No!" Jackie screamed, but not in response to Kat's question.

Two arms reached around Kat from behind. The man had seen their argument as a chance to free himself from the vulnerable situation he'd been placed in. One arm tightened around Kat's neck, and the other pried the gun from her fingertips. The man stepped away from Peter and Jackie, Kat stumbling with him as he brought the gun to her head. The fear in his eyes was undeniable, and despite the fact that he had his arms wrapped around Kat's neck, he was still trembling.

Kat finally had answers, but she still hadn't cried. Even with a gun to her head—her life only a pull of the trigger away—she still hadn't shed a tear. She was nothing but a fiberglass mannequin.

Jackie at least expected a human response from Peter, but his face was hollow, eyes vacant. He watched Kat's fading life in front of him with no urgency to lend her a hand.

The police car doors opened from behind the fence, their sirens accompanying Sunshine Auto's warning signal to compose a haunting lullaby.

Without looking at the screen, Jackie swiped to the second page of Capsule and tapped the emergency button a second time.

01:00:02

KAT OPENED HER eyes to a blanket of stars, a sparkly collection of salt floating in a bowl of dense ink. She raised her back from the grass, sitting with her palms crushing delicate shards around her. Several feet away stood a steep ledge. The end of the world. And although she couldn't see the waves crashing against the cliffside, their hammering slams matched the tone of a warning siren.

Kat tucked the wisps of hair away from her cheeks.

I'm here.

The image beyond the cliff was the same one Emmeline had imagined on her drive that homecoming night.

Lothen Heights Campground.

Kat stood. Nothing lit her vision but the glittering water, leaving her in a world of black-and-white. She turned her back to the cliff, searching for a sign of Peter and Jackie, but she met nothing but the menacing imprints of redwood trees, their silhouettes cutting hollow holes into the sky.

Nicholas killed her. Kat faced the cliff again and walked to the edge of the grass clearing. The rage overpowered her fear of falling as she lowered herself onto the ground and dangled her heavy boots off the ledge. Surely the game had brought her to Emmeline's desired destination for a reason.

The last time Kat had been here was two and a half years ago, after Jay had appeared at their doorstep for the first time. She and Emmeline had stood at this very ledge under the beaming sun, but the ocean held an incomprehensible beauty at night. As the moonlight bounced from wave to wave, Kat understood why Emmeline would come to a place like Lothen Heights to clear her mind. Being so much higher than the water—so much closer to the moon—was mesmerizing.

Kat fell into a state of awe as she basked in the view. She forgot about the blood that had dripped down the side of her sister's face. She forgot about what Nicholas Moon had done—or had failed to do—that night. She forgot about her argument with Peter at Sunshine Auto. Forgot about the countdown. Forgot about the game.

The words flowed naturally from her lips, and after starting, she could no longer stop.

"Sometimes when I visit my family"—Kat lost herself in the water's bright reflection—"they compliment my new car."

Kat's vision filled with pure white, isolating herself inside her thoughts. For the past two years she had studied the poems by memory—line by line, word by word—but until tonight, they had always been meaningless. With her hand gripping the ledge—the part where the soft grass of the clearing met the sharp rock of the cliffside—Kat recalled a few lines from the longest of the five poems.

"And as I wonder where you went when you left on vacation that day, I wonder where I will go for mine."

The first memory Capsule had given them was Peter Moon's fifteenth birthday, when he'd assumed Nicholas was heading on a date. *"But that's not why I'm dressed up today,"* Nicholas had told him. *"After breakfast I'm heading on a trip."*

"Apparently Isabella's family was vacationing in Pelle Cove the same time my uncle was," Peter had said after they'd opened the Level Three capsule.

Kat closed her eyes, trying to avoid the truth, but her mouth pieced the puzzle together against her will. "Oh, how I wish I could do something right. To play the hero instead of the villain." Kat recited the last few lines of the poem, her voice breaking every few words. "So if I can't be the hero, if I can't do something right, if I can't be proud—then oh, how I wish in place of the villain I play the victim."

Peter's soft voice filled her mind. *"But my uncle—he didn't make it back."*

The clues had been there all along. On her first trip with Jay they'd found the five poems tucked under a baby-blue hydrangea, Emmeline's least favorite color. They had easily deduced that the poems had been written for Emmeline—that she was the stranger—and the flowers had confirmed that the author was someone who hadn't known her well. But what kind of person would leave behind flowers for a stranger?

Perhaps someone like Nicholas Moon.

Kat gulped. "Sometimes I forget my own face. I gaze into the mirror. I see your life, your eyes. I feel what you felt when you left that day." She scooted backward, pulled her feet up from the ledge, and brought her knees to her chest. A menacing red hue tinted the water. "And I wave goodbye."

She thought back to the argument she'd had with Peter only moments ago. She'd claimed that his uncle had been a murderer. That for the past two years, Peter had been trying to live up to the impossible standards of a psychopath. A psychopath who drove away from Emmeline when he could have helped. A psychopath who sacrificed himself to save a twelve-year-old girl from a storm. That same psychopath who'd spent his remaining days following the accident burrowing himself in his own grief.

It doesn't make sense. Kat wrapped her arms around her legs. She finally had answers, yet now that she knew the full truth, she didn't feel the sense of enlightenment she'd longed for. The tears refused to swarm down her cheeks, and the void expanding in her stomach filled her with an emptiness worse than any tears could bring. *Why can't I cry?*

Kat knew where her sister was headed that night and why she was headed there. She'd learned that Nicholas Moon had made a mistake and had spent the next six months of his life regretting what he'd done. Nicholas had written the *Dear Stranger* poems that haunted Kat and Jay since the day they'd found them, but these answers did nothing but make the blood rush to her head. She wasn't angry at Nicholas for what he'd done, not at Peter for the person he thought Nicholas was—but at herself. Even with answers, even with a vivid memory of her sister's crash, as though she'd been there—Kat still felt nothing but numb.

I really am a monster.

The red hue at the horizon intensified. She raised her chin to find a source of light rising from beneath the cliff—a sixth capsule that glowed with an aura similar to the one they'd seen at Sunshine Auto. This one, however, was a cranberry red, shining in sharp contrast against the creamy moon. It hovered several feet away from the ledge.

Kat jumped to her feet and reached for the capsule with a weak arm, already knowing it was too far. She leaned over the edge. The jagged rocks below protruded from under the waves with bodies sharper than knives.

And she started to wonder.

Had this game been designed for them to win?

Or had they fallen into a sick trap?

A few soft footsteps tapped the grass behind her, and Kat turned around to find Jackie standing by the trees.

"Hey." Jackie stepped forward onto the grass clearing with a forced grin. "Is everything okay?"

"It's over," Kat said. Jackie was the one person who could open the reward capsule, but the reward was nothing more than a death trap.

"No, it's not." Jackie held her phone in the air. The countdown revealed that they had just under an hour left. "We still have time."

"Time means nothing." Kat stepped aside, unblocking Jackie's view of the sixth capsule.

It was at this moment—as Jackie's eyes widened at the sight of the game's cruel plan—when Kat realized that Capsule owned them. The game had taken hold of their lives, threatened them, and toyed with them. The reward capsule floating over the ocean was proof that to the game, they were nothing more than a fun science experiment. And Jackie had it the worst. She was the player. A character the gamer believed they had control over, when in reality all actions were limited and built into the design. She played with the illusion of free will.

"It doesn't make sense." Jackie's voice was steady, logical, but her quivering eyes denied her calm aura. "What kind of game has a reward the player can't claim?"

Kat crossed her arms. This wasn't an innocent arcade game on Jackie's phone. Sure, Capsule had similarities to games Jackie had played before, such as challenges, rewards, even a storyline to follow—but this game was *real*. Of course Capsule was capable of eliminating the ability for them to win.

"Maybe it's a test." Jackie tossed her phone onto the grass and watched the screen fade to sleep. "If I open the capsule and the game ends, I'll never land."

Kat's heart sank. "It's too risky."

"This whole game has been risky!" Jackie shouted, her voice more piercing than the sharp rocks that broke the waves below them. "I knew it was risky when I started the countdown in the first place, but I did it anyway, and I'm not gonna back out right at the end. I'm doing this."

Earlier at Sunshine Auto Kat had said, *"We're just your entertainment, aren't we?"* Her anger had blinded her so much she'd failed to recognize the sacrifices Jackie had made for her and Peter today. Jackie had chosen to help them get to the sixth location even after they'd abandoned the game in rage—even after they'd abandoned themselves.

But do people risk their lives for entertainment? Throughout the day it was Jackie who had kept them on track, and now she was willing to take a leap of faith for them. To threaten her own life to stop the threatening of theirs. *Do people jump from cliffs with no protection, all for a game?*

Jackie took a few steps back, her shoulders loosening as she positioned one foot firmly in front of the other. As she ran toward the ledge, Kat's mind cleared for the first time in ages. She didn't know how to feel about the answers she'd received tonight. She didn't know how to feel about the fact that she still couldn't cry. But right now, at this moment—watching her friend rush toward her own doom—all Kat knew was that she cared about Jackie.

Jackie Mendoza, the girl she'd met in the hallway this morning, but felt as though she'd met a lifetime ago.

Kat stepped in front of Jackie, pushing her hands against her shoulders and forcing her to a halt.

"Let me go!" Jackie forced herself forward, but Kat held her stance firm in the middle of the clearing.

"It's *game over*, Jackie." Kat folded her fingers around Jackie's shoulders. "I won't let you do this."

Jackie stopped struggling. Her dark eyes held the entirety of space, and Kat found herself lost in them.

Before she could gather her thoughts, a sharp pain seared through her ribs. Kat dropped to her knees and gripped her side, teeth clenched. As she faced the ground, her glasses slipped from her nose and tumbled onto the grass. It took Kat a moment to process that Jackie had elbowed her to get away. That Jackie had slipped from her grasp. That Jackie's *life* had slipped from her grasp.

Kat raised her chin from the ground to find Jackie's blurry figure standing in the middle of the grass clearing. Jay's flannel flowed from Jackie's waist as a violent wind attempted to push her away from the ledge. She held her figure strong, lips pulling into a straight line as she concentrated on making the jump.

"Jackie?" Kat dug her fingernails into her side, applying pressure to ease the pain. "Stop!"

As Jackie ran for the ledge, Kat reached to grab her ankle but only managed to graze the side of Jackie's sneaker. By the time Kat hopped back onto her feet, Jackie had already reached the edge of the cliff and swung off into the air.

REWARD CAPSULE

JACKIE STOOD IN *a room made of shadows. The walls and floor beneath her resembled the infinite night sky, but the pressure against the bottom of her sneakers insisted that she wasn't floating. She raised her palms to her face, and the lack of control over their shakiness left her petrified. A moment ago she'd been soaring through the night sky with the capsule in her grip, but now the capsule was gone.*

Her clothes matched what she'd been wearing earlier today—sweatpants, a dull blue top stained with blood, and Jay's checkered flannel tied around her waist. Even her arm was wrapped with the same gauze, but when she felt around the wound, the sharp pain wasn't there anymore.

Jackie dropped her hands to her side and stepped forward, stopping as her phone buzzed in her back packet. She frowned at the memory of tossing it onto the grass clearing.

How did it get here? *Jackie's fingers wrapped around the device in her back pocket and pulled the screen to her eyes.*

CONGRATULATIONS, PLAYER. YOU PASSED THE TEST.

Jackie lowered the screen to her side and searched the room for a sign of someone, but the air around her was nothing but empty space.

"What test?" Jackie's voice echoed, slowly fading but never falling completely silent. "Is someone there?"

Her phone buzzed again. A new line had faded underneath the previous one. **PLEASE CLAIM YOUR REWARD.** When Jackie lifted her eyes from the screen a second time, a capsule hovered in front of her face. This one was different from the others. It was smaller—the size of an actual pill—with a black body and a red cap.

Another buzz. **PLAYER, YOU MAY BRING ONE SUBJECT HOME WITH YOU. THE CHOSEN SUBJECT MUST TAKE THE CAPSULE WHOLE TO MARK THE END OF THE GAME AND REVERSE THE DAY.**

Jackie took a step away from the capsule.

One subject?

She gripped her phone tight enough to make her fingers go numb. "I did everything you wanted me to!" Jackie screamed into the infinite room. "I went to all of your stupid locations, and your reward is to only let me save one of them?"

Tears welled in her eyes, but she didn't acknowledge them. This game really had set them up to fail. Capsule was winnable after all, but what was the point of winning if either Peter or Kat would disappear?

The capsule remained hovering at eye-level, rocking subtly back and forth as though it were hanging from a string. With a grunt Jackie swiped the pill from the air. The floor of darkness removed itself from existence in acknowledgment of Jackie accepting her vicious defeat. She fell backward into the void and shut her eyes, stars flashing in her mind as a familiar gust of cold air rushed around her, the phone in her tight grip vanishing, leaving her fingers limp.

00:45:13

THE JAGGED CLIFFSIDE encased the area of sand by the shore of Lothen Heights, trapping Peter inside the mouth of a beast. With every step closer to the water he found himself backing two steps away. The sand squished and cried beneath his shoes.

"Jackie, are you there?"

The wind sucked the air away whenever Peter tried to breathe, so he held his breath, scanning the dense water ahead of him for a sign of Jackie. All he could see was a mass of swirling black fluid, its contents only found in his imagination.

She'll be okay. Peter ripped the sneakers from his feet and tossed them onto the sand. *She has to be.*

He stepped forward, his ankles meeting the bubbling water. "Jackie!"

With every crash and pull of a wave against his calves, Peter was drawn deeper, further beyond control, but he reminded himself that the false sense of the ocean floor's movement was only his mind playing tricks on him. The water reached his knees, leaving the upper half of his body covered in goosebumps.

It won't end like this. If it did, he wouldn't be able to live with himself for the mere forty-five minutes he had left.

About fifteen minutes ago the emergency button had brought Peter to the shoreline where he'd spotted a silhouette standing at the edge of a cliff towering in the distance. When a second silhouette had appeared at the clearing he still hadn't made the connection until a flash of red appeared out of thin air and hovered several feet away from the ledge. A sixth capsule. By the time Peter realized the two figures had been Jackie and Kat, it was too late for him to shout.

He'd seen Jackie leap.

He'd seen her fall toward the water.

But he hadn't seen her land.

A patch of water failed to reflect the moonlight, breaking the shimmering pattern on the waves. Upon closer inspection Peter identified the patch as Jackie's body. She floated peacefully, the strong rushes of water always slowing down just in time to reach her with nothing but a gentle nudge against her side.

Peter leapt deeper into the water, and the sandy floor beneath him vanished. A wave crashed into him, submerging his head, forcing him to assimilate into the cold. He broke the surface with a gasp, eyes burning, turning his head to find the figure he'd seen only moments ago.

But when he looked at the floating girl's face, he didn't see Jackie.

He saw *her*.

Isabella.

Peter could feel the blood of Nicholas Moon pulsing through his veins. He felt the same level of breathlessness, the same urgency, the same boldness that Nicholas had felt that day. In that moment Peter had become the man he had always wanted to become, but instead of embracing his transformation, he fantasized about stabbing his arms and draining the blood from his system as though it were pure venom injected into him against his will.

Peter tried to fight, but every struggle against the truth weighed him down, threatening to drag him to the bottom of the sea. He couldn't deny that the man who had crashed into Emmeline's car and had done nothing was the same man Peter shared his DNA with. The waves punched him, bullied him, forced him to accept the strength he so badly wished to leave behind.

Peter swam, the blood in his veins pumping faster, the venom spreading to his fingertips. He embraced the breathlessness, the urgency, the boldness that Nicholas had felt that day. He embraced it all, and when he reached the floating figure on the water's surface, Jackie's face was back.

Peter wrapped his arms under her shoulders from behind and pulled her toward the shore. The water didn't fight him anymore. He was one with it, and as he reached the shallow end, lifted Jackie from the water, and set her onto the rocky sand, he couldn't help but feel proud of Nicholas for the gift he'd given Isabella.

Peter dropped to her side, reaching for Jackie's left arm to check her pulse. Her heart was still pumping, and she was breathing normally with her chest rising and falling in a steady pattern. Her right hand rested on the sand in a fist, fingers tense.

"Hey, can you hear me?" Peter shook her shoulder, her head bobbing against the sand. "Jackie?"

In an instant Jackie shot up, their foreheads slamming into each other.

Jackie clutched her head with her left hand, eyes clamped shut, but Peter's relief overwhelmed his pain. He scanned the cliff in the distance, where the silhouette of Kat he'd seen earlier had now disappeared. She must have gone searching for a path leading to the shore. As much as he didn't want to think about the possibility of facing Kat again, he knew that right now, Jackie was more important.

"I don't get it." Peter lowered his chin, gauging the dangerous distance of the fall before facing Jackie. "What the hell just happened?"

"You didn't see it?" Jackie tucked her fist into the pocket of her sweatpants and struggled to get back onto her feet. Peter stood to help her up, the sand sticking to his dripping clothes. By the time Jackie regained her balance, she'd removed the hand from her pocket, her fingers now relaxed at her side.

Peter wrapped his arm around her shoulder and guided her toward the stony wall ahead of them. "See what?"

Only one trail led to the main campground at Lothen Heights. It was steep, but definitely more manageable than climbing up the way Jackie had come.

A salty gust of air passed as they approached the start of the trail, marked by a warning sign that read, *Stones may slide. Take caution.* Peter stopped to make sure Jackie could handle the climb. He was trembling from the cold, but Jackie—she was quivering out of control, her bottom lip shaking with every rapid breath. She leaned against the cliffside. "Just give me a moment."

Peter nodded. Whatever happened after she'd jumped wasn't normal, and although he was pleased she'd survived a seemingly unsurvivable fall, he worried she might have long-lasting injuries. His eyes landed on the dripping gauze wrapped around her right hand.

"Let me see that." Peter reached for her arm, which she held toward him without so much as a wince. He unraveled the loose gauze to reveal the skin of her forearm, completely healed. "Must be the work of the game. I think you'll be okay." He tossed the wet strips onto the sand.

"How much time do we have left?"

"We'll deal with that later." Peter surveyed the distance to the top of the trail, ignoring the pit of guilt that burrowed itself into his stomach. "You think you can handle it?"

"I'll be fine."

Peter held his hand out, and Jackie looked away.

"Really?" Peter shook his hand in front of him again, emphasizing the gesture. "Don't make this weird. You know we can't have the player dying right before the end of the game."

Jackie rolled her eyes and took his hand. "You're stupid."

"And you're stubborn."

Peter set his sandy sock on the first stone, wondering whether he would have been better off with his sneakers, which were still lying by the shore. At this point it didn't matter. They didn't have much time left anyway.

As Peter and Jackie scaled the trail together, the fatigue finally caught up to him. Peter might have stopped to rest for the remainder of the night if it weren't for Jackie's panting behind him. The game had spared her, but that didn't mean Capsule intended to show mercy. He needed to get her medical help.

The trail grew less steep as they neared the sea of trees above them, but Jackie still continued to stumble, her slippery sneakers sliding with every step. She gripped Peter's hand firmly to keep from tumbling down the rocky path they'd climbed.

Peter couldn't suppress one distinct question that whirled through his mind. Earlier today he and Kat had abandoned Jackie at the spring dance, and what felt like minutes ago—and probably was—he'd been screaming at Jackie as though the only reason she helped him was because she enjoyed playing the game.

"Are you feeling okay?" Peter tightened his fingers around her hand as he felt the strength in her grip fading. "We're almost there."

He looked over his shoulder at Jackie, recalling what he'd told her after receiving the Level Five memories. *"That's all you care about, isn't it?"* Peter blushed. *"You're just in this for the game."*

Jackie's damp hair fell over her shoulders, her eyes vacant as she grimaced in pain. After all he'd said, why would Jackie take such a stupid risk for him? Why would she jump for someone so rotten, someone who had never even thanked her once?

By the time they'd reached the comforting grass and trees of the Lothen Heights Campground, Jackie had lost most of her energy. Her hand slipped from Peter's grip as she leaned forward and dropped onto her knees. She pressed her palms into the grass, trying to force the strength back into her.

Peter kneeled by her side. He wanted to say something encouraging, to tell her that everything would be okay, but that would be a lie. Where were they supposed to go? How would this game end? The countdown was ticking, and now Jackie was losing energy faster than Peter was supposedly dying.

Kat emerged from the trees, arms swinging frantically by her sides as she ran, Jackie's phone in her grip. When she noticed Peter and Jackie, she rushed forward and kneeled next to them.

"After she jumped, Capsule had a new pop-up called *warning*. All it said was *seek fire*." Kat pointed into the dark trees ahead of them—the same dark trees she'd come running from. "I saw a campfire on the way over here. I think it's a sign."

Peter had hardly heard a word Kat had said. All he could think about was how similar she looked to Emmeline. She'd always tried to be more like her sister, but under the moonlight that night, she resembled Emmeline more than ever, and Peter couldn't pinpoint why.

Kat's brows furrowed, breaking the image of Emmeline and shooting Peter back into action. Now wasn't the time for distractions.

Peter and Kat stood on opposite sides of Jackie and helped her back to her feet. Jackie was still awake, but her eyes were glazed over, and her thoughts wandered somewhere else. With their arms around Jackie, Peter and Kat dragged her stumbling body between the trees in silence, only occasionally glancing in each other's directions.

The campfire was only a few-minute walk into the forest, a flickering orange blur sitting next to an RV parked in the middle of the woods. By the time they neared closer, a figure sitting on a log in front of the fire stood and rushed toward them.

The woman looked to be around her fifties. She had cheekbones sharper than kitchen blades and raven-black hair as thin as printer paper. Her wrinkles grew more defined as she caught sight of Jackie's condition and came to a dead stop. At this point the girl was nothing more than a walking zombie.

"My goodness, what happened to you three? Lothen isn't the place you visit for a midnight swim." The woman headed toward her fire faster than she'd arrived from it, motioning for them to follow. "Please, you three warm up. It's mighty cold out tonight."

The woman stepped into her RV to grab a spare blanket while Peter and Kat placed Jackie against one of the logs facing the campfire. In only an instant the color returned to Jackie's cheeks. As she blinked more frequently, Peter took a few backward steps into the shadows of the trees and sighed with relief.

"Well," Peter said as Kat joined him by his side. "That was *something*."

She shook her head. "No kidding."

Peter and Kat stood next to each other by the trees. Not close, but not *I-hate-you* far. They watched the flickering fire from a distance as the woman returned from her RV with a quilt. She wrapped the warm fabric around Jackie's damp clothes, encasing her in a red-and-white striped cocoon. After sitting on the dirt next to Jackie, the woman's mouth moved, but her voice was inaudible from so far away.

Jackie had jumped to save them. She'd fought for Peter's and Kat's lives more than they'd ever fought for themselves, and Peter admired that about her. He'd been wrong. Jackie really did care after all.

As Peter's and Kat's minds wandered in different directions, Peter realized that nothing had changed. They were still the nephew of the criminal and the sister of the victim, but they were also Jackie's friends. Subjects in the game. Students misunderstood by their peers, struggling to move on from their shattered pasts.

What parts would they allow to define them?

The goosebumps disappeared from Peter's arms. What he felt that night—the strange relief that came with giving up—it warmed him. He welcomed the satisfaction that came with accepting that he could never win the war he was fighting, and neither could Kat. If Nicholas had called the police, Emmeline could still be alive today. If Emmeline hadn't swerved into the other lane, Nicholas could still be alive today. There were no winners. And as hard as he'd tried to convince Kat that Emmeline's death was her fault and her fault alone, it wasn't that simple. Perhaps he'd been fighting someone on the same side all along.

Peter finally worked up the courage to face her. Kat's hair had fallen over her shoulders, frizzy from the chaos of the day, and the cat eyeliner she'd worn earlier was now smeared. Kathabelle Pike. A girl dealing with the truth behind her sister's death. Dealing with the pain of answers. Peter had insisted that Nicholas was innocent, but that wasn't what Kat needed to hear. What she needed was a real friend.

"I understand if you hate me," Peter said, and when Kat faced him, he directed his focus to the flames. "I was being—"

Kat leaned over and wrapped her arms around him. "Are you kidding me?" She buried her face into his chest, her voice muffled by his shirt. "People have hated you enough."

Peter froze, too stunned to hug her back. By the time Kat stepped away and dropped her arms, there were tears in her eyes.

She didn't wipe them away.

"I thought I needed answers to feel again." Kat smiled at Jackie. "But I was wrong."

Jackie chatted with the woman from the RV in front of the campfire. With a light smile spreading across Jackie's face, she came to life again. Jackie had never deserved any of this. She had never deserved the game. But as recklessly selfish as it was, Peter was glad Jackie had been the one chosen as the player.

"It feels weird to say this." Peter grinned. "But congrats on crying?"

Kat threw her back against the tree behind her. "Oh shut up, Peter." She wiped her tears with the crinkly sleeve of her windbreaker.

"Really though." Peter leaned against the tree standing next to hers. "I'm happy for you." He looked down at his socks, which were now covered in sand, dirt, and a new collection of evergreen needles. Normally that would've annoyed him to death, but he smiled at its stupidity.

"Of course you are." Kat sniffled. "Nice socks, by the way."

"Thanks. It's a new trend. I call it *natural soles*."

Kat chuckled, but the humor wasn't really there. "And I—well—you know—"

"Careful." Peter crossed his arms with a grin. "You're starting to sound like me."

Kat crossed her arms too. "I just hope you know that your uncle's past doesn't define you."

The smile tumbled off Peter's face. That line—he'd been dying to hear it for the past two years. They were the words he'd been craving without even knowing it.

"I know." The words were a mere croak from his mouth as he rested his head against the prickly tree bark and shut his eyes. "And about what happened earlier. The—you know—"

"Kiss?" A heavy breath left her lips, cloaking the humor in her voice. "Yeah, about that. I think we were both a little caught in the moment."

"I wasn't."

"What?"

Peter burst into laughter. "Joke." He opened his eyes to the tree branches above him, their silhouettes erasing clumps of stars in strips. "That was a joke. We're probably better off as friends. Especially now, you know?"

The unlock *click* of a phone. "Maybe if we didn't have answers, things would be different."

Peter stepped away from the tree and caught a glimpse of Jackie's phone in Kat's hand.

00 HOURS : 29 MINUTES : 44 SECONDS

Time trickled between their fingertips, and although Peter would rather pretend the countdown wasn't there, they'd have to face fate eventually. He watched Jackie smile and chat with the woman by the fire. She'd sacrificed so much for them, but Peter and Kat would have to make a choice.

Jackie raised her chin, meeting eyes with Peter before he could avoid her gaze. "Weird how that works, isn't it?" His breath stopped as he brought a hand up in a stiff wave. "After the memory at Sunshine nothing really changed, but it feels like everything has."

"It's like the game was designed to turn us against each other." Kat's voice grew raspy as she tucked the phone into her pocket and forced a smile in Jackie's direction. "First you against me, and now Jackie against us."

Peter's hands rolled into fists at his sides. He faced Kat, his face burning as he blurted the idea he'd been dreading to share. "But the game doesn't have to win."

Kat grinned weakly at the dirt. Peter had broken a barrier they'd been mutually afraid of crossing. "I'm guessing that means we're on the same page?"

"Definitely." Peter nodded, and his clenched hands unraveled. "But how do we tell her?"

00:27:16

IT WAS NICE to see Peter and Kat standing next to each other peacefully. When Jackie had first woken up in the main parking lot by the *Lothen Heights Campground* sign, she'd thought her only option was to finish the game alone—that Peter and Kat's anger would keep them from cooperating—but she'd thought wrong.

Jackie adjusted the quilt over her shoulders while the woman next to her shared the story of her failed business. The stranger had spent seven years pouring every dime into creating a new social media networking site that ultimately flopped. With no resources left, she thought her only option was to work a job she hated, but instead she made the insolent decision to travel the country in her RV.

Losing everything had given her the opportunity to live a lifestyle that brought her joy.

"I guess I realized that the past has power over us, but it doesn't change who we are," the woman said. "Only we can do that."

Jackie had been fully invested in the woman's story, smiling along with the beauty of her words as the fire warmed them, but then she remembered the reward capsule. Her hand—concealed under the quilt—reached inside the pocket of her sweatpants, ensuring the capsule hadn't fallen out on the way up from the shore. A breath slipped between her lips as her fingers fondled the game's reward. She lost herself in the flames, sweat accumulating on her forehead despite the cold air.

The woman stopped mid-sentence. "What's with the grim face?"

Jackie burrowed the capsule deeper into her pocket and rolled the quilt into a ball on her lap. "It's nothing."

"Surely there's *something* on your mind if you decided to go swimming at one of the most dangerous California beaches." The woman held a sharpness inside her gaze. Kind, yet calculating, and Jackie knew she couldn't get away with lying to her.

"I'm not even sure where to begin," Jackie said.

Before the woman could respond, Peter and Kat appeared across the other side of the fire. They sat next to each other on a log, and the dazzling sparks rising from the campfire formed a wall that separated them from Jackie. Their smiles wrenched a blade right through the last of her enthusiasm. She'd have to tell them the truth.

"Thanks for the help," Kat said to the woman.

"Not a problem. Sometimes we go to the most beautiful places when our minds take us to the ugliest. I think it's safe to say you three haven't had an easy time lately." The woman stood and dusted the dirt from her jeans. "But if there's one thing I've learned, it's that some parts of our past are better off forgotten."

The flames crackled, consuming the wood that fueled it.

"Can we stay here for a bit?" Peter asked.

"I'm heading off to bed, but you kids take your time. And feel free to help yourself to the snacks in that bag there. I've had far too many s'mores of my own." She pointed to a paper bag leaned against the log Peter and Kat were sitting on. Before Jackie could mutter *thank you,* the woman had already disappeared into her RV, leaving the trio alone around the fire.

"Well," Kat said, "she's nice."

"Yeah." Peter's eyes narrowed on the flames. "And she's right."

Peter and Kat didn't look at each other, and it was starting to make Jackie uncomfortable. At Sunshine Auto, Capsule had exposed a dangerous truth—knowledge they might've been better off not knowing in the first place—but it no longer dragged them down, and although it brought Jackie relief, she also knew their resolution was temporary.

"*Anyways.*" Kat stood from the log, breaking the tension. Her eyes wandered to the paper bag sitting on the ground by her sneakers. "You guys hungry?"

As Kat removed the marshmallows and graham crackers and arranged them onto the log neatly as though it were a kitchen counter, Jackie stared at the fire, pondering how to break the news. The timing didn't feel right, but would it ever? If they wanted to win the game, either Peter or Kat had to take the capsule—and soon. Yet despite this urgency, Jackie couldn't gather the strength to ask Kat for her phone back.

Peter held a twig out toward Jackie, a marshmallow pierced into the end of it. Jackie raised a palm and leaned back, refusing his offer and avoiding eye contact. She pressed her back against the log, the fire burning her face as Peter and Kat's gentle chattering filled the night air, but she didn't scoot away. She embraced the heat. The subtle pain distracted her from the capsule resting in her pocket.

"I haven't had s'mores in forever," Peter said.

By the time Jackie returned to her senses, Peter had a s'more in his hand, the ingredients in a jagged alignment, the marshmallow more brown in some parts than others.

He brought the sweet graham cracker sandwich closer to his lips. "Ten grams of sugar and a tenth of the average person's daily caloric intake."

"Don't ruin my favorite dessert please." Kat popped the last bite of her s'more into her mouth.

"It tastes as good as the nutritional label implies." Peter spoke while he chewed. "Yeah, that's definitely ten grams of heaven."

"You don't like s'mores?" Kat asked Jackie.

"Not really."

Jackie lied.

Kat and Peter sat against the log on the other side of the fire, laughing and stuffing their faces with chocolate as they reminisced on the memories they'd shared today. Not the memories the game had given them, but the ones they'd made. They talked about stealing Owen's car, shoplifting from Closets & Beyond, and trying to outdrive the police car in the outskirts of Ravensburg. They talked about meeting Isabella in front of Grove Aid and the fact that Whitney had shown up at the Grovestown dance. But all Jackie could think about was the countdown.

"Oh Jackie, you should've seen the act Peter and I pulled on that guy at Sunshine Auto." Kat clapped her hands against each other as the hysteria struck her. "I used that weird memory wipe power-up on him, and then Peter and I pretended like he was the one in the wrong."

"I will admit that my acting was impeccable." Peter's brows furrowed. "Is Jay alright, by the way?"

"Yeah, we kinda ditched him in Grovestown," Kat said, "didn't we?"

When Jackie had first woken up at Lothen Heights her phone had rung with a call from Jay, confused on where they were. Supposedly Sunshine Auto was swarming with police officers, so Jackie had advised him to focus on himself and find a way to leave unnoticed.

"He called me when I first woke up." Jackie's throat tightened as she spoke, trying to keep the words from leaving her throat. Trying to protect her. "I told him that Capsule took us to Lothen Heights and that he shouldn't worry. That I was about to end the game."

Jackie closed her eyes and let the fire's rage fight off her chills. Discussion about ending the game had somehow become untouched territory.

Even without seeing them she could sense their presence across the fire. Peter Moon and Kathabelle Pike. They had passed each other in the halls of Brookwood High hundreds of times, but they'd been living as though the other didn't exist. Tonight, sitting by the fire, the two were united through the game. The same game that was about to rip them apart a second time.

Jackie lifted her chin and opened her eyes to the stars. They were brighter in Lothen.

The absurdity of it all was that this morning she'd been planning to play this game alone. But if she'd reached the cliff without knowing them now—if all she had were the memories Capsule had given her at every level—would she have jumped? Would she have taken that leap for them?

"As weird as today's been, I'm glad I had the chance to meet you guys." Jackie lowered her head, a sense of ease overtaking her. Time was running out, and she knew what she had to do. She knew she would have to let them choose. The capsule in her pocket had never been hers, and it wouldn't be right to give it to the person she felt was the best fit. No—she'd tell them the truth and allow them to come to their own conclusion.

"Of course." Peter ran a hand through his hair. "I mean, if I had the chance to meet myself, I'd be pretty happy too."

Kat elbowed him, and they both laughed.

"Okay, so this might be a crazy thing to say," Peter added, the unsteady humor in his voice fading, "but I consider today the best day of my life. And it's *definitely* the best birthday."

"Same, minus the birthday thing." Kat nodded. "And Jackie, I'm sorry about what happened at the dance. I know for a fact now that if the game had chosen anyone else as the player, Peter and I would've never stood a chance."

"Kat's right." Peter's eyes glimmered. "You're probably the most determined girl I've met."

"Whoa!" Kat pointed her finger at Jackie with a grin. "A compliment from Moral Moon? Now that really means something."

As conceited as it felt to admit, Peter and Kat were right. The pair had always clashed, nice to each other in one moment and at each other's throats with the sharpest knife from their kitchen drawers in the next. Jackie had been the one to focus solely on the game, to keep them on track and moving forward together as a team. Jackie was the one to click the emergency button a second time when they had been too distracted by their merging pasts.

Jackie was the one to take a leap of faith when they would've accepted defeat.

For a moment Jackie smiled. It was so genuine. So calming. *They really do care.* But the satisfaction had a time limit.

"Guys, there's—there's something you should know." Jackie reached into her pocket. "I only have—"

"I lied earlier." Peter picked up his marshmallow-roasting stick and held it over the fire, watching the tip ignite. "I saw."

"We both saw," Kat said. "And we decided neither of us should take it."

Jackie wrapped her fingers around the capsule, her face going stiff. They'd seen her in that strange room? They'd known this entire time?

"I realized that Capsule has been here to mess with us from the start. It wants a violent finale. It wants hate." Kat pulled out Jackie's phone and wrapped her tense fingers around the screen. "But we don't have to let it control us anymore."

"But then we'll lose." Jackie stood from the log, the quilt sliding off her lap and onto the dirt. "You'll disappear. Both of you."

"Jackie, you have our memories." Peter tossed the remainder of the twig into the fire before standing from the log. She could see his face clearly now, not one wrinkle between his brows. He was so calm. Idiotically decisive. "You know us better than anyone else, and as long as you remember us, our friendship will live on through you."

Kat stood by Peter's side. "Capsule will never be the winner of this game, even if it claims to be."

"You guys are crazy." Jackie shook her head as they spoke. "After all we've been through, you wanna give up? We can't just lose the game after everything we—"

"Jackie. Stop." Kat walked around the fire and offered the phone to her. "I'm sorry, but we're not changing our minds."

"Can we just enjoy the time we have left?" Peter asked.

Jackie pushed Kat's hands away, refusing to accept the countdown. "There should be two!" She reached into her pocket and pulled the capsule out, pinching it in front of her nose and dreaming about strangling it. Choking it to death. But right now, the object she hated the most was also her only hope.

"Well there's not!" Peter's bold voice ripped Jackie's focus from the capsule as he joined them on their side of the fire.

Jackie lowered her hand, meeting Peter's quivering eyes. They'd harvested the flames.

"There's only one," he said.

Jackie's fingers loosened around the capsule. Her plan had been to let them choose, and they'd made their choice. If that's what they wanted, she'd have to respect their decision. Capsule was horrible, cruel, vicious—but their reality had been set, and they couldn't change that. Her nose fell to the ground, embarrassed that they'd accepted their fate before she had.

"I'm sorry." Jackie tucked the capsule back into her pocket.

"It's okay." Kat held the phone toward Jackie again. This time, Jackie took the device from her with a weak grip and checked the countdown.

00 HOURS : 07 MINUTES : 14 SECONDS

The three sat on Jackie's log in silence, and soon enough two minutes had flashed by. Time was so precious now. So delicate yet so dangerous at the same time.

Peter cleared his throat. "I told myself that I'd never be caught dead wearing this outfit, but look at me now."

Neither Jackie nor Kat could bring themselves to laugh at his failed attempt to lighten the mood. They simply watched him as the grin faded from his face.

"I've been thinking," Peter continued. "Sure, my uncle's not all that great—maybe he did do some horrible things—but his past didn't make saving Isabella any less meaningful." He ran his thumb along the lines in his palm as though he'd accepted the features as a part of him for the first time.

When Jackie turned to Kat, she had silent tears running down her face. Tears at such a random time—so random they had to be unintentional.

"I still don't know whether I can forgive Nicholas." Kat reached to wipe away her tears, but stopped herself, allowing them to reach her chin. "But I do think I'm ready to forgive myself."

Jackie raised the phone screen to her chin, holding her breath as she swiped to unlock the phone. The countdown ticked closer to zero.

00 HOURS : 03 MINUTES : 44 SECONDS

Peter and Kat leaned against her shoulders, watching the numbers drain away.

Jackie gripped her phone tighter. "I'm gonna miss you guys."

"Hang in there, Jackie." The warmth in Peter's voice left her eyes tearing up.

She purposefully lost her gaze inside the flames, unable to watch the countdown fade away. She wished they could've had a chance to spend time together outside of the game. That they could've had a chance to spend time together without the noise of the past and the future. If only they could've shared more moments together like this one.

She had so much to thank Peter and Kat for. If it weren't for them she never would have fixed her broken relationship with Jay. She never would have proved to herself that she didn't have to be like the boy who had sat with hollow eyes at the back of the Grovestown gym. With their help Jackie had proved to herself that she could gain the trust of two strangers. That she could befriend both the most hated boy and the most popular girl from Brookwood High all in the course of one day.

Jackie's shoulder's lightened. She raised the screen in her hands.

00 HOURS : 00 MINUTES : 00 SECONDS

The shift wasn't as dramatic as Jackie had expected it to be. The countdown simply faded away to make room for a new line of text to appear.

GAME OVER.

When Jackie turned to her sides, no one was there.

Peter and Kat had vanished into the midnight air as though they'd never been there in the first place. They had truly disappeared. This time, permanently.

And now Jackie was alone. She was just as alone as she'd been before starting the countdown, but now she was no longer blind to what she'd been missing.

Jackie couldn't stare at the **GAME OVER** screen for too long. The words mocked her.

The capsule sitting in her pocket mocked her.

She tapped the screen, desperate for a solution. She swiped, but even the second page of power-ups had vanished. There was no way to fix this. Her battery percentage dropped to two percent.

The phone vibrated. Jackie stood from the log, breathing heavily as her thumb paused over the green answer button. *Eugenie.* She tapped and brought the phone to her ear.

"Hey, if it isn't JackieLantern. Finally picking up my call."

Eugene's smile could be heard through his voice alone, and Jackie couldn't stop the tears from rolling down her face.

"Sorry, I know you've probably had a crazy day." Eugene's voice stiffened as Jackie brought the phone closer to her ear. "I just wanted to let you know that I've been doing some thinking lately, and I realized it's probably best if we stop this gaming thing. You know, our lives are only gonna get busier, and—"

"My phone's about to die." Jackie wiped the tears away from her face with her free hand.

"Uh—okay." Eugene spoke faster. "I just—I think we should take a rest from Mystery Bullets and meet some new people. Or at least try to."

Jackie took a deep breath. "I have to go."

"Jackie, wait. Don't—"

Without even ending the call, Jackie chucked her phone into the woods. The device crushed itself against a tree, but she didn't bother to survey the damage. Her hand fell to the capsule in her pocket, plucking it from its safe cavern. If only Capsule had never shown up in the first place. If only she'd known that she'd lose everyone in the end anyway. If she'd known, she never would've started that pointless countdown.

Jackie raised her fist over the fire, threatening to drop the capsule, but she couldn't bring herself to let go.

12:58 PM

MR. BERKSHIRE ANNOUNCED Peter Moon and Kat Pike missing on Monday, April 5th of 2021.

Their phones had been found by a search team off the side of Quasso Drive, and none of their experiences on the night of April 2nd had ever been associated with Jackie. She was absent in Closets & Beyond's security footage, and the owner of Sunshine Auto claimed he'd only seen two teenagers that night—never three. Perhaps Capsule had worked its magic one final time.

Jay had driven to Lothen Heights late that night to find Jackie after calling her ten times with no success. He'd been crushed to hear the news about Peter and Kat's disappearance, but after a few days he focused on the positives—that Jackie hadn't been caught for the crimes she'd committed, that she had enough money saved to buy herself a new phone, and that their parents had believed their silly excuse for coming home at nearly four in the morning. But no matter how many great points Jay brought up, Jackie only felt lucky to have known Peter and Kat in the first place.

This time, as cruel notes accumulated on Peter's locker and students commented on Kat's Instagram photos begging her to come home safely, Jackie finally understood how wrong people were about Peter and Kat. Rumors spread throughout Brookwood in the exact same way Jackie remembered them spreading. The theories were crazy, but none rivaled the crazy truth—that a vicious game called Capsule had vanished Peter and Kat into the night air, and that Jackie had been there when it happened.

On the last day of April, exactly four weeks after Peter and Kat's disappearance, Jackie had been standing at Peter's locker when a shadow loomed over her. She turned to face the short-haired girl. The book club member had given up on scrubbing the messages away, but she'd occasionally stop by.

I didn't write anything, Jackie thought. That's what she'd said to her last time, but now it was merely a thought. What left her mouth was something new, something she'd been wondering for the past few weeks.

"Do you really care about him?" Jackie asked.

The girl nodded and rested her hand on Peter's locker. "I really hope he comes back."

Jackie frowned at the messages. "But when did you ever talk to him?"

"Huh?"

"I mean, I know you went to book club together, but did you ever try to—like—be his friend?"

"Be his friend, huh?" The short-haired girl's hand fell from the locker with a chuckle. "No, that's impossible. I've seen people try to get close to him before, but it never works out. It would take someone really special to reach him."

As Jay drove Jackie home that afternoon, she scrolled through Instagram posts about Kat on her new phone. The first photo of Whitney's friendship carousel featured her and Kat smiling together, the red hue in the background hinting that they'd taken the selfie at Cherry Ice. In the caption Whitney spoke about how her best friend of two years had now been missing for four weeks straight. She explained how hurt Kat had been as a result of her sister's death. How someone who'd been through such a heavy hardship couldn't possibly deserve to go missing.

Whitney Navarro. Kat's best friend of two years, and she didn't understand that Emmeline's death didn't hurt Kat in the way she thought it had. Kat's best friend of two years, and on the night of Kat's disappearance she had shown up to the Grovestown dance with nothing but gossip and the urge to spread Kat's family drama.

"Isn't it weird?" Jackie said.

Jay looked over at Jackie as he pulled into the driveway. "Isn't what weird?" He stopped the car, and they remained seated to chat for a bit, something the siblings had been doing far more often lately.

Jackie thought about the short-haired girl scrubbing notes from Peter's locker and Whitney's social media posts about Kat. "Isn't it weird how the people who look like they care and act like they care never actually tried to get to know them?"

"Yeah." Jay nodded slowly, eyes on the steering wheel. "Ironic, isn't it?"

Jackie remembered how Jay had tried to connect with Kat after Emmeline's death but failed. All of the times Jay had tried to connect with *her* but failed. It wasn't until now that Jackie truly admired the amount of effort Jay put into making and maintaining his connections with people. Peter truly was wrong in his Moral Moon entry about Jay. People liked Jay for a reason, and it had nothing to do with calling people nicknames and dressing pretty.

Jackie headed straight to her room that afternoon. On her desk were two textbooks and a glass of water—no PC greeted her anymore. She'd sold it on Craigslist and had replaced it with a cheap Chromebook. She only needed a computer for school anyway.

Eugene had messaged her several times on Discord apologizing for what he'd said that night. He offered to play Mystery Bullets again, but Jackie had already moved on. She was done with the internet. Done with technology. All it did was damage.

The Moon Monkeys YouTube channel and Peter's Moral Moon blog had corrupted him.

Kat's Instagram had become a hub of a life she pretended to live that wasn't reality.

And Jackie—she had used her video games as an escape from what really mattered. They had kept her from becoming closer to Jay. They had kept her from finally having an open-hearted discussion with her parents, which she had done last week, and in the process of doing so had lifted a giant weight from her shoulders. Eugene had been right. The world didn't revolve around the internet.

We have the sun for a reason.

After she'd deleted Discord, all that remained from her video game life was the capsule. She'd come home with it in the pocket of her shoplifted sweatpants that night. It was the last piece of evidence that everything she'd gone through was real, and as much as the sight of the capsule brought her pain, she couldn't will herself to throw it away. She'd placed the capsule alone on an empty bookshelf in her room.

Jackie was about to get ready for another afternoon run, but she stopped by her bedroom mirror at the sight of something new. For the first time, she saw in the reflection a girl who tried. A girl who not only acted like she cared but cared and took action. She wasn't like Whitney or the short-haired girl, and for a brief moment she saw a piece of Jay in herself. A piece that she'd always envied, but could never describe with words.

A few knocks on her door. Jackie turned away from the mirror. "Yeah?"

The door swung open, but the face that greeted her wasn't Jay's.

"Hey." A pause. "If it isn't JackieLantern."

Jackie took a single step forward. "How did you—"

"I don't live in Florida." Eugene smiled lightly. "But you've probably figured that out already."

And it was him.

The boy.

Staring at his curly brown hair and the dull glow in his eyes, she couldn't deny it. His voice was slightly deeper than it sounded on their online calls—richer, with more dimension—and he was taller than Jackie had imagined him to be, but it was him.

Eugene.

Jackie froze. He was her best friend. The boy who she'd spent four years gaming with on a daily basis, keeping in touch with during free time in class through occasional Discord messages. He was the boy who had always pushed her to make new friends, even though she'd never listen.

But he was also the same boy who she'd met the night of the Grovestown dance. The boy who had shown up to make friends and failed. The boy who had retreated to the grimy lockers at the back of the gym, staring at Clay River and admitting that he was done with people. Done trying. He was him.

Eugene.

To the rest of the world he was just a high school boy. But to Jackie, he was an anomaly.

A contradiction.

A best friend and a stranger.

"I lied, by the way. My best friend isn't Nolan Russo." Eugene stuck his hands into the pockets of his jeans with a weak grin. "There is no Nolan Russo."

He was wearing a white shirt with the words *I paused my game to be here* written in red text. His curly hair tickled his tan face as though each strand had a life of its own. When he smiled, his teeth were blindingly white. It took Jackie a moment to realize that he wasn't fake.

Over the past month she'd learned to forget that Eugene was a real person, that a heart was beating behind the screen. She'd tossed him aside along with her games, but she'd made a mistake. She'd cut ties with the one person who had always pushed her to be happy, even at his own expense.

That night at the Grovestown dance, Eugene had overheard Jay call Jackie's name. That's when he'd made the connection that the girl he'd met by the lockers that night was none other than JackieLantern, and he'd realized that Jackie had finally broken free from her shell. As sad as it must have been to lose his best friend that night, he still smiled as he waved goodbye. *"Your friends are lucky to have you."*

About two hours later, Eugene had called her to end their gaming sessions. To end their friendship. He was happy for her, and he didn't want to risk dragging her back into her old ways.

"I just didn't want you to be like me." Eugene's focus drifted to his shoes. "You know—a loner. So I tried to push you to make more friends, and when it finally happened I thought I'd have to end things between us too. By the time I realized how stupid that was and reached out to you again, I was already too late."

Eugene had taken the extra step. He not only cared, but he cared enough to go through the effort, the fear, the risk of reconnecting, and Jackie could appreciate that now more than ever.

"How'd you find me?"

"I'm a computer nerd." Eugene raised his chin with a shrug. "I have my ways. A little coding here, some hacking there…"

Jackie crossed her arms, and he sighed, giving in to her suspicions.

"Your Instagram handle matches your Discord ID. I found your brother in your following list and DMed him."

Fair game.

"And I'm really sorry that I wasn't being honest. I made stuff up because I was always scared you'd find out who I really was. It was stupid. Who the hell does that?" He let out a short chuckle. "I completely understand why you'd ignore me after that call. I tried to cut things off out of nowhere, and—"

"It's not your fault." Jackie raised her voice, shocking the life back into Eugene's eyes. "It's a long story, but I—I haven't been ignoring you because of what you said. It's because I lost a game. A really important one, and it's been taking me some time to fully get over it."

"Wait. You've been ghosting me because you *lost a game*?" Eugene frowned at Jackie's desk before approaching it. "All of this, for a game? And what's with this lame-ass Chromebook? This piece of trash probably can't handle anything more than a few games of online Tetris. What happened to your PC?"

"Sold it." Jackie laughed. Now that Eugene had pointed it out, her extreme measures to distance herself from video games sounded ridiculous even to herself.

Eugene shook his head as he turned around. "Why didn't you just play the game again?"

"Dude, I wish it were that simple." Jackie joined him by her desk and watched the water tremble in the glass sitting next to her Chromebook.

"Look, do you remember when I was trying to beat Donkey Kong Country on my old Super Nintendo? It took me weeks on the first try, and I lost the game two levels before reaching the final boss." He raised his voice to the same volume that usually ended up getting distorted through Jackie's headset, but now it sounded like nothing more than *obnoxious*. "Ran out of balloons. But you know what I did? I started up again, right back at the beginning."

Jackie peered at the capsule resting on her bookshelf. "It's not exactly the type of game you play again."

"Jackie," he said in that annoying mothering tone of his. It'd been a while since she had last heard that one. "It wouldn't be a game if you only had one shot. Of course you can play again."

Jackie pictured the **GAME OVER** screen she'd seen that night by the campfire. There hadn't been any other extra buttons. No prompt to replay the game. Now that her old phone was gone she had nothing left but—

The reward capsule.

Jackie sprinted to the bookshelf in the corner of her room. She grabbed the capsule, which was covered in dust, but blowing on it seemed to do the trick. It was sanitary. Well, sanitary enough.

"You better change your username to EuGenius."

Eugene frowned as Jackie made her way back to the desk. "What?"

"Thanks, Genie. Really." Jackie raised her chin to face him with a smile. "You just saved my life."

If it weren't for Eugene, Jackie would have never noticed yet another pattern to the game. Capsule had always pulled one trick after another. First, Capsule had placed the reward capsule over a cliff. Second, Capsule had only offered to save one of its subjects. Both had been tests to determine how much the three of them cared for each other.

And the **GAME OVER** screen was the final test of all—the test that proved whether Jackie not only had enough determination to care about Peter and Kat, but to take that extra step and reach out, even if it seemed hopeless—just like Eugene had. Just like Jay always had.

Was Jackie the type to give up so easily? Was she the type to let everything fade away even though she'd been gifted a morsel of hope, a slight chance of success? Oh, the pieces were coming together brilliantly. Beautifully.

You silly game. Jackie squinted at the capsule resting between her fingertips. *All this time, you were nothing but a test.*

"Saved your life from what?" Eugene leaned toward her, trying to decipher what she was doing with her hands. He couldn't see the capsule.

The game's magic was still at play.

"Bro, just hear me out, alright?" Jackie could hardly contain her excitement, stumbling over her own words, mind racing faster than her muscles could match. "What if it's not even a matter of playing the game again? What if it's more like the—that credit roll fakeout in Donkey Kong Country? Like the part when—when you think the game's over but it's actually just a trick?"

Jackie didn't need Eugene's confirmation to know that she'd finally cracked the code. Capsule had never made a mistake. The game had cleaned up every mess it'd created, leaving behind no trace of its existence apart from the reward capsule. A brutal game like Capsule would never offer Jackie a sentimental souvenir. No, the game was still on. The credits had been rolling, but she hadn't won or lost yet.

"Thanks for finding me, by the way. It really means a lot." Jackie popped the capsule into her mouth, and it bounced on her tongue as she spoke, slurring her words. "I mabe sure we meet again."

Eugene furrowed his brows as Jackie wrapped her hands around the glass of water. "Are you okay?"

Jackie raised the glass to her lips. "Neber been better."

08:57 AM

"DOZING OFF, ARE you?"

Jackie raised her head from the wooden desk to find herself in Mr. Berkshire's classroom. The time was 8:57, twenty-seven minutes after class had first begun. Mr. Berkshire stared at Jackie with sharp eyes and crossed arms, but she didn't remember falling asleep. Luckily, his frustration was temporary. His eyes wandered to the desk at Jackie's right.

"That's strange. He's always on time." Mr. Berkshire uncrossed his arms and referred to the seating chart resting by his laptop. "*Peter Moon.* Does anyone know if he's sick?"

The boy next to Jackie broke into a laughing fit, the lemony lights of the classroom shimmering on his golden glasses. "He's been sick since 2004."

That line.

She'd heard it before.

When the door to Mr. Berkshire's room swung open, the memories came pouring back to Jackie. The boy who entered the room—the one in the red t-shirt—his name was Peter Moon. He'd disappeared from Jackie's life. Twice. He was a greatly disliked student from Brookwood—to put it softly—as well as one of two unlucky subjects in a cruel game. Capsule—that's what it was called.

And he was a friend.

"Sorry I'm late." Peter slammed the door behind him, drowning the laughter to its end. He hurried to the desk next to Jackie's, and for a moment their eyes met before he sat to unpack his belongings.

The fog cleared from Jackie's memory. The date on the whiteboard read *April 2nd*—the day Capsule had erased Peter and Kat by the campfire at Lothen Heights.

Jackie reached into her leather rucksack for her phone, which was still wrapped in a lavender case. She'd purchased a new phone after destroying her old one but hadn't bothered to buy a case for it yet, which meant this *was* her old phone, and in mint condition.

Jackie unlocked the phone under her desk and swiped to her screen filled with mobile games. Capsule wasn't there. The spot next to Clash of Clans was empty.

For the remainder of class Jackie marinated the story in her mind.

Surely I haven't imagined it. Jackie shook her head as the bell rang. *No, it had to be real.*

Jackie stuffed everything into her rucksack and ran after Peter to the door. She followed him through the hall, her footsteps bold. The sneakers on her feet were clean, not yet muddied from the chaos of the game.

"Hey." Jackie raised her voice without hesitation. She'd do anything to reach him. "Peter!"

As Peter turned around, Jackie stopped, and a sudden jolt shoved her a step to the side.

"Shit!" A girl winced and gripped her own shoulder. "You don't just stop in the middle of the hall like that."

Jackie regained her balance, and her eyes widened at the sight of the girl's perfect blond locks dangling from a ponytail, her glittering green eyes, and the artistic arrangement of freckles on her cheeks. It really was her.

Kathabelle Pike.

"Oh yikes, bad luck." Peter approached them with crossed arms. "Looks like you bumped into the famous, entitled feline."

There it was—that same line.

Well played, Capsule. Jackie grinned as her eyes hopped between their faces. *Well played.*

Peter raised his brows. "Do you need something?"

"Jackie, you have our memories." Her eyes watered as she recalled what Peter had told her at the campfire that night. *"You know us better than anyone else, and as long as you remember us, our friendship will live on through you."*

Kat released her arm with red cheeks. "And why are you smiling like that?"

Jackie stared into their eyes, her grin widening. She'd found a way to beat the game. Now she could meet Peter and Kat again, but this time, the right way. Without the app.

"Hi." Jackie raised her arm with a short wave. "I'm Jackie."

ACKNOWLEDGMENTS

I STARTED WRITING *Capsule* sixteen months ago at the age of seventeen, clueless as to how many people would later be involved with the project. I can proudly say that the story is no longer mine alone, but the work of everyone in this acknowledgment section for contributing a piece to the jigsaw puzzle that now sits in your hands.

Let's start with my family. Mom and John for listening to me rant about writer problems they didn't need to hear, and Dad for giving me a logical approach to the business side of publishing. Shoutout to my siblings—Monica, Marie, Lucas, Levi, and Eli, my aunt and uncle—Robin and Thomas Bottorff, and my grandparents—Eleuterio Torrefranca, Norma Torrefranca, and James Hensley.

I am honored to have worked with a group of incredibly creative people throughout the publishing process at Lost Island Press. Ivan Cakamura for his talented cover design—once again, Katie Flanagan for her critical writing feedback, Nora Sun for marketing guidance, Zoe Anastasia for proofreading, and Kim Sowon for her overwhelming support.

I would like to acknowledge my beta readers who read an early version of this novel and provided constructive criticism—Siddharth Singh, Mayah Robinson, Reeha Dalin, Naomi Kenyon, E Bennett, The Chicken, Avery Elise, Nina J. Jeran, Paulien Goossens, Imān Ayesha, Ben Clarke, Angeline Sieman, Sowon Kim, Zara Štumberger, Olivia Nahrgang, H.R. Lock, Akkriti Tiwari, Luis Rodrigues, Franck Picardat, Aaron Saechao, Gabriel Darrett, Germaine Han, Era Reid, Erin Willis, Skye O'Riley, Moina Fatima, Gaia Camaya, Rosalinda Perri, Nishi Nandineni, Ruby Shaw, Carissa Matson, Katie Flanagan, Miriam Fernandez, Carol Keirn, Richie O'Brien, Edvardi Jackson, Ti'Laha Hayes, Aurora Dayspring, Brandon Nguyen, Kate Larsen, Treasure Elohor Onothome, Molly Jesus, Sabrey Moiraine, Alice Smidebush, Akeem Cammock, Beka Lynne, Chinmayi Veluri, Haley Richards, Joe Lines, beta readers who chose to remain anonymous, and advanced readers who supported *Capsule* before the release. I am forever grateful for your time.

Eugene is a special character to me as he represents the amazing connections I've made through the internet. One of many is Ralph Torrefranca—a writer, filmmaker, and musician who DMed me on Instagram with the message, **Hey Mel! I wonder if we're related**. I appreciate Ralph and the other Cuffed Up band members—Sapphire Jewell, Joe Liptock, and Vic Ordonez—for allowing me to incorporate lyrics from their songs *Small Town Kid* and *Danger, Danger* into Jackie's life. I would also like to mention the online friends whom I've had the pleasure of meeting in person. Sebastian Delgado, a writer and filmmaker whom I collaborated with on a short screenplay adaptation of my debut novel *Leaving Wishville* in late 2020. Abigail Ann, a fellow writer and entrepreneur whose work ethic I truly admire.

Friendship is a core theme in *Capsule*, so I find it fitting to end by thanking the amazing friends who have helped me bring this story to life. Brandon Nguyen—whom this novel is dedicated to—for supporting me in both my creative and personal lives, especially during high school. Joy Kabigting for her willingness to tackle any challenge with me, whether it be filming a fun YouTube video, brainstorming ways to fix a plot hole, or planning our crazy move to Thailand. And lastly, Angie Eggers and Eliza Negrete—my childhood friends whom I met before I could even read—for walking this journey with me from the beginning.

ABOUT THE AUTHOR

MEL TORREFRANCA is an entrepreneur and novelist from the San Francisco Bay Area. When she's not writing dark and mysterious young adult fiction, she runs the publishing house Lost Island Press and films YouTube videos documenting her personal experiences. Mel discovered her passion for writing at the age of seven and published her debut novel *Leaving Wishville* before graduating from high school. She also drinks way too many lattes.

meltorrefranca.com
youtube.com/meltorrefranca
instagram.com/meltorrefranca